Five Grounds

Scott Rempell

ISBN: 1479201723
ISBN-13: 978-1479201723

For Debra

Although *Five Grounds* is a novel, the storylines are grounded in true historical and contemporary events. The Author's Note at the end of the novel describes these in greater detail.

Prologue

SITTING ON HER bed, Lin could not make out the words. Her mother was huddled in the far end of the room, whispering with a stranger. Lin did not trust this mysterious man, the way he kept glancing over his shoulder to look at her. The house reeked of cigarette smoke by the time he left.

Her mother walked over to the bed, an expressionless gaze fixed on Lin. The unsettling look had become all too common since her father disappeared. "We need to find a sturdy bag for you to pack," said Lin's mother.

"Pack for what?" Lin asked.

"You have to go away."

"Where? For how long?"

Her mother didn't answer.

"What about the Moon Festival?" Lin asked. Growing up in the isolated countryside of China's Fujian Province, Lin was never able to make many friends. Like most children in the area, she stopped attending school at a young age, instead working in the fields with her parents. With her home secluded on the steep ridges of the rice fields, the annual festivals were some of the only times when she would socialize with other teenagers. She had been looking forward to the Moon Festival for some time—lighting firecrackers, eating pomelos, sucking on pomegranate seeds, and squeezing the red bean paste out of flaky moon cakes. Especially now, she needed something positive to look forward to. Anything to take her mind off her father.

"Festival?" Lin's mother scoffed. "I'm afraid that won't be possible."

"Why?" Lin asked, not sure she wanted to hear the answer as she thought about all the horrible things her mother could have discussed with the mysterious stranger.

"In three days, you will be leaving China forever."

SOFIA WALKED TO the front pew of the church that served as the centerpiece of Escuinapa, a small town in northwestern Mexico. She knelt down on the cool stone floor, hands clasped, looking up at the stained glass windows that formed a semi-circle around the altar. Between her palms, she clutched *La Sombra de San Pedro*, a pocket prayer booklet dedicated to Saint Peter, the patron saint of travel. "Blessed *San Pedro*, grant my body the strength to persevere on the long journey that lies before me and the power to overcome all obstacles that stand in my way. Grant my children the will to carry on without me and the judgment to avoid the temptations lurking behind each corner of Escuinapa. Amen."

Touching her brow, Sofia slowly performed the sign of the cross and struggled to her feet. She walked over to the side of the church. Comforted by the giant statues of the patron saints overhead, she lit a candle and closed her eyes.

"Mama," Eva said, putting her hand on her mother's shoulder. "Are you ready?"

Sofia smiled.

"Are you sure you're up for this?" asked Eva. "It's a very long way."

"It is a long way," Sofia said, playful sarcasm in her raspy voice. "Several thousand kilometers if I read the map correctly."

"I'm serious." Eva could no longer mask her sadness. She had done her best to keep her composure in front of her younger brother Manuel. But now, watching her mother hobble around the church like a woman twice her age, Eva struggled to hold back her tears. She hugged Sofia, resting her forehead on her mother's frail shoulder.

With Eva's shaking body clutching her tightly, Sofia could not stop herself from crying. She knew Eva was mature beyond her years. *But she's still a young teenager,* Sofia thought as she stroked her daughter's thick, brown hair. *A teenager who will be in Mexico without her parents.*

"It doesn't matter if I'm ready," Sofia sobbed. "We both know what I have to do." *And why I have to do it.*

TESFAYE WAS SLEEPING when the phone on his nightstand began to ring. His eyes snapped open as he sat up, leaning uncomfortably on his elbows. He glanced at his wife, Ayana, sleeping beside him. Then he lifted the receiver as fast as he could to make sure it did not ring again. "Hello."

The voice on the line spoke softly, but Tesfaye immediately knew who was calling him. "Geteye?" he asked. "Everyone is sleeping, let me take this in the other room. I'll call you right back."

Muffled by her pillow, Ayana let out a curious groan, her half-hearted attempt to find out why someone would call at such an early hour.

"Sleep, my dear," Tesfaye whispered reassuringly. He walked down the hall to his study and sat at his desk. Tired and lightheaded, the sound of a dial tone in his ear momentarily mesmerized him. After a few seconds he snapped out of his daze and dialed Geteye's number. Barely half a ring echoed in his ear before Geteye answered.

"Tesfaye."

"A little early, no?" Tesfaye asked, clearing his throat.

"I would not have called if it wasn't important."

"I know," Tesfaye said. "What is it?"

"We're not safe anymore," Geteye said, his voice stone cold.

Tesfaye did not respond as he digested Geteye's words. It was the call he hoped would never come.

"Are you there?" asked Geteye.

"Yes, yes, I'm here."

"Did you hear what I said?"

"I heard you," Tesfaye said, his palms growing sweaty. He had envisioned this conversation since the day he began working at the Ministry of Defense. But still, Tesfaye remained skeptical that Geteye's angst was warranted. Everyone at the ministry knew that he had a tendency to exaggerate.

"It's not just us," Geteye continued. "Your family isn't safe either."

Tesfaye immediately perked up, the thought of his family's safety washing away the fog that had clouded his thoughts since he awoke. "The rebels?"

"Ay, the Tigray." Geteye paused. "We have to get out of Ethiopia now, Tesfaye. This morning."

Chapter 1

Thirty Thousand Feet Above Southern France, September 1999

TESFAYE STARED DOWN at his hand gripped tightly around the plastic cup. The flight attendant had poured him a glass of ginger ale twenty minutes ago. He took a sip. The ice cubes had already melted, dissolving almost all the carbonation. He wasn't thirsty anyway. He continued to stare at his hand. It had been many years now since *they* cut off the tip of his finger. He still could not get used to the sight of it.

"Trash, any trash?" asked the flight attendant, a forced smile paining her face as she briskly navigated the narrow aisle. Tesfaye released his grip from the plastic cup. "Here, Miss."

Fiddling around his pants pocket, Tesfaye pulled out a crumpled picture of his wife Ayana, and two daughters, Afeworki and Yenee. Years of folding and unfolding had made the picture fragile and faded the smiling faces of his family.

Tesfaye had not seen his wife and daughters in more than eight years, since the day he received a phone call from his longtime friend and colleague at the Ethiopian Ministry of Defense, Geteye Tge. His memory of that morning was like an album skipping under the weight of a record player's warped needle, replaying in his head over and over again. And the part of the album that replayed the most over the years was his argument with Geteye.

"YOU HAVE TO get out of Ethiopia!" Geteye shouted, growing frustrated by Tesfaye's stubbornness. "Any day now they could be in Addis Ababa. Tesfaye, I beg you."

Tesfaye had been a senior official at the Ministry of Defense for many years. He was almost certain he would know if the rebels were within days of the Ethiopian capital, Addis Ababa. But he did not want to take that chance with his family's safety. Not when Geteye was so peculiarly adamant about the danger.

"Geteye, my friend, make the arrangements for my family, three tickets."

"You mean four . . ."

"Geteye!" Tesfaye blurted out, immediately regretting that he raised his voice loud enough to possibly wake the children. "Please," he continued, softening his tone, "if what you say is true, then I don't want to waste any more time arguing. Make the arrangements for a flight this morning and for housing in Kenya."

"The arrangements have already been made, Tesfaye. We will be heading for the town of Thika, a short drive from Nairobi. I pray you will come to your senses and meet us there soon."

Tesfaye hung up the phone, startled by the resolute nature of Geteye's plea. He ran down the long corridor that separated his study from the bedrooms.

Ayana was fast asleep. Tesfaye stared at her lying so peacefully in bed. For a moment, he thought about letting her sleep. *Everything will be fine, why should I listen to Geteye's clamoring? He always overreacts.* "Maybe," Tesfaye whispered to himself, "but Geteye's paranoia has saved me before."

Tesfaye had known Geteye since his days at Holetta, one of Ethiopia's most prestigious military academies. Both had been singled out at the academy as astute tacticians who possessed the wit and resourcefulness of natural born leaders, but Tesfaye's brash disposition in his younger years made him particularly prone to butting heads with his superiors, and it seemed as though Geteye always managed to help get him out of trouble.

Tesfaye raised the blinds, letting dawn's ambient light coat the bedroom. He gently shook his wife's shoulder. "Ayana," he whispered.

Ayana blinked her eyes to adjust to the light. She stared up at Tesfaye. "I heard you shouting. Who was on the phone?"

"I need you to pack, only essential items."

"Pack? What do you mean? What's going on?" Ayana sat up and looked around the room, as if to make sure she wasn't still dreaming. "Tesfaye, who was on the phone?"

"It's probably nothing," Tesfaye said calmly, "but I want you to go to Kenya with the children for a few weeks."

"A few weeks!" said Ayana in disbelief. "You're sounding mad."

"The rebels have made some progress in their positions."

Ayana gasped as if all the air in the room had suddenly been sucked out. For a moment, she sat in silence. "Are they close to us?" she finally asked.

Tesfaye tried to convey a sense of certainty in his voice. "No, no. It's a tactical retreat. Mengistu pulled back the military from some of its positions to stretch the rebel forces." Colonel Mengistu Haile Mariam had been in power in Ethiopia since a successful coup in 1974. With hundreds of thousands of military personnel at his disposal, he governed Ethiopia with an iron fist.

The truth was, Tesfaye was not sure about the strength of Mengistu's military positions. Although he was a senior official at the Ministry of Defense, Tesfaye had noticed that his access to the inner workings of the government's security apparatus gradually dwindled over the past few years. "I just want you to go to Kenya as a precautionary measure," Tesfaye assured Ayana.

Staring at Ayana, Tesfaye's lips locked tight together. His thin goatee quickly absorbed beads of sweat that formed in a divot under his nose. As Tesfaye ground his teeth, Ayana could see his protruding jaw muscles flexing. A vein in his thick neck pulsed slightly.

Ayana examined Tesfaye's intense gaze. She knew the look well. It was uncharacteristic of Tesfaye's usual playfulness with her. "Okay. Okay, Tesfaye."

"Wake the kids, have them pack as quickly as possible."

The floorboards creaked as Tesfaye darted back down the long corridor to the front of the house. He opened the front door and stepped outside onto the porch. When he heard the front door shut behind him, he began running up the long driveway, past the garage, toward the front gates of the villa. He ran until he reached the guesthouse, which was shaded by the evergreens planted along the villa's perimeter wall. Tesfaye knocked on the front door of the guesthouse.

"Negasi, are you in there?" Tesfaye had hired Negasi to be his chauffeur shortly after he joined the ministry. Negasi stood six and a half feet tall with arms that looked like miniature tree trunks. Tesfaye felt more at ease knowing Negasi was there to protect the children when he was called away from Addis Ababa on official business. Throughout the years, Negasi's job description grew to include general grounds-keeping responsibilities around the property. "The gentle giant," Ayana would call him.

Tesfaye knocked again. "Negasi," he said, a greater sense of urgency in his voice. Tesfaye opened the door and looked around. On the table, he saw a few scraps of bubbly *enjera* flat bread, but no Negasi. "Dammit, where is he?" He hurried back to the garage, hoping to find Negasi cleaning one of the cars, but the lights in the garage were off. Sweating profusely, Tesfaye ran around the property toward the small pond behind the house. There, he saw Negasi doing push-ups. "Negasi!" shouted Tesfaye. Out of breath, he gestured wildly for Negasi to come toward him.

"Yes, Tesfaye?"

"I need you to drive Ayana and the girls to the airport."

"Of course. What is happening?" asked Negasi, knowing there were only a short list of emergencies that could get Tesfaye so riled up.

"Just a precaution. The rebels have advanced their position a little. Now listen," Tesfaye said sternly, "I don't want you to say anything in front of the children about the situation with these rebels."

"You are not going with them?"

"And abandon my country? Where is the honor?" But Tesfaye knew uncertainty plagued all of his potential options and he needed more time to think things out. He also needed more information. What if the rebels were defeated and he had abandoned his country? He could never return. Or perhaps he would be deported back and thrown in jail, or reduced to begging in the streets of Addis Ababa like so many he passed every day on his drive to the ministry. *Or likely something worse.* Nonetheless, Tesfaye did not want his family to stay in Ethiopia while he thought out his options.

Negasi ran to the guesthouse and grabbed the keys to the 1989 midnight blue Mercedes Benz, the 560 SEL model owned by less than one hundred people in the entire country.

Ayana struggled to open the front door as she balanced her suitcase on her knee.

"Wait, my dear," Tesfaye said as he approached the front door. "Let me help you." He brought Ayana's bag to the edge of the driveway as Negasi parked the Mercedes in front of the house.

A large bag strewn over her shoulder, Afeworki came out to the car and forcefully swung her belongings to the ground, more concerned with alleviating the weight of the bag than she was about the safety of her possessions.

With the same sense of urgency and purpose he applied to all his tasks, Negasi darted out of the car and placed the bags in the trunk, carefully laying each down as if they were fragile segments of valuable crystal.

"Where is Yenee?" Tesfaye asked Afeworki.

"She doesn't want to go, Papa."

"Wait in the car," Tesfaye said as he ran inside, back toward the bedrooms. He stopped at the edge of the doorway of Yenee's room and watched her sitting on her bed, playing with an African doll dressed in white robes.

"I'm not going," Yenee pouted. "Mama says we are going on vacation, but I can tell she is fibbing. Her hands were shaking and she wouldn't look me in the eye." Yenee was eight years old, three years younger than Afeworki, but Tesfaye knew that she was the sharper of the two.

Tesfaye grabbed Yenee's suitcase from the corner of the room and kneeled down in front of the young girl's bed. He ran his hand over her braided hair, which was pulled back in a ponytail. "Yenee, you know your mother. Despite her strong front, she gets nervous when the wind blows through the kitchen." Yenee smiled. "Everything is fine. You can have the window seat on the plane if you behave and come outside."

"Alright, Papa," Yenee said.

Tesfaye placed Yenee's suitcase in the trunk. When Negasi opened the back right door of the car, Yenee jumped inside and rolled down the window. "Papa, you're coming, aren't you?" asked Yenee, her voice cracking. Afeworki quickly moved over to the window by Yenee, and the two children waited impatiently for their father's answer.

Tesfaye placed a hand on each of his daughters' cheeks. "I have some business to take care of, but I will come soon. I promise."

Unconvinced, Yenee opened the door and grabbed hold of Tesfaye's leg. "No, you need to come with us now. Please come with us."

Tesfaye picked up Yenee and tried to comfort her. He could feel the tears on his shoulder, seeping through his shirt. "Look at me, Yenee." Tesfaye gently pushed up on Yenee's chin so that her eyes met his. "Look at me," he repeated. "I have always tried to teach you the importance of responsibility. Our country has put its trust in me and I have a responsibility to help protect it."

"But . . ."

"You remember the importance of honoring one's obligations?"

"Yes, it's just . . ."

"Now I need you to be strong." Yenee loosened her arms, which had been clenched around Tesfaye. Her body slowly slid down until her feet touched the cobblestone walkway below. After she reluctantly got back into the car, Tesfaye stuck his head inside the open window and kissed Yenee on her forehead. He walked over to the front passenger seat, reached in the car, and gently caressed his wife's neck, massaging her earlobe with his thumb.

"We will see you soon," Ayana sighed, forcing herself to smile.

Tesfaye smacked the roof of the car twice with his hand and Negasi shifted into gear. The Mercedes sped down the long dirt driveway toward the front gates, dust spewing into the air. Tesfaye stood at the edge of the driveway until the dust had again settled into the bone-dry ground.

I will see them soon. I just need some time to think.

Tesfaye could not have foreseen the consequences of his decision that morning, but the circumstances of his past were already conspiring. A chain of events set in motion nearly two decades ago was about to catch up to him. Soon, the conspiracy would reveal itself, and he would spend years desperately trying to unravel it.

Chapter 2

Fujian Province, China, September 1999

L IN FELT THE tapping on her arm. Her eyes opened for a moment, but she quickly succumbed to the heaviness of her eyelids and pulled the blanket up to her chin.

"Lin," her mother, Mei Peng, said softly. "It's time. Get out of bed. We must leave shortly."

Reluctantly, Lin pushed the blanket off her body and sat at the edge of her bed. She lifted herself up, accidentally stepping on the small bag of clothing she had packed the night before. On the other side of her one-room house, steam rose from a cast iron pot. "No time to let the water boil," Mei said, pouring Lin a cup. "Drink up. We are leaving in two minutes."

As she sipped her tea, Lin's attention gravitated to the family's bookcase, which reached within one inch of the ceiling. But there were no books. Two of the shelves lay cracked on the floor, a reminder of the consequences of her father engaging in conduct the government deemed subversive. A reminder of the last time she saw her father.

"Get dressed," said Mei sternly.

Lin struggled to get her arms through her favorite shirt, a mint green imitation silk with a bronze embroidered centipede running down the left side. Her father had given it to her as a present three years ago on her fifteenth birthday.

After she finished getting dressed, Lin retrieved her tea, but Mei immediately grabbed the cup from her hands. The tea had barely silenced her hunger pains. "*Ma*, I'm not finished."

"There's no time, Lin, it's already dawn. Grab your bag and do not make a sound." Mei wrapped a scarf around her head. Her bangs covered most of the wrinkles that had begun to form on her forehead and the bridge of her nose.

The front door creaked as Lin followed her mother out of the house. A faint fog masked the plush green vegetation that lined the hills. Wedged between dense patches of trees, rice fields sliced through the earth. The layered fields bore the rigid angles of the Mayan ruins, creating from afar the appearance of a staircase designed for giants.

Lin tried to keep up with Mei as she scurried down the soft soil. A knot tightened in Lin's stomach and the few items she had packed were already beginning to weigh heavily on her shoulder. Mei turned around and saw that Lin had fallen behind. Refusing to give Lin any time to rest, she stopped and waved incessantly for her daughter to walk faster. Once Lin caught up to Mei, the two stood in the tall grass several yards from one of the dirt roads that cut through the hills.

"Is this the road?" Lin whispered loudly, struggling to catch her breath.

Mei quickly placed her index finger on her lips. "Shhh," she said, pointing to a hill in the distance. "He's waiting for us on the other side."

Lin had barely taken a full stride toward the dirt path before Mei pulled her to the ground and placed a coarsened hand over her mouth. Lin gasped for air and removed Mei's hand. She looked over at Mei, who was again pressing her finger firmly on her lips. "Shhh."

A clicking noise grew louder. Lin slithered through the tall grass and peeked her head out to investigate. In the distance, she saw two men standing on either side of a cow. Mei grabbed the collar of Lin's shirt and pulled her back to the safety of the thick grass, out of sight from the road.

Lin and Mei lay still while pink and orange shades of the morning sky began to light the hillside. The knot in Lin's stomach was so tight that it made her dizzy. The clicking sound was getting louder. Lin began to sweat as she let out a soft groan. A moment later, she vomited in the moist soil and watched droplets of her morning tea trickle down the blades of grass.

As she wiped her mouth, Lin could feel her mother's penetrating gaze. Mei's eyes were bulging and her eyebrows had settled halfway up her forehead. Lin wasn't surprised. This was not the first time she had thrown up in front of her mother, and her mother had never shown her any sympathy in the past. For as long as Lin could remember, she had battled frequent bouts of anxiety. It would start as a tickle in her chest, a second before her heart would start to race. Then she could feel the sensation slither through her body. Once it started, Lin was powerless to stop it. The thought of not being able to control it only led to more stress, and so the feelings spiraled beyond her control.

Crouched over in the tall grass, Lin wanted to stop fighting the tears that were welling up in her eyes. She wanted to cry about the cold sweat on her brow, the nausea consuming her body, and the uncertain future that lay before her. But most of all, she wanted to cry about her *fù qîn*—her father. Lin looked over at her mother, who kept her disapproving facial expression fixed on Lin. *Fù qîn, I wish you were here now.*

Through a small slit in the thick grass, Lin could make out a boot laced tight. The boot brought back memories of the uniforms worn by the *cadre*—the local government officials in China—when they burst through the front door three months ago, the last time she saw her father. *Were those the boots they were wearing?*

"What did you hear?" asked the man wearing the tight-laced boots.

"I don't know . . . nothing," replied the other man. "Keep going."

The wheels of a wooden cart clicked as the cow following the two men pulled it along the dirt road. When the tight-laced boot disappeared from Lin's periphery, the sound of the clicks began to fade into the distance.

"We must go," Mei said. "I only hope the snakehead has not yet departed." Lin had suspected that the mysterious man smoking cigarettes in her house three days ago was a snakehead. In the Fujian Province, everybody knew about the snakeheads. It was the name not so affectionately given to members of the Chinese underworld responsible for illegally transporting people out of the country. Ideally located on China's eastern border adjacent to the Pacific Ocean, the Fujian Province had become a hub for international smuggling operations that took advantage of nearby airports and waterways.

Lin and Mei walked up the hillside, struggling to keep their footing. Once they reached the top, they stared downward at a steep slope. "There," Mei pointed.

Lin squinted to see the outline of a van parked by the bottom of the hill. Suddenly, the lights of the van flickered and the unmistakable sound of an engine starting sent a wave of panic through Mei's body.

"Wait!" Mei screamed.

So much for being quiet, Lin thought.

Mei had already made it halfway down the hill by the time Lin secured her bag on her shoulder. Lin stumbled down the hill after Mei, losing her footing several times in the wet soil. For a moment, Lin took her eyes off the ground when she heard her mother pounding on one of the van's windows.

As Lin's heels lost traction, she fell on her back and slid to the bottom of the muddy slope by the edge of the dirt road. Lying on the ground and breathing heavily, the overwhelming sensation of nausea returned. The muscles in her abdomen tightened, and she was again retching, the latest pool of vomit converging on the van's front tire.

The window of the van rolled down slowly. Lin watched the man sitting in the van inhale a deep drag of his cigarette. He was the same man who had previously visited her home three days ago. His face was round and puffy with stubble lining his upper lip. The man smirked and Lin could see that he was missing several teeth. He looked down at the vomit soaking into the soil and rolled his eyes back to Mei. "You are late."

"I'm terribly sorry."

"Do you have the down payment?"

Mei reached into her pocket, pulled out an envelope, and handed it to the man.

He opened the envelope and flipped through the bills with his thumb. His playful smirk disappeared. "This is not enough."

"But you said . . ."

"I know what I said, but the circumstances have changed."

"That is all I have. I have nothing else. Nothing!"

"It will cost . . ." The man paused and a conniving grin soon returned to his face. "An extra year of service," he continued.

Mei looked down at Lin, who was lying on the ground and in no hurry to stand up. "Alright," Mei sighed. Although she was convinced that it was the best course of action for Lin, Mei still felt guilty. She stared down at her daughter, knowing very well that it was Lin who would have to bare the burden of the additional year of service. "Alright," Mei repeated softly as she helped Lin to her feet.

The man got out of the van and opened the back door. "Get in," he said, gesturing to Lin.

Mei placed her hands on Lin's shoulders and spoke sternly. "You will be fine, everything will be fine." Her hands slid down Lin's arms until she was clenching Lin's forearms. "You must honor your family."

"But with Father gone, you will be all alone."

"That is why you must honor *him*. Don't worry about me."

Lin wished in these last few moments that her mother would relax her cold stare and display some form of sadness watching her daughter leave. But Mei's gaze remained stern. Lin had always felt a distance between her and her mother, a feeling that had intensified shortly after her father disappeared.

Mei pulled a sheet of paper from her pocket, a name and telephone number scribbled on the upper left-hand corner. She folded the paper and stuffed it into Lin's bag. "Do not lose this," instructed Mei. "Do you understand?"

Her voice inhibited by the lump in her throat, Lin simply nodded.

Unsatisfied by Lin's feeble acknowledgement, Mei persisted. "Do you understand?" she asked more forcefully.

"Yes. I understand."

The man took one last puff of his cigarette and flicked the butt onto the muddy road. "In the back," he grumbled, clearing his throat.

Two other passengers were already inside. Huddled in the far corner of the back row of seats, a young woman stared straight ahead. She wore a long tattered cloth robe that partially cloaked a pair of broken sandals. Smudges of dirt covered her bronze face. She hugged her knees tightly to her chest with her thin arms, her black hair draped over her shoulders. She appeared to Lin no older than twenty.

The other passenger was a young man who sat with his legs crossed and his back arched. Although he was staring at Lin, his gaze was not piercing. He had atypically wide hazel eyes and ears that stuck out. The tip of his nose hung down slightly below his nostrils, a feature that Lin found particularly dignifying for reasons she could not articulate. As Lin appraised the young man's soft eyes, a momentary feeling of comfort washed over her, helping to alleviate her racing pulse.

Lin hoisted her bag into the back of the van and stepped inside. The door shut. The man got back into the passenger seat and turned to the driver. "We are late, drive fast." He stuck his head out the window and looked at Mei. "If your daughter vomits in my van, I will add another year!" The driver let out a boisterous laugh. A moment later, the engine roared as he clumsily maneuvered the clutch and gas pedal.

The sky continued to grow brighter as the van sped away. Lin brushed off the mud that had dried to the side of her body as the van swerved back and forth to avoid large rocks in the dirt road. She nervously watched the two men sitting in the front of the van smoking cigarettes. Quietly she sat, contemplating everything she thought would take place over the course of the upcoming days, unaware that she would witness events that would shock and disgust her, and do things that she would regret forever.

So much has to go right for this to work.

Chapter 3

Sonoran Desert, Arizona, September 1999

SOFIA TRIED TO swallow, but there was no more saliva. Her throat burned. Her cracked lips were starting to puff out. She clung to her last bottle of water. *It must be close to noon*, she thought.

The sun was directly overhead, burning the patches of her scalp that her thinning hair left exposed. She had been wearing a hat when she departed Mexico a day and a half ago but quickly discarded it after she began to develop a rash from the brim rubbing against her sweaty forehead. Sofia regretted this decision. She would trade the irritation caused by the hat for a moment of shade.

Each step she took was a struggle. Although Sofia was only thirty-seven years old, she weighed no more than ninety-five pounds. Her small frame had slowly withered since she became sick. *Getting to the United States is my only chance to live.*

It took Sofia more than two years to save enough money to finance her trip to the United States. Paying for the bus ticket to the border town of Sonoita was the easy part, an uncomfortable fourteen-hour drive north, up Highway 15, listening to horn percussions blasting on passengers' oversized boom boxes.

The money she would need for the rest of her voyage after she reached Sonoita was harder to calculate. She heard stories from friends about the cost of hiring smugglers, who were known as *coyotes*. The dramatically varied prices were a glaring uncertainty in what Sofia believed to be an otherwise meticulously calculable plan.

Sofia was not sure she had enough money to make it all the way to the United States when she left her hometown of Escuinapa. But her physical condition had worsened considerably in recent months, and she could not wait any longer. Many coyotes promised her safe passage to the United States, but Sofia decided to go with the one who gave her *"el gran paquete"*—a package deal. The coyote threw in a complimentary Social Security card, which he assured her was the key to increased employment opportunities in the United States—"along with other benefits," he told her.

Placing her hand on her brow, Sofia did her best to shield her eyes from the sun. She squinted, looking back and forth as she tried to locate the coyote. Hours had passed since the last time Sofia saw him. She had been following one of the other *ilegales*, Maria, who was also lagging behind. Maria was traveling with her eleven-year-old son, Fernando, who needed to stop and rest more frequently. Fernando's mother had neatly parted his straight black hair before they set out for the United States. But now, his hair was clumped and knotted, specks of sand caked to his sweaty forehead and his earlobes. Sofia was grateful that Fernando's skinny little legs could not keep up with the dozen other travelers who were able to keep pace with the coyote.

In every direction, all Sofia saw were bushes, shrubs and cacti sprinkled along zigzagging dirt paths that cut through the rocky, mountainous terrain. She struggled to navigate the small boulders lining the side of a moderate incline. She was only a few feet away from the top when Fernando ran back in Sofia's direction and inadvertently barreled right into her.

After Fernando knocked her over, Sofia lay on her back staring at the sun, her feet positioned higher on the slope, sending a rush of blood to her forehead. Sand covered her tongue and she could not muster enough saliva to spit it out.

When Maria crawled back over the top of the hill, Fernando was bending down to rub his shin, which he had scraped on a jagged rock after he bounced off of Sofia. "Get down, Fernando. Be quiet," she said before noticing Sofia's helpless body sprawled out on the side of the dune. "My goodness, Fernando, what have you done?" Maria reached into a bag draped over her shoulder and pulled out a canteen. She elevated Sofia's head onto her lap and helped her take a sip of water.

For a moment, the grains of sand crunching in Sofia's mouth did not bother her. The water had quenched the ongoing burn in her throat and Maria's head was shielding Sofia's eyes from the sun.

"What's wrong?" Sofia asked. "Why are you coming back?"

"*Bandidos*," Maria said. "The bandits are heading toward the coyote and the others."

Gunshots echoed throughout the valley.

Fernando tugged on Maria's shirtsleeve. "Mama, I'm scared."

Maria didn't respond.

Sofia reached for Maria's other sleeve. The burning feeling had returned to her throat and her heart was pounding. As she looked up at Maria, Sofia felt as helpless as a child. Little did she know, their lives would be intertwined until the end of their days.

"Mama, what are we going to do?"

Maria stroked Fernando's hair and gently pressed her other hand on Sofia's forehead.

"Pray to *San Pedro*, my dear. Pray they do not follow the tracks back to us."

Chapter 4

"**L**ADIES AND GENTLEMEN," the flight attendant announced, "we are starting to make our final descent into London. Please take your seats and ensure your seatbelts are fastened."

The flight from Nairobi to London passed quicker than Tesfaye anticipated, taken up by his effort to methodically search his thoughts for any bit of information he might have overlooked, anything to help explain the circumstances that forced him to flee Africa.

After departing the plane, Tesfaye scuttled through the long corridors of Heathrow Airport, mindful that he did not have much time until his connecting flight. Finding a departures screen, he scanned the list to find the gate number of his flight to New York. Sandwiched between two flights departing on time was his flight, *cancelled*. "Shit."

The airline representative was mechanically apologetic, insisting there was nothing she could do. She booked Tesfaye on the first flight the following morning. After a few drinks at the bar, Tesfaye plopped down in an uncomfortable chair in the terminal, watching travelers whisk by.

The hairs on his neck stood on edge when he noticed the silhouette of an exceptionally large, dark-skinned man approaching him. Making eye contact, Tesfaye's heart sank. "Negasi?" asked Tesfaye, not sure why the question came out of his mouth. The man looked the other way and kept walking.

Tesfaye violently scratched his head and sighed. *Keep it together Tesfaye*, he instructed himself. A lump formed in his throat. *I should have gotten out of Ethiopia with Geteye and my family. I should have forced Negasi to come with us to Kenya.*

AFTER NEGASI DROVE away, Tesfaye ran inside and headed straight to his study. He sifted through his rolodex and found the number for Mohamed Da'al. A military man all his life, Mohamed had been a trusted advisor of Mengistu for years—one of the only Muslim men permitted to join Mengistu's inner circle. He would know the seriousness of the rebel incursions in the north, Tesfaye thought.

Tesfaye frantically dialed Mohamed's home phone number. The phone kept ringing and Tesfaye was about to hang up. "Hello," a voice groaned.

Tesfaye realized how early it was and that he had probably woken Mohamed. "Mohamed, is that you?"

"Tesfaye? What time is it? Is everything all right?"

Tesfaye wanted to tell Mohamed that he sent his family to Kenya and that he would have gone with them if he didn't fear the potential repercussions. But he refrained from disclosing his true fear. Mohamed had been a good friend, but life under the Mengistu regime had made everyone cautious about disclosing their thoughts and feelings, even those with high positions in the government. Tesfaye did not want to test Mohamed's loyalty to Mengistu and find out whether he would provide the paranoid ruler with information about Tesfaye's recent actions in order to gain favor.

"I didn't realize it was so early. Go back to sleep my friend and I will talk to you later."

"That's quite alright, Tesfaye," Mohamed said in the midst of a yawn. "I'm awake now. What's on your mind?"

"Probably nothing to even think twice about, but I recently heard a story about rebels in the north. I'd be curious to know whether you've heard anything on the subject in the last few days."

"Ah, the TPLF. What are the Tigray trying to accomplish, eh? The poor bastards are just bitter they don't control the government. Looting the countryside certainly isn't going to change that." For centuries, the Amhara ethnic group had dominated all political and cultural aspects of Ethiopia, leading to widespread animosity and distrust of the ruling class by other ethnicities, including the Tigray. With his multi-ethnic background, Mengistu was supposed to change this dynamic after he forcefully took control of the government. However, distrust among most countrymen remained strong and led to the creation of numerous ethnically-based liberation fronts throughout Ethiopia.

Tesfaye forced himself to laugh. "Very true. I don't know what they want to accomplish. Do they actually think they will take over the government? Mengistu will never allow that, no?"

"Let them try. I've heard the Tigray are at least a few weeks away from Addis Ababa, and we have 30,000 soldiers in reserve here that could easily crush whatever resistance has not been completely wiped out by that point. With all the money we've gotten from the Russians, they don't stand a chance. Poor, misguided bastards."

Tesfaye talked to Mohamed for a while longer about local gossip at the ministries and other pleasantries about their families to make sure he was not suspicious of the early morning call. When Tesfaye hung up the phone, a wave of relief washed over him. If nothing else, Mohamed had confirmed his hope that he had at least a couple of weeks to assess any progress made by the rebels in the north. But still, Geteye's insistence that he leave immediately continued to weigh heavily on his mind. While it may have been a wise decision for him to accept the position at the Ministry of Defense nearly fourteen years ago, he now felt trapped by his prominent role in the current government. Applying the pragmatism that Ayana always admired in him, Tesfaye decided that he had to formulate a contingency plan. *If the rebels are successful*, he thought, *I will be ready.* He grabbed a small suitcase, packing some basics in the event he would have to make a quick escape. He would have Negasi do the same when he returned from the airport.

For the next week, Tesfaye religiously listened to the radio and soaked up bits of information he would gather from colleagues at the ministry. He felt sick every time he thought about his family in Kenya. He knew he could not talk to Geteye over the phone because the line could be tapped. There were confirmed reports that Mengistu's security forces had periodically monitored the phone conversations of his ministers and high-level officials to protect himself against any subversive activity.

Eight days had passed since his family flew to Nairobi. Tesfaye grew even more anxious. Many of the rumors flowing through the ministry were contradictory. Several prominent officials had not been seen in days. *By the end of the week, I will have to make a decision.*

On the ninth day, Tesfaye awoke and turned on the radio. "I repeat," the voice on the radio said, "we have received reports that the Tigray have entered Addis Ababa." His eyes bulging, Tesfaye listened for another minute. He heard nothing about the government sending reinforcements to crush the rebels. No calming words of assurance from Mengistu. Just an animated radio broadcaster claiming that the airport was now under rebel control.

Tesfaye ran to his office and located Mohamed's number. His hand trembled as he dialed. He let the phone ring for a full two minutes, but nobody answered. The front door slammed shut. Loud, thumping footsteps let out the familiar creaks in the corridor approaching Tesfaye's study.

"Tesfaye!" shouted Negasi as he entered the study. "They have taken control of the airport."

"I've been listening, I heard it too."

"What should we do?"

Tesfaye thought for a moment. "Negasi, your family is from Awasa, right?"

"Very close."

"Then that will be our destination. Awasa isn't far from Kenya." Tesfaye dug through the closet in his study, emerging with a map of Ethiopia that he laid out on his desk. "We will head south, southeast by car to avoid the Tigray and then loop back around to Awasa. I'll rest there for a night and then continue south to Kenya to meet my family in Thika."

"I appreciate your looking out for me, but I'm going with you to Kenya," Negasi insisted.

"This is not up for debate," Tesfaye snapped, "you'll be safe in Awasa and I don't know what's going to happen when I get to Kenya. Go get your bag, we're leaving now. You did pack a bag like I told you to?"

"Yes, Tesfaye."

"Bring it to the car. I'll be outside in two minutes."

A rush of adrenaline was surging through Tesfaye's body. He had planned for this possibility, but every action now felt exponentially more demanding. *Did I pack everything I need? Where did I put my passport?* He wandered aimlessly around his study. *Focus Tesfaye.* Taking a deep breath, he ran down the corridor and grabbed his bag from the front closet. His hand was turning the handle of the front door when he paused. He darted back to his bedroom and retrieved a picture of Ayana and the children. Quickly removing the picture from the frame, he placed it in his pocket and hurried out the front door to wait for Negasi.

The wheels of the Mercedes began to spin as Negasi gunned the accelerator and tried to get traction on the heated dirt driveway. The tires glided for a moment on the dry dirt before coming to a stop in front of the house. Negasi jumped out and put Tesfaye's bag in the trunk while Tesfaye got into the car. Negasi sped away toward the front gates of the property. As they approached the entranceway, a jeep drove through the front gate heading straight toward the Mercedes.

Negasi slammed on the brakes.

The Mercedes skidded and came to a stop inches from the front grill of the jeep. Having forgotten to buckle his seatbelt, Tesfaye's head lurched forward and slammed into the front dashboard. Slightly stunned, he grabbed his head and stared down at his shoes for a moment. When he looked up, the strong morning sunlight was shining directly in his eyes. Flashes of light flickered all around, distorting his vision. As the flashes began to fade, Tesfaye squinted and used his hand to shield his eyes from the sun.

Two jeeps were parked in front of the Mercedes. The smell of fumes emanated from their idling diesel engines. Three men sat in both jeeps, each carrying an AK-47 proudly pointed to the sky. With one exception, they were all wearing dark t-shirts, sweat stains circling their necklines. The man in the front passenger seat of the jeep that Negasi almost hit was dressed in a muted olive army uniform, a pair of gloves covering his hands. His aviator sunglasses masked a patch that covered his left eye.

The uniformed man shouted something to the others. Tesfaye could not make out what he said, but he could hear how sternly he said it and how quickly the other men obeyed. The doors of the jeeps opened and the men approached Tesfaye and Negasi with their AK-47s pointed at the car.

"Tesfaye, what should we do?" whispered Negasi, staring straight ahead and trying not to move his lips.

There was no time to formulate a strategy. For all his planning, Tesfaye had not accounted for this. *How did I manage to get trapped in my own front yard? Why are they at my house of all places?* "Just let me do the talking," Tesfaye whispered back.

"Out!" someone shouted.

Negasi quickly got out of the car and stood by the open driver's side door. Tesfaye joined him. Two of the men were searching through Tesfaye's car. They removed the bags that Tesfaye and Negasi had packed so many days before and threw them in front of Tesfaye's feet.

The man in the olive military uniform walked over to Tesfaye. "Good morning," he said. "I see you are going on a trip. I am so sorry to disturb your vacation plans." The other men laughed.

"No vacation," Tesfaye said. "I have some business to take care of in Kenya." Tesfaye did not want to disclose where he was going, but he knew his answer had to be plausible and he could not think of another stable country in the region.

"Kenya." The man in the military uniform snickered. "Of course." He glanced at the two bags lying in front of Tesfaye. "Are both of these yours?"

Tesfaye knew he could not pass off Negasi's abnormally large clothing as his own if the men searched the bags, so he decided that, at this point, it was in his interest to be candid. "No, sir."

The uniformed man looked disapprovingly at Negasi. "Does your driver always accompany you on your business flights to Kenya?" he asked Tesfaye.

Tesfaye struggled to swallow. "As it happens, I'm driving to Kenya. I have always had a fear of flying so I try to drive whenever I can. It is less convenient to drive, but what can you do?"

"Yes, yes, what *can* you do?" asked the man in the military uniform in a mocking tone as he looked around at the other men, who provided more approving laughter. "What can you do?" he repeated, taking a step closer to Tesfaye and removing his aviator sunglasses. His sarcastic smile disappeared, replaced by the unsettling gaze of his one bloodshot eye. "I will tell you what you can do. You can give me the information I want, or you can take one last breath before I put a bullet through your head."

"Information? What . . ."

"Where is Geteye Tge!"

Geteye? His pulse suddenly elevated by the unexpected inquiry, Tesfaye pictured Geteye sitting at a kitchen table in Kenya with Ayana and the kids. *Why does he want to know about Geteye?* There was no way Tesfaye would tell this man where in Kenya to find his dear friend. He would certainly not reveal the location of his family. Tesfaye had made a promise to his daughter Yenee—to all of them—that everything would be alright.

"What is your name, sir?" asked Tesfaye with as much confidence in his voice as he could muster. Although he was genuinely curious about the identity of this man, Tesfaye immediately regretted his question.

The butt of an AK-47 smacked against Tesfaye's jawbone. His head snapped around and he felt an excruciating pain shoot through his neck. For a moment, he was again facing the long driveway leading to his new cobblestone walkway. Tesfaye fell to his knees and his throat began to ache from the whiplash.

Two of the gun-wielding men brought a stunned Tesfaye to his feet and the man in the military uniform stared at him. "I do not ask questions expecting a question in return. Do you understand?"

Tesfaye nodded affirmatively.

"You do not need to know who I am," he continued. "All you need to know is what I represent. That is change. I represent the end of Colonel Mengistu and the end of all those who have allowed him to steal our livelihood and rape our women without consequence. Do I make myself clear?"

Tesfaye again nodded that he understood.

"I will ask you again, where is Geteye Tge?"

"I don't know," Tesfaye pleaded. "I swear I don't know."

The vein next to his bloodshot eye pulsing, the uniformed man clenched his lips. He pulled a large machete from his belt.

Tesfaye could see his reflection in the bloodstained machete blade. *He's going to kill me*, he thought, feeling some pride knowing he would die without revealing the location of his family. His momentary satisfaction quickly turned to sadness as he thought about Ayana and the children. *I broke my promise.*

"Very well," said the man in the military uniform. Without hesitation, he stepped over to Negasi and sliced his throat open with the machete.

"Negasi!" screamed Tesfaye.

Grabbing his throat, Negasi dropped to his knees. Blood poured down his hands and trickled onto his shirt. Negasi looked over toward Tesfaye. One of the men kicked Negasi's shoulder and watched him fall over.

There were a few gargling sounds. Then silence. Negasi's body lay lifeless on the ground.

"Negasi," Tesfaye whispered.

Tesfaye's legs could barely support his solid frame. His hands were trembling and tears started to build in his eyes.

The butt of an AK-47 hit Tesfaye in his stomach. He gasped for air. His body was being lifted off the ground and all he could see was the dirt beneath him.

"Throw him in the back."

Tesfaye's head was pressed against the back seat of the jeep, an AK-47 lodged on his tailbone. The smell of diesel again permeated the air. He gasped to catch his breath. The jeep began to move. Then, everything went black.

"IN A FEW minutes, we will begin boarding for our nonstop service to New York."

Tesfaye had dozed off and the gate agent's announcement over the loudspeaker startled him. He stared back down at his index finger and shook his head. "Negasi," he mumbled.

Chapter 5

LIN HAD NEVER been more than ten miles from home. She sat quietly in the back of the van, gazing out the windshield. The vehicle soon got off the dirt roads and began to glide smoothly on the pavement. An hour later, Lin could see the outline of a city in the distance.

The young man sitting next to her sat motionless, his legs coiled together. Lin was amazed at his seemingly effortless ability to keep his back arched. He opened his eyes. "Are we leaving from Fuzhou?" he asked calmly.

The snakehead in the passenger seat turned around to face the boy. A wide grin forced his puffy cheeks upward. "Yes," he said. "But we have one more stop to make first."

Lin turned to the young man. "Is that Fuzhou?"

"I think that's Changle City," he replied. He stared at Lin for a moment. "I'm Shaoqing. You are?"

"Lin. My name is Lin."

Shaoqing pointed to the girl in the back of the van wearing the long robes. "That is Ai."

After their brief introductions, the passengers again sat in silence as the van approached Changle City. Tucked between mountain ranges near the eastern border of the Fujian Province, Changle City is an eclectic mix of old world attractions and modern conveniences, with ancient palaces and pagodas interspersed among high-rise apartment buildings and shopping centers.

The outlines of the buildings in the distance grew more detailed. The van entered the city, heading north, rows of planted trees and bushes separating the road from the wide sidewalks. Pristinely landscaped parks decorated with circular fountains broke up the city's growing urban feel. Driving past Changle Hospital to a residential neighborhood in the heart of the city, the driver stopped the van on the side of the road, turning off the engine as the snakehead sitting in the front passenger seat exited.

Lin heard laughter outside the van. Out of the corner of her eye she saw the snakehead bowing repeatedly. When the side door opened, Lin's heart fluttered.

The first feature Lin noticed was Jiang's chiseled jaw line. His dark complexion complemented his rich brown eyes and thick eyebrows. His hair was spiked by a product that made it look wet. Lin stared at his fingernails. *So clean*, she thought.

Standing by the front door, the snakehead blew a puff of smoke in Lin's eyes. "What are you looking at?" he barked at Lin. "Get in the back. Come now, go, go," he ordered as Lin scurried to the back of the van next to Ai, making room for Jiang by the side door.

The van sped out of Changle City and continued east on a monotonous two-lane road. With nothing else to do, Lin stared intently at Jiang's spiked hair and the straight edge where his hairline ended and his neck began.

Lin wasn't sure how much time had passed before the van came to an abrupt halt in a deserted dirt lot surrounded by forest.

"Everybody out," ordered one of the snakeheads. He opened the side door and the four passengers made their way out of the van.

The driver and the puffy cheeked snakehead quietly sat on the hood of the van, tapping their feet and impatiently checking their watches every few minutes until a Volkswagen Santana pulled up next to them. The Volkswagen was a small and boxy car, low to the ground, with a jade grey exterior rusting all around. The driver's side door creaked open as an elderly gentleman exited the car. With the assistance of a cane, he walked over to the van. The three men talked for a few seconds and nodded at each other.

"Get in the car," the snakehead shouted at Lin and the others, pointing toward the beat-up Volkswagen.

The man with the cane shook his head. "We're late, very late." Beckoning Jiang, he opened the front passenger door. Lin had pulled the right rear door halfway open before the cane smacked her hand, and the door was slammed shut. "Too dangerous, we don't want to draw attention at our destination. You'll have to ride in the back," he said as he walked around the Volkswagen and opened the trunk. "Come now."

Taken aback when she looked down, Lin could see the fumes spewing from the tailpipe of the Volkswagen. But after Shaoqing jumped into the trunk without hesitation, Lin reluctantly followed, placing her head next to Shaoqing's on the side of the trunk farthest from the tailpipe.

"There's no way I'm getting in there," Ai insisted.

The man with the cane slowly walked over to the driver side door. He reached into the Volkswagen and emerged with a gun, which he pointed at Ai's chest. "My dear, we don't have time to argue. If you don't get in the trunk, then we'll be late. If we are late, then you will miss your ride. If you miss your ride, then you will not repay your debt. If you cannot pay your debt, then you are useless to me." Smirking, he continued. "If you are useless to me, then I might as well shoot you now."

When Ai approached the trunk, the man with the cane pushed her inside and slammed it shut. Lin could smell Ai's feet, which were inches from her face. Adding to Lin's discomfort, Ai's knee was lodged on her tailbone and Shaoqing's thick hair was nearly suffocating her. With her thigh unavoidably pressed against Shaoqing's rear end, she closed her eyes and pretended she was leaning against Jiang. But no daydream could trick her fragile stomach. She prayed she wouldn't vomit in Shaoqing's hair.

Every bump in the road sent Lin's head banging against the unpadded floor of the trunk. She wedged her arm under her ear to soften the blows. Each time the Volkswagen came to a stop, the smell of fumes would fill the trunk and Ai would let out a groan that was barely audible over the vibrations of the engine. Lin could hardly stand the smell from her own vantage point during the deep breaths she had to take to stop herself from vomiting. She could only imagine what Ai was going through.

Lin's heavy breathing became rhythmic. Like the ticks of a pendulum, she used each breath to count the sluggishly passing seconds. Breathe in, *one*, breathe out, *two*, breathe in, *three*, breathe out, *four*. Each second became its own nightmare as she nervously lay in the trunk, terrified she would throw up on Shaoqing. Terrified the man with the cane would beat her for fouling up his trunk. Terrified she would be sent back to her mother in shame. Her heart rate rising, she again felt as though she were about to cry. *This can't be happening*, she thought as Shaoqing's hair tickled her nose. She was still in China and the journey was already too much for her to handle. So she again focused on her breathing, counting out each protracted second. *Thirty-four, thirty-five, thirty-six, thirty-seven.* What she wouldn't give to be propped against the dry stone wall her father built outside the kitchen window, sitting next to him, discussing one of the books he would make her read as a substitute for her lack of formal education.

After an onerous forty-five minutes, Lin heard the creaking noise of a gate opening before the Volkswagen continued to move. Not long after, the car came to a stop and the engine vibrations ceased. When the man with the cane opened the trunk, Lin covered her eyes until they adjusted to the light.

"Out," he said.

Lin waited for Ai to get out of the trunk, but she wasn't moving.

A few pokes of the cane yielded no response.

"Hmm," he said, placing his cane on the ground. He took a vial out of his pocket and placed it under Ai's nose. Moments later, she groaned.

"You gave us a scare," the man with the cane snickered. "Now get out of the trunk before someone sees us. All of you, follow me."

For the first time in her life, Lin took in a deep breath of the salty ocean air. The man with the cane led Lin and the others through a maze of large metal shipping crates stacked in rows on the grounds of the port. Lin watched a large crane lift crates onto a ship as she followed the man with the cane down a narrow path that protruded out into the ocean.

A fishing boat nearly thirty feet long was tied to the dock at the end of the path. Patches of rust blotted the boat's exterior where a once fresh coat of paint had long since faded away. Lin could make out at least five other people on the vessel. Her heart began to beat faster as she thought about crossing the ocean in this rickety old fishing boat.

A lanky, slender man leaned on a guardrail lining the end of the dock. He pointed at the man with the cane. "We were about to leave."

The man with the cane bowed his head. "My apologies, Lee. An opportunity arose and we made an extra stop along the way," he said, pointing his cane toward Jiang. Lin remembered that the man with the cane hadn't yet arrived at the dirt lot by the time her van pulled in, which meant he was purposefully concealing his responsibility for their apparent late arrival. Looking at the man with the cane, Lin could see the trepidation in his forced smile, and she sensed that he was afraid of Lee. It then occurred to Lin that she was about to board a ship with a man feared by other snakeheads. It was a realization that did not sit well.

The man with the cane continued, "I assure you, it was a very profitable extra stop." Fumbling around his pocket, he tucked his cane under his arm and handed Lee an envelope. "I think you will find this more than makes up for the slight delay."

Lee sifted through the envelope. His face looked withered and leathery, the sides curled inwards as if he were sucking violently on a straw. A narrow face made Lee's eyes appear enormous. He turned around and faced the fishing boat. "Fei Pin!" he shouted.

Lin had a bad feeling about Fei Pin as soon as she gazed at his squirrely round face. His mouth never seemed to fully close and his belly bulged beneath his overly tight, untucked button-down shirt. She stared at the large crevices in Fei's bellybutton and slowly moved her gaze upward to find Fei's eyes staring right back at her. As Lee and the man with the cane talked, Fei continued to stare at Lin and smile, his mouth wide open.

"Fei Pin!" Lee shouted again. Fei immediately turned to Lee and bowed his head. "Take this," Lee ordered, handing Fei the envelope. Fei nodded and walked back to the end of the dock, gazing at Lin over his shoulder until he stepped onto the boat.

"They all have their stories?" Lee asked.

The man with the cane nodded. "I imagine so."

"Good."

Lee turned his attention to Lin and the others. "On the boat!" he ordered.

Fei Pin pulled a cord on the fishing boat's motor several times before it started. Dark plumes of smoke rose from the engine. The deck began to vibrate and the sound of the engine intensified as the boat gathered speed.

The sunny skies of the coast slowly turned grey as they got further from shore. Lin couldn't tell if it was raining or if the drops of water sprinkling on her face were from the boat cutting through the ocean. She looked around at the other travelers clinging to the sides of the boat. *Were they happy to be here? Frightened like I am?* she wondered. She couldn't tell. All she saw was a collection of muted, expressionless faces staring out onto the ocean, occasionally wiping a tear from the corner of their wind-whipped eyes.

Fei Pin made no effort to reduce the speed of the boat when it approached choppy waters. Lin tried to time when the boat would hit a wave to avoid landing on her tailbone. Her timing improved over the next several hours as the boat traversed through the dense mist hovering above the ocean. Then, for no apparent reason, the boat stopped.

Lee didn't attempt to hide his frustration. "Where is it?" he barked at Fei Pin. "We should have been there twenty minutes ago!"

"I must have missed one of the buoys," Fei Pin said, staring at a compass.

"Are you trying to get us caught? If the Coast Guard finds us Fei Pin, I will personally see to it that you are sodomized the first night we're locked away!"

Fei Pin's eyebrows drew closer to each other, the skin on the bridge of his nose protruding outward. He placed his hand on his chin and stood silently for a moment. "Everyone be quiet." The sound of another motor was faint over the splashing noises of the rocking boat. "I hear it."

Fei Pin turned the boat around, maintaining a slow speed to minimize the vibrations of the motor. His eyebrows were still furrowed, as if their proximity was directly related to the strength of his sense of hearing. Lin watched Lee try to pierce the mist with his wide eyes.

As the sound of another engine grew louder, Lee waved his hand at Fei Pin. "Cut the motor!"

Through the mist, Lin could make out a maroon object; it seemed barely one story out of the water, but considerably longer than the boat she currently occupied. As they drifted closer, the outline of the ship came into focus, a gigantic vessel floating three stories out of the water. Above its maroon hull, the ship was colored deep blue, blending into the surrounding waters of the Pacific Ocean. On the side of the boat, stenciled in white letters, it read *The Bamboo*.

Other small fishing boats lined the exterior of the large ship. Crewmen from the larger ship were hoisting passengers onto the deck three stories above.

"International waters," Lee said. "Everyone up. Quickly!"

Lin grabbed the end of the rope that several crewmen had lowered from the ship's deck. The rope was split at the bottom into a 'v' shape, with a loop at the end of each of the two strands. She placed her feet in the two loops and clung tight to the wet rope as the crewmen hoisted her to the deck.

Much to Lin's dismay, Fei Pin joined Lee on the deck. Lee waived down to the remaining person on the small boat, who started the motor and sped away, back toward Fuzhou.

Once all the other travelers were hoisted onto the deck, they followed Lee down a steep metal staircase, past a poorly lit interior level filled with wooden shipping crates. Continuing down the steps one more level, Lee led them through a narrow corridor lined with small rooms that served as the crewmen's living quarters. A group of the crewmen were squeezed into one of the rooms, bantering as they drank whiskey and played cards. When Lee passed by, the crewmen all quieted down, like a group of students caught misbehaving by the principal.

Ahead was a large metal door at the end of the corridor. When Lee reached the door, he spun the handle, cursing as his skinny frame struggled to pull it open. "Why is this door closed?" Lee murmured to nobody in particular.

On the other side of the door, natural light illuminated a closed hatch on the ground. Lee dropped to his knees, groaning as he spun the metal wheel. He lifted the rusty hatch and looked back up at the passengers, gesturing with his hand. "Get in."

Lin didn't understand how natural light could be shining in the middle of the ship this far below deck until she was standing next to Lee by the hatch. Looking up, she saw an empty space that was like a vertical vestibule, a hollowed-out chamber that stretched all the way up to the deck. And on the deck, there was another hatch that if closed, would cut off all the natural light now shining on this inner chamber. Next to Lin, there was a metal ladder that extended from hatch to hatch, the entire height of the inner chamber. The snakeheads purposefully designed it this way, carving out a hole in the middle of the deck so the travelers could climb straight to the deck from their living quarters without having to go anywhere else on the ship.

Eager to soak in one last second of natural light before leaving the chamber, Lin glanced up at the grey sky. "Get in!" Lee ordered, pushing the back of her neck. Below the hatch, Lin could see a thick iron pole, about seven feet long, with foot holdings that extended to the floor of the passengers' apparent living quarters. After she felt the floor of the living quarters with her toes and secured her footing, Lin immediately covered her nose, taken back by the pungent smell of stale sweat. Green halogen lighting filled the room, magnifying the eyes of the other passengers and revealing a pile of cardboard pieces stacked in the corner.

Lin gazed up at Lee standing at the top of the open hatch, smoking a cigarette. Exhaling a deep puff, Lee glanced down, smiling as he locked his bulging eyes on her. He flicked his cigarette butt down at Lin and grabbed the handle of the hatch.

A moment later, the hatch slammed shut. The green lights grew brighter. And Lin's nausea returned.

Chapter 6

COWERING IN FEAR from the sound of gunshots echoing throughout the Arizona desert, Sofia sat motionless with Maria and Fernando. They all prayed for what felt like hours until the sound of the bandits' ATVs faded into the distance.

"Are they gone?" moaned a delirious Sofia. "I need to get out of the sun."

Maria and Fernando helped Sofia to her feet. They walked to a nearby patch of shrubs and lay down in the blotches of shade. Surveying Sofia's emaciated body sprawled out under the shrubs and barely conscious enough to speak, Maria thought about abandoning her, trudging forward to catch up with any survivors. But she quickly dismissed the idea, reasoning that anyone who survived would have run away from the gun-toting bandits as fast as they could. At this point, they'd likely be separated, aimlessly walking through the desert, praying that they were heading in the right direction. And in their heightened desperation, she and Fernando would be easy targets—for their water, their food, or perhaps something else more nefarious. *I'm on my own*, Maria accepted, praying she would remember the right direction from her past hikes through the desert.

"We should stay here to be safe and get some rest," Maria said, removing a wrinkled blue sheet from her bag. "By three tomorrow morning we'll need to start heading to the pickup location."

"What time is it?" asked Sofia. "I need to meet Rosario in Tucson." Sofia struggled to piece together the plan she had discussed with her friend Rosario. "Wait, wait, what day is it?" she asked.

"Don't worry," Maria assured her, recognizing that the heat had battered the coherency of Sofia's thoughts. "We'll be on time. The coyote was going to stop soon anyway. You'll feel better after you get some rest."

Maria stared at Fernando sitting on the blue sheet, pouring handfuls of sand over the shrubs. *He looks so tired*, Maria thought, unsure Fernando would have had the strength to keep walking even if she had decided it would be best to abandon Sofia. Her chest suddenly felt hollow as tears began streaming down her face. *Oh my God! How could I do this to my son? Is this really happening? Am I actually sitting in the middle of the desert?* She thought about all the things that could go wrong, like a discombobulated young man who survived the bandits going the wrong way, finding them in the middle of the night, raping her, killing her, beating Fernando. Or maybe she'd take them in the wrong direction, back into the heart of the Sonoran, where she'd have to watch her son die of dehydration. When the thoughts became too much, she slapped herself across the face. "Snap out of it," she told herself. *You're in charge now. You need to be strong.*

The desert cooled after sunset, but Sofia had a difficult time falling asleep on the hot sand. She was lying on her side and a pain was shooting through her neck. Choosing not to expend the energy needed to adjust her body, she accepted the discomfort until she fell asleep.

Vivid dreams woke Sofia throughout the night. Her children's screams muffled by men's laughter, her husband's body lying dormant in a pool of blood. These recurring images had subsided over the last couple of years, but they started to appear more frequently once her failing health made the circumstances of her predicament more real.

Sofia's eyes opened when she heard Maria and Fernando whispering. Although she felt slightly rejuvenated, her eyelids were heavy and she would have welcomed the opportunity to rest longer.

Maria tapped Sofia's shoulder. "Are you awake?"

Sofia blinked several times and tried to focus on the outline of Maria's face. The desert was pitch black except for a small circle of light illuminating from the flashlight Maria pointed at the ground.

"We need to leave soon," Maria said as she munched on a bag of peanuts. "Here," Maria offered, holding out the bag. "The salt will help prevent dehydration."

Like a hungry dog devouring a piece of meat thrown in front of it, Sofia immediately grabbed the peanuts. While she shoved handfuls in her mouth, she noticed what looked like chunks of tobacco spread over the ground around her. "What's this for?" she asked Maria.

"It helps to keep rattlesnakes away. I even rubbed some on your ankles."

"How do you know how to do all these things?"

Maria smiled. "Let's just say this isn't my first time crossing the desert. But I have never seen bandits before. I heard they are everywhere."

Listening to Maria, Sofia realized that despite her earlier planned efforts, she was completely unprepared for her journey to the United States. "How many times have you crossed the border?" asked Sofia.

"Four times before this trip. Well, three times I guess. Once I turned around and went home because everyone told me I didn't have the right supplies. This is your first time crossing?"

Sofia nodded.

"What are you going to do in the United States?" asked Maria.

"I don't know," Sofia conceded. "I don't care. I'll clean toilets. I just need to get help from a doctor." Sofia stared down at the circular bones protruding from her emaciated wrists.

"I didn't want to say anything."

"No, it's fine. I know you can tell by looking at me that I'm sick. Everybody can tell."

"What's wrong?"

Sofia sighed and tried to force a smile. "Don't worry, what I have is not contagious."

Fernando began cursing as he tried unsuccessfully to unknot a plastic bag full of stiffened tortillas that Maria had packed. "Watch your language," Maria whispered sternly. "Give me that," she said, opening the bag and handing Fernando a tortilla. "Do you have any children, Sofia?"

"Two. My daughter Eva is sixteen, and my son Manuel is thirteen. *I cannot believe I'm leaving them behind.* "They're home with my sister." Looking at Fernando, Sofia suddenly felt the need to justify why she didn't take her kids with her. "It cost so much to make this trip and there's no money for them to come up now." Sofia sighed. "But what good am I to them if I'm dead, right?" she asked, seeking Maria's approval.

"You would be no good at all." Maria patted Sofia's hand. "Everything will work out just fine. You'll see."

Sofia wasn't used to displays of kindness from people outside her family. Ever since word of her condition spread through town, she had been treated as a pariah.

Maria glanced at her watch. "It's almost three-thirty, we should go. Luckily for us, the coyote was able to guide us most of the way. I think I remember the way from here. I've done this route before. We should get going."

The one flashlight was their only guide through the desert in the darkness. They walked for twenty minutes before the flashlight suddenly illuminated the bloody legs of the coyote. Seeing his bullet-ridden body sprawled over a pile of jagged rocks, Maria quickly moved the beam away before shoving Fernando's face into her chest. "Take my hand and close your eyes," she instructed. With his head pressed against her chest, Maria turned to Sofia. "Check their bags for water," she whispered.

Kneeling down next to the coyote, Sofia swatted at the flies swarming around his body. She grabbed a half-empty jug of water from his backpack. *Better him than me*, Sofia thought, feeling momentarily guilty about her indifference at seeing the coyote's dead body.

"*Agua*," Sofia heard a voice whisper.

"Maria," Sofia said, "hand me the flashlight." Sofia walked around the gruesome bodies of murdered travelers bunched in the area, their feet exposed because the bandits had taken their shoes.

When Sofia saw a finger move, she focused the beam on the man's face. He was lying on his back, staring up. The eyes on his young face were rolling back into his head, his lips swollen so badly that Sofia thought a poke of a needle could pop them. "*Agua*," the man whispered again. Sofia searched the nearest bag and found a canteen. She drizzled the water into the man's mouth. "*Gracias*," he mumbled.

Sofia sighed, the humanity returning to her heart. She thought about how this man was somebody's son, maybe some woman's husband. She knew what it felt like to kneel over the mangled body of a loved one. *Maybe his family is luckier than mine*, she thought, reasoning that they won't have to live with the graphic images that still haunt her.

"Knife," the man whispered.

"What?"

"Knife," he repeated, pointing to his pants pocket.

Sofia reached into his pocket and pulled out a switchblade.

"Here," the man said, moving his shaking hand to his chest, tapping the breastbone over his heart.

"No," she said, shaking her head vehemently.

"Please."

"No."

"It hurts so bad . . . so bad."

Sofia wrapped the man's fingers around the switchblade and rubbed the back of his hand. "I'm sorry," she said as she stood up and walked back over to Maria. "We need to go," Sofia barked, walking away from the bodies as fast as she could, undeterred by the fact that she had no idea where she was going. But she soon regretted her impulsiveness. Suddenly, a sharp pain permeated her shin and she immediately dropped to her knee.

The coyote had warned Sofia and the others to be mindful of the cacti growing throughout the entire route. Now, dozens of cactus spines were embedded in her shin. The barbed edges of the cactus spines made it difficult for Sofia to grip them with her frail fingers.

"I think this is the best we can do out here," Maria said after managing to remove a few of the least entrenched spines. "When you get to the United States, use melted wax to remove the rest, and make sure it doesn't get infected."

Infection? No, no, this can't be happening right now. The pain in her leg added to all the other ailments afflicting her body. The sunburns on the areas of her head where she had lost her hair were starting to blister. Her lips were cracked and swollen from dehydration. Overwhelmed, she began to cry. "I can't do this anymore," she sobbed. "I can't make it. Just go." Wheezing uncontrollably, Sofia wiped her nose on her sleeve. "Just go," she repeated, lying down on her back.

"I'm not going to leave you here, Sofia," Maria said, even though part of her wanted to. She reached into her bag and felt along the bottom until she found a couple of vitamin pills. "Take these."

"What are they?"

"They're painkillers."

Sofia looked away, but she didn't refuse the pills. Maria forced them into Sofia's mouth and lifted her head so that she could take a sip of water. "In a few minutes you won't even notice the pain in your leg. Come now, we need to get to the meeting spot."

"Look at this," Fernando said to Sofia as he lifted the cuff of his pants to reveal another pair of pants underneath. "The cactus can't hurt me!"

Observing Fernando's unassuming playfulness in the middle of the desert, Sofia's feelings of hopelessness dwindled, and she started to think about her own son. *If not for myself, then at least for my children.* She stood up and slowly put pressure on her shin as the flow of her adrenaline spiked. "I'll fight through the pain."

Sofia and Maria walked quietly for the next three hours while Fernando intermittently practiced whistling. Maria scolded him at first for making too much noise, but she eventually gave up, almost welcoming a break in the desert's perpetual silence. Soon the strength of the flashlight beam faded as the rising sun began to color the clouds.

"That's it," Maria said, pointing ahead.

Squinting, Sofia could make out a stretch of dirt whose only defining characteristic was a few tire marks. *"That's* it?"

"I remember this road," Maria said assuredly. "This is where the truck showed up the last time I made this trip."

The heat intensified as they waited by the dirt road. Sofia lied down on her back and placed her bag over her head to protect her scalp.

An hour went by. Then two.

"Are you sure we're in the right spot?" asked Sofia.

Maria scratched her head and squinted her eyes as she looked around. "This looks familiar. I remember those," she said, pointing at a large patch of toadflax flowers grouped by the side of the road.

Sofia didn't feel particularly assured. Her own water supply was long gone and the coyote's water jug was all that remained.

"No," Maria said after a few minutes of silence. "I'm not sure this is the spot. I'm not sure of anything right now."

Hearing Maria panic for the first time, Sofia grew frightened as the reality of her situation set in. She was in the desert, dehydrated, barely able to support her own weight. She could very well die right here, in the middle of nowhere. She would never see her children again, and they would never learn what became of their mother. It was a scary proposition, one that hadn't felt quite so tangible when she heard people casually talk about crossing the border in search of lucrative jobs.

The coherency of Sofia's thoughts dulled as the sun mercilessly heated her body. She had almost lost consciousness by the time Fernando started yelling.

"Mama, Mama!" he shouted, pointing up the road.

The hot air refracting off the approaching object created the appearance of moving waves, but it soon became clear that it was a van. Maria grabbed Fernando and stood by the side of the road next to Sofia's sprawled-out body.

After the van stopped in front of them, two Hispanic men stepped out and walked over to Maria. One was a good six inches taller than his companion, who had a birthmark covering his right temple.

"*Que tal?*" asked the taller man suspiciously as he looked around. "*Que pasa aqui?*"

"Where's Carlos?" asked the other.

"Bandits," Maria answered, assuming Carlos was the name of the coyote.

The two men immediately drew guns from their belts. "Where?" asked one of them anxiously. "When?"

The other man pointed his gun at Maria's head. "Did you leave a trail? Did they follow you?"

"Trail?" asked Maria, shaking her head. "No, no trail."

"Look at her," said the man with the birthmark, pointing at Maria, whose head was teetering back and forth, "you think she would know if she was followed?"

"We have to get out of here," the taller man said. "Let's just cut our losses and go."

"Leave them?"

"Carlos is gone, we're not going to get any money."

"Please," Maria pleaded, "you can't just leave us here, I'll get you money!" Maria pointed toward Sofia, who was still lying on the ground. "*She* can get you money! She told me she has access to money, lots of money!"

The two men looked at each other. "Whatever," one of them said. "Just throw them in the back, we'll decide how to deal with them later."

One of the men grabbed Sofia's arms and dragged her to the van. He picked her up like a ragdoll and rolled her body into the back. Rummaging through Sofia's pockets, he grabbed her wallet. "You too," he said to Maria. "Give me your wallet."

After complying with the man's order, Maria helped Fernando into the back of the van and followed him in.

As the doors shut and the van sped away, Maria tried to make Sofia drink what little water they had left. She wanted Sofia to be as coherent as possible when she apologized—when she tried to explain that she panicked and that she didn't mean to tell these men that Sofia had access to a lot of money.

The van ride wouldn't be long. Maria needed to think of a plan.

Chapter 7

THE YOUTHFUL TWIN boys in the row in front of Tesfaye stopped their incessant whining about their eardrums popping when the wheels of the Boeing 747 glided smoothly onto the runway at JFK International Airport. Still clenching the picture of his family, Tesfaye had no memory of the flight attendant asking him repeatedly to close his tray, or that she eventually closed it for him.

A young couple across the aisle playfully nuzzled their noses together. They smiled at each other as the woman stared intently at the diamond sparkling on her ring finger. Tesfaye wondered whether their pithy interaction caught anyone else's attention. He doubted they fully understood the significance of the moment they shared. In fact, he was sure they didn't. They couldn't. Not like Tesfaye could. He had an appreciation that could only come from retrospect, when sharing such moments was no longer possible.

It was a particular look that initially drew Tesfaye to Ayana. A particular look when he was a young professor at Addis Ababa University.

ONLY TWENTY-SEVEN YEARS OLD at the time, Tesfaye had quickly developed a reputation as one of the most respected professors at the university. His classes would be among the first to fill up. Students would regularly tell him that they picked up life-changing lessons in his class, a sentiment that might have led to bigheadedness were it not for Tesfaye's self-deprecating nature.

It wasn't just his knowledge of history that elicited unparalleled enthusiasm and participation from his students. Tesfaye was, by all accounts, exceptionally dedicated to his students, passionate about mentoring them and helping them find direction. He figured it was his military background that stirred in him a desire to mold leaders out of cadets—an analogy he artfully reinvented to apply to the quite different, liberal clientele attending the university. His practical understanding of warfare no doubt contributed to a unique perspective on the significance of numerous historical events.

It was almost the end of the fall semester in 1972 when Tesfaye saw Ayana for the first time. The afternoon began when several of his former students convened in his office for one of their regularly scheduled weekly chats.

"*Tediyas*, professor," the former students said, grabbing pieces of honey bread from Tesfaye's desk. The group started meeting the previous year when they were enrolled in Tesfaye's history class, but the tradition continued when they all showed up to his office the next semester on the same day and time they had always met, as if nothing had changed.

"So what's the topic of conversation today?" asked Tesfaye.

"The best way to pass exams so your father doesn't whip out the belt," suggested one of the former students.

"He doesn't use his belt because of your grades, he's just trying to beat the ugly out of you," joked another to everyone's amusement. "Now there's a better topic of conversation—at least for the non-ugly ones—how about the best way to get a woman?"

"Let's keep it civil," Tesfaye reminded everyone. "I know we're all friends here, but I do have to create the appearance of being a serious professor." Tesfaye took a bite of honey bread. "Besides," he continued, "that's an easy one. Just don't try."

"*Easy?*"

"Engage her like you would any other friend you respect," Tesfaye explained. "If the chemistry is there, the rest will surely follow."

"Words of truth," said Beniam, one of Tesfaye's former students. Even though Beniam's distinctive jawbone and big brown eyes garnered the attention of many women, it was his auburn hair that made him stand out in a crowd. "Women can sense when you're trying too hard."

"You *would* know what a woman is thinking," said one of the other students, "since you color your hair like a woman." All the other boys laughed.

"Make fun all you like," said Beniam, playing with his hair, "but only one of us has a date tonight with the most beautiful girl in school."

"Desta?" asked one of the boys.

Beniam grinned devilishly and several of the boys grumbled in disbelief—and a little jealousy. "Besides, my hair looks good."

Tesfaye and Beniam shared a look of mutual understanding. In private conversations, Beniam had confided in Tesfaye the true reason he dyed his hair. When Beniam was a child, authorities stormed into his parents' home, accusing his father of plotting with the commanders and ministers who orchestrated an unsuccessful coup attempt against the Emperor. As punishment, they burned the house to the ground in front of Beniam and his mother—with his father still inside. Beniam told Tesfaye that his auburn hair serves as a daily reminder of the flames that took his father's life, providing him with "fire in his belly" to motivate him to fight for what he believes in, and to honor his father's memory. Firm in his conviction but slightly embarrassed by his reasoning, Beniam made Tesfaye promise he would not tell another soul.

"The key is confidence, gentlemen," Tesfaye said. "Be comfortable in your own skin. It doesn't matter if you're wearing a burlap sack as long as you act confidently. It's no different from what I taught you about any goal you want to achieve—you need a vision, a plan, and a strategy to execute." Tesfaye tore off another chunk of honey bread. "And it wouldn't hurt to be a little better looking than Beniam," Tesfaye joked, leading to more laughter and playful pointing.

"So Professor, where are you now in your history class?" asked Beniam.

"We are looking at conflicts caused by historical claims to land."

"Like the Jews and Palestinians," said one of the former students.

"Or China and Tibet," Beniam rattled off.

"India and Pakistan fighting over Kashmir," added another.

"You boys have good memories," Tesfaye said. "I'm glad something actually soaked into your brains besides Desta. Okay, for a cold Meta beer, what other country laid claim to part of Kashmir after the British got out?"

"China?" Beniam said hesitantly.

"That's right, not bad."

Tesfaye's conversation with his former students got him thinking about the often rocky relationship between India and China, and the animosity created by India hosting the Dalai Lama's government in exile since the time he fled Tibet in 1959. As often occurred when a conversation triggered his interest, he wanted to delve deeper into the issue, particularly since he could incorporate any new information into his lesson plans for his next history class. After his discussion with Beniam and the other students, Tesfaye went to the university library to do some research. Walking down the aisles of books in the history section, he quickly scanned the shelves, kneeling down to get a better look at the books on the bottom. Resting on one knee and visibly agitated, Tesfaye lifted his head to see a young Ayana, barely twenty-two years old, placing books onto the shelves at the other end of the aisle.

Ayana paused and smiled girlishly. "You look troubled." Ayana's skin was a milky, dark olive. With her hair pulled back tight in a bun, the faint rouge covering her high cheekbones glowed.

A normally intrepid Tesfaye was at a loss for words.

"Do you need some help?" asked Ayana.

"I'm not having much luck finding a book I'm looking for."

Ayana pointed to the previously checked-out books on the cart that the head librarian asked her to return to their designated location, an assignment she tried to finish quickly, since she had only been working in the library for two months, and she was still trying to make a good impression. "Maybe you're looking for one of these."

Realizing that he was still kneeling on the worn carpet of the library, Tesfaye stood up and walked over to Ayana. "Unfortunately, I don't think that is likely."

"How can you be so sure?"

"According to the card catalog, I'm looking for a book that wasn't checked out." Tesfaye glanced toward the stack. "I'm sure it's around here somewhere. Students are always putting books back in the wrong place." He scanned the books directly in front of him. "But they usually get the general location, so I was hoping I could find it on my own."

"Of course," Ayana replied. "If anyone would know how to find a book in the library, it would be you, Professor."

"You know who I am?"

Ayana didn't answer. Blushing slightly, she unwittingly tilted her head toward the ground, her eyes focused intently on Tesfaye. When her innocent smile unearthed two perfectly round dimples in her cheeks, Tesfaye found himself unable to swallow. *That* was the look.

The two were inseparable after meeting in the library that day. A common love of literature sparked numerous conversations lasting well into the night. Ayana had heard about Tesfaye's passion in the classroom and his dedication to students. She was awed that he brought the same level of intensity to everything he did. Most importantly to her, he always displayed tenderness.

Tesfaye would discreetly visit Ayana in the library at random times throughout the day. Occasionally, Ayana would pinch herself just to make sure that she was not dreaming—that this tall, strapping man who had caught the attention of all the women at the school was actually interested in her. But there was never any doubt in Tesfaye's mind. He saw in Ayana something regal, an Amhara princess. She exuded a poised demeanor that appeared uniquely natural, complimented by a sharp wit. Luckily for Tesfaye, she had an unforced appreciation for his brash honesty. It was no surprise that they married six months later.

It was an exciting time for Tesfaye and Ayana to be opening a new chapter in their lives. A very exciting time at the university. The student body was abuzz with talk of revolution and change.

Haile Sellassie had been the Emperor of Ethiopia for decades. When the rains failed the previous summer, a massive drought led to hundreds of thousands of deaths in the Ethiopian highlands. Although famine was not new to Ethiopians, there was something particularly unnerving about the Emperor's indifference to the suffering of his people, while he was living lavishly in extravagantly decorated palaces, servants dutifully catering to his every whim. For the first time in a long time, the grunts and frustrations of the masses were louder than a whisper, with the university serving as one of the main hotbeds of discontent.

Their animosity fueled by decades of aristocratic rule, many students found comfort in the tenets of equality espoused by Marxism. Tesfaye was not convinced, but he made sure that his political opinions and individual ideals remained out of the classroom.

It was during this time from 1973 to 1974 that Mengistu Haile Mariam, a charismatic military officer of no particular importance, helped to orchestrate the overthrow of the government and the execution of the Emperor. It seemed an unlikely scenario that a soldier who had only obtained the rank of major would serve as the chairman of a secret committee, the Derg, with a hundred or so other low-level officers from all divisions of the military.

Once in power, the Derg pushed a brazen socialist agenda, nationalizing industries, rural land, and eventually even urban tenements. They enlisted help from students at the university, many quite radical and eager to help.

Tesfaye grew troubled by the Derg's meddling in the school. Ayana could pinpoint her husband's mood based on the slightest changes in his facial expressions that only she noticed. Sitting on the couch and reading in their one-bedroom flat in Addis Ababa, Ayana observed Tesfaye biting the inside of his lip and squinting slightly with his right eye, giving away his internal angst. Ayana prodded, "What's wrong?"

Tesfaye stared at a pile of nuts he was fiddling with in the palm of his hand.

"Tesfaye? Is anyone there?" she asked playfully.

Smiling, he tore himself away from his daydream. "I'm concerned."

"About what?"

"The students. This country. Everything."

Ayana didn't understand. Everyone at the university seemed so excited about the radical transformations taking place all throughout the country. "Why would you be concerned about the students?"

"Because they are so young, and so passionate." Tesfaye put up his hand, as if to stop Ayana from asking the question that naturally flowed from his answer. "I fear that because the students are so wound up about the idea of change, they will not pay attention to how these changes are actually implemented." Tesfaye leaned closer to Ayana. "What you read in these books—socialism, Marxism, whatever name it is called by—the way these principles work out in real life is always different than the ideals that seem so perfect in written form."

"But you must admit, you cannot be surprised that socialism is appealing to people now."

"Forced mediocrity? Sure, that's brilliant," he said sarcastically as he leaned back and smiled at Ayana. "I'm more of a democracy man myself."

"Bah," Ayana winced. "I don't like any system where good people end up at the bottom." When Tesfaye assured Ayana that he would never let her be at the bottom, she touched his hand as her smile gave way to the dimples on her cheeks.

AYANA'S DIMPLES WERE barely visible anymore in the weathered photograph Tesfaye still clung to in his hand on the airplane. He put the picture back in his pocket, waited his turn to retrieve his bag, and exited the plane.

Thumbing through his doctored passport, nervous butterflies menaced his stomach when he saw the long, slithering line of people waiting to meet an immigration agent tasked with weeding out those who had not earned the privilege of entering the United States. The agent he would meet in a few minutes might as well be Saint Peter himself, wielding the power to open up to Tesfaye a new world and a new beginning, or send him back to wherever he came from.

Tesfaye scanned the agents, methodically watching their facial expressions and timing the number of seconds it took them on average to stamp a passport and send tired travelers on their way.

There was the heavyset Hispanic man who over-enunciated his greetings, grinning from ear to ear. *A little too happy*, Tesfaye thought. He bore the shallow happiness of a sad clown masked by a painted smile.

Next to the Hispanic man was an older, skinnier white fellow with a mustache that did little to cover the craters punctuating his face. This agent made no attempt to hide his disdain for his job, and Tesfaye thought it best to avoid serving as the patsy who would break up his otherwise monotonous day.

Tesfaye felt the butterflies disappear when he saw the female agent. As apathetic as anyone he'd ever seen. She was overweight, with a plump face that masked what was likely a much more youthful woman. Her dark brown eyes matched her complexion. *My African Queen.*

After surveying the remaining agents, Tesfaye was still banking on his African Queen to swing open for him the gates to America. As a backup, he centered in on a young, Asian man who appeared to be getting over a cold and looked in no mood to exert much energy.

Timing the African Queen proved harder than he anticipated. An agent was randomly calling on people to stand in different numbered rows to await inspection. There were only so many excuses Tesfaye could use to allow the people behind him to cut in front without drawing suspicion. After all his careful planning, Tesfaye was unable to ultimately determine his choice of agent. So he waited in line for the sad clown.

The nervous butterflies were the extent of Tesfaye's emotions about his situation. He wasn't scared. After what he'd been through, a simple inspection was not the type of event that would instill fear. Not even close. Not after living through the Red Terror. Tesfaye knew it would be bad when he watched Mengistu smash the bottles of red liquid onto the streets of Addis Ababa and declare the official start of the Red Terror campaign. But nobody anticipated just how bad it would be.

Chapter 8

IT COULD BE worse, Maria thought. She could have gone the wrong way. They could still be in the middle of the Arizona desert. The fact that they even survived an ambush by bandits was impressive enough. But it wasn't just about her survival. She had to think about her son, Fernando.

Maria had no doubt that the men in the front of the van belonged to a much larger criminal syndicate. In her prior crossings, the coyote and the men arranging transportation would hold all the travelers in a safe house in Arizona until each paid in full. The first thing the coyotes would do was confiscate everyone's identification. The coyotes seldom experienced any problems collecting fees for the voyage. Most people were smart enough to arrange payment upon arrival in the United States. In the rare event that something went wrong, the coyotes didn't hesitate to explain the scope of their network and the potential repercussions for travelers' family members back home if payment was not forthcoming. Maria knew it wasn't just talk. There was evidence of that. She heard all the stories, and occasionally she saw the consequences play out in her Mexico City neighborhood.

The current situation was different. There was no precedent for Maria's current quandary. These men lost a lot of money. And they were not happy. She and Sofia represented their only possible source of revenue.

Maria did not have any family back home in Mexico City. It was just her and Fernando. For the last three years, Maria left Fernando with her great aunt for a few months while she migrated north to do seasonal work. She had spent the last two winters in Colorado working as a cook in the cafeteria of a ski lodge. When her great aunt died during the past summer, Maria decided this would be her last trip across the border. And this time, Fernando would come with her for a permanent relocation up north. Although Maria was overjoyed to travel to the United States with her son, she felt sick knowing that the men in the front of the van might use Fernando's well-being as a bargaining chip to secure money.

Maria knew what she would have to do. She stared at Sofia's frail body. *This is the person I will rely on to save my beautiful Fernando and me?* "Sofia," Maria whispered, "can you hear me?"

Sofia was starting to feel better now that she was out of the sun and a little more hydrated. "Of course I hear you, I'm not dead."

"How much money did you owe the coyote?"

"Huh?"

"Money," Maria repeated. "How much money did you agree to pay him after he brought you to the United States?"

"Nothing. I already paid the coyote all the money. He wouldn't take me unless I paid up front because I look so sick. He thought I might die in the desert."

"*Nada?*" asked Maria, realizing just how upset the men in the front of the van were going to be. "Do you have any access to money?"

"I spent every *peso* I had on this trip." Sofia noticed the apprehensiveness covering Maria's face. "We're in trouble, aren't we?"

Maria stayed quiet and smiled, trying to avoid upsetting Fernando. "We'll be fine. Just promise me you'll go along with whatever I say when these van doors open, okay?"

Sofia hesitated. "Okay," she said softly.

The van came to a halt and the engine noise ceased. The front doors opened and then slammed shut. There were muffled voices, then silence. Five minutes later, the doors again opened and shut, the engine revved, and the van was moving. A few moments later, the van was reversing. Sofia took a few deep breaths as the back doors of the van opened.

"*Vamos, andelé,*" said the man with the birthmark as he looked around in all directions. "Go straight in the open door. No funny stuff." He was pointing to the open door of the rented Motel 6 room in downtown Tucson, Arizona. Sofia, Maria, and Fernando dashed into the room.

The taller man directed them to sit on the tan and maroon checkered bedspread. He switched on the television and turned up the volume.

"There were twelve of you when you left Mexico. Our cut was three hundred per person. That means we should have made . . ."

"More than three thousand," said the man with the birthmark.

"You hear that? More than three thousand dollars," he said as he took out his gun and pointed it at Sofia and Maria. "I've got a family to feed. I gotta pay the bills, you know? But I'm going to give you a discount. Twenty-five hundred and you get to walk out of here alive."

"I can get five hundred for you, no problem," Maria said. Pointing toward Sofia, she continued. "She can get you the other two thousand."

"What?" asked Sofia.

"Don't let her fool you," Maria said, "she was bragging in Sonoita about all the money her family had in the United States."

Sofia's feeling that Maria was setting her up overtook her previous promise to go along with whatever Maria said. "That's not true! She's lying!"

"Really? I'm lying? That's why I know that you have a wealthy sister coming to pick you up and that your cousin owns a condo on the beach."

Sofia was at a loss for words. "You know that's not true." She turned to her captors. "It's not true."

"You selfish bitch! Withered hag! You might not have much life ahead of you, but I have a little boy to take care of. I'll pay you back if that's what you're worried about, just stop lying."

"Enough," the taller man said sternly. "You," he said, pointing at Sofia, "I'm giving you two days to get the money."

Sofia's head was spinning. *This is craziness.*

"Can my son stay with me?" asked Maria. "He behaves most of the time, and he usually doesn't wet the bed, and he's been really improving with his night terrors—he rarely screams in the middle of the night anymore."

She's trying to get rid of him, Sofia thought. *Could this actually be part of a plan?*

The two men looked at each other. "I'm not dealing with a kid," said one to the other. "Send him with the sick lady. If something goes wrong, it's better the kid doesn't have to watch what will happen to his mother."

Fernando grabbed Maria, burying his face in her chest, just as he had done when they found the coyote's body in the desert.

One of the men handed Sofia a piece of paper. "Call this number when you get the money." He took Sofia's wallet out of his pocket and removed her identification card. "Don't make me have to hurt your family in Escuinapa. If you go to the cops, your family will be dead within the week. I assure you our boss will do anything to make sure people know what happens if they choose to work with the police. You understand?" he asked, turning his attention to

Fernando. "Besides, I'm sure you wouldn't want this kid to know that it was your fault we had to cut off his mother's ears."

Sofia was amazed that Fernando was able to stay so composed. She could see him struggle to hold back the tears, his bright blue eyes glazed over, his lips quivering.

"*Comprendo*," Sofia responded, placing the phone number in her pocket.

Maria hugged Fernando and whispered something in his ear. "Promise me," she said, gazing at Fernando's scared face until he responded.

"I promise," Fernando said.

The man motioned toward Sofia and Fernando. "We're leaving. I want both of you to sit in the front of the van and act normal." He opened the door of the motel room and led them outside. "So," he continued when they were all in the van, "where is your pickup point supposed to be?"

"The Convention Center," Sofia responded. "I'm supposed to look for a beige minivan with wood paneling on the side."

Sofia's eyes were tranced on the white lines in the middle of the expressway that rapidly shot underneath the van. She couldn't believe the situation she was in. Her husband was dead, her kids were in a different country, yet a random boy was now sitting next to her, his body wedged between her and the passenger door. Sofia's leg was hurting too much for her to focus on concocting a way to raise two thousand dollars in two days. She was sure cactus spines were still embedded in her shin.

The man circled the Tucson Convention Center, stopping at the corner of Church and Cushing. "There it is," said the man, pointing to the Convention Center parking lot across the street. "Now get out, you have two days."

Sofia took Fernando's hand and hobbled across the street. "C'mon honey," she said, "help me find the minivan. Just look for wood paneling."

"What's wood paneling?" asked Fernando.

"Never mind, honey."

The variety of cars was overwhelming. In Escuinapa, it seemed as though everyone drove old beat-up pickup trucks, and it was usually one of the old Fords or a Chevy Cheyenne. No matter what the original color, the dirt roads quickly immersed the trucks in a light brown coat.

Even before Sofia saw the wood paneling, she spotted Rosario pacing back and forth, snacking on a bag of pretzels. Rosario was much larger than Sofia remembered and each step Rosario took required her to build momentum to get her hips swinging in the right direction. Her distinct, full lips remained the focal point of her otherwise plain, round face. Years of heavy smoking had chiseled away her youthful complexion. Faint crows feet now cornered her brown eyes.

Sofia and Rosario had been best friends since they were kids. Growing up together in Escuinapa, they lived on adjacent farms. Like all little girls in Escuinapa, the two always dreamed of hitting it big and ending up in *El Norte*—the United States. But this childhood dream only came true for one of them. Rosario's husband was a United States citizen who happened to be vacationing in the nearby coastal city of Mazatlan when Rosario was working as a waitress in one of the beach resorts.

"Rosario!" Sofia shouted.

Rosario stopped pacing. She hadn't seen Sofia since the sickness dramatically transformed her appearance. "Ay, Sofia," Rosario said, her hips gaining momentum as she walked over to embrace Sofia. "Look at you, so thin. We'll have to work on fattening you up." Rosario looked down at Fernando. "I didn't know you were bringing your son," she said as she knelt down. "Look at you, Manuel, all grown up," she said with a straight face, even though she remembered Manuel looking quite different.

"I'm not Manuel," Fernando said politely.

"You're not, are you."

"No," Sofia said. "That's Fernando. We need to talk."

Chapter 9

IT WAS THE employment visa that allowed Tesfaye to speed past the immigration agent at the airport without a hitch. Although his passport wasn't genuine, the United States government officially authorized the visa. There were times Tesfaye doubted he would ever get it. Many years had gone by since the contact he met in Kenya told him he could get him into the United States. The man assured Tesfaye that he had a connection to a company in Queens, New York that could get him a worker's visa. Of course, the visa wouldn't be under Tesfaye's real name; it would need to match up to his fake Kenyan passport. In return, Tesfaye was required to be patient and understand that the wheels of the immigration bureaucracy in the United States turned slowly.

Having made his way out of JFK International Airport, Tesfaye followed the instructions his contact in Kenya had given him, boarding a bus to Jamaica, Queens. After exiting the bus, Tesfaye walked aimlessly through the city streets. Even though he previously spent many nights in Kenya studying New York City maps, he could not make sense of the directions, regretting the amount of time he had dedicated to studying the streets of Manhattan. Although he knew he was lost, part of him didn't care.

Cars packed the streets and honked unrelentingly at other vehicles guilty of the slightest infraction. People crowded the sidewalks, walking briskly and talking loudly. Delivery boys on bikes fearlessly dared oncoming traffic, brazenly swerving around jaywalking pedestrians. Despite the commotion of the city streets, there was something peaceful about the chaos surrounding him. Tesfaye felt like a ghost floating unnoticed through a whirlwind of activity.

Tesfaye's wandering led him down a poorly lit alleyway that cut between two main streets. For the first time in almost an hour, he paused and surveyed his surroundings. The enclosed walls of the alleyway immediately triggered long suppressed memories from two decades ago and shot vivid images to the fore of his mind. Images of the last time he was confined in the narrow pathway of a back alley. Images of the Red Terror.

THE BEGINNING OF the cold season in October was typically a welcome time in Addis Ababa. The rainy season has come to an end and the February hot spell is pleasurably in the distance. Residents flock to the city square for the annual *Meskel* festival, held to commemorate Empress Helena's recovery of the holy cross on which Jesus was crucified. In 1976, however, the dancing, feasting, and commemorative bonfire did not proceed as planned. Fear inhibited these mass gatherings.

Rebel groups seeking to challenge the Derg's claim to Ethiopia began openly assassinating public officials aligned with Mengistu and his fellow committee members. Some of the main rival groups passed out subversive literature to undermine the Derg. When Mengistu smashed the bottles filled with red liquid and declared that the Red Terror had officially begun, anyone associated with these groups immediately became enemies of the revolution—even the university students who previously expressed such excitement about the prospects of a new beginning after the fall of the Emperor two years prior.

Ayana and Tesfaye came to dread their daily walk to the university in the morning. The air developed the stench of death. Bodies lined the streets. Those courageous enough to brave the streets of Addis Ababa avoided talking above a whisper or making eye contact. Innocent pleasantries with a passing acquaintance could result in placement on *the list*.

The list was a product of the lowest organized level of the Derg's new socialist government. When the Derg decided to nationalize all the urban dwellings, they created *kebeles*, neighborhood associations designed to listen to the needs of the local community and help resolve problems. But after the Red Terror began, the role of the *kebeles* changed. The Derg armed members of the *kebeles* and charged them with rooting out all the counter-revolutionaries, morphing these groups into roaming death squads.

Living in a perpetual state of fear for months on end proved too much for Ayana. The steady flow of bodies in the streets was enough to break even the strongest of wills. With final examinations wrapping up, Tesfaye had been staying late at the university to grade papers. He had barely gotten one foot in the door by the time Ayana lost it.

"I can't live like this anymore," she said, pacing back and forth. "Every day there are bodies in the street. They just leave them there, all day, to be picked at by the hyenas."

Tesfaye shut the front door behind him.

"Hello to you too."

"I'm serious."

"I know. It's disgraceful."

"Disgraceful?" Ayana said sarcastically. "Did you hear what happened to Melke, that nice woman down the street?"

Tesfaye nodded. "Of course, she disappeared."

"She disappeared because she went to retrieve her son's body from the street. They watch the bodies you know. These *kebeles*. They watch to see who comes to get the bodies and then they snatch those people up too. And poor Miss Wolaya . . ."

"Don't even tell me they executed *her*," Tesfaye interrupted. "She must be seventy years old by now."

"No, they didn't. But when she went to retrieve her son's body from the street, to properly bury him, the *kebele* forced her to pay the price of the bullet they used to execute her son." Ayana was now close to tears. "The price of the bullet," she repeated in disbelief. "Can you believe that!" Ayana looked out the window and sighed. "I can't go to work anymore. All these students, missing."

Tesfaye tried to comfort her. He too struggled with the steady drop in classroom attendance. "Don't assume the worst. Many students have relatives in other parts of the country. I'm sure they left as a precautionary measure."

"But you know that's not true, at least not for all of them. What about Beniam?"

She's right. Tesfaye had come home several months ago particularly troubled that auburn-haired Beniam and the other students had not showed up for their weekly get-together.

"You were right, Tesfaye. The students' passion is unabating. They want change, but this Red Terror campaign—this attempt at censorship—is certainly not what got them so enthusiastic after the Derg took over." Along with the rest of the faculty, Tesfaye noticed the gradual shift in students' attitudes toward the Derg in the two years since Mengistu's successful coup. While their enthusiasm for reform remained intact, they had grown increasingly skeptical of a regime that became more controlling and ruthless. "I've seen the rallies at school against the Derg," Ayana continued. "I'm sure you have too, and I would bet that Mengistu also knows what's going on."

Tesfaye put his arms on Ayana's hips. He knew she was right. Some of his most promising students had disappeared. "We'll get through this. To be honest, I think it's almost over. You must admit, there have been less killings recently."

"Who knows? Maybe they're hiding the bodies now instead of leaving them in the street. Maybe there are more killings and we don't even know about them all. Maybe . . ."

Tesfaye put his finger over Ayana's lips. "They are not hiding any bodies. The whole purpose of their actions is to make the bodies visible to everyone in the city as a symbol of what happens when you cross the Derg."

Ayana swatted at Tesfaye's finger and walked away. "I don't care, I want to leave. I want to get out of this city. The semester is almost over. It would be the perfect time."

"I have a full course load next semester. Students have already signed up for my classes. What would they think if I weren't there next semester? I can't abandon them."

"You can't abandon *me* either, and I need to get out of here."

Tesfaye walked over to Ayana. "In a few days I'll be done grading papers. We'll go up north to your cousins in Wolo. We'll stay there for a few weeks until the beginning of the next semester and then we'll reassess our situation.

"No, no, no! You cannot put it off. You must tell the university tomorrow that you will not be there next semester."

Tesfaye was not used to seeing Ayana so animated. "Ayana, I don't understand why you're being so insistent. Where is this coming from? Addis Ababa has been a morbid place to live for some time now. What's wrong with reassessing our situation in a few weeks? Are you pregnant or something?" Tesfaye joked.

Ayana didn't answer, and Tesfaye's smile faded. "Are you?" he asked again.

"I don't know. Maybe. I haven't gone to a doctor, but it's possible. Even if I'm not, Tesfaye, just thinking about how it's possible I'm pregnant has made me realize that this isn't worth it. I know you are dedicated to your students and I know they all look up to you, but as cliché as it might sound, all I want is to make sure you come home to me in one piece."

Tesfaye stared intensely at Ayana. "You're pregnant," he said as the smile returned to his face.

Despite her heightened anxiety, Ayana couldn't help but smile back. "I told you, I'm not sure."

"And you aren't just saying that you might be pregnant as an excuse to get me to take a leave of absence?"

Ayana lightly swatted Tesfaye on the shoulder. "How could you say such a thing?"

"I'm just kidding," Tesfaye laughed. "Okay then, we'll go in a few days."

"And you'll tell the university tomorrow that you'll be taking a leave of absence?"

"If I have time."

"Please try. I don't want to mention to anyone that I'm taking time off before you do."

Tesfaye could have made time the next day if he wanted to. Instead, he avoided the matter completely by immersing himself in his students' papers. Walking home that night, he felt giddy thinking of himself as a father. These thoughts initially clouded his otherwise astute senses. When he again focused on his surroundings, he could hear the footsteps behind him. A quick glance over his shoulder revealed the mundane sight of two men walking a block behind.

Tesfaye first became nervous when he picked up the pace. The two men behind him also started walking faster. The faint light still emanating from the setting sun was insufficient to make out the faces of these men, but Tesfaye now thought he saw a pistol in one of their hands.

The decision to run was not well thought out. Tesfaye had no particular location in mind. He flew through the streets of Addis Ababa and the men chasing him kept pace. When he looked back, he saw four men running after him. Tesfaye wondered whether he had initially missed the other two, or whether they joined the chase midstream.

Nearly out of breath and barely able to lift his legs anymore, Tesfaye turned into a dark alley to hide, hoping the men following him had fallen far enough behind. He crouched into a ball behind a stack of newspapers. Hearing voices in the distance, he did his best to avoid breathing loudly. The footsteps got closer.

Standing over Tesfaye, the men waited silently for him to rise to his feet. The beats of Tesfaye's heart echoed in his ears. His eyes were teary and his throat bone dry. Staring up at the walls of the alleyway, Tesfaye experienced a claustrophobic sensation he had never felt before. *If only my confinement were figurative*, Tesfaye thought. Yet here he was, trapped in an alley, cornered by four men, about to become another statistic in Mengistu's Red Terror campaign.

"Why?" asked Tesfaye, hunched over and breathing heavily. "At least extend me the courtesy of telling me what I have done before leaving me in the street for the hyenas."

The man closest to him stood expressionless. "You need to come with us."

STARING UP AT the sliver of New York sky visible between the high walls of the Queens alleyway, Tesfaye felt the same claustrophobia overtake him. Unable to catch his breath, he fell to his knees. When the tightness in his chest subsided and his hands stopped trembling, Tesfaye brushed himself off and reevaluated the directions his Kenyan contact had given him.

Chapter 10

AFTER LISTENING TO Sofia's incoherent attempt to explain what happened to her in the desert before she arrived in Tucson, Rosario calmed her down and drove to the Days Inn. Sofia and Fernando stood by the bathroom sink of the room Rosario rented, taking turns filling their plastic cups with water and downing each cup in two or three gulps. After Sofia got into the shower, Rosario sat Fernando in front of the television and went to the local pharmacy to pick up some toiletries and medical supplies for Sofia's leg.

When Rosario returned, Sofia was sitting next to Fernando on the bed, watching cartoons. She examined Sofia's shin. "Heavens, you must feel better after taking that shower."

"Much better," Sofia said. "You have no idea, Rosario. You would not believe what I've gone through."

"At least now I can understand what you're saying. I think you were in desperate need of water—several gallons of water." Smiling at Fernando, Rosario reached into her purse and grabbed a bag of potato chips she purchased at the pharmacy. "Would you like some?"

Fernando nodded and began devouring the chips.

Rosario took the wrapping off a waxing product she bought at the pharmacy. "I'll go get us a proper meal after dealing with this leg of yours. So how did you come to be with this handsome boy?" she asked, using a tiny spatula to spread the wax on Sofia's shin.

Sofia took a deep breath. "We all set out from Sonoita with the coyote and everything was going fine until the *banditos* killed the coyote and all the others besides me and Fernando and his mother, and then we barely made it to the van that was supposed to pick us up, and then they took us to a motel room and demanded money, and now they are keeping his mother as a prisoner, and they let us go, and now . . . well . . . we have two days to get them the money."

Resting on her knees, Rosario gazed up at Sofia with her mouth wide open. She ripped off a chunk of wax.

"Ay, ay, ay!" shouted Sofia.

Rosario showed Sofia the cactus spines in the wax. "How much money?" she asked.

"Two thousand dollars."

"And what happens if you don't pay?"

"The kids, they're in danger. The coyotes know where I live. They'll hurt Eva and Manuel if I don't pay."

"Hurt your kids? In Escuinapa? You believe that?"

"Things have changed since we were children."

"I know. I know they have." Examining Sofia's facial expression, Rosario tilted her head and smiled. "I know that look, Sofia," Rosario said.

"What look?"

"You don't have to say anything, I know exactly what you're thinking. You know I would do anything for you, but I don't have that kind of money to give." Rosario grabbed another section of the wax. "We need to think of another plan," she said as she ripped off the wax.

"Ay!" Sofia shouted again.

"What are you doing?" asked Fernando.

"I'm getting well, dear," Sofia said, "enjoy your chips." Sofia laid back on the bed. "How many of these do we have left?"

"Just one."

"Let's get it over with already." Sofia winced as Rosario ripped off the last piece of wax. "Rosario, you must have *some* savings."

"*I* must have some savings? No, my husband does, and not much at that. Do you know what would happen if he came home and found out that our savings were gone? He's never hit me before, but I'm sure taking his money would tempt him."

"*None* of it is yours? You have a job, don't you?"

"A part-time job in a beauty parlor. I suppose I contributed a few hundred over the years."

"Rosa, it's not just my kids." Sofia cupped her hand to shield her mouth from Fernando. "His mother," she whispered, running her finger across her throat.

"Oh, I see."

"When is your husband coming home?"

"Two weeks, give or take." A truck driver for more than a decade, Rosario's husband frequently had to leave her alone for weeks at a time.

"I'll repay your money before he comes back."

"How? It took you forever to save enough to make it to the States."

"Have I ever lied to you before? For the kids, please. If I don't get you the money, I'll leave before your husband gets home, and you can tell him that I robbed you."

"Do you realize how ridiculous that sounds? Besides, where would you go? You know I would never let you live on the streets." Rosario looked over at Fernando watching cartoons, small pieces of chips covering his shirt. "My husband has an account that I don't have access to, but I'll check to see what's in the joint account."

Sofia reached over and hugged Rosario. "*Santa* Rosario," she said, kissing Rosario on the neck.

The next day, Sofia waited in the motel room with Fernando while Rosario went to the bank. Rosario returned forty minutes later. "Well?" asked Sofia.

Rosario took an envelope out of her purse. "Nine hundred dollars, that's all I could get. I hope it's enough."

"Me too," Sofia said, walking over to the phone by the bed. She dialed the phone number given to her by the men holding Maria.

"*Hola*," said a voice.

"I have nine hundred, it's all I could get."

"You have thirty minutes, bring it right now to the Motel 6 on 22nd Street, Room 28."

"Wait, is that enough? Is that enough!" she persisted. But it was too late. He had already hung up. "We have to go," Sofia blurted out, already limping toward the door.

Sofia and Rosario drove to the Motel 6 and pulled into the parking lot. They did not want to leave Fernando alone in their rented motel room so they reluctantly brought him along.

"Stay here, honey," Sofia said to Fernando.

Clutching the envelope and fighting through the pain in her leg, Sofia hobbled over to the walkway that lined the rooms of the first floor, scanning the room numbers on each door. Rosario kept pace behind her.

"What number are we looking for?" asked Rosario.

"Twenty-eight."

"These are all low numbers, twenty-eight must be on a higher floor."

"That's impossible. We were in a ground-level room yesterday." After she scanned the remaining rooms on the first floor, Sofia realized that Rosario was correct. They headed for the steps and walked up to the second level.

It didn't take long to find room twenty-eight; the two Hispanic men were standing outside, smoking cigarettes. When they saw Sofia and Rosario emerge from the staircase, they flicked their cigarette butts off the ledge and walked over to them.

"Well," said the man with the birthmark.

Sofia handed him the envelope. "Like I told you, it's only nine hundred. It's all we could get. Please tell me it's enough."

He looked in the envelope and glanced at his taller cohort, who nodded back at him.

"Is it enough?" asked Sofia a second time.

Scratching his birthmark, he put the envelope in his pocket and smirked at Sofia. "*Hasta luego*," he said sarcastically as they headed for the steps.

Sofia grew aggravated by the men's cryptic answers. "What about Maria—the other girl—does she owe you anything more?"

"Don't worry," one of the men shouted from the stairwell, "we worked something out with her."

Confused, Sofia looked at Rosario for reassurance that she wasn't the only one baffled by the men's behavior. "What just happened?"

"I don't know," said Rosario. "Let's just get this woman and get out of here."

Sofia turned the doorknob of room twenty-eight, but it was locked. She knocked on the door. "Maria." There was no response.

Her fist clenched, Rosario stepped in front of Sofia and banged repeatedly. "Hello! Is anyone in there?"

Moments later, the door swung open. A man stood in the doorway, soaking wet, a towel around his waist. "What the fuck?" he said.

"Is there a woman with you?" asked Rosario.

"What?"

"Maria," said Sofia.

"Who?"

"Middle-aged Mexican woman," added Rosario.

"I'm the only one here," he barked, visibly irritated that he was forced to abandon his shower. "You've got the wrong room."

Sofia wedged her arm in the doorway, stalling the man's attempt to finish his shower. "Listen," he said, "get the fuck out of here or I'm gonna call the police." Rosario lowered Sofia's arm and the door slammed shut. "I'm calling the front desk right now," they heard him say through the door.

Turning their heads, they watched as the Hispanic men's van sped out of the parking lot.

"Fernando!" both said at the same time. They rushed down the steps back toward the minivan. Each let out a deep sigh when they saw that Fernando was still sitting in the back seat.

"Are you okay in there?" asked Sofia.

"Where's Mama?"

"She'll be here soon."

"She will?" Rosario whispered to Sofia.

Sofia was now in a full-blown panic. "What are we going to do?"

"The original room," said Rosario, trying to remain calm. "You said they brought you to a room on the first floor. Which one?"

Sofia scanned the ground level of the motel, nothing but peach walls spotted with identical blue pastel doors. "I didn't see the room number, we were hurried into the room so quickly."

"Think," Rosario prodded. "Anything distinguishable? Was it near an end of the building? Were there cracks in the concrete in front of the door? Anything?"

"I don't know. I don't know!" shouted Sofia in frustration. "I could barely stand when they brought me here."

Rosario tapped on the glass. "Fernando, honey, can you come out here?" He opened the door and dangled his legs out the side of the minivan. "Do you remember which room you were in yesterday?"

Fernando scanned the rooms. Without hesitation, he pointed to a room by the far left corner of the building.

"Are you sure?" asked Sofia.

"Yes."

"How can you be so sure?" asked Rosario.

"The bottle," he said, pointing to an empty two-liter bottle of Coke wedged in a divot between the parking lot and the walkway that lined the peach walls of the motel. "I remember stepping over it yesterday."

With Fernando following them, Sofia and Rosario walked briskly toward the room. Without hesitation, Rosario knocked on the door. There was no response. She got down on her knees and peeked her head under the door. "It looks dark," she said. "What's the room number?"

"Seventeen," Sofia replied.

"Where's the front office?" asked Rosario, not expecting anyone to know the answer. Building momentum with her arms, Rosario swung her hips from side to side and picked up the pace. Accepting that Fernando was going to find out what happened to Maria one way or another, Sofia grabbed Fernando's hand and tried to keep up.

The assistant manager was reading a magazine behind the counter when Rosario marched in. "Good morning," he said, calmly standing up and tipping his cowboy hat.

"Hello, good morning to you," Rosario said with a big smile. She turned around, glancing at Sofia and Fernando standing outside the glass door of the front office. "We're looking for a friend. She said she would be in room seventeen, but nobody's answering the door. Would you mind calling the room for us? Maybe she's sleeping," said Rosario jokingly, trying to mask the feeling of urgency churning in her stomach.

"Room seventeen," he said as he opened the motel's logbook. "There's nobody in that room. They checked out last night."

"Maybe you can help me. My friend—who was staying in that room—was supposed to give me something very important, something I let her borrow. Would you mind opening the door, just so I could peak inside and check quickly."

The assistant manager took off his hat and scratched his head. "The room has already been cleaned. If the previous occupants left anything in the room, it would be behind this desk. And I assure you, there's nothing behind this desk."

"Did you see a woman check out of the room?"

"Nope."

"Did they leave a credit card number?"

"They paid in cash. And even if they didn't, I wouldn't be giving you that information," he said disapprovingly. "You wouldn't by chance be walking around the motel, banging on doors, would you?"

"What? No. Of course not."

"Because I've been getting some calls."

Rosario wasn't getting anywhere and she could tell she was testing this man's patience. "Please, for a poor old woman, just tell me whether you saw the Mexican woman who was in that room."

"Ma'am, you're not that old, and I wasn't even working last night. I think it's time for you to leave."

"But . . ."

"Before I call the police."

Rosario walked out of the front office. "We need to get out of here."

"Where's Mama?" asked Fernando again.

"She's busy right now," Sofia said, trying to stall for time.

The three drove back to Rosario's motel room and ordered pizza. Once Fernando fell asleep, Sofia and Rosario stepped outside to try to figure out what to do.

"Do you have any way to get in touch with Maria?" asked Rosario.

"No."

"So now what?"

"I don't know. I have enough problems of my own, but I can't just abandon this child."

"Sofia, you can't take him with us."

"Well what do you propose?"

"I don't know. Leave him at an orphanage."

"I can't do that. He reminds me of my Manuel when he was younger. Besides, what if Maria comes back? Maybe I can take him and leave a number with the front desk of the motel."

"*My* phone number? You want to leave a trail back to my house, after we knocked on all those doors and I acted like a lunatic at the front desk? What if this woman—Maria—turns up dead somewhere and they start putting the pieces together? Are you trying to think of ways to get kicked out of the country and get me thrown in jail?"

Sofia and Rosario couldn't think of any good options. But they would have to do something and they would eventually need to have a serious talk with Fernando. It was obvious to both of them that he already sensed something was very wrong.

Sofia also had other problems to think about. She needed to raise nine hundred dollars in two weeks. But she knew that none of these problems would be solved tonight and she prayed that a good night's sleep would clear her mind. If only she would be able to sleep.

Chapter 11

B Y THE TIME the ship unmoored from international waters off the coast of China's eastern seaboard, eighty-eight smuggled Chinese were crammed into the dingy living quarters. Lin instinctively stayed close to long-robed Ai and hook-nosed Shaoqing, the three sharing an artificial camaraderie as a result of their time together in the trunk of the Volkswagen. Much to Lin's surprise—and delight—Jiang also stayed close to them instead of joining a much larger group of travelers who had also resided in Changle City prior to boarding the ship.

Lin was glad to be part of a group. She counted only thirteen other women and the presence of so many men in cramped quarters deepened the ongoing unease she had felt since the day her mother finalized the smuggling arrangements with the snakehead. A handful of the other women on the ship were from Changle City. When the travelers initially settled in the living quarters, Lin saw Jiang talking to one of them, Ming Tso, a strikingly gorgeous teenager who had unusually full breasts and thick lips that looked like pieces of candy, the outer edges colored a rich dark brown, coating a soft pink interior. Lin immediately grew jealous, although part of her wanted to become friends with Ming Tso, thinking halfheartedly that being close to Ming would somehow make her more desirable. Maybe under different circumstances they could have been friends, but it was not meant to be. Lin would soon be forced to do something that would make Ming swear that she would never speak to Lin, or look her in the eye, or even recognize Lin's presence if they were in the same room.

Lying on her cardboard bed the first night at sea, Lin began to cry again. She buried her face in her arms, hoping none of the other passengers saw her. Her body convulsed wildly as she tightened her muscles to ensure she did not make any noise. By the second day, many of the other passengers had also huddled together in groups based loosely on their geography. In addition to the Changle City crew, there were factions from Mawei, Lianjiang, Tingjiang, and Fuzhou City. The passengers all took note of the group from Tingjiang. It was hard not to. There were eight of them, all men in their twenties, one more brutish than the next.

Crewmen came down three times a day with food and fresh water. Everyone waited patiently in line to get a ration. The meal was usually rice, but on the third day the crewmen treated the passengers to a small portion of fish, a luxury they didn't know would be their last.

Jiang took a bite. "Not bad," he said, wiping his hands on his sleeve. "But now we're going to smell like fish for the next week."

Shaoqing looked up at Jiang and raised his eyebrows. "You think we'll be off this boat next week?"

"That's what the snakehead told my parents," Jiang said. "What were you told?"

Shaoqing continued to pick at his fish. "They told me nine days, but I was taught snakehead math."

"What's that?" Lin asked.

"Take the amount of time that you're told you will spend traveling to the United States and double it, at least."

"Maybe if they gave us something to do, this ship wouldn't be so bad," Ai said. "It's so boring down here."

The rocking of the ship on the open seas didn't bother Lin at first, but by the fourth day, she and the other passengers were struggling to adapt to the growing ocean waves. Seasickness became the norm and the stench of vomit soon permeated the room.

Once every three days, crewmen would escort the passengers out of the living quarters to wash. The sun was a welcomed change to the dim light and unpleasant smells. Standing on the deck, it would take Lin nearly a minute to adjust her eyes to the light. A pleasant ocean breeze masked the smell of fecal matter building up in the corners of the ship.

The crewmen made no attempt to mask their enjoyment when they watched the female passengers bathe. Most of the male passengers took off their shirts to clean their bodies. Although Lin and the other females remained almost fully clothed, the crewmen would delight in the moments when they would lift up their shirts to soap under their arms. Lin did not even feel comfortable putting water on her body in front of Fei Pin, who stood quietly with his arms folded over his protruding belly, his squinting eyes fixed on her, just as they had been the first time he saw her on the dock in Fuzhou.

Bathing in salt water gave Lin a slight skin irritation, which quickly turned into a full blown rash. She found herself constantly scratching her body, which only served to further irritate her skin. Sharing Lin's plight, the other passengers all developed rashes.

Jiang tapped Lin on the shoulder. "Would you mind scratching my back?"

Lin immediately blushed. "Sure," she said, unable to stop her voice from cracking.

Jiang's body instantly relaxed when Lin ran her fingernails down his back. "Ahhhh. This is great," he said.

Her pulse now elevated, Lin tried her hardest to stop her hands from sweating as she slowly moved them around Jiang's shoulder blades, pausing at the ridges that lined the muscles of his upper back. As with her time in the van on the way to the dock in China, she again found herself staring at the back of his neck.

"Let me scratch yours for you," Jiang said as he turned around. "I wonder how long it's been since we got on this boat," he said after a minute of silence.

Lin checked the ground next to her cardboard bed where she had been etching a new line for every day they were on the ship. "Ten days."

"Where are they anyway with our food and water? I'm so thirsty."

The crewmen did not provide the passengers with any more food on the tenth day of the voyage. On the eleventh day, only two meals were served as well. The amount of fresh water they dispensed was also shrinking. Corresponding with this decrease, the behavior of the passengers began to change when their meals arrived. Although they still formed an orderly line, the hungry passengers now ran to get to the front of the line whenever the hatch to the living quarters began to creak open.

On the twelfth day at sea, the order maintained by the unspoken understanding among the passengers broke down.

Chapter 12

TESFAYE WAS NOT required to show up to the company that sponsored his sham employment visa. Instead, his contact had set up a job for him as a cab driver. The contact gave Tesfaye little guidance about the job other than a map of New York City. However, one point was stressed repeatedly. Under no circumstance was Tesfaye to reveal his true identity to his fellow cab drivers. Some were immigrants from Ethiopia, Eritrea, or Somalia. The last thing Tesfaye needed was to poke at old wounds that time had finally begun to heal.

Try as he may, Tesfaye could not tune out the raucous conversations of passengers who treated the back seat of his cab like their own living room. A youthful thirty-something woman was nearly brought to tears by feelings of inadequacy. She had no idea what cause the charity event she was going to would be benefiting, but she was convinced that her dress would draw snickers from her fellow attendees for its bold colors and Spanish-influenced style. Then there was the couple who furiously brainstormed the best tactics to ensure their child got into the *only* acceptable preschool in the city. He was equally amused when he listened to a young fashionista gab about her blind date's stinginess, even though he took her to a restaurant that would cost Tesfaye a week's salary.

Tesfaye would happily take on all the worries of his passengers in exchange for one more chance to see his family. Driving a taxi gave Tesfaye time to think. Too much time. He had already fit together some pieces of the puzzle. The time he spent in Ethiopia after the rebels threw him onto the backseat of the jeep had shed some light on Geteye Tge. Whether the information he learned about Geteye was true or not was a different story. If it were true, Tesfaye could understand why the man with the eye patch who slit Negasi's throat was so interested in finding Geteye.

More pieces of the puzzle were filled in when Tesfaye arrived in Kenya. But the gaps about Geteye remained and Tesfaye attributed them to his own oversight. Perhaps the signs were evident but unheeded. What Tesfaye wouldn't give for the chance to go back to the time when he and Geteye first became entangled in that mess.

WHEN HE WAS trapped in the alleyway, Tesfaye was convinced that the men who chased him through the streets of Addis Ababa would kill him. Now that Tesfaye was sandwiched between two of them in the back seat of a Peugeot, he was confused but relieved. If he were to be executed—and become another victim of Mengistu's Red Terror campaign—he knew it probably would have happened behind the stacks of newspapers in the alley where the four men had cornered him.

The faint outlines of the buildings were barely noticeable as the driver flew through the streets of Addis Ababa. The Peugeot ascended a hill that overlooked the city, toward an iron fence that formed a perimeter around an enclosed building. At the top of the hill, the driver signaled to a pack of AK-47 wielding men dressed in street attire guarding the gate to the compound. When the gate slowly creaked open, Tesfaye immediately knew where he was—the Grand Palace. Modest by comparison to the residences of royalty in Europe, the former Emperor's Grand Palace stood two stories tall, comparable in size to the White House.

The brakes squeaked as the Peugeot came to a halt in front of the palace and parked between a military jeep and a rusting tank. All four doors opened in unison.

"Follow me," said one of the men.

Flanking Tesfaye, they led him up a set of semi-circular steps, past two gold statues that greeted guests as they entered the residence. Once inside, they marched straight to the far end of the palace, past a door that led to the old wine cellar that the Derg now used to hold former high-ranking officials from the Emperor's regime. They marched down a wide hallway to a set of double doors adorned with intricately carved wood paneling. Two men released their grip from Tesfaye's arms as another knocked firmly on the door.

"Enter," a voice shouted.

As the door opened, Tesfaye first saw the olive colored pants tucked firmly into a pair of combat boots propped up on the desk. The sleeves of his uniform were rolled up to his elbows and the muscles in his forearm flexed as he played with his stubby mustache. Looking up at Tesfaye, he motioned with his eyes for him to sit in one of the chairs on the other side of his desk.

"I assume you know who I am," said the man.

"Yes, of course. You are Mengistu Haile Mariam." Seeing Mengistu up close, Tesfaye was surprised at the softness of his eyes—not at all the stinging gaze he pictured from the man who assassinated all his rivals to take control of the country, or the man who launched the Red Terror campaign. His face was narrow and appeared even more elongated by his slightly receding hairline.

"You are probably wondering what you are doing here. No?" Mengistu asked.

Tesfaye shrugged his shoulders, remaining silent.

Mengistu reached into a box on his table and pulled out a cigar. "Would you like one?"

"No thank you, sir."

"Are you sure? Comrade Fidel makes the best cigars."

"There would be no point in wasting such a good product on someone who does not smoke."

"Nonsense," Mengistu exclaimed, "these cigars are the reason people start smoking." After clipping the end of the cigar, Mengistu handed it to Tesfaye. One of the men who had chased Tesfaye into the alley came over and lit the cigar for him.

"That is good, isn't it?" asked Mengistu, lighting his own cigar and putting his feet back onto the table. "What is your background, Tesfaye?"

"My background, sir?"

"Your ethnic background."

"I am half Amhara and half Oromo."

Mengistu smiled. "Ah, you are like me then, diverse like our country." Mengistu's ethnicity had long been a topic of much debate. Tesfaye heard endless rumors and speculation about Mengistu's background, running the gamut from direct lineage to members of the Amhara aristocracy to him being the bastard child of a slave.

"This diversity should be a strong point for our country, an asset that propels Ethiopia to greatness." Mengistu stood to his feet and stared out the window. "Unfortunately, our late Emperor thought it better to exploit and denigrate many of our brothers and sisters for the sake of a select lucky few." Turning back around, Mengistu pointed at Tesfaye. "You are a history teacher, are you not?"

"I am."

"So then, given this history of repression, would it be any surprise to learn that different ethnic groups are rebelling all over the country?"

"I suppose not," Tesfaye replied, sensing there was only one acceptable answer to the question.

"Of course it wouldn't," Mengistu declared. "Right now, the Somalis are encouraging rebellion in the Ogaden region, the Oromos are fighting in the south, and the Eritreans in the north are calling for independence. Even the pesky Tigray are trying to form a ragtag liberation front."

Mengistu sat back down at his desk. "As we both know," he continued, "all of these territories have been part of the Ethiopian Empire for thousands of years."

Tesfaye knew Mengistu was glossing over the recurring battles with surrounding ethnicities and neighboring armies over the last two millennia that continuously altered the territorial sovereignty of the state currently known as Ethiopia. But he wisely concluded that he was in no position to correct Mengistu.

"You have an interesting background," Mengistu said, looking at a piece of paper on his desk. "You were first in your class at Holetta Military Academy, but shortly after graduating you decided to leave the military and become a professor of history. Did you know I also graduated from Holetta?"

"I had heard that, sir."

"But I was not first in my class," Mengistu said as he let out an awkward cackle. "So tell me, why did you leave the military?"

"I suppose I felt I could better serve the country educating our future leaders."

"I see. Our future leaders." Mengistu's facial expression turned slightly less pleasant. "These students certainly have the will to lead, but do they choose to fight for the right cause? The answer appears to be *no*. I hear about daily protests at the universities to our newly formed committee. I hear about students joining rebel groups. So I wonder where your loyalty lies. Do you believe in loyalty to your country?"

"Of course," Tesfaye responded, again feeling the answer he was supposed to give was a foregone conclusion.

"I ask because we are at the dawn of a new era and it will take loyal people to make sure our country fulfills its goals—the goals of a socialist state that *will* create equality for all citizens. The problem is that not all of our citizens understand that our new system will be beneficial. They are stuck in the mentality of the past. They look at the exploitation of ethnic groups and remain distrustful of those in power. And what is the result? Ignorant liberation fronts."

Mengistu took a puff of his cigar and stared intently at Tesfaye. "We need to save the people from the leaders of these rebellions. We need to save our great country. *Ethiopia First*, Tesfaye."

"Of course, sir," Tesfaye responded, unsure what else to say.

"I will not mince my words. If you graduated first in your class at Holetta, then you must be a born leader with an acute insight into military tactics. Your professorship shows your deep understanding of the history of warfare. Combining these two, I see a person uniquely positioned to assist our government in its quest to create a new, stronger Ethiopia."

"I am honored you would think of me," Tesfaye said, trying his best to quash Mengistu's apparent hesitance about his loyalty.

"Good. Good. Because it is important to be able to distinguish your friends from your enemies. Take the Americans for example. Would you consider them to be a friend or an enemy?"

Tesfaye sensed a test. Relations with the United States had dwindled in recent years as newly elected President Jimmy Carter ratcheted up his criticism of Ethiopia's human rights record. Mengistu's recently formed alliances with the Soviets and Cubans made his feelings toward the United States readily apparent. "The Americans cannot be considered a true friend," Tesfaye remarked confidently, "because they only provided Ethiopia with aid when it was in their military interest to do so."

"Very good," Mengistu said, gnawing on the tip of his cigar. "I couldn't agree more. I think you will do well at your new post."

"My new post, sir?"

"You are going to serve in the Ministry of Defense as one of my advisors. How does that sound?"

Listening to the job "offer," a wave of relief washed over Tesfaye as he became certain Mengistu had no intention to execute him. But Tesfaye knew a military leader willing to kill his rivals to assume power is unsurprisingly capricious in his view of the loyalty of those surrounding him.

Tesfaye thought about Ayana and their possible new baby. He saw only one option to secure their immediate safety. "The new post will be a great opportunity to contribute to the cause, sir. I am honored you selected me to help Ethiopia reach its full potential."

"That is fantastic. Now, I have selected another candidate who will be working closely with you."

"Sir?"

"Someone else whose career I have found very impressive. Do you remember who you beat out for top honors at Holetta?"

Tesfaye remembered well. The person's failure to secure top honors was a regularly joked about topic at get-togethers. "Geteye?"

"Correct, Geteye Tge. I do not have time to round up everyone on my list of future advisors, so I will task you with tracking him down."

As Mengistu stood and extended his arm, Tesfaye quickly did the same. "You will need to find him quickly. I expect both of you to report to your new offices at the ministry next week. You can take the cigar with you." And with that, Tesfaye exited Mengistu's office and began to plan how exactly he would break the news to Ayana that they would not be leaving Addis Ababa as planned.

Chapter 13

ROSARIO HAD PAID for two additional nights at the Days Inn in Tucson. Sofia pleaded for a third night, even though she knew it was likely pointless. They called the Motel 6 twice each day from different payphones, asking if a woman who fit Maria's description had made any inquiries about them. Nothing.

The Motel 6 was the only thing connecting them to Maria. Fernando insisted he had no other family, that it had always been him, his mother, and his elderly aunt. But his aunt recently passed away and now his mother was gone. He had no identification on him and he couldn't think of anyone to call. His surname—Perez—was about as common in Mexico as Smith is in the United States.

Rosario couldn't afford to keep paying for a motel room, considering she gave most of her available funds to the two men who were supposed to release Maria. So when the manager at the Motel 6 assured them on the third day that Maria *still* hadn't showed up, they decided to drive back to Rosario's home in Phoenix with Fernando.

Sofia's motherly instincts cautioned her against abandoning this child, but it wasn't just the fact that Fernando reminded her of her own son. Maria had, for all intents and purposes, saved Sofia's life in the desert. Sofia had no doubt that she would have died without Maria's guiding hand providing her with water, protecting her from the snakes and scorpions scurrying in the desert throughout the night, and motivating her to continue when the cactus spines pierced her shin.

At Rosario's insistence, they did not leave a forwarding phone number or address at the Motel 6. The plan was to keep calling back to check in with the front desk for any sightings.

Neither of them were optimistic that Maria would ever show up. The border between Mexico and the United States was the new Wild West. People were a commodity. The coyotes and their criminal networks exploited the unassuming travelers, knowing full well their illegal status would prevent them from seeking police protection. And if the police found one of the bodies of these unidentified Mexicans discarded throughout the vast desert wasteland, a thorough investigation was not going to be at the top of their list of priorities.

It was heart-wrenching to explain to Fernando that his mother might not be coming back. But as the minivan left Tucson, Sofia knew she had to level with him. Fernando cried for most of the ride to Phoenix. There was little she could do to comfort him. Déjà vu all over again. The numbing inability to provide consolation to a grief-stricken child felt eerily reminiscent of the darkest period in her life.

True to her word—and much to Rosario's surprise—Sofia repaid the nine hundred dollars within ten days. Rosario knew how she got the money. She sold three brand new laptop computers that she mysteriously acquired to several of Rosario's friends at the beauty parlor at a steep discount. What Rosario didn't know was how Sofia managed to come into the possession of these pricey items. Sofia insisted she won them at a raffle at a local electronics store. Although Rosario was skeptical, further inquiries after a day of prodding seemed moot.

It was five o'clock on the morning of Sofia's twelfth day in the United States. She couldn't sleep. This was the day she had been waiting for. The day she dreamed about for years. She would finally see a doctor in the United States. A month ago, after the plans for Sofia's journey north took shape, Rosario booked her an appointment at Helping Hands Medical Clinic, a non-profit organization dedicated to helping immigrants unable to afford medical care.

As the sun rose, Sofia got out of bed, unable to control her excitement anymore. She tiptoed out of the second bedroom, circling the blowup mattress in the middle of the floor that served as Fernando's bed. Rosario and Fernando came down an hour later to the smell of *huevos rancheros*—an over easy egg sitting on a fried tortilla doused with cheese and homemade salsa—which Sofia had spent the morning preparing. She resisted the urge to sample her specialty, mindful that she was not supposed to eat before getting blood work.

After Rosario dropped her off at the clinic, Sofia sat in the waiting room, trying to mask her excitement in front of the other patients who did not share her enthusiasm about their morning appointments. Ten minutes later, the nurse helped her fill out paperwork and then escorted her to an examination room to draw blood.

"All done," said the nurse after she filled four vials. "The doctor will be in shortly."

After a few minutes, the doctor opened the door. A long, white jacket covering his khaki pants, he had the thick, perfectly parted black hair of the doctors she would gawk at on American soap operas.

"*Hola*, I'm Doctor Garcia," he said, extending his hand, "it's very nice to meet you." Sofia immediately felt comforted by the doctor's willingness to shake her hand.

He examined her for a few minutes and then consulted the chart prepared by the nurse. "So it says here that you have HIV?"

"Yes."

"Okay. And do you know how and when you contracted HIV?"

It seemed a perfectly reasonable question, one that Sofia should have anticipated. But she hadn't, and the thought of explaining the circumstances made her sick to her stomach.

Chapter 14

LIN AWOKE ON the twelfth day at sea to the omnipresent rocking of the ship. The cracks in her dehydrated lips stung and licking them only provided momentary relief. She rested on her back on top of her piece of cardboard, staring up at the green, halogen lights. To avoid drying her lips further, she tried to breathe through her nose. *Damn*, Lin thought, *bathing day*.

Lying on her back made Lin more aware of the hunger pains gnawing her stomach. She sat up and looked around. Jiang was fast asleep. The few people Lin observed moving refrained from making a sound. The passengers did whatever they could to prolong the periods of sleep and minimize the amount of time they had to spend awake in the dark living quarters with nothing to do.

Slowly the passengers began to awaken and talk quietly. Lin saw Jiang and Shaoqing talking softly to each other. Curious, she crawled over to them.

"What are you whispering about?" she asked.

"We're trying to figure out the best way to make sure we get food," Jiang replied. "Look." Jiang pointed to the area beneath the closed hatch. "See those three huddled over there. They had been sleeping on the other side of the room, away from the entrance. I think they are trying to get closer to the entrance now to avoid the scramble when the snakeheads bring us something to eat."

"And something to drink," Shaoqing added. "I'd give up a meal for twice as much water."

Lin nodded. "Me too. So what are you going to do?"

Jiang pointed to an empty space on the floor behind the iron pole with foot holdings used to get down to the living quarters from the hatch. "Everyone always lines up in front of that pole and that area looks full right now. But if we go quietly to the empty space behind the pole, we can spring to the front of the line as soon as we hear the hatch open."

Shaoqing shrugged. "It's very risky. It will look as if we're cutting the line."

"Not if we're in front of the ladder before the hatch is opened," Jiang said. "We just have to be attentive and move fast."

"I don't know," Shaoqing said.

Jiang raised his hands. "What don't you know? All I know is that I want to make sure I get food. And I know that everyone down here is as hungry as me. Do you think these snakeheads care if we stay in line? They were smiling yesterday when everyone was pushing and shoving. I bet they've been bringing us less food and water for their amusement, just so they can watch us bicker."

"You're probably right," Shaoqing conceded. "Perhaps your plan will work, but maybe we should test it out with fewer people just to make sure."

"What did you have in mind?"

"Instead of all four of us going over there, why not try it today with two people and see if anyone notices. The other two will just wait in line and hope that there is some rice left."

"Fine," Jiang said. "But the two people going will need to go now before more people wake up. Who's coming with me?"

Shaoqing abdicated. "I'll stay back."

Although Lin felt apprehensive about the plan, her heart was racing at the chance to sit next to Jiang until the crewmen came down with food. But with her stomach in knots, she didn't have the courage to speak.

Jiang was looking at Lin when Ai sat up. "I don't know how many more days I can take," Ai said as she rubbed her eyes.

"Ai," Jiang whispered. "Are you hungry?"

"Of course I'm hungry," she replied sarcastically. "What kind of question is that?"

"Follow me," Jiang said. "I'll explain when we get there."

Lin watched Jiang and Ai crawl between half-sleeping bodies toward the back of the pole. She felt relieved to still be sitting at her familiar resting area, but puzzled that Jiang didn't even ask her if she wanted to go with him. She noticed that Shaoqing was faintly smiling as he watched Jiang crawling around the living quarters.

"Why didn't you want to go if you agreed with Jiang that his plan might work?" Lin asked.

"I don't really think his plan will work."

"It sounded like you did."

"By the time Jiang shared his plan with us, he had already decided what he was going to do. I could tell I was not going to change his mind. I just needed a way to take myself out of the plan without making it look as if I didn't agree with him."

Listening to Shaoqing confidently explain himself, Lin suddenly felt a strong appreciation for his seemingly effortless, methodical reasoning. "How is it that you always remain so calm?" she asked. "I don't think I've ever seen you get angry, not even remotely upset."

"Even those with self-control get upset."

"You're being modest. I remember when the crazy old man with the walking stick ordered us to get in the trunk of his car. I was so scared, but you jumped right in."

"I suppose I had accepted my fate. We were in the middle of nowhere and these men had the only means of transportation. We have financial arrangements with them. They had the means to use violence against us. There was no other option. Fear cannot change this fact."

"Maybe, but if something frightens me, I can't help but feel scared. You make it sound as if fear is a choice."

"Do you ever meditate, Lin?"

Lin's stomach sank. She pictured her father sitting in the corner of their home during one of his frequent meditation sessions, his legs crossed and his back vertically stretched as high as it could go. Having not thought about her father for a couple of days, Lin felt guilty that she had let her hunger pains overshadow the respect she should have been showing him.

"Lin?"

Startled, Lin looked up at Shaoqing. "Hmm?"

"Meditation. Have you ever meditated?"

"No," Lin said. "I have no interest."

"Really? None?"

When Lin was younger, her mother often scolded her for making a scene when they traveled to the closest market. After standing still for any significant period of time, Lin would feel a twinge in her stomach and chest that could only be alleviated by moving around—another attribute of her condition that she had convinced herself made her uniquely peculiar. She would often vocalize her discontent while standing next to her mother in the market, watching her mother heckle with other farmers and shopkeepers. As he always did, Lin's father tried to persuade her that her feelings were not uncommon, and that he too used to be the same way as a child. When he told Lin that meditation could help alleviate her internal tension, she gladly accepted his offer to join him occasionally during his meditation sessions.

But Lin was in no mood to open the door on that subject. Although she had no problem discussing meditation with Shaoqing, she felt the need to put up a wall to protect herself from any possible questions that may force her to discuss the circumstances of her father's disappearance. Not enough time had passed. Since the grey morning when the passengers were herded into the living quarters like cattle, Lin had managed to gradually compartmentalize the reality of her predicament as the repetition of each day started to make her situation seem all the more normal. She didn't want to revert back to the thoughts causing her to nearly break down when she was on her way to the dock in Fuzhou, inundated by the fumes of the Volkswagen driven by the man with the cane. She didn't want to start thinking about the fact that her father had been missing for months, that her mother forced her to leave the only home she'd ever known, that she was in the middle of the ocean so far from China, and that she had no idea what was going to happen to her if she even managed to get off the ship safely.

"No," she repeated, "I have no interest in meditation," she said with forced contempt, well aware that she was never any good at lying.

"If you say so," Shaoqing said. "I would have thought differently."

"You would be mistaken."

Lin and Shaoqing sat in the malaise of the living quarters until the unmistakable creaking of the hatch sent passengers scrambling. Starving and thirsty, they huddled tight and pushed forward to get closer to Fei Pin and two other crewmen, who were handing out large spoonfuls of rice.

Awaiting her ration, Lin was sandwiched between Shaoqing and another female passenger. Out of the corner of her eye, she saw Jiang and Ai rush out of the pack, Jiang looking over his shoulder as he scarfed down his rice. Letting the momentum of the pack push her forward, Lin directed her attention to the two passengers who were running toward Jiang, yelling in his direction. She tried to make out what they were saying, but the room had grown noisy.

All of the sudden, Jiang stopped moving. He had barely turned around by the time a fist struck his jawbone. Lin watched as he dropped to the ground, and the two passengers who had been following him quickly jumped on top of his sprawled-out body.

"Fight!" someone screamed. The living quarters erupted. Passengers began yelling. Afraid the ensuing turmoil would somehow interfere with their meal, many started to push toward the front of the food line. But the passengers' actions only exacerbated their initial concerns. As the panic cascaded, several people were thrown to the ground. The shrieks of trampled passengers echoed off the walls.

Lin was staring at a young man on the ground clutching his bruised arm when she lost her own footing. She made several attempts to get to her feet until she was unintentionally struck in the back of the head by a boot. Instinctively, she tucked into a fetal position and covered her head with her hands. She clenched her eyes tight and tensed her muscles to minimize the blows of fellow passengers stepping on her back and legs.

There was a large crash as the tin pot used to serve rice spilled onto the floor. Passengers scrambled to the ground to scoop rice with their hands. More fights broke out as everyone realized their meal was being washed away.

Shaoqing grabbed Lin by the collar of her shirt and hoisted her up to her feet. He led her to the side of the living quarters, away from the epicenter of the brawls.

"Enough!" shouted the crewman, causing all the passengers to calm down. "Your actions today have cost everyone their meal. Since you are not able to maintain order, the rules from now on are going to change." Fei Pin grabbed the empty tin pot and followed the other crewmen out of the living quarters.

Lin and Shaoqing rushed over to Jiang. "What happened?" Lin asked Ai, who was kneeling beside him.

Ai's face had turned pale. "I don't know, it all happened so fast."

"Jiang," Shaoqing said. "Jiang!" he repeated after getting no answer. "Are you okay?" he asked, assuming Jiang's jaw would be throbbing.

Jiang let out a murmur. "My stomach," he said, lying on his side, doubled up in pain, his knees coiled together by his chest.

Shaoqing looked down at Jiang's hands folded over his stomach. When he unfolded them, he saw a pool of blood building by the lower right side of Jiang's abdomen. After a peek under Jiang's shirt, he quickly looked away.

"What is it?" Lin asked.

"Jiang's been stabbed."

Chapter 15

"**A**RE YOU OKAY?" the doctor asked Sofia.

"I'm fine," she insisted.

But she was not fine. Even though she had not yet uttered a word about how she contracted HIV, she already felt the humiliation rising in her.

THE TOWN OF Escuinapa hugs the center of Mexico's northwestern border. Adjacent to the Pacific Ocean, it sits in the Mexican state of Sinaloa, known as the Tomato State. True to its name, the region boasts one of the most concentrated areas of tomato farmers in the country. Sofia's husband, Israel, was a tomato farmer who worked the same land his father had before him. Israel didn't fit the typical mold of most farmers in the region. He didn't have the leathery, ultra dark skin that years of working in the sun without sunblock would produce. His face was spared the premature wrinkles that transformed middle-aged farmers into old men before their time, and his hands were free of the hardened layer of dirt and grime that had settled under the fingernails of fieldworkers who had given up trying to remove it every night. At Sofia's insistence, Israel did his best to take care of himself, blanketing his face and neck in sunscreen, regularly sporting large-brimmed cowboy hats. Selfishly perhaps, she wanted him to maintain the handsome face she had fallen in love with.

Israel and Sofia led a relatively simple life. Like many, they worked long hours in the fields, attended church regularly, and congregated in the small town center on special occasions. And like all the other townspeople, they knew that the drug cartels were running a sophisticated trafficking operation all around them. Locals would joke about how easy it was to spot the men who belonged to a cartel. All you had to do was stand in the middle of any town in Sinaloa and look toward the peak of the nearest hill. There, you would find them, living in the biggest houses, driving the nicest cars. At night, they would frequent the local discothèques, spending more cash in a night than others could dream about seeing in a month.

In Escuinapa, it was a man named Guillermo who enjoyed this decadent life. As the townspeople often did with their local drug lords, the citizens of Escuinapa gave Guillermo a nickname. Playing off the shortened version of his name, Memo, everyone referred to him as *El Memo*.

The morning of September 10, 1994, was like any other. Sofia woke up early to prepare *chorizo* and eggs for the children before sending them off to school. She was cleaning the kitchen when she saw Guillermo's Camaro approaching the farm. Guillermo pulled to the side of the road next to the field being tended by Israel and waived for him to come over to the car. The conversation didn't last more than ten minutes, Sofia watching nervously the whole time.

When Guillermo drove away, Sofia walked briskly to Israel. "What did he want?"

"He invited us over for dinner."

"You think that's funny?"

"He was just asking about the trucks."

"The delivery trucks? Why?"

Although Israel shrugged off her question, Sofia had an idea what Guillermo was after. Produce from the farm was regularly loaded into trucks destined for the United States. When it came to making money, members of the cartel were very creative. They used all means at their disposal to transport drugs into the United States.

Sofia's initial instincts were validated. Over the course of the next few months, Guillermo frequently returned to the farm with some "additions" to their regular shipments of tomatoes. At first, she fought with Israel for helping Guillermo, but Sofia mainly picked fights to vent her own frustrations. She knew Israel didn't choose to help the cartel. His services were not optional. The only concession Israel could get from Guillermo was that he wouldn't come to the farm when their children were home.

The first sign of trouble occurred on a pleasant December morning while Sofia was busy in the kitchen preparing food for Christmas dinner. Startled by the sound of a shouting voice, she went to the front porch to investigate. There, in the fields, she saw Guillermo yelling at Israel, repeatedly poking Israel's chest with his index finger. Guillermo looked over toward Sofia and began pointing at her. Israel grew visibly agitated by whatever Guillermo had just said, presenting a much more aggressive posture than Sofia had ever seen him display in Guillermo's presence.

True to his nature, Israel made light of his confrontation with Guillermo when Sofia asked him what had happened. He admitted it concerned money, but assured Sofia that it only involved a misunderstanding about a tiny amount and that Guillermo was just trying to act like a tough guy.

The months went on and everything seemed to return to normal—as normal as life could be now. Sofia still felt uneasy by the image of Guillermo poking her husband's chest. Despite Israel's assurances, she felt perpetually unsettled, convinced he was hiding something from her.

The incident that occurred the next spring was more serious. This time, Sofia saw Guillermo pull out a gun and wave it in her husband's face before speeding off in his Camaro. Israel didn't wait for Sofia to come out and start questioning him. He walked into the house and headed for the kitchen. Sofia followed, watching him go straight to the refrigerator and grab a Carta Blanca.

"Son of a bitch," he said, taking a swig.

"Are you in trouble?"

"He's crazy."

"What?" asked Sofia impatiently as Israel took another sip of his beer. "Israel, talk to me!"

"He thinks I'm stealing money from him."

"Stealing? From *him*? Who would be stupid enough to do that? You're not that stupid, are you?"

"Will you look around? Do you see a television less than ten years old? A couch that doesn't have ripped upholstery?"

"Then why does he think that?"

"Something with the trucks, the checkpoints."

To tide the flow of narcotics, Mexican authorities established recurrent checkpoints along all the major roads leading north to the United States. Agriculture shipping trucks and other vehicles capable of hiding large quantities of the cartels' products were frequently subjected to searches. The cartels viewed these potential searches as more of a nuisance than a real problem. Bribing the officers stationed at these checkpoints was just another cost of doing business.

"A checkpoint?" asked Sofia. "Why does that have anything to do with you?"

"He thinks I'm skimming the bribe money."

"And why would he think that?"

"Because the drivers' grease money is being depleted too quickly. *El Memo* and the others, they have a whole system. They know how many checkpoints a truck must pass before reaching *El Norte*. They know how much money it takes to bribe officers in different precincts if something is found, and they think they know the likelihood of a truck being randomly stopped and searched. They even know where they can ignore certain checkpoints because they have the entire police force on the payroll."

Israel rolled his eyes and sighed, finishing what remained of his beer. "I told him, I don't know what to say, I didn't do it. There's so much money going through so many different sets of hands. What if the trucks are getting stopped more frequently than he thinks? For goodness sake, what if the drivers are just pocketing some of the bribe money? How can he hold me responsible for *that*? I grow tomatoes and live in a shack!"

"You *never* took any money?" Sofia asked.

"Last December I might have taken a few pesos. But that was one time, and I only did it to get Manuel that silly Power Ranger toy he wanted for Christmas."

"*Idiota*," Sofia murmured under her breath.

"What?"

"So what are we going to do?"

"I don't know."

"Should we leave?"

"And go where? With what money? Maybe if I actually stole his fucking money we could go somewhere else."

Even if Sofia and Israel decided to leave, their plan would have been thwarted unless they left immediately. That night, as Sofia put Manuel and Eva to bed, she heard the front door burst open, followed by the piercing sound of a gunshot.

"Mama!" Eva cried out.

"Both of you listen to me," Sofia said quickly. "Hide under your beds. Do not come out of this room under any circumstances. Do you understand? Now get under the beds!"

Sofia shut the bedroom door behind her and ran to the front of the house. Guillermo stood in the entranceway with a gun in his hand, flanked by two of his fellow drug pushers. Israel was lying on the floor, grabbing his shoulder, blood trickling down his fingers.

"Israel!" she screamed, kneeling beside him.

"There's only one thing worse than a thief," Guillermo snickered, "and that's a thief who refuses to make amends."

Drug dealer logic, Sofia thought. *That's why all the towns in Sinaloa have a church built or repaired by people affiliated with the cartels. So they can justify everything else they put us through.*

"On my mother's grave," pleaded Israel, "I did not take your money and I don't know who did!"

"Of course," Guillermo sarcastically quipped. "You have *no* idea. All these farmers in this area, all the trucks heading north, and strangely I'm only having problems with the ones leaving from your farm."

"Please, it could be anyone on the route skimming off the top."

"Are you saying I don't know how to run my organization?"

"What? No, of course not, I'm just . . ."

"Because it sounded like that's what you're saying."

"That's what it sounds like to me," said one of the men flanking Guillermo.

"Please, I'm just saying that there are so many things that could have caused the problems with the bribes and it's such a small amount of money for you anyway. I'll get to the bottom of it, just give me a chance."

Guillermo shook his head. "That's always how it starts, isn't it? A little bit here, a little more from there. Next thing you know, people are starting to skim more than just a few pesos because they think they can get away with it. I can't run a business like that."

"No, *El Memo*," agreed one of the others, "that's no way to run a business."

"I need order," Guillermo said.

"Fucking order, man," agreed another.

"I need everyone who touches my money from here to *El Norte* to know that they can't fuck with me. It's like cockroaches. If you don't take care of the problem right away, it multiplies until you're surrounded. I can't trust my supply chain to a hoard of cockroaches, now can I?

"Take anything you want—take my house, my truck, take it all!"

"Sorry *Israelito*, that ship has sailed. It's time to make an example out of you."

Guillermo grabbed Sofia, threw her on the couch, and forcibly removed her underwear while the other two men pointed their guns at Israel. "There's no need to close your eyes Israel, we're all friends here." Sofia knew what was going to happen next. Guillermo slowly undid his belt and proudly let his pants fall to his ankles, his penis already erect. With his hands, he grabbed Sofia's knees and tried to spread her legs apart.

"No!" Sofia screamed defiantly.

Before she had a chance to say anything else, Guillermo had wedged his knee between her clenched thighs and grabbed her by the throat, smiling as he watched Sofia gasp for air while her eyes bulged. "Yeah," he said, "struggle a little. Let me see your fighting spirit."

The others cheered Guillermo on as they waited their turns. Eventually accepting her fate, Sofia refrained from making any more noise, deciding it was more important to ensure that her children did not have to listen to her cry out. She closed her eyes, letting her mind wander far away from the horrors afflicting her body. She pictured herself with Rosario when they were kids, racing to the top of the hill to catch fireflies—before the hilltop was taken over by Guillermo's big house. Before there was a driveway filled with fancy cars.

SOFIA KEPT SOME of the details to herself. Parts of the story she hadn't even told Rosario. But she provided Dr. Garcia with the general overview of that terrible night in 1995.

"It can be a sick world," said the doctor. "I've heard a lot of bad stories over the years." He patted her hand. "The important thing is that you're safe now and we're going to work on getting you better. A few more questions and we won't ever have to talk about this again. Any drug use? Needles?"

"No."

"Ever have a blood transfusion?"

"I don't think so."

"Did your husband ever get tested for HIV?"

"He didn't have HIV," Sofia said defensively. "It was those fucking drug dealers."

"I'm just asking. What about unprotected sex with anyone other than your husband during the marriage?"

Although she didn't mind answering, Sofia was slightly taken back by the question, a devout Catholic upbringing stirring in her a conditioned uneasiness. "Heavens no."

"I know these are not the most pleasant questions in the world, but it's helpful to pinpoint all possible origins of contraction." Dr. Garcia put down his chart. "Okay, I can't say exactly which drugs I'm going to prescribe to you until I see your blood work, but I can tell you that it will likely be a combination of anti-retroviral drugs designed to reduce the virus in your bloodstream. These drugs aren't going to cure your disease, but hopefully they will dramatically reduce your symptoms."

The words coming out of the doctor's mouth were like silk caressing her body. This man was actually going to help her cheat death. A few words scribbled on a prescription pad would grant her the privilege of remaining in her physical body a little longer. Sitting in the doctor's office, she was suddenly overwhelmed. Her eyes watered. "Bless you," she said to the doctor, a few tears emerging from her rapidly blinking eyes.

"I'm just doing my job," Dr. Garcia remarked. "Everyone deserves a second chance in life." Folding his legs, Dr. Garcia took off his glasses and started to clean the lenses with a tissue. "What are your plans here in the United States?"

"I don't know. I've just been so focused on getting to a doctor."

"A few years ago we started noticing a correlation between a positive outlook on life and a patient's survival rate. One of the biggest contributing factors to a positive outlook is employment. I don't know why—maybe because it gives a person direction, a feeling of purpose, or simply because money makes people happier. But it got us thinking that if we are trying to heal our patients, we shouldn't limit ourselves to prescribing medicine."

"I'm not sure I follow."

"Well, it occurred to us that if a job helped our patients live longer, why not develop relationships with businesses in the area that are sympathetic to our mission here. Do you have any skills, Sofia? Anything you're really good at?"

"Cooking, cleaning, farming. I guess I know how to sew a little, and I've done some beadwork before."

Dr. Garcia put his glasses back on and stroked his chin. "I may be able to help you."

Chapter 16

BEADS OF SWEAT trickled down Jiang's forehead. He took quick breaths that were precisely spaced apart, as if he were trying to perfect his Lamaze technique. "Do you have any idea how much this hurts?" Jiang asked.

His eyes bulging, Shaoqing stared at the wound. "We need to stop the bleeding."

"How?" Lin asked.

Shaoqing shook his head. "How should I know?"

Ai blew her nose and rubbed her eyes. She had remained quiet since she witnessed the stabbing, but watching drops of blood from Jiang's side stain the ground brought her thoughts into focus. "Apply pressure," Ai suggested. "Isn't that what you do?"

"We need a shirt or something to wrap around the wound," Shaoqing said. "Where's your bag, Jiang?"

"I don't know," Jiang grumbled as he surveyed the area. "I thought it was next to me."

Shaoqing, Lin, and Ai checked all around the surrounding area, but Jiang's bag was nowhere in sight.

"The bag doesn't matter right now," Shaoqing said. Without hesitation, he took off his shirt and tried to maneuver it around Jiang's abdomen.

Observing Shaoqing's bare chest, Lin and Ai gave each other a quick glance. When he wore his baggy clothes, Shaoqing appeared as proportionately emaciated as many of the men who came from the poorer areas of China's rural countryside. But the contours of Shaoqing's muscular body reminded Lin of a Bruce Lee picture she once saw as a child.

Shaoqing knotted the shirt firmly around Jiang's abdomen. Jiang clenched every muscle in his body, fighting the pain as best he could.

"Did you see the knife?" Shaoqing asked Jiang.

"I think it looked like a triangle," he answered in the midst of his panting. "It was hard to tell with that ogre on top of me."

"I know those blades, that's good," Shaoqing said, not surprised the attacker had used a blade that was easily concealable.

"Good?" Jiang asked in disbelief. "Why is that *good?*"

"Because Jiang, that means the wound is not very deep."

Jiang stared at Shaoqing with a perplexed look on his face. "How the hell do you know that?"

"The length of the gash. Imagine the tip of a triangle digging into your flesh. As the tip goes deeper, the expanding angle of the triangle will cause a wider split in your skin. The triangle blades are small, but if one of them goes all the way in, then your wound ends up being at least twice as long. Either way, none of this will matter if we don't stop the bleeding."

After twenty minutes of applying pressure, Shaoqing loosened the shirt and peeked underneath.

"How does it look?" Jiang asked.

Shaoqing rewrapped his shirt around the wound. "Better."

Lin and Shaoqing stood up and walked away from Jiang. "How does it really look?" Lin asked.

Shaoqing shook his head. "You don't have to be a doctor to see that he needs medical attention."

Some of the passengers tried to mask their gaze, but many openly stared at Jiang. From the middle of the large Changle City group that had been huddled together since they boarded the ship, a lanky boy stood up and walked over to Shaoqing and Lin.

"You're name is Shaoqing, isn't it?" asked the boy. Shaoqing nodded and the boy continued. "I'm Bao," he said. "How is Jiang doing?"

"The Pacific Ocean is a bad place to get stabbed," Shaoqing replied.

"So he was stabbed by that creep from Tingjiang."

Shaoqing and Bao glanced at the ensemble of men from Tingjiang Township hoarding space in the far corner of the living quarters. Wide smirks adorned their faces, which were couched in mockingly rigid visages of superiority. Each had atypically wide necks and thick arms with no muscle tone.

"They all look like apes," Shaoqing snickered.

"I don't know what the little snakeheads are going to do with us to maintain order," Bao said, "but we know there's safety in numbers. Most of the fifteen or so of us from Changle know Jiang, or at least heard about his family when we were growing up. I can't say for sure why they attacked him, but I can tell you that Jiang's father owns a very well-known, successful business, and I would bet that at least one of those Tingjiang apes knew that too." Bao inched closer to Shaoqing. "Someone saw one of the apes take his bag," he whispered.

"Stabbing Jiang just because they wanted his bag? Seems a little much."

"Who knows?"

"In any case, I couldn't agree with you more. We should stick together, whatever comes next."

Curious about all the whispering, Ai walked over to Shaoqing and Lin after Bao left. "What did he want?" Ai asked.

"He's scared," Shaoqing said, quickly surveying the living quarters. "Everyone's scared."

"Wait," Lin said, looking at the hatch. "Do you hear that?"

When the hatch opened this time, there was no pushing or shoving. The passengers waited quietly as ten crewmen climbed down, three carrying guns, and the other seven brandishing iron rods.

Lin recognized two of the crewmen. Fei Pin stood toward the back of the group with his mouth open, belly protruding, grappling his iron rod with both hands. And then there was Lee, the concave-faced elder man who Lin had not seen since he forced everyone down the hatch when they first boarded the ship. A gun tucked into his waistband, Lee led the other crewmen toward the group from Tingjiang Township without looking at anyone else.

Lin tried to whisper without moving her lips. "What do you think they're talking about?" she asked to nobody in particular.

"*Ma zhais*," Shaoqing whispered back, also trying to curtail his lip movement.

"*Ma zhais?*"

"Enforcers," Shaoqing grumbled.

Lee spoke for a few minutes with Dong, one of the largest of the eight brutes from Tingjiang. After Dong bowed toward Lee, the crewmen passed their iron rods to the Tingjiang group.

As the crewmen headed for the open hatch, Lin thought about Jiang lying helplessly by the wall. She took a deep breath and stepped forward. "Wait!" she said.

The crewmen stopped their forward progress, Fei Pin's mouth now opened even wider than usual.

Feeling all the eyes suddenly locked on her, Lin became lightheaded, her knees wobbling back and forth. She opened her mouth, but forgot momentarily what she wanted to say. "Our friend is hurt," she managed to eke out after she regained her composure. "We need some medical supplies."

Lee stepped directly in front of Lin, holding his gun in his right hand. "What is all the fuss here little girl?" he asked.

Lin pointed at Jiang. "We just need some medical supplies, or thread and a needle. Please, sir."

Lee smiled as he surveyed Jiang trying to mask his bloodstained shirt. "Look, Fei Pin, the profitable last minute addition." Fei Pin and the other crewmen cackled. Their genuine indifference to Jiang's suffering frightened Lin. When the laughter died down, Lee's smile quickly disappeared. "Now you listen up little girl, from now on you talk to them," he said, pointing at the group from Tingjiang who were now armed with iron rods. He looked around at the crowd of passengers staring at him intently. "That goes for all of you!" he shouted. "From now on, they will be in charge of making sure there is order here. There will be no more incidents like the one before. And to show we are serious, nobody gets anything to eat or drink for the rest of the day. No washing today either. You can wallow in your own filth." Lee paused to let his words sink in with the frightened passengers. "Only well-behaved people get to eat," he continued. "If you want to eat tomorrow, there better be no more trouble."

The familiar crashing of the hatch slamming shut sent a wave of helplessness through Lin. She felt anxious enough to go to the bathroom right there in the middle of the living quarters. Barely able to support her own weight, she sat down next to Jiang. "I'm sorry."

Jiang stretched out his bloody hand to touch Lin's wrist. "Don't be. Thank you for trying."

"What now?" Ai asked. "We can't ask those Tingjiang animals for medical supplies. Obviously they'll say no."

"Maybe, but we have to try," Shaoqing said. "I'm going over there."

Without hesitation Shaoqing stood up and walked over to the group from Tingjiang. Lin and Ai looked at each other and struggled to their feet to follow him.

Proudly displaying their iron rods, the Tingjiang crew formed a line when they saw Shaoqing walking toward them. Dong, who was now the apparent leader of the group, took a step forward. He did not wait for Shaoqing to explain what he wanted. "We were taking bets on whether you'd have the courage to come over here." Dong glanced at the others. "I guess I lost the bet," he said, the Tingjiang crew laughing behind him.

"We don't want anything from you," Shaoqing said. "We just want you to ask the snakeheads for medical supplies. You owe Jiang that much."

Dong's eyes bulged wide and his lips clenched together. "I don't owe Jiang *anything*, do you understand?"

Shaoqing put his hands up. "Okay, you don't owe Jiang anything. But you do have his bag and I'm sure there's money inside. So why don't we call it even? You keep everything in the bag in exchange for asking the snakeheads for medical supplies."

Dong looked at Jiang's bag clumped in the corner several feet behind him. "That bag? I think you're mistaken. That's my bag. I brought it on the ship with me."

Shaoqing began to walk away. "Wait," Dong said. "You want medical supplies?" Shaoqing paused and turned back around. "No problem," Dong said, smirking at Ai and Lin. "All we want is some favors from your two beautiful friends." Several members of the group snickered with approval at Dong's suggestion.

Shaoqing didn't answer Dong. He bowed slightly, walked away, and sat back down next to Jiang with Lin and Ai. "If they won't give us the medicine, we'll have to go and take it ourselves," Shaoqing said.

"Impossible," Lin insisted.

"Impossible unless you want to catch a beating," Jiang added.

Shaoqing smiled. "I have a plan."

Chapter 17

JIANG REMAINED UNCONVINCED by Shaoqing's claim to have a viable plan to obtain medical supplies. "Having a plan doesn't mean the plan will work," Jiang said. "I had a plan for getting food. Little good that did me."

"We *did* get food though," Ai reminded Jiang. "So what is your idea, Shaoqing?"

"When is the only time we can get out of this pit?" Shaoqing asked.

Lin cringed when she thought about the answer. "Bathing," she said with a wince. "When we have to bathe in front of open mouth Fei."

"Exactly," Shaoqing said. "So we have to act during that time. Today was supposed to be the day we washed up on the deck. I think it's a good bet that tomorrow they'll bring us to the deck instead. So let us assume that will be the case, and if not, we can reassess our options tomorrow. The question becomes what exactly do we know about this ship and crew, and how will that help us achieve our goal."

Ai chimed in. "One of the snakeheads stands by the open hatch while we're led up and down to make sure nobody tries to get out of this cellar."

Shaoqing nodded. "Right, and there are two snakeheads watching us on the deck when we bathe."

"Two?" Lin scoffed. "More like ten."

"Ten?" asked Shaoqing.

Ai nodded. "Lin's right. I think they all come up to the deck to watch the women bathe." Ai lowered her head. "It's very humiliating."

"Interesting." Shaoqing stroked his chin for a moment. "What about the snakehead who is supposed to be watching the hatch? Have either of you seen him on the deck when you're up there?"

Lin and Ai looked at each other. "I don't know," Lin said. "Honestly, I try not to pay attention."

Ai deliberated intently. "There was one time, when one of the girls got a lot of water on her shirt. I remember a commotion. I think I remember seeing the snakehead who watches the hatch come over and stare."

"Was he already on the deck or did someone call him up?" Shaoqing asked.

Ai shrugged her shoulders and looked at the ground. "I'm not sure."

"Are you sure you never saw him on the deck any other time when you were washing?"

"No," Ai admitted. "I'm not sure. He may have been there. I don't know."

"So we know that the snakehead guarding the door might leave when females are washing on the deck," Shaoqing summarized. "And we know that he will go up to the deck when he thinks there is something worth watching up there. So we can hope that he is gone or we can make sure we create a distraction that will get him up there."

Jiang let out a moan as he struggled to speak. "Forget it," he said softly. "I don't want you taking this risk for me. I got myself into this mess and I'll deal with the pain. Besides, the pain takes my mind away from thinking about how hungry I am."

Shaoqing put his hand on Jiang's shoulder. "We have a long time left on this boat and I'm sure I'll find myself in a situation where I need your help. So how about this? You promise me that you'll help me when you're all healed and I get myself in trouble, and we'll call it even."

Jiang clenched his lips together and nodded his head. "Agreed," he said.

Listening to Shaoqing delve into the details of his plan, Lin could not help but admire his brazen willingness to take on such a perilous venture for Jiang. Nonetheless, she was having trouble understanding why Shaoqing was so willing to propose risking his neck for someone he had only met two weeks ago. *Would I have the courage to propose such a bold action?*

"I think you have failed to consider," Jiang added, "that even if you are somehow able to get out of this hole undetected, you still need to find the medical supplies."

"I've seen them," Shaoqing said confidently. "We all have. When we first came onto this ship—when we were following that skinny guy with the freakish eyes—we walked down a hallway where all the little snakeheads sleep. The doors were open and I saw a medical kit in one of the rooms."

"You're sure?" Jiang asked, considering whether to buy into Shaoqing's confident manner.

"I am. One of the snakeheads was using a large medical kit to block his cards. I was focusing on the game they were playing and the medical kit was on the table."

Happy to contribute, Lin chimed into the conversation. "But that doesn't mean the medical kit would be in that room *now*."

"Perhaps not," Shaoqing conceded, "but where else would it be?"

"Anywhere," Ai said.

"That's true," Shaoqing agreed, "but if I had to make a bet, I'd bet the medical kit is in one of the rooms in that corridor. Since those rooms yield the highest probability of success, I think they should be the target."

"Of course," Ai said, "being able to go look for a medical kit can only work if nobody is still in the snakeheads' living quarters."

"Which is based on the success of the distraction," Lin added.

Shaoqing nodded. "Precisely."

Lin glanced across the room at the boys from Tingjiang. "This isn't going to work, even if we come up with a good distraction. If you were to go, Shaoqing, you would need to figure out a way to sneak out of here without being detected by the Tingjiang *ma zhais*."

"And," Ai added, "even if you could get out of this room undetected, you would also need to get back down here without the *ma zhais* seeing you."

Jiang grimaced in pain as he struggled to lift himself to a seated position. "Don't worry about the Tingjiang apes," he said. "I'll take care of them."

Chapter 18

THE TWO COLLEGE freshmen were visibly drunk when they clunked into the backseat of Tesfaye's cab.

"Bleeker and Thompson," said one of the boys.

"What's up man?" the other asked Tesfaye. "Kanja," he said, reading Tesfaye's assumed identity from the taxi information sticker hanging from the rearview mirror. "Where you from?"

"Kenya," Tesfaye responded, hoping there would be no traffic on Ninth Avenue to prolong the drive downtown.

"They speak English in Kenya?"

Tesfaye did not feel like explaining that he was really from Ethiopia where all university classes were taught in English. "Yes, many people in Kenya speak English."

"Did you live in a teepee?"

The other boy began laughing uncontrollably. "Dude," he said to his friend, "what are you talking about? It was the Indians who lived in teepees."

"Whatever, you know what I mean."

"You're such a dumb-ass," his friend was barely able to spit out in the midst of his laughing spree.

"Come on, you know what I mean, those little huts, made of tree branches and twigs and shit." He turned his attention back to Tesfaye. "Well buddy, is that where you grew up? Did you raise a family in one of those little huts back home?"

Tesfaye smiled. "No, I did not raise a family in a hut."

"NO PEEKING," TESFAYE instructed Ayana, covering her eyes as he drove through the open gates and down the dirt path of the villa. "Okay, you can open your eyes now."

Ayana immediately fixated on the two columns that flanked the front entrance. Offsetting the house's bright white exterior, mahogany paneling surrounded the windows, painted the same rich auburn that enveloped the rectangular shingles on the roof.

"Tesfaye, what are we doing here?"

Tesfaye grinned as he grabbed Ayana's hand. "We are here because this is your new home."

"What?" Ayana queried, barely able to control her jubilation.

Tesfaye ran around the car, opened the passenger door, and helped a very pregnant Ayana to her feet. "So what do you think?"

Her jaw dropped as she surveyed the house. "What do I think?" she repeated sarcastically.

Tesfaye took Ayana for a tour of her new home and the guesthouse that Negasi would soon occupy.

"I don't know what to say," Ayana said.

"You don't need to say anything. All I am doing is giving you what you deserve."

"I couldn't think of a more perfect place to raise a child. You must be good, Tesfaye. You must be very good."

"What do you mean?"

"For us to be able to afford this, Mengistu must really love you."

"I'm just doing my job," Tesfaye said, feeling no need to display conceit to Ayana. But his counsel to Mengistu was undeniably well received. A few days after he and Geteye assumed their positions at the ministry, Mengistu summoned them and launched into a tirade about Fidel Castro and Soviet President Podgorny for daring to suggest that he settle his differences with Somalia. Mengistu could not understand how these countries could expect him to forgive Somalia for intruding onto Ethiopian land. The mighty Ethiopian state would not become a puppet government simply because the Soviets wanted to see a united communist federation throughout all the countries in the Horn of Africa.

It was Tesfaye who pointed out to Mengistu why giving in to such demands would not be necessary. Historically, such coaxing only works when the countries fighting are on equal footing. Here, however, Ethiopia's population dwarfed the several million people inhabiting Somalia. If the Soviets were *forced* to choose between the two countries, Tesfaye was almost certain they would choose Ethiopia. When Tesfaye's prediction turned out to be correct, his stock immediately soared in Mengistu's eyes.

One month after moving into their new home, Ayana gave birth to a healthy baby girl. An even seven pounds, Afeworki was the pride of Tesfaye's world, an added motivation for him to excel at the ministry.

But his concerns about the regime's course of action remained. Tesfaye still had his doubts about the long-term success rate of governments that strictly adhere to Marxist thinking. It was a careful balancing act to ensure that his individual beliefs did not cloud the advice he provided Mengistu.

By the winter of 1977, the Soviets were pumping hundreds of millions of dollars in military aid into Ethiopia, as the helping hand of the United States officially clamped shut. Mengistu assembled his most trusted advisors to create a plan to defeat the Somalis and other rebel groups fighting in the southern provinces of Ethiopia.

Tesfaye and Geteye had formulated a plan to let Ethiopian militias take the lead. As Tesfaye let Geteye explain, if you are going to base your political structure on nationalism, then you want the people to have a stake in the government's success. The militias crushed the Somali positions and ran them out of the southern provinces. It was a strange sight, Tesfaye thought, to see the citizens form a militia—trained by the North Koreans and financed by the Soviets—to fight alongside thousands of troops from Cuba, all in the name of Ethiopia.

Tesfaye knew that the joy of victory would be short-lived. With vast swaths of southern Ethiopia now firmly under the Derg's control, the nagging rebellions in the north would need to be addressed more forcefully. But he was happy. Afeworki was healthy. His relationship with Ayana was stronger than ever. Mengistu seemed willing to try and win over the hearts and minds of the citizenry. A national literacy campaign had been put into place. All in all, the country seemed to exhibit faint glimmers of hope. But all of that would soon come crashing down. The famine of 1983 would change everything—more so than Tesfaye would realize for a long time.

Chapter 19

"HELLO AGAIN, SOFIA," said Dr. Garcia. "Let's talk about your test results."

"I have tonsillitis, don't I?"

"A sense of humor, that's very important," he said, putting on his glasses to read her blood work. "Well, to confirm what I believe you already know, you do indeed have HIV. Your CD4 T-cell count is quite low."

"What does that mean?"

"It means that I want to get you started on a drug regimen today."

"Good, I want to start today, right now."

"I would be remiss if I didn't go over the potential side effects from some of these drugs."

Sofia put up her hand. "If you tell me, then I'll be thinking about them. I told you yesterday about all the different types of illnesses I've had."

"You did."

"Are the side effects going to make me feel worse than how I feel now?"

"Not likely."

"Am I going to live longer if I take these medications?"

"Everyone responds differently, but that could very well be the case."

"Then there's nothing left to discuss."

Dr. Garcia shrugged his shoulders. "Okay then," he said, taking a pen out of his pocket. "There is one other thing. I mentioned yesterday that I might be able to help you find a job." He scribbled down a phone number on a sheet of his prescription pad. "As it turns out, I found something that would be perfect for you," he said, handing the sheet to Sofia.

"What's this?"

"It's the phone number of a friend of mine in downtown Phoenix who manufactures and sells Native American crafts. When your immune system starts to show signs of improvement, I'm going to want you to give him a call."

"How long will it take for the drugs to work?"

Dr. Garcia hid his trepidation well. Sofia's T-cell count was nearly the lowest he'd ever seen in a new patient. It took him a considerable amount of time to brainstorm a suitable employment vicinity free from any chemicals or pollutants that he might let slide with other patients.

"I have to give the typically ambiguous doctor's answer—it depends. Right now, the most important thing for us to do is get you on a regimen and carefully treat the abrasions on your shin. An infection could be fatal."

Chapter 20

L IN COULD SENSE the glow of the green lighting even though her eyes were shut. She lay on her back in silence, delaying as long as possible the start of a new day. She had grown increasingly accustomed to the hunger pains and the rocking of the boat, but she felt particularly nauseous this morning. Anxiety consumed her body when she thought about the plan she and the others would try to execute. Jiang might not make it to the United States without medical attention.

Even if we get the medical kit, he still may not make it. After all, we are not doctors.

Lin knew that her anxiety was not only based on the state of Jiang's health. The image of her mother's unwavering look of disapproval made her keenly aware of the utter contempt her mother would feel if Lin engaged in actions that could diminish her chances of reaching the United States.

Jiang's loud breathing interrupted Lin's streaming thoughts. She opened her eyes and glanced at Jiang lying on his back, the tips of his fingers pressed firmly on the ground as if he was trying to claw his way out. Crawling next to Jiang, she placed her lips close to his ear to avoid waking the others.

"Jiang," Lin whispered.

Jiang opened his eyes. As he turned his head slightly in Lin's direction, a tear rolled out of the corner of his eye, down his temple. "I'm not going to make it off this boat," he said with a cold confidence that startled Lin. "I'm in so much pain. I feel so weak."

Lin tried to comfort him. "Don't talk like that. There is no reason for you to think that way. You're just saying that because you're in pain right now." Lin wondered if she would be as willing to help Jiang if her attraction to him was not so strong.

Jiang grabbed Lin's leg and squeezed it as tight as he could. "You don't understand," he whispered sternly. "There is a reason those apes from Tingjiang attacked me and it had nothing to do with being the first to get food from the snakeheads. I knew Dong before we got on this ship. I knew him very well. He is not going to let me get off this boat alive."

"What?" Lin asked. "What are you talking about? And why don't you talk to Shaoqing about this?"

"Because he won't listen to me. Well, he won't take my concerns seriously. He will assume I am speaking out to avoid the appearance of being selfish and asking others to sacrifice for me."

"But we all talked about this yesterday. You agreed on the plan. You even helped set up part of the plan."

"I know, but I have been lying here awake in pain all night thinking about it. You don't understand," Jiang repeated, "they are not going to let me get off this boat alive."

"You're right, I don't understand. What happened between you and Dong?"

Ai let out a yawn and rubbed her eyes.

Jiang had not loosened his grip on Lin's leg. "Just promise me you will try to convince Shaoqing to call off his plan. Please."

"I'll try."

The noise in the living quarters grew louder as passengers gradually awoke, murmuring within their groups about the length of time they would have to wait until the snakeheads brought them food. After several hours, the hatch opened and a faint beam of light slightly dulled the green halogens. The passengers all remained still when the snakeheads brought down food. Open-mouth Fei Pin and another crewman placed a pot of rice and several jugs of water on the floor. Immediately, they looked over at Dong. With his Tingjiang cohorts following him, Dong walked briskly toward the hatch, giving passengers sitting in his way a slap on the back of the head. Fei Pin climbed up with the other snakehead and shut the hatch behind him.

Lin watched Dong and the others shovel rice into their mouths and take big gulps of water. "Are they going to leave anything for us?" she whispered.

After consuming half of the rice and water left by Fei Pin, Dong ordered the Tingjiang boys to distribute the remaining food among the rest of the passengers. Ai, Shaoqing, and Lin stood in line patiently with everybody else. Ai got to the front of the line first. She was given a small cup of water and a scoop of rice was placed in her palm.

"Can I have another portion for . . ." Ai gestured toward Jiang with her head.

The boy dispensing rice smirked at Ai. "Here," he said, dumping another spoonful into her already full palm. "No extra water." Frustrated but not wanting to start any trouble, Ai walked away, securing the rice between her hand and stomach to keep her meal from falling on the floor.

Lin and Shaoqing both got their rice and water quickly and began walking back toward Ai and Jiang. Shaoqing had already started eating by the time Lin caught up to him and tapped him on the shoulder. "I need to talk with you. Alone."

Shaoqing stopped walking but continued to eat. "Is something wrong?"

"Jiang doesn't want us to go forward with the plan. He . . ."

Shaoqing cut Lin off. "Of course he would say that, it is the honorable thing to say. But that doesn't mean we should do nothing and create a greater risk of him dying."

Lin was again taken back by Shaoqing's insistence on helping a recently acquired friend. "I think it's more complicated," she said.

"Why do you say that?"

"Because he has a history with that guy from Tingjiang who stabbed him. He told me that even if we do succeed, they will hurt him again, and there is no point in risking . . ."

Shaoqing again interrupted Lin. "You mean he thinks they will hurt him a second time, but he does not know that to be the case. In his mind, he sees the future course of events unfolding in a particular way, and he cannot imagine an outcome that does not fall within the narrow path he believes already set for his future. It is natural that as the event grows closer he will think of new and different ways to convince himself that it will not work or should not be tried. I will not give in to such doubts."

Lin stood momentarily speechless by the subtle and reserved forcefulness of Shaoqing's manner of speaking when he was sure about his position. She searched for something clever or convincing to say. "Jiang did sound very sure about not wanting us to go forward." Lin didn't even feel convinced by her own response.

"For this plan to work, everyone involved must be thinking clearly about what they need to do and feel confident that it will work. You do think it will work, don't you?"

"Sure."

"Then let's go sit back down and finish our food."

Jiang stared up at Lin as she walked toward him. He raised his eyebrows as a means of inquiring about Lin's conversation with Shaoqing. Lin shook her head slightly to indicate that Shaoqing had not been convinced.

Seeing Jiang's condition, Ai gave him almost all of her water. Shaoqing and Lin also saved small sips for Jiang. Lin wanted to save more, but the momentary euphoria she felt as the water trickled down her throat made it difficult for her to stop drinking.

The four travelers sat quietly after finishing their meager portions of rice. Much to Lin's surprise, Jiang didn't express his reservations about the plan to Shaoqing.

Sitting in silence, Lin debated the best way to breathe. If she took breaths through her mouth, then the painful irritation of swallowing with a dry throat would only increase. If she breathed through her nose, then she had to endure the putrid mix of body odor, urine and other smells intensifying every day in the living quarters. Lin had not fully resolved her internal debate when the hatch of the living quarters again opened.

"First group!" a voice shouted. "Men first." The group from Tingjiang immediately rose up and walked over to the open hatch.

Shaoqing rose to his feet and looked around. "I will try to go to the deck in the next shift so that we'll have time to work out the details of our plan," he said before walking away toward Bao and the rest of the Changle City crew.

Ai let out a moan.

"What is it?" Lin asked.

"Nothing," Ai responded. She waited for Jiang to lie back down and then tapped Lin on the shoulder. Lin leaned toward Ai, who cupped her hands around Lin's ear. "I shouldn't have given Jiang all of my water," Ai whispered. "Words cannot express how thirsty I am."

"Then why did you?" Lin whispered back.

Ai blushed. "I guess I want him to like me."

Lin tried to fight the images of Ai and Jiang together that had now conquered her thoughts. "Oh," Lin said, not wanting to hear any more talk of Ai's feelings for Jiang. "You also need to think about your own health before giving all your water away."

Dong and the rest of the Tingjiang crowd came back down through the hatch. Shaoqing waited for them to clear away before walking toward the exit.

"Next group!" a voice shouted.

Shaoqing and nine other males climbed up and returned about fifteen minutes later. Looking as refreshed as any of them could be after two weeks on the ship, Shaoqing sat down next to Lin, Ai, and Jiang.

"Well?" Lin asked.

Shaoqing smiled. "I glanced down the hallway of the snakeheads' living quarters. Most of the doors are open."

"That's good," Ai said.

Shaoqing scratched his forehead. "At least we have something going in our favor."

Group by group, the passengers took their turns going up to the deck. Lin nervously clutched her knees with her forearms, waiting patiently as the last group of men eventually returned from the deck. *"All* females!" shouted the ominous voice hovering above the hatch.

Lin took a deep breath, reviewing one last time what she was supposed to do.

Chapter 21

ETHAN SHAW FIDDLED with his pen as he stared out his office window. He could see a reflection of his bald head in the pane glass. He recently shaved his head after he decided to abandon his futile effort to save his rapidly receding hairline. All the men in his family started to lose their hair in their early thirties. Ethan had hoped he would be an exception. Even though his genes acted right on cue, almost everyone who cared to comment thought he looked better bald.

He diverted his attention to the cars idling at the corner of Dowd and York, impatiently waiting their turn to merge onto the New Jersey Turnpike. He knew he would eventually have to brave the chemical infested strip of the Turnpike that had contributed to New Jersey's undesirable reputation as the armpit of America. The immigration detention facility where he worked was located in the heart of the city of Elizabeth, next to Newark International Airport and only a few miles from New York City. If he left in the next half-hour, he could make it home to North Bergen in time for a quick shower before heading to a bar for the Monday night football game.

But he knew he needed to stay late and tackle the huge stack of case files sitting on his desk. He flipped through the tabbed manila folders, looking at the glum faces of each immigrant on the wallet size headshots stapled to their immigration files. Myriad of stories covered the crinkled pages tucked in the manila folders—each story a heartfelt plea by an illegal immigrant who hoped to avoid deportation.

Ethan's anti-immigration biases couched his opinion of each desperate appeal for mercy. He assumed that every story he read was either embellished or an outright lie. He started to scan the case files. On the top of his stack was the file of a Serbian woman named Jasna Jovanovic. Her fair skin almost blended into the off-white backdrop of her photograph. Ethan was drawn to her wide sympathetic eyes, staring straight ahead, as if she were asking the photographer to save her. She appeared on the government's radar after a botched shoplifting attempt. According to her file, she had recently fallen in love and married an American citizen. Ethan smiled when he noticed that she married her American love less than a month after her immigration troubles began. Now this man would have to bear the brunt of Ethan's marriage fraud investigation.

Ethan rolled his eyes as he examined the picture stapled to the next file, the boney young face of Igor Trivosky, a Russian Jew who claimed that the police threatened to put his testicles in a vice if he failed to leave town. "Bullshit," Ethan said to himself, snickering at the picture, as if Igor's two-dimensional mug shot could respond. Ethan did not doubt that the neighborhood kids bullied little Igor. He'd read enough to know that anti-Semitism was widespread in the former Soviet bloc. He could see this scrawny kid getting picked on no matter where he grew up. Now Ethan would be picking apart every detail of his story. If Ethan found enough inconsistencies, he could convince a judge that little Igor would be safe back in the Motherland.

Then there was Ngandi Totuku, who claimed he was tortured in the Congo, and Farrad Silakum, who insisted that he faced persecution in Egypt for being homosexual. The stories went on, circling the globe, depicting the breadth of human suffering, illustrating the lengths that immigrants go to for a chance to live in the United States.

Ethan's thick skin had only hardened further since he graduated from Brooklyn Law School. It took him four years to graduate, half-awake through night classes while he worked full-time on the Secaucus police force. He spent the last five years working for the Immigration and Naturalization Service, the immigration agency housed in the Department of Justice. The job suited him well. His appetite for fighting illegal immigration was the reason he went to law school in the first place. It was a hunger that had festered since he was a teenager. He almost never talked to anyone about the origins of his anti-immigration fervor, though he suspected most people had read about it in the newspapers at one time or another.

The INS job gave Ethan a mix of assignments that helped keep things interesting. He was responsible for field investigations and courtroom appearances. He liked the idea of being in control of the process from start to finish. He couldn't picture himself sitting in one of the cubicles that lined INS headquarters in Washington, D.C., where most investigations got stuck in red tape. He didn't need a central bureaucracy looking over his shoulder. In the INS field office, one supervisor was all that stood between him and total freedom.

The pile of manila folders on Ethan's desk had been steadily growing. He used to clear his case docket quickly, but a new investigation had garnered his attention. For the last seven months, Ethan had become obsessed with the idea of breaking up an international syndicate that he believed was operating in the United States, stealing the identities of United States citizens and ruining their lives.

The investigation came to him by chance or, as he liked to think of it, through meticulous attention to detail. While he was going through the financial records of an immigrant in one of his case files, he noticed that the Social Security number on an old telephone bill did not match up to the Social Security number that the immigrant put on his recent tax returns. Ethan ran a check on the Social Security numbers and discovered that the number on the telephone bill belonged to a man in Los Angeles. When Ethan called the Los Angeles number, the man told him how he spent years fighting delinquent accounts that someone had opened using his Social Security number.

Ethan approached his supervisor at INS and asked to pursue the issue further. His supervisor was furious that Ethan would launch an investigation without prior authorization. Eventually his supervisor calmed down and thought about what Ethan might have stumbled on. He gave Ethan limited leeway to investigate further. As Ethan discovered more fraudulent uses of Social Security numbers by illegal immigrants, his supervisor let him form a small taskforce to investigate. Everyone on the taskforce still had to clear their regular caseloads. Ethan promised the team he would bare the brunt of the extra work by taking some of their cases. And so he sat at his desk, scanning the stack of manila folders, regretting his promise, knowing there was no chance he would watch the football game.

There was a knock at the door. Ethan looked up and saw Ryan Bard walk into his office, his wavy brown hair neatly parted on the side as usual. Ryan was six feet tall and lanky. He had a few inches on Ethan, but Ethan's stocky frame had outmuscled Ryan during a number of impromptu drunken wrestling matches over the years. Ryan was Ethan's closest colleague at INS and one of the members of the identity theft taskforce.

"You going home soon?" asked Ryan.

Ethan continued to flip through the stack of case files. "Nah," he said, barely acknowledging Ryan.

"I heard back from her."

Ethan quickly shot him an annoyed glance and gestured at the door. He waited for Ryan to shut the door before responding. "What did she say?" asked Ethan in a hushed voice.

Ryan smirked. "We're good."

"When?"

"Midnight."

"Tonight?"

"Tomorrow."

"Money?"

"The usual."

"Alright. Swing by my apartment tomorrow at eleven-thirty."

Chapter 22

LIN'S STOMACH WAS in knots, her hands trembling at the thought of going up to the deck.

"All females," the impatient snakehead repeated, "up to the deck to wash up. We are running late so I want all the girls at once." *Running late?* Lin thought, recounting the voice's assertion. *Running late for what? We are in the middle of the ocean!*

The soothing warmth of the sun coating her forehead momentarily comforted Lin. She squinted her eyes, keeping them nearly shut at first to adjust to the light. Through the open slits of her eyes, she could make out the smirks of the male crewmen who began to emerge from their living quarters when their fellow snakehead shouted for all the females to come to the deck.

Lin stood on the deck with Ai and the other female passengers. She watched crewmen climb up the ladder to join big-eyed Lee and open-mouth Fei Pin.

"Are all the snakeheads up here?" Ai asked Lin, trying not to move her lips.

"I don't think so," Lin responded.

"So we still need to create a distraction?"

"I guess."

"I want everyone to wash well," Lee said sternly. "The boys are starting to complain that it smells downstairs. We don't want to upset the boys, now do we ladies?"

Lin reached into one of the buckets of water and dunked her hands. She washed her stomach for a moment while Ai stood next to her doing the same. Ming Tso, the beautiful woman from Changle City who made Lin jealous, was kneeling next to them, scrubbing the grit that was caked to the bottom of her feet. Lin and Ai observed Ming Tso innocently trying to get through the bathing process as quickly as possibly. They then glanced at each other, observing mirroring expressions of guilt, knowing that Ming Tso was unwittingly about to become part of their distraction simply because she happened to be next to them.

"C'mon," Ai said to Lin, "do it now."

Lin grabbed the bucket of water next to her. "Give me that!" Ai shouted, giving Lin a slight push.

"Fine!" Lin shouted back as she hurled the water in Ai's direction. Ai moved out of the way, knowing full well what Lin planned to do, and the soapy water doused Ming Tso as she crouched on the ground, soaked from head to toe. Rising to her feet, Ming Tso wiped the salt water from her eyes and looked down at her drenched body. Her wet shirt clung to her skin, revealing the outline of her breasts.

The crewmen gawked. "Are you going to let this insult pass?" one of them asked Ming Tso. "Where is your honor?"

Fei Pin chimed in. "Maybe she enjoys being dishonorable!"

"I'm sorry," Lin said to Ming Tso. "I was frustrated with Ai because she stole the soap I was using and the water was irritating my skin."

Ming Tso snickered, unsatisfied by Lin's feeble explanation.

"This water?" asked Ai as she grabbed another bucket and tossed the soapy water in Lin's direction. Lin flinched slightly and the water splashed under her left arm, soaking the side of her body. The crewmen laughed uncontrollably at the sight of Lin and Ai's staged fight.

"Water fight!" Fei Pin shouted. More crewmen darted up to the deck to survey the commotion, including the one who had been guarding the open hatch.

SHAOQING WAS LYING down by the open hatch when he heard Fei Pin shout that a water fight had broken out on the deck. He intently surveyed the shadow of the crewman watching the hatch, which dimmed the ground of the living quarters by Shaoqing's feet. The shadow disappeared completely when the crewman reached the top of the ladder and ran onto the deck to watch the water fight.

Convinced the crewman had abandoned his post, Shaoqing glanced over at Jiang, who in turn winked at Bao and tugged his earlobe, the result of an overly elaborate plan that had been concocted the night before by a group of travelers who had no doubt grown increasingly paranoid and fearful of their temperamental hosts. Continuing the long line of signals, Bao repeatedly tapped his right temple with his index finger without looking directly at a small group of his friends from Changle City who were standing in a circle near the Tingjiang gang. With Bao's gesture, the Changle City boys initiated the plan that Jiang had concocted the night before.

"Thief!" one of the Changle boys scoffed at another. "Give it back!" he shouted, pushing one of his friends into Dong, the Tingjiang group leader.

The Tingjiang boys' attention quickly gravitated toward the staged fight, and Shaoqing climbed up the prongs of the pole as fast as he could. When his head emerged above the hatch, he paused momentarily to look for signs of any crewmen. Seeing none, he rocketed to his feet and bolted down the corridor that hosted the living quarters of the crewmen.

Dong grit his teeth and flexed his jawbone as he stared wide-eyed at the boy who had bumped into him. He grabbed the boy by the throat and stuck his finger between the boy's eyes. "I want you to convince me that I shouldn't split your head open with an iron rod."

"I did not mean any disrespect. Please, I will make it up to you."

"Well, what did you steal?" asked Dong.

"What?" inquired the boy, stalling for time to think of an answer.

"He called you a thief before pushing you. So what did you steal?"

"Nothing. I didn't steal anything. I don't have anything. He, he was talking about when we were back in China. He thought I stole a girl from him, a girl he used to be with."

Dong glanced over at Jiang. "He stole a girl you say," Dong remarked, releasing his grip from the boy's throat. Snickering at Jiang, Dong continued. "I think that is an offense punishable by death, or a good thrashing at the very least." He then focused his attention on the boy who instigated the staged fight. "Don't you agree?"

The instigator responded, "Being on this boat has made me a little crazy. I'm not thinking straight. He didn't steal any girl from me. I had not been with her for nearly a year. It was my fault."

"Very well then," Dong said. "Have it your way. But I expect that you or one of the other rats from Changle will be giving me something of value to make up for this needless infraction into my personal space."

"Yes," remarked one of the boys from Changle. "I see no reason why that cannot be arranged."

"And don't forget," Dong said, again looking in Jiang's direction, "stealing someone's girl is punishable by death."

AFTER PAUSING MOMENTARILY in the corridor of the crewmen's living quarters, Shaoqing headed for the room where he believed he had seen the medical kit on the day they all began their voyage from China. There was a stack of playing cards on the table but no medical kit in sight. Shaoqing scanned the room. Behind the small table, two mattresses lay on narrow planks protruding from the wall, one plank three feet above the other. A couple of rusty shelves lined the wall closest to the door. Shaoqing inspected the shelves for any sign of medical supplies. Underneath several empty whiskey bottles, he saw the butt of a gun. Gripping the handle, he massaged the metal barrel with his fingertips.

Don't be stupid, what are you going to do with a gun? "You don't have time for this," Shaoqing reminded himself. "Keep looking." He put the gun back on the shelf and tiptoed into an adjacent room. After fruitlessly searching the shelves, he fumbled inside several duffel bags clumped together by the beds in the back of the room.

Shaoqing was rummaging around the dirty clothes and empty cigarette packs in one of the duffels when the barely audible grumblings of a snakehead caught his attention. As the voice grew louder, he darted out of the room, back down the corridor. When he approached the hatch, he found himself eye-level with the foot of one of the snakeheads, a set of dirty toes searching aimlessly for the next rung of the ladder.

For a moment, Shaoqing stood paralyzed in the hallway as a surge of adrenaline clouded his thoughts about what to do next. He had thought about potential obstacles that might prevent him from getting back to the hatch, and he had also brainstormed a potential alternate route. *Run the other way*, Shaoqing had told himself, *away from the hatch and up the staircase on the other side of the corridor.* However, even for his straightforward, feeble contingency plan, it was proving much more difficult for him to go through the physical motions of executing the plan. Myriad questions raced through Shaoqing's mind in a millisecond, too fast for him to fully compute the questions or assess potential answers. *Do I have time to make it down the entire corridor to the steps before the snakehead sees me? Will the snakehead hear my footsteps if I run full speed?*

Gathering his composure, Shaoqing ran back down the corridor. Deciding he didn't have enough time to make it all the way to the staircase, he scurried back into the room with the duffel bags. After wedging himself under the bottom metal bed, he placed two of the duffels in front of him to shield his body from view. An object dug into his lower back. He reached around and grabbed it to allow himself to hide closer to the wall underneath the bed. Shaoqing smiled as he pulled a box in front of his body. *The medical kit.*

STANDING ON THE deck with the crewmen and other female passengers, drenched as a result of Lin tossing water on her, Ming Tso looked at Lin in disbelief. "What are you doing, Lin?" Ming asked, trying to cover her chest with her hands.

"I'm so sorry," Lin implored, "it was Ai's fault. Look at me, I'm soaked as well."

"My fault!" Ai shouted. "You should think twice before using something that isn't yours. I wanted to get this bathing over with and get back downstairs, but I cannot do that without soap, now can I?"

"But it was *my* soap," Lin said. The previous night, Lin and Ai had rehearsed what they were going to say to each other, but Lin was nervous to the point of mental paralysis, unable to recall even the basic script as all the eyes of the crewmen and other female passengers were fixed on her. She stood silently as Ai stared at her, waiting for her to say something. After a moment of silence, Ai pushed Lin on the shoulder.

"Forget it," Ai said. She took the soap she had picked up off the ground and threw it toward the other side of the deck. "Now nobody gets the soap."

Fei Pin was laughing so hard that he fell to the ground.

Lin couldn't think of anything else to say. She and Ai pretended to reconcile their fake differences so that it wouldn't appear strange to the crewmen when they would later be sitting together in the living quarters.

A number of the crewmen, including the man who had been watching the open hatch, walked back toward the ladder. Lin felt a lump forming in her throat. *I only hope we gave Shaoqing enough time to find the medical kit and bring it back to the living quarters.* But she hadn't, and Shaoqing was forced to hide behind the duffel bags.

SHAOQING LAY CURLED in a ball under the bed. His heart was pounding. He worked hard to control his breathing to ensure he didn't make a sound.

The voices of the crewmen grew louder and Shaoqing could hear a distinct conversation. He couldn't tell where the crewmen were, but he was certain they were not in the room where he was hiding.

"I'm growing tired of this game," Shaoqing heard one of the crewman exclaim. "When will we be allowed to have some fun?"

"You say this every time we do this voyage, and that is precisely why you are not in charge. If you were in charge, we would never maintain order."

"That was one time. One time with that girl. We all learned our lessons from that trip. That will not happen again."

"We are very close to the States, it won't be much longer. Stop your complaining and deal the cards."

Shaoqing moved one of the duffels slightly and peered out. Seeing no crewmen, he slid out from underneath the bed. With the medical kit in hand, he headed for the door.

THE WOMEN ON the deck resumed their normal routine, bathing quickly while keeping their bodies as unexposed as possible. Fei Pin stood by with eight other crewmen. He was drinking a large glass of water.

"Who is thirsty?" Fei Pin asked sarcastically. "Anyone?" Several of the women stared at the cup of water Fei Pin was drinking, but none of them responded. "Nobody?" he said, turning to one of the other snakeheads. "Perhaps we're giving them too much water. None of them are thirsty." Fei Pin walked individually to each of the women and asked if they wanted water. Unsurprisingly, each had confirmed that they would accept water by the time Fei Pin stood in front of Ai. "Well?" Fei Pin asked. "How about you?"

"Yes," Ai said softly. "I would like some water."

Fei Pin looked at Lin. "You?"

Lin nodded her head. "Of course."

"I will bring water to everyone who wants it. A full cup each. All you have to do is lift up your shirt. Just for a few seconds."

Lin felt embarrassed by the very thought of succumbing to Fei Pin's wishes. She was not alone. Despite the widespread dehydration among all the women on the deck, two of the other women declined the offer to lift up their shirts in exchange for water. Most, however, begrudgingly accepted Fei Pin's proposal.

"Well?" Fei Pin asked Ai. "How about you?"

Lin watched Ai licking her cracked, dry lips. She thought about Ai giving Jiang all of her water earlier that day. *If she regretted that decision before, I can only imagine how upset she must be now.*

"A full glass?" Ai asked.

"Yes," Fei Pin replied, his mouth open wider than usual.

Ai looked down at the soapy deck. "Fine," she said softly, barely above a whisper. "I'll do it." The other crewmen huddled behind Fei Pin as Ai lifted her shirt. Lin looked away, as if she was sharing directly in the shame of the incident. She looked back a few seconds later to find Fei Pin staring at her.

"How about you, my dear?" Fei Pin asked. Although Lin drank more water than Ai had earlier that day, her thirst still overshadowed everything else, her burning throat serving as a constant reminder of her seemingly perpetual state of dehydration—as if she needed a reminder.

Observing Fei Pin standing in front of her now, his mouth *still* wide open, Lin remembered sitting with her father in the rice fields by her home three harvests ago. A mouse was skirmishing around several tall blades of grass protruding from an otherwise barren patch of dirt when all of a sudden it stopped. Lin observed the mouse shiver and look hastily in all directions. Within a second or two, the mouse dashed into a nearby hole in the ground. Moments later, a hawk dove down to the spot on the ground where the mouse had paused, its outstretched claws clamping down on the air where the mouse had been shivering just one second before.

"Do you know how that mouse escaped?" Lin's father asked her.

"It went into a hole."

"Yes, but how did it know to go into the hole?"

"I guess it heard the hawk."

"Do you think the sound of a hawk flying through the air is that distinct from all the other sounds in nature?"

"Maybe."

"Well, do you think the mouse was able to recall the exact sound a hawk makes in less than a second and react accordingly?"

"I don't know, Father, it's just a mouse. It was shivering. It was scared. It must have heard something that sounded suspicious and reacted."

"Exactly, Lin. Exactly."

"Exactly? I don't understand."

"It was instinct. It knew something was wrong and it reacted. The mouse acted on its instincts. Did it know exactly what was wrong?"

Lin shrugged her shoulders.

"You don't know, Lin?" her father continued. "Well, neither do I," he said, chuckling to himself. "People have instincts too, you know."

"I know."

"These instincts are a funny thing. Your initial reaction to a situation may very well be wrong. Mine have certainly been wrong many times. But human beings have an advantage over other animals such as that mouse."

"What's that?" Lin asked.

"We can look back on our reactions and ponder them in great detail. Hopefully we can learn from them. Sometimes though, we make the same thickheaded choices over and over," her father said as he again chuckled. Lin was accustomed to her father dancing around the main point he was trying to make, so she remained silent.

"However," he continued, "over the course of one's life, you will find that your instincts will serve you well. It is one of the gifts bestowed upon us, all animals, and however much the limited capabilities of our minds struggle to understand our animal instincts, sometimes we must trust in them, even if we do not fully understand how they work, or the role they play in maintaining harmony between us and everything around us."

Fei Pin closed his mouth. "Well? I don't have all day, my dear." Lin had been weary of Fei Pin ever since that initial day on the dock when she first locked into an uncomfortable gaze with his sagging eyes. She desperately wanted water, but thinking of her father, she trusted her initial reaction to Fei Pin's proposal and declined his offer.

"That is too bad, my dear," Fei Pin said, shaking his head back and forth. "I am sure you will enjoy watching all the other girls quench their thirst."

Several of the crewmen handed the participating female passengers full plastic cups of water. Lin watched Ai put the cup to her lips and swallow almost a third of the water in her first gulp. Ai slowed down after that initial chug, turning to Lin when there was only one sip left.

"Here Lin," Ai said, "take the rest."

Lin did not hesitate to finish the water. "Thank you, Ai." And it didn't take long for her to begin feeling groggy and weak. She looked over at Ai and the other women. Those who drank full cups of water had already fallen to their knees or were lying on their sides on the deck. Ai, who had also fallen down, grabbed Lin's calf.

"Lin," Ai said. "What's going on? I feel dizzy, too weak to stand. All I want to do is lay down and rest," she said as she began to giggle.

Fei Pin and the other crewmen stood silently with their arms folded, watching all the women squirm around like fish out of water, except for Lin and the other two who had refused to expose themselves.

Lee pointed at the two women other than Lin who were still able to stand. "Fei Pin, take them down." Fei Pin grabbed each by the arm and escorted them to the ladder.

Lin felt slightly weakened and tired, but the single sip of water she took made her far more cognizant of her surroundings than the other women. Through her clouded perception, Lin could not believe what she was witnessing as the crewmen walked over to the women and started to remove their clothing.

The warm, sweaty hand gripping her arm caught Lin off guard. The outstretched bellybutton Lin saw in her peripheral vision made the identity of the person grabbing her apparent before she even had a chance to turn her head. When she did, the smell of Fei Pin's heavy breath overshadowed the stench of his dirty clothing.

"I've been waiting a long time for this," Fei Pin said, grabbing Lin's other arm. He thrust his hand down into Lin's underwear.

While she struggled to keep her thighs as close together as possible, Lin managed to slip her wrist from Fei Pin's sweaty grip. She clawed at his face with her long nails, digging as far into his flesh as her minimal strength permitted. Fei Pin began to curse loudly.

"Fei Pin," Lee said sternly. "Why are you fooling around with that girl? She barely drank. You are needlessly wasting your time."

Fei Pin rubbed his hand over the scratch marks on his face and examined the streaks of blood on his fingers. He stared intently at Lin. For once, his lips clenched tight together. "This isn't over," he said as he grabbed Lin by the hair and shoved her toward the ladder. "Get back down."

Lin scurried to descend the ladder faster than Fei Pin. When she stumbled to adjust her footing, Fei Pin would keep climbing down, stomping on Lin's fingers. Unable to keep pace because of the drugs running through her bloodstream, Lin fell down and landed next to the open hatch of the living quarters.

When Fei Pin got to the open hatch, he used Lin's hair to pull her to her feet. He grabbed her by the throat and pinned her up against the wall. "I see," Fei Pin snickered, "up there you have the strength of an ox, but now you can't even make it down a ladder." Fei Pin pushed Lin down the open hatch. Lin smacked her arm on several prongs of the metal pole before landing on the ground next to Bao.

"Are you okay?" asked Bao. "Did you see Shaoqing up there?"

Lin strained to breath. Her throat began to swell from Fei Pin's sweaty fingers digging into the sides of her neck. "Shaoqing isn't down here?" Lin asked as she coughed.

"No, but I have the medical kit."

How could Bao have the medical kit if Shaoqing hasn't returned?

"This isn't over, my dear," Fei Pin yelled at Lin. "Come on, let's have some fun," Lin heard Fei Pin say to one of the other crewmen. The sunlight quickly disappeared as the hatch slammed shut.

WHILE LIN WAS still on the deck battling Fei Pin, Shaoqing was standing at the edge of the doorway listening intently for any sounds other than the conversation of the two crewmen playing cards. The crewmen's banter emanated from a room between Shaoqing and the open hatch he needed to get to in order to avoid being caught.

With the medical kit under his arm, Shaoqing dashed down the corridor, away from the open hatch and the talking crewmen, in the direction where he and the others had originally boarded the ship. He bolted one level up the metal staircase to the second interior level. Weaving between the wooden crates that lined the corridor, he tiptoed back toward the ladder that passengers had to climb in order to bathe on the deck.

Gripping a rung of the ladder, Shaoqing peeked down. He saw a snakehead guarding the open hatch as he smoked a cigarette and hummed to himself. Placing the medical kit beside him, Shaoqing sat down and rubbed his eyes with the palms of his hands. *Think Shaoqing, think.*

"Get back down," Shaoqing heard Fei Pin say from the deck. The sound of Lin moaning was getting louder. Shaoqing leaned over the edge of the shaft, let go of the medical kit, and watched it drop through the open hatch, hitting Bao's foot before coming to rest on the ground of the living quarters. Pushing off the ladder to get momentum, Shaoqing dashed a few yards back down the corridor and ducked behind one of the wooden crates, shielding his body from sight.

The shaft echoed from the sound of feet hitting the hollow metal rungs of the ladder. "Up there you have the strength of an ox, but now you can't even make it down a ladder," Shaoqing heard Fei Ping say to a drugged Lin. "Come on, let's have some fun." Then, Shaoqing heard the unmistakable sound of the hatch slamming shut.

Fei Ping climbed back up the ladder to the deck, followed by the crewman who was guarding the hatch and the two others who were playing cards downstairs. Shaoqing waited for the sounds of the crewmen to fade. He walked back over to the ladder, climbed up a few rungs, and discreetly peeked his head out onto the deck.

Disbelief was Shaoqing's initial reaction when he looked over toward the women. They were lying helplessly on their backs, legs spread open, some screaming with what little energy they had, as the crewmen took turns having their way with each of them.

Shaoqing's feelings quickly morphed to anger. He looked away and climbed back down. *The shame*, he thought. His fists were clenched; his head pounded. He ran back across the corridor, down the stairs, and into the room where the crewmen had set up the table to play cards. The butt of the gun was still exposed between the empty whiskey bottles. Without a moment's contemplation, he grabbed the gun and ran to the now-closed hatch. The sound of women screaming on the deck was muffled slightly by the strong ocean breeze and the boisterous laughter of the crewmen. Shaoqing put his hand on a rung of the ladder to begin climbing to the deck, but he paused and took a deep breath. He listened to the pleas for help and surveyed the gun he was clasping in his hand.

Shaoqing had only held a gun one other time in his life, and it was recently. Three weeks before he began his voyage to the United States, he had decided to purchase a gun. It did not take long to find a firearm. He was willing to overpay for the sake of expediency and many surly characters were eager to make a handsome profit for a quick sale.

Within a week, Shaoqing had obtained the gun he wanted. A silencer would not be necessary. There were no houses within half a mile of his uncle's mansion. Nor did Shaoqing think anyone would dare come to his uncle's house unannounced, even if they had heard a suspicious noise.

Shaoqing paced in his bedroom, his fingers gripping the firearm. He pulled the trigger of the unloaded gun several times to practice. *Okay, I'm ready*. His hand trembled as he inserted an eight-bullet cartridge. He walked out of his bedroom past several doors down a long hallway, pausing by the top of a banister. The banister lined a staircase that winded around a great foyer. Standing at the top of the staircase, Shaoqing was level with a giant chandelier that would illuminate a statue of a terracotta warrior standing six feet tall in the middle of the foyer. At this late hour, however, the chandelier was dark. The only light in the house was emanating from the study his uncle frequented at night before going to sleep.

By the time he was halfway down the staircase, Shaoqing could smell the sweet tobacco his uncle would stuff into his pipe. The smell of alcohol would not become apparent until he neared the entranceway of the study. Although thousands of books lined the walls of the study, Shaoqing had never seen his uncle read a single one of them. With the loaded gun tucked into the belt of his pants, Shaoqing stood in the entranceway, his heart pounding.

"I can see you standing there," his uncle said, refraining from making eye contact with him.

"May I enter, Uncle?"

Shaoqing's uncle did not answer his question. "I have not seen much of you lately," his uncle said. "When I come home you are already in your room, and you have already left the house by the time I wake up."

Shaoqing took a few steps into the study, even though his uncle had not given him permission. "I have been busy."

"That is a lie. You have changed your routine. An alteration in one's routine is not the sign of being busy. It is a sign of avoidance. And you have been playing your little game of avoidance ever since you ran out of the factory last week." Shaoqing's uncle took a sip from a tall glass of rum. "Avoidance, Shaoqing, is the path a coward takes."

Reaching behind him, Shaoqing pulled out the gun. He let it point toward the rug away from his uncle.

Shaoqing's uncle laughed. "Very resourceful," he remarked. "I am impressed. Of course, it is much easier to plan the details of acquiring the gun then it is to formulate a plan for what you are going to do with the gun after you've used it. Have you thought about that?"

"You are going to make them sick," Shaoqing said.

"You didn't answer my question. Have you thought about what you are going to do with that gun?

"They could die, hundreds, thousands, tens of thousands."

"You need to think about what you are going to do with the gun, Shao-qing!" his uncle repeated sternly. "If you shoot for the head, you will have to clean the pieces of my skull that will fly across the room. The blood from the bullet hole will leak onto the upholstery of the couch after I slump over, and you will not be able to move this couch by yourself. Even if you could, it would look quite suspicious when investigators come and find an empty space in the middle of my study. Alternatively, you can shoot for my stomach. That will probably do it, but it could take some time, and it can get a little messy. Right here is one of my favorites," he continued, pointing to his wrist. "Right by the artery. It is incredibly painful and you can watch me bleed to death. But that, too, can be messy, and unless some of the books you have been reading concern how to remove bloodstains from a seventeenth century Persian rug, I imagine that will not be a viable option either."

Shaoqing raised the gun and his uncle smiled. "Why are you smiling?" Shaoqing asked.

Shaoqing's uncle placed his glass of rum on the table and walked toward him. "I am smiling because we both know the truth."

"That you are a murderer," Shaoqing scowled, cocking the gun's hammer.

"No. We both know that *you* are a coward. That you are too weak to do anything with that gun."

"Why did you do it?"

"Why did I do *what*? Provide for my family? Give you everything you ever wanted? Make sure there was enough to support my whore of a sister-in-law? We are entering an era of Chinese dominance in the world. In the *world*, Shaoqing. And do you know why that is the case? Because of me. Because of me and others like me who do what needs to be done. Now give me the gun so you can minimize the shame you should feel for interrupting me and try-ing to pass judgment on what I do."

When his uncle went to grab the barrel of the gun, Shaoqing did not try to stop him. He sat up all night in his bed letting the pain of the bruises his uncle had just given him serve as a reminder of the repercussions of choosing a course of action he did not have the will to complete.

The memory of that night with his uncle still fresh in his mind, Shaoq-ing took in another deep breath of the salty ocean air and released his grip from the rung of the ladder.

"I can't do it," he said to himself. He stared up the shaft, picturing what was going on above on the deck, and then he dropped his head in despair. *You're right, Uncle. I can't do what needs to be done.* Shaoqing tucked the gun in his waistband and opened the hatch. Bao glanced up at him for a second and then casually looked away. Using one of the unnecessarily elaborate gestures they had worked on the night before, Bao signaled to Shaoqing that it was not safe for him to come down yet.

Bao waited until the other passengers redirected their curious gazes away from the open hatch. Then, he signaled the Changle City boys who previously staged the fight. The Changle City boys proceeded to walk over to Dong.

"This is for you," one of them said, both bowing their heads slightly as one of them handed Dong a watch. "It is the most valuable thing that any of us have."

Dong stroked the watch with his thumb. "I already have a watch."

As the conversation between Dong and the Changle City boys continued, Bao signaled to Shaoqing that it was safe for him to make his return. Shaoqing jumped through the open hatch and fell hard to the ground, barely avoiding hitting the butt of the gun on the protruding arms of the metal pole. He quickly propped himself up next to Bao and engaged in a fake conversation.

Dong held up the watch. "Do any of you need one of these?" Two members of the Tingjiang crew went to grab it. "Wait," Dong said sternly, "I'm not giving it away. You'll have to trade for it."

"So this will suffice?" asked one of the Changle City boys.

"Maybe," Dong replied. "I will mull over your offering in light of the severity of your previous infraction."

Shaoqing was breathing heavily. "What happened up there?" Bao asked him. "Lin walked straight over to those two girls without saying a word to me or Jiang and the other girls have been up on the deck for longer than usual."

"What happened up there?" Shaoqing repeated. "Nothing honorable, let's leave it at that," Shaoqing scoffed as he walked over to Jiang and sat down next to him.

"It worked," Jiang said. "I can't believe it worked."

Shaoqing stared at the ground. "Yes," he said. "It did."

"Was it on the card table like you remembered?"

"Later when everyone is going to sleep, we'll tend to your wounds," Shaoqing said, ignoring Jiang's question.

"I already looked inside the medical box," Jiang said. "There's thread, bandages, and some medicines, although I have no idea what the medicines are for."

"Hopefully one of them can help stave off infection. But we'll deal with it later." Shaoqing stood up and traipsed around before sitting against one of the walls away from Jiang. "I am a coward," he mumbled to himself.

The remaining women returned to the living quarters several hours later. Some of them had bruises on their faces and others were clinging to their ripped shirts in an ineffectual effort to avoid exposing their shoulders and chest. Ai did not speak to anyone when she returned. Instead, she staggered to the edge of the living quarters and wedged her body into the corner, her head facing the wall. Many of the other women did the same, curling up on their pieces of cardboard with shirts and pants over their faces, trying to cocoon themselves from the outside world.

When the living quarters grew quiet and most of the passengers had gone to sleep, Shaoqing inconspicuously helped Jiang tend to his wound.

"Are you going to stitch it up?" asked Jiang.

"There's no point," Shaoqing said.

"How do you know that?"

Growing up with his uncle, Shaoqing had more experience with medical ailments than he cared to admit. "You're not bleeding anymore, so stitches won't be necessary. At this point, we just need to make sure that it doesn't get infected." Shaoqing opened a bottle of saline solution. "Are you ready?" he asked.

"Let's just get this over with."

"This is going to sting," warned Shaoqing.

When the saline solution hit Jiang's abdomen, his body tensed and he grabbed Shaoqing's hand. "Stop," he said, fighting back the tears.

Shaoqing handed him a shirt. "Bite on this."

The sweat dripped down Jiang's forehead as he did his best to refrain from making a sound while Shaoqing cleaned the wound. Shaoqing mixed a soap packet from the medical kit into the saline solution and gently rubbed the gash, clearing away the crusty blood clots that had formed along the perimeter. When he dressed Jiang's abdomen, parts of the bandage turned red.

"I thought you said the bleeding had stopped," said Jiang.

"I must have aggravated it. It should stop soon. Trust me, it's much more important to make sure it's clean." Shaoqing carefully studied the medicine bottles and took out a pill that he thought helped to fight infection. "Here, take this," he said, handing the pill to Jiang.

"I don't have the saliva to swallow."

"Take your time. Try not to chew it, but do what needs to be done to ingest it before you go to sleep tonight."

An hour later, Lin rejoined Shaoqing and Jiang, but Ai remained curled in a ball in the corner of the room. Lin observed Shaoqing's sympathetic expression staring back at her. She opened her mouth to say something, but stopped to refrain from crying.

"It's okay," Shaoqing said, "you don't need to say anything. Just try to sleep."

Shaoqing lay still with his eyes closed. The darkness was a welcome barrier between him and the rest of the passengers. All he wanted to do was go to sleep, but his mind was racing. He could not stop thinking about what he had witnessed on the deck, and that he failed to stop it. Little did he know, another problem would soon present itself. The plan to get the medical kit had not gone off without a hitch. Suspicions had been raised. And Shaoqing would soon have to face the repercussions.

Chapter 23

THE NUMBERS ILLUMINATING from the electric alarm clock provided the only light in Tesfaye's studio apartment in the Jamaica neighborhood of Queens. He watched the minutes change. It was now three o'clock in the morning. Each contortion of his body into a new position brought the hope of sleep, but only for a moment. Warm milk, deep breathing, reading a magazine, Tesfaye tried them all to no avail. It was the fourth night in a row he clung helplessly to the promise of a full night's rest.

He could not pinpoint a particular thought causing him such consternation. Countless memories passed in and out of his mind in what felt like a lifetime of regrets overshadowing the joyous moments he shared with friends and family. The inability to sleep was bad enough, but the onset of heart palpitations was particularly troublesome. An all-consuming wave of panic, as if he needed to flee a scene of fated peril before his chest caved in.

The next morning, after a mere ninety minutes of sleep, Tesfaye skipped his shift at work. Although he was new on the job, he was in no condition to drive and thought prospective passengers would happily avoid a zombie playing the role of chauffeur. He was sitting on his bed, eating dry cereal out of the box, when he suddenly felt the need to get out of his studio, even though he had nowhere to go, nobody to talk to.

Walking through the streets of Queens, Tesfaye came across the steps of the Church of Saint Ann. He stood in the street and fixated on the church's large wooden doors as pedestrians deviated from their linear paths on the sidewalk to avoid running into him. In contrast to the godless tenets of the socialist political platform he served for so many years, Tesfaye felt surprisingly comforted by the spiritual enclave nestled on the other side of the doors.

The priest was standing by the front pew, conversing with a gentleman holding a broom whom Tesfaye assumed was a janitor. After the man walked away, Tesfaye strolled up beside the priest.

"Excuse me," he said.

"It's a little early. We won't be starting morning mass for two hours," the priest said.

"I'm not here to pray, Father. To be honest, I'm not even sure what I'm doing here." The priest remained silent, waiting for Tesfaye to continue. "It's just that I cannot sleep. Even when I'm just sitting in my apartment, I'm constantly agitated. I can't seem to shake the feeling."

"Where are you from, my son?" asked the priest. "That is, where are you from originally?"

"I'm from—I'm from Kenya," Tesfaye said hesitatingly, feeling some discomfort lying to a priest.

"I don't know many people who are unsure about their homeland, although I've come across quite a few in this community who would like to forget. Where are you *really* from?"

"Ethiopia."

"Are you one of those people?" asked the priest in a deliberately gentle manner. "One of the immigrants who would like to forget where they came from?"

Tesfaye thought about the priest's question. "I don't want to forget, Father. I just want to go back and change what happened. I want one more chance to do it all over again."

"Regret is a powerful emotion, it can be very draining on the soul. If you have sins to atone for, then perhaps you would like me to hear your confession."

"I don't know if I can do that." *I'm not even Catholic.*

"All the more reason why you should."

Not surprisingly, Tesfaye felt anxious as he stepped into the confessional. Then he repeated the phrase he had heard so many times on television. "Forgive me, Father, for I have sinned."

THE SUMMER OF 1983 was mercilessly dry in the northern Ethiopian provinces of Tigray and Eritrea. The Derg's agriculture policies were an utter failure and vast swaths of crops failed. Millions faced starvation.

Tesfaye saw a situation eerily similar to the famine in the early 1970s that led to the overthrow of the Emperor. *Trying to win the hearts and minds of citizens on the brink of starvation is an exercise in futility*, he thought. At high-level meetings, he frequently tried to draw attention to the plight of the starving masses, but his concerns were repeatedly brushed aside. More pressing matters were at hand.

Mengistu was consumed by preparations for the tenth anniversary of the revolution. Leaders and top honorees from all the socialist states in the world descended on Ethiopia for the elaborate affair—top leaders from Moscow, Cuba, and East Germany, officials from Vietnam and North Korea, and other dignitaries from various African countries.

After the festivities wound down to a triumphant close, Mengistu summoned Tesfaye, Geteye, and several other officials to the Grand Palace to discuss the famine. The officials gathered outside Mengistu's office, recanting the success of the anniversary gala. Geteye discreetly pulled Tesfaye aside.

"Yes?" Tesfaye asked, his eyebrows raised in anticipation of Geteye's motive for a side meeting.

"A cautionary word, my friend—I wouldn't mention it if I hadn't heard a similar sentiment expressed by others."

"Spit it out then."

"I believe your repeated attempts to bring up the famine to Mengistu in the midst of his planning that little anniversary party was perceived by some as ill-timed and perhaps a little too forceful."

"Are you aware that hundreds of thousands of people have already died in the highlands?"

"Tesfaye, I am not here to argue your point, but we both serve at the pleasure of the Chairman."

"That goes without saying. We are certainly here at the pleasure of Mengistu. But I am not participating in a popularity contest for advisor most liked by his peers."

"Do what you wish with my advice, but I wouldn't want you to go into this meeting and say something you'll later regret. That's the only point I'm trying to make."

"Of course," said Tesfaye, realizing he was acting defensively. "I appreciate the cautionary word."

"Come now, after Yenee was born, I distinctly remember you saying you were going to relax more," Geteye joked.

Tesfaye smiled and patted Geteye on the shoulder. "I guess I just don't know how to do that."

"Gentlemen," Mengistu exclaimed, as he opened the door to his office. "Let's get on with it."

Encircled by his advisors, Mengistu lit his cigar and characteristically put his feet on the table. "So, is the famine as bad as I hear it is?"

One of the other advisors cleared his throat. "The rains have failed to fall for two years now. One year probably would have been sustainable, but this second year of drought has made the situation very bad."

"Very bad, you say," Mengistu remarked. "It is certainly bad if you ask the Americans. I hear word of the famine leaked out and has become fodder for international news programs. Can we avoid more people dying without taking aid from the Americans or those pretentious Europeans?"

"I don't see how that would be possible," the advisor said, causing Mengistu to clench his lips.

"Regardless of where the aid comes from," Geteye added, "it would behoove us to make sure it is dispersed properly. If aid gets into the hands of the rebels, the resistance will become stronger."

"Then how do you suggest we deliver aid to the areas in the north under rebel control?" asked another advisor.

"We don't," Mengistu said forcefully. "We don't give them aid."

"Colonel," Tesfaye chimed in, "a failure to provide aid will only result in the people turning against us."

"Yes, I know Tesfaye, we want to convert their souls, but do you actually believe that citizens living in the parts of Tigray controlled by rebels will attribute the aid to *us*? No! They will thank the Tigrarian People's Liberation Front! And we will be no better off."

Mengistu stood to his feet, a clear sign he was unhappy with the information he was getting from his advisors. "I want more ideas," he said to no one in particular. Tesfaye opened his mouth to speak, but closed it immediately, hoping his facial contortions had gone unnoticed. "You have a mothball stuck in your throat, Tesfaye?" Mengistu asked. "Out with it."

Tesfaye licked his lips. "Well, in a situation like this, our goal is to crush the ranks of the rebel factions and to make sure nobody else joins their liberation fronts. At the same time, when it is problematic to bring food to the hungry, the most direct alternate course of action would be to bring the hungry to the food."

Mengistu stared blankly at Tesfaye as the advisors shot each other perplexed glances. Then, Mengistu smiled. "Ah," he said. "Aha! I get it. The famine can be an excuse to move people out of the rebel infested north to areas in the south that have not been hit by the famine. That is brilliant, Tesfaye!"

"Also," Geteye added, "it would look as if our actions are directed solely at helping the people."

"And it would help fulfill our political goals of land distribution by giving northerners their own plots of land in the less populated south," said another advisor.

Hasn't the famine taught you anything about bad land distribution policies? Tesfaye snickered internally.

"Sir," Tesfaye said, "you asked me to brainstorm potential courses of action and that is what I did. But before we all get too self-congratulatory, I really think we need to think through this a little more. There are a lot of intangibles here. Tearing people away from their homeland could be extremely problematic. Such a mass migration would also require considerable and meticulous planning. If it isn't done right, we could find ourselves worse off than when we started."

"Don't worry about the details," Mengistu said assuredly. "You underestimate the people's desire to till their own land."

"It's not that sir, I just . . ."

"Tesfaye," Mengistu interrupted. "You are one of the only people I know who cannot seem to take a compliment for a job well done. You are all excused."

As the advisors filed out, Tesfaye waited for Geteye to finish a glass of water. "What are you doing tonight for dinner?" Geteye asked Tesfaye as they headed for the door. "I would love to have you over for dinner, with Ayana and the girls of course. I wouldn't want Ayana to think that I'm a mooching bachelor who doesn't know how to repay her hospitality."

"Geteye," Mengistu blurted out. Tesfaye and Geteye stopped in the doorway and turned around. Mengistu circled his desk and approached them. "A quick word."

Tesfaye exited the office and watched as Mengistu shut the door in his face.

TESFAYE AND THE priest walked down the aisle between the benches of the church. "How many people died as a result of the forced migration?" asked the priest.

"I don't know. It was a very large number."

"Do you hold yourself responsible for all these lives?"

"I gave him the idea."

"But it sounds like he had been wanting to do it for a long time. It also sounds like you weren't too eager to share your views with him."

"Father, about my sleeping problems, is there any way you could get me some medication, something that will help me go to sleep?"

The priest stopped his casual walk down the aisle. "I'm afraid I can't, you'll need to see a doctor for that." Looking down at Tesfaye's severed index finger, the priest continued. "But I do have an idea. I obviously don't know the full story of what happened to you, but based on what you told me, you might be eligible for something called asylum."

"Asylum?" Tesfaye queried, having an idea what the term meant from his time in Kenya.

"Think of it as our country's way of welcoming those from around the world who've had some very bad things happen in their lives."

"Bad things. Sounds like I would qualify."

"Well, I'm not qualified to tell you that either, you'll need to ask a lawyer."

Tesfaye shook his head. "I don't have money for a lawyer."

"I figured not. If you'll accompany me to my office, I believe I have a list of organizations that offer free legal services to immigrants."

Chapter 24

ETHAN SHAW AND Ryan Bard sat on the hood of Ryan's Ford Explorer, parked in the middle of an empty lot in back of a Friday's restaurant in Hackensack, New Jersey. They sat in silence. Ethan fidgeted with his thumbs. "What time is it?" asked Ethan.

"Quarter to midnight—no, ten till."

Five minutes later, they saw the headlights of a beat-up Honda Accord. The woman in the passenger seat got out of the car and nervously approached Ethan and Ryan.

"You have something for us?" asked Ryan.

The woman nodded as she handed him an envelope.

Ryan grabbed two envelopes from his jacket and looked at the names written on them. "This is for you," he said, handing her one of the envelopes. "That's your sister, Angela, in the car?"

"Yes."

"This is for her."

The woman smiled. "So we are legal now?"

"You're legal," Ethan said, "but you commit one crime and they will rip these papers up faster than the time it takes to buy you a bus ticket back to Mexico. I will personally make sure they do."

"I understand, sir. I will be the best citizen. Thank you, thank you so much, from the bottom of my heart," she said, tears welling up in her eyes.

Ethan made the same threatening statement every time. It was part of the code he developed to justify the side scheme he and Ryan concocted a few years ago. He knew he lacked the diplomacy to advance much further up the government pay scale. In exchange for five thousand dollars apiece, Ethan provided immigrants with green cards they otherwise would have to wait years to get, if they were eligible at all. But under his code, Ethan would only help immigrants who had never committed a crime. He ran multiple background checks on all of them, taking advantage of his access to a handful of FBI criminal databases.

Ethan knew that his code wasn't foolproof. An illegal immigrant who hasn't committed any crimes may do so in the future. Illegal immigrants might have clean criminal histories simply because they have never been caught. He quashed these concerns by trusting his instincts to spot a violent criminal. The violent ones were usually men who couldn't account for what they did all day. He would look for the shifty eyes, the mischievous smirk, the gang clothes and tattoos, and even certain cars.

Ethan flipped through the bills in the envelope. There was a strong look of disappointment on his face. "What's this?" he asked.

"Sir?"

"There's five thousand here."

"Yes, that is what Mr. Ryan said, five thousand."

"Each," Ryan said, pointing to the woman in the car.

"Each!" gasped the woman. She pleaded with Ethan, "Mr. Ryan said five thousand."

"It is five thousand," Ethan responded sternly. "Five for you and five for her. *Comprende?*"

"I don't understand."

Ethan knew that she understood perfectly well and he had no patience for talking in circles. "Listen, you take your papers, and when you get another five thousand, contact us again the same way you did last time, and we'll give you the papers for her."

"Sir, please, there must be some way I can get the papers for her."

"There is, get another five grand."

"I had to sell my car just to get the five thousand. Please, sir," she said as she kneeled down in front of Ethan. She took his hand and gripped it tight, resting her forehead on the back of his hand. "I beg you."

Ethan pulled his hand away. "You're barking up the wrong tree."

"I don't understand."

"Trying to make me sympathize with you isn't gonna work. Your friend will just have to wait a little longer."

"There must be something else I can do," she said, looking up at Ethan, unzipping the fly of his jeans.

"What are you doing?" Ethan said. The woman didn't respond. Ethan half-heartedly tried to move away as a rare feeling of guilt washed over him. He looked at a despondent Angela sitting in the driver's seat of the Honda with her head down. He knew they were both trying to imagine that they weren't in a dimly lit parking lot.

Chapter 25

SHAOQING LAY ON his piece of cardboard, overtired from the mayhem of the previous day and a bad night's sleep. As other passengers awoke, he kept his eyes closed, even though he knew there was little chance he would be able to get any more sleep.

"Do you know the difference between you and a rat?" asked Dong.

Shaoqing opened his eyes to the unwelcome sight of Dong and the other Tingjiang boys standing over him.

"You're tongue-tied I see," Dong said. "Well then, let me give you the answer. It's quite simple. When you trap a rat, after a certain amount of time, the rat accepts his fate. It stops looking for a means to escape. You, on the other hand, cannot seem to accept the fact that you are trapped." Dong kneeled down and looked Shaoqing in the eye. "But you are a rat, Shaoqing. You are stuck down here and *I* am your master." Dong took the triangle blade out of his pocket. "Did you think nobody would notice you jumping down the open hatch? That little game you and the Changle City rats played with that staged fight."

"What do you want, Dong?"

"You mean what am I going to take. Maybe you are unaware, but you have been helping to protect a low life." Dong looked over toward Jiang. "He stole my sister's honor."

"That's a lie!" Jiang exclaimed, drawing the attention of the other passengers.

"I would keep my mouth shut if I were you," Dong replied, pointing the blade in Jiang's direction.

"So what do you intend to do, Dong?" asked Shaoqing. "Take Jiang's life? Make him suffer because you have the power to do so?"

"That's right," Dong responded, "I do have the power to do so. Jiang is destined for a fate to be determined by me, and so are you. When the snakeheads come down with our food, I will inform them of your actions yesterday. Do you have any idea what they'll do to you?"

Dong pointed at Lin. "And you! You dishonor yourself by associating with this scum. I should do the honorable thing and punish you for your actions. I saw you return before the other girls. That means you aren't tainted. At least not yet." The Tingjiang boys cackled at Dong's not-so-subtle insinuation.

Dong sat down and remained silent, gazing intently at the ground. A few moments later, a devious smile covered his face from ear to ear as he basked in the glory of what he perceived to be a brilliant idea. "Although I can take whatever I want, I will not do so here." Dong locked his gaze on Jiang. "Instead, I will leave the decision to Jiang. You have two options, Jiang. You can accept the punishment you personally earned *and* let your friend suffer at the hands of the snakeheads after they find out what he did yesterday. Or, you can absolve yourself of your past infractions and keep Shaoqing's actions hidden from the snakeheads by sacrificing Lin to us so that we may have our way with her and finally have some fun on this never-ending trip."

"What?" Lin hissed. "You truly are an ape! No, you are less than an ape. You, you are . . ."

Jiang raised his hand for Lin to calm down. "You cannot ask me to make this decision."

"I'm growing impatient." Dong stood up, walked over to Jiang, and placed the blade of his knife close to Jiang's throat. "This is fun, isn't it? So what is your decision?"

Having quietly observed Dong and Jiang, Shaoqing lunged to his feet, retrieved the gun from his waistband, and pointed it at Dong's head. "There is only one decision you need to worry about now, Dong," Shaoqing scoffed, "and that is whether you desire to take your last breaths today. I suggest you loosen your grip on that blade immediately."

Lin picked up the triangle blade that Dong unhesitatingly dropped.

"What is this?" Dong snickered. "You stole a gun from the snakeheads? You don't think they'll notice it's missing?"

"There are many guns on this ship. Do you think the snakeheads know how many? Do you think they remember where they store all the guns? Under which empty whiskey bottle they dropped a gun in a drunken stupor? You give the snakeheads too much credit, just like you give yourself too much credit. And you forget that the relevant question for you right now is not what happens in the days to come, but what will take place right now."

"If you shoot me, the snakeheads will hear the gun go off and come to investigate."

"Maybe so, but you will be dead, and the snakeheads' curiosity will be of no value to you. I, on the other hand, risk death by not doing anything if you tell the snakeheads I left the living quarters, and that means that I have nothing to lose."

A crowd gathered around Dong and Shaoqing. Dong surveyed the onlookers and scowled at Shaoqing. "Do you think I'm afraid of you?"

"Yes," Shaoqing replied without hesitation. "I do think you're scared. You are scared and you are a coward. You prey on those who do not have the means to stand up for themselves. You take pleasure in causing fear and you steal with impunity. You justify taking Jiang's life by saying that he dishonored your sister, yet you would take Lin's honor because it amuses you and you now know that the snakeheads don't care at all about the wellbeing of the women on this ship. True strength is doing what is right even when you don't have to. It's having the means to act with no repercussions, but choosing not to give in to the temptation. And that, Dong, is why you are weak. That is why you are a coward."

Several of the passengers now huddled around Dong and Shaoqing quietly applauded Shaoqing's scolding of Dong, mindful to control the noise level of their jubilation in order to avoid drawing attention from above.

"Look around you, Dong. How many of these people would jump at the chance to bleed you slowly? Since I'm holding the gun and you have no weapon, it would be easy for me to give all of them the go-ahead." With a look of vengeance in his eye, Shaoqing lunged at Dong, spun him around, and pressed the barrel of the gun to the back of his head. His lips now millimeters from Dong's ear, Shaoqing continued. "But I am not weak," he whispered as his hand began to tremble. "Do you hear me? I am *not* weak," he repeated forcefully.

Shaoqing pushed Dong to the ground and took a few steps back. "You are going to return everything that you and your friends have stolen from the other passengers. Then, you will remain in the corner of this dungeon. The only time you will move is when the snakeheads come to bring down food. And when they do, you will eat the same amount of food as everyone else, but you will get your portion last. A gun will be pointed at you at all times by someone who is willing to pull the trigger. I promise you the gun will be used if you try to say anything to the snakeheads."

After the uproar caused by the confrontation subsided, Shaoqing quietly stood watch over the Tingjiang boys. Moving for the first time since returning to the living quarters, Ai walked back over to the piece of cardboard she called a bed, closed her eyes and curled herself into a ball without saying a word to anyone. Jiang took a shirt out of the bag Dong had begrudgingly given back to him and placed it under Ai's head before sitting next to Lin.

"He's a better man than I am," Jiang said.

"Why do you say that?" Lin asked.

"Let's just say Dong's sister was slightly more honorable before I met her." Lin rolled her eyes and Jiang continued. "The truth is, she seduced *me*," he said with a big grin on his face. "Dong is right though, I do bear responsibility for letting what happened between me and his sister become public. It was shameful for me as well."

Jiang lay next to Lin until she fell asleep. Managing to get to his feet after several bouts of dizziness, he walked over to Shaoqing. "Dong will wait until we bathe again," Jiang said. "When he and the others are up on the deck, alone with the snakeheads, he will tell them everything we've done and we will have to deal with the snakeheads."

"You're right. I'm sure that's what he's thinking."

"So what's your solution?"

"Simply to allow Dong to maintain the false hope that he will have another opportunity to bathe on the deck."

"I don't follow."

"I overheard one of the snakeheads. We are close to the United States."

"The United States," Jiang repeated.

Shaoqing looked at Jiang and smiled. "The United States."

Chapter 26

IN THE NEARLY three weeks since Sofia tearfully departed Escuinapa for the United States, her children Eva and Manuel slowly adjusted to life under the watchful eye of their aunt Miranda, the family taskmaster. They accompanied their aunt into town to help her carry groceries from the market. Inviting soft blue, red, and peach colored storefronts were sprinkled among older, more worn buildings with deteriorating walls that exposed their brick underbelly. Children piled onto bicycles, two or three at a time, wobbling down the street past vendors selling *taquitos* and seafood from their food carts.

Next to the market, a group of middle-aged men gathered under a canopy set up along the sidewalk, anxiously watching the soccer match.

"Can we watch, Aunt Miranda?" pleaded Manuel.

Miranda squinted her eyes. "Five minutes, then I want you to come help me with the groceries."

After ten minutes, Eva and Manuel walked back toward the market.

"Check it out," Manuel said, pointing to a brand new, black Ford F-150 pickup truck speeding down the road, pulling over in front of the market. "It's *El Memo.*"

The engine still running, the drug pusher Guillermo exited the truck, music blaring out the open windows. "What do we have here?" he asked, Manuel and Eva both looking at the ground. "So you can't even look at me?" he asked Eva. "How often do you get to see someone as sexy as me up close?" he said sarcastically. "C'mon baby, what are you doing tonight? How about I take you out for a night on the town?" Guillermo leaned toward Eva and whispered in her ear, "I bet you taste as sweet as your mother."

Eva took a few steps back before running into the market.

Guillermo shook his head. "Women," he said to Manuel. "You like women?"

"Yeah," Manuel answered, still avoiding eye contact with Guillermo.

"You have a girlfriend?"

"No."

"Why not?"

Manuel shrugged his shoulders. "I don't know," he quietly replied.

Guillermo patted his chest. "I do."

Intrigued, Manuel raised his eyes, observing Guillermo rubbing the tip of his thumb back and forth against the tips of his other four fingers. "Money," Guillermo said. "The girls want to know you can show them a good time, take care of them. I bet you want to make some money of your own, don't you?"

"Sure, I guess."

"Then why don't you come work for me? You'll have so much money you won't know how to spend it all." Guillermo squatted down, using his hand to balance himself. "Unless you want to spend the rest of your life picking tomatoes."

"What are you doing here?" screamed Miranda, running full speed toward Manuel and Guillermo.

"This must be *Tia* Miranda," Guillermo said. Manuel didn't even flinch when Guillermo rattled off his aunt's name because he knew that everyone knows everyone else's name in these small towns.

Miranda grabbed Manuel's collar. "Get in the car!"

Guillermo winked at Manuel. "We'll talk later, *carnal.*"

"You're sick," Miranda said. "How fucked up are you, trying to recruit Manuel, after everything you put this family through?"

"You mean everything Israel put the family through."

"Everyone in this town might be scared of you, but I'm not. I see you for what you really are."

"And what's that?"

"A lucky son of a bitch who happened to know someone in the cartel, who would otherwise be turning tricks in the back of the discothèque for other faggots."

"You fucking cunt," Guillermo said, shaking his head. "You're lucky I'm in a good mood today, otherwise I'd slit your throat right here in front of everyone."

"You want to terrorize the town, recruit all the other boys to become drug pushers, fine, do it, ruin their lives. Just leave my nephew alone. That kid may have been too young to know what you did to his mother and father, but eventually he's going to find out."

"That's right. Eventually he will find out, and then he'll want to come after me, seek revenge. I should kill him right now, eliminate the threat."

"He is no threat to you."

"We both know that's bullshit." Guillermo looked up at the clear sky. "Don't worry. It's a beautiful day and I'm feeling good." Becoming more serious he continued, "But let me be clear, either you convince him that Israel was responsible for everything that happened, or eventually I'll have to deal with the situation my way."

Chapter 27

SHAOQING PICKED THE passengers he trusted the most to take shifts pointing the gun at Dong. At least two people were watching him at all times. None of the Tingjiang boys tried to fight back or cause any trouble.

Despite the recent triumph over the *ma zhais*, the mood in the living quarters remained somber. The length of the journey had taken its toll. The passengers complained less and generally talked less. Conversations that did take place were barely louder than a whisper. Ai and some of the other female passengers had not uttered a word since they returned from the deck two days ago.

Most of the passengers were still asleep when the ship stopped moving. A few moments later, the hatch opened, and Lee climbed down. "Everybody wake up!" he shouted, grading a tin cup over the prongs of the pole. "Pack your belongings and come up to the deck. This hatch will be shut in ten minutes. Anyone still inside will end up in Taiwan."

The passengers all rushed to pack what little belongings they had. One by one, they climbed up and gathered in the shaft above the open hatch, spilling out into the surrounding corridors. After everyone emerged, they followed Lee up to the deck.

In what had become a regular pattern of begrudging abdication, the Tingjiang boys followed Lee without raising a fuss. None of them even attempted to alert the snakeheads to the fact that Shaoqing was carrying a gun. The anticipation of arriving in the United States was exciting enough to quash Dong's desire for retribution.

Lin couldn't help but smile as she climbed the steps. She pictured the shore of the United States welcoming her at the top of the staircase. The shoreline, however, was not there. Lin gazed out onto the seemingly endless waters of the Pacific Ocean in all directions. There was no land in sight. Soft shades of purple and red from an unobstructed morning sun adjoined the water behind eight motorboats that were rocking in the waves next to the ship.

Lee waited impatiently for all the passengers to ascend the stairs and gather on the deck. "Everyone into the boats."

The tired travelers slowly filled the motorboats, climbing down the same ropes used to hoist them onto the ship from international waters off the coast of China so many weeks ago. Weak from their journey, several lost their grips on the withered ropes and fell into the water. As they labored to swim to the waiting hands of fellow passengers already squeezed onto the motorboats, the snakeheads cackled with amusement at their plight.

The passengers huddled together to fit on the small, decrepit motorboats, the smell of fumes from the aging motors permeating the air. As Lin's motorboat sped away from the ship, her eyes grew teary from the strong wind blowing in her face. She looked back and watched Lee's concave face and bulging eyes fade into an insignificant dot. Fei Pin never showed his face again after threatening Lin by the open hatch. Lin prayed she would never see him again.

Nearly an hour went by before Lin could see land. From a distance, all she could make out was the canopy of a forest off the coast of Oregon. As her boat sped closer to shore, she saw the jagged edges of small boulders pressed against the ocean's edge.

The sound of the engine dulled as the boat approached the shore, coasting toward a small strip of sand that extended twenty feet inland. With a flick of a switch the engine noise stopped and the snakehead maneuvered the engine's propeller out of the water.

"Everybody out," ordered the snakehead. "Grab a side of the boat." Knee deep in salty water, Lin clutched a rusty edge of the boat and helped push it onto the sand with what little energy she had left. She leaned over to catch her breath, watching the other boats being strewn along the shore. She grabbed her bag from the boat and followed the snakehead up a maze of boulders and rocks that covered the hill. The faint glow of dawn did little to illuminate the dirt paths in the forest. The adrenalin Lin felt from being on U.S. soil aided her trek through the trees and bushes. In this moment, she was relieved her mother forced her to pack minimal clothing.

After thirty minutes of trudging through the forest, the dirt path opened up to a large picnic area where a convoy of idling vans was waiting to transport the passengers to their next destination. Two snakeheads stood by the vans, handing out brown bags to the hungry travelers. "Take a bag and get in the vans," one of them said.

Lin found Shaoqing and stood in line with him to get a brown bag. In the moment before they were ushered into one of the vans, Lin quickly surveyed the crowd and saw that Jiang and Ai were far behind.

The van was off-white with heavily tinted windows, the words *Richardson Plumbing* stenciled on the side. Sitting in the back corner of the hard floor of the seatless van, Lin opened her brown bag. Inside, she found a bottle of water and a sandwich with one piece of bologna between two stale pieces of bread. She had nearly consumed the entire bottle of water by the time the van was full with bodies. The driver did not wait for the other vans before speeding away. Lin turned around and watched Jiang standing in line for his dried-out sandwich until he was no longer in sight.

The next two days were a blur. Lin drifted in and out of sleep. Winding mountain roads and trees were replaced by endless cornfields and flat open land, as the van headed east from Oregon through Nebraska.

Lin awoke and glanced at Shaoqing, who was nursing his bottle of water. "Here," Shaoqing said, offering the water to Lin, "take a sip."

"Thanks." Lin pressed her knees on the floor and gazed out the back window at the white lines in the median of the road that were shooting past her. "I cannot believe I am in the United States," she remarked, smiling to herself. "My mother would be proud if she knew what I went through to get here."

"I'm sure your parents could never imagine all the crap we had to endure these last few weeks," Shaoqing said.

A pit formed in Lin's stomach as her thoughts drifted to her father. The sun radiating down through a cloudless sky onto the cornfields reminded her of that morning nearly four months ago, the last day she saw him.

LIN AWOKE EARLY that morning, joining her father, Chang, in the fields. Standing in the shin-deep water needed to properly irrigate the rice, Lin and her father tended the patty fields, picking rice plants that had sufficiently matured and wrapping them together in bushels.

Although Chang had only recently celebrated his fortieth birthday, he moved at the speed of a man many years older. Lin worried about his health. She had vivid memories as a young child of hearing her father complaining about constant aches and pains in his joints. Chang did not let his discomfort affect his work in the fields every day. His deliberate actions and methodical approach made up for his lack of speed.

Nor did Chang allow his health problems to interfere with his favorite pastime. At night, he would return home tired, covered in mud, anticipating that he would enjoy some rice porridge and pickled tofu with a cup of tea. After dinner, he would sit on the floor, reading quietly in the corner of the house by the bookshelf.

For as long as Lin could remember, her father had immersed himself in books about religion and philosophy. As Chang had explained to her, the majority of his youth was overshadowed by Mao Zedong's Cultural Revolution, where academics, economists, and scientists were hunted as bourgeois elements of society that needed to be eliminated. Once the Cultural Revolution ended in 1976, Chang begged his father to teach him how to read. Like most of the villagers, Chang's father was almost functionally illiterate, so he permitted Chang to study three nights a week with a friend named Guozhi who lived nearby.

Once Chang began to read, he couldn't get enough. By his fortieth birthday, he had amassed a collection that was quite exceptional for a poor rural farmer—the works of Lao Zi, Sun Bu'er, and several other prominent Chinese philosophers, books covering Mahayana and Theravada schools of Buddhism, Taoism beliefs and practices, even a few readings on Christianity.

Mei had urged her husband to buy literature that may improve his health if he insisted on spending what little money they had on books. In light of Mei's persistence, Chang had obtained several books on *qigong* over the past year. Admittedly, Chang had always been curious about the practice of *qigong*, and Mei did not have to do too much convincing. All Lin's father had told her about *qigong* was that it sought to promote health and general wellbeing through the practice of carefully circumscribed meditation practices.

Observing her father working in the fields that morning, Lin thought she noticed a slight improvement in his mobility since he started practicing *qigong*. *Wishful thinking, perhaps.*

Chang let out a groan. "I think we've done enough before breakfast. How about we go inside and eat. I think your mother's steaming pork buns."

Lin followed her father up the hillside, but Chang was walking away from their home.

"Father, where are you going?"

"A quick stop at Guozhi's. He said he has a new book for me."

Guozhi lived on an adjacent hillside a half-mile away. An avid believer in *qigong*, Guozhi had amassed a large collection of literature on the subject. Guozhi took pride in his practice of *qigong* and was delighted to lend Chang several books written by Guo Lin, Liang Shifeng, and several other *qigong* masters.

"Guozhi," Chang called out through an open crack of the rickety front door.

Guozhi opened the door and smiled, displaying a mouthful of gums sprinkled with a handful of teeth that seemed destined to fall out soon. "Greetings, Chang." Guozhi looked over toward Lin, bowed his head slightly, and motioned for both of them to come inside.

The shabby exterior of Guozhi's house masked a deceptively elegant living space. An emerald green oriental rug with a gray floral design adorned the center of the floor. Two cast iron tea stands stood in the far corners of the house, each supporting a cream-colored porcelain vase. Between the tea stands, a hardwood table hugged the far wall, books neatly stacked underneath, the tabletop decorated with small animal figurines.

Although the interior of Guozhi's home was not much bigger than the meager dwelling of Lin's family, it appeared roomier because the space was only shared by two people. Seven years ago, Guozhi's wife passed away, and the couple never had children. Guozhi shared his home with a nephew who was already out tending the fields.

After the first time Lin visited Guozhi's home, she had asked her father how Guozhi could afford all these things. Chang scolded her for prying into another man's personal life. The contents of Guozhi's home remained an ongoing mystery that puzzled Lin each time she visited with her father.

Guozhi was on his hands and knees rummaging around the floor. He reached under the springs of his nephew's mattress and pulled out a book. "Ah, here we are," he said, dusting off the front cover. "I think you will enjoy this. The Master focuses on . . ."

Before Guozhi could finish his sentence, the front door burst open and smacked against the wall. The top hinge detached from the doorframe. The lower hinge quickly gave way and the door fell to the ground. Lin noticed a pair of tightly laced boots step over the front door. Six more pairs soon followed. "Guozhi Yu," the apparent leader of the cadre group said. Guozhi remained silent, but bowed his head slightly.

"Good morning, Guozhi, I am Yending. I am very sorry to disturb you this morning," he caustically snickered, "but I must request your presence at the Security Bureau."

"I don't understand. I've done nothing wrong."

"Quite the contrary," Yending said, speaking slowly and over-enunciating his words. "You have engaged in activity subversive to the State."

"I would never engage in such conduct."

"Do you deny that you are a practitioner of Falun Gong?"

Guozhi paused. "I, I do not deny it. But I would never seek to overthrow the government." The quiver in Guozhi's voice shifted to outright indignation. "Falun Gong is my religion. It helps me find peace and maintain my health."

With a tiny gesture by Yending, one of the cadre charged toward Guozhi and wacked him in the stomach with a baton. The other cadre ransacked Guozhi's home, confiscating any item that appeared to hold value, and smashing everything else to pieces.

When the house was in complete shambles, Yending bent down and smiled at Guozhi, who was slumped over and struggling to repopulate his lungs with air after the blow to his stomach. "Falun Gong is certainly not a religion," Yending said, pacing back and forth. "It's a dangerous cult!" He gave Guozhi a moment to survey the damage to his home. "Do you deny passing out literature on Falun Gong?" he asked sternly.

"I do not."

"Do you deny participating in a protest at Tianjin with other Falun Gong practitioners?"

"No, I do not. But the protest was entirely peaceful. All we sought was for the newspapers and the radio station to retract the lies they were spreading about Falun Gong. Entirely peaceful. Nobody would dispute that."

"But there have been hundreds of protests all over the country by your fellow Falun Gong practitioners. Hundreds!" Yending stopped pacing. "These are not the actions of a true religious faith trying to maintain harmony with the government."

Lin and Chang stood silently in the corner of the room. They watched Guozhi take deep breaths to maintain his composure and refrain from crying.

Yending's voice softened. "You have been brainwashed. Li Hongzhi has led you astray. He created this Falun Gong movement—this Falun Gong cult—to trick you into following him as if he were divine. I am here to rescue you, Guozhi. You must renounce Falun Gong."

Guozhi's lower lip quivered. "I cannot do that."

Any inkling of kindness Yending momentarily displayed disappeared when Guozhi refused to renounce. The baton Yending gripped tightly smacked Guozhi across the face and knocked him to the floor. Chang pressed Lin's face to his chest to shield her eyes. Guozhi's arms wobbled as they tried to prop his torso off the ground. Blood and saliva dripped from his mouth. Then he let out a deep cough, and two teeth fell onto the bloodstained floor.

"Hold him down, grab his arm," Yending ordered. When a cadre official placed his knee in the middle of Guozhi's back, his arms immediately gave way. Another cadre placed his knee on Guozhi's shoulder blade, pinning his left arm to the dusty floor.

The cracking sounds of Yending's baton striking Guozhi's left hand were eerily lucid. And they continued until each finger was broken.

"Please!" Guozhi screamed. "Stop. I'll renounce. I'll renounce!"

"Stand him up," Yending directed. Guozhi was sobbing as the cadre lifted his body off the ground like a marionette. "I suppose you require medical attention. Do you want to go to a hospital?"

Guozhi nodded. "Yes," he replied in a barely audible voice.

Yending resumed pacing back and forth. "If I am not mistaken, I believe that Falun Gong practitioners believe in the value of more traditional healing," he snickered. "Are you sure you do not want to put your faith in *that* superstitious nonsense?"

Guozhi didn't answer.

Yending articulated each word sternly and quickly as if he were a judge doling out a sentence at the conclusion of a trial. "The Falun Gong movement is responsible for the deaths of thousands of Chinese citizens. All of these people needlessly died because they forsook medical treatment that could have saved their lives. Instead, under the guile of the superstitious nonsense of your evil cult, they were tricked into turning to Falun Gong to help them. You, Guozhi, as a Falun Gong practitioner, have contributed to these deaths. For these evil deeds and your subversive attempts to undermine the stability of our great country, I am placing you under arrest."

Two cadre each grabbed Guozhi under one of his arms and dragged him out of the house. "Tell my nephew where to find me," Guozhi murmured in Chang's direction.

Yending turned his attention to Chang, who was still hiding Lin's head in his chest. "Your name?"

Chang lowered his head. "Chang Ou."

"And where do you live?"

Chang pointed toward the general direction of his home.

"It's unfortunate you would subject such an innocent, young girl to such unruly characters," Yending hissed. "Shall we take a walk?"

The half-mile walk back home felt like an eternity. Lin's hands were trembling, the urge to go to the bathroom overwhelming. Surrounded by cadre, she kept her head pointed to the ground, relying on her father's guiding hand to lead the way. Tight-laced boots clogged her peripheral vision.

With the exception of a momentary lapse the night Mei's own father died, Lin could not recall her mother displaying any significant outward emotion. That is, until the cadre burst in through the front door. The door hitting the wall startled Mei, jolting the pot of tea in her hand. Hot water splashed her wrists and caused her to lose her grip. Mei screamed when the pot fell to the ground and hot water splattered onto her right foot and ankle.

Yending pointed to the rickety chair next to the stove and motioned for Mei to sit down. He surveyed the home and walked directly to the bookcase. "This is quite a collection of books," Yending remarked. "Quite a collection. There are many people in these parts who don't even know how to read."

Yending grabbed a book on the teachings of Buddhism and faced Chang. "Someone who reads this many books would undoubtedly want to share his wisdom with others. Do you like to teach others, Chang?"

Chang sensed a trap in the cadre's question. "I have no interest in teaching others," he said. "I'm a simple farmer."

Yending methodically scanned the title of each book in Chang's collection. He picked another book off the shelf and stared at it. "*Zhuan falun,*" Yending said, "authored by Li Hongzhi. How long have you been a Falun Gong practitioner, Chang?"

"Guozhi gave me that book some time ago. I have never been a Falun Gong practitioner. I am a farmer." Chang stuck out his hands, trying to reason with Yending. "A farmer," he repeated.

"You are not a Falun Gong practitioner? Yet you admit you have read the book Li Hongzhi has declared to be the bible of the Falun Gong cult, and you associate with individuals who admit they have engaged in conduct meant to undermine the government."

Chang stood silent with his head down.

"Well?" Yending prodded.

Even though his head did not move, Lin could see Chang's eyes turn and focus on her and her mother trembling in the corner of the house, their feet idle in a pool of spilt tea. "I have read this book," Chang conceded, "and I have associated with known Falun Gong practitioners. I am guilty of these crimes. I accept the repercussions of my actions."

Chang willingly followed the cadre out the front door. Without thinking, Lin started to chase after him. Her progress was halted by Mei's strong arms wrapped around her waist, and then by the pain in her knee after she slipped on the wet floor.

The years Chang spent collecting books were washed away in an instant. The cadre confiscated all the books on the shelves and then knocked over the bookcase.

The tea on the ground soaked through Lin's clothing. Each breath was a challenge with Mei's arms around her waist. The shock momentarily halted the tears, but an unbroken stream soon followed. And they continued until she fell asleep that night.

LIN BLINKED QUICKLY to avoid crying in front of the others in the van. Revisiting the day the cadre took away her father reminded Lin how much she still did not understand. She had heard her father speak of *qigong*, but never Falun Gong. *What exactly is Falun Gong? Is it possible my father was involved in a movement to overthrow the government?* Lin had begged her mother to explain to her why the cadre took her father and why the cadre were so concerned about Falun Gong. But her mother refused to talk about any of it. Not a word.

Lin pressed her forehead against the window of the van. The uncertainty surrounding the events of the recent past gave way to butterflies in her stomach. The moment she would step out of the van would be the start of her new life in a country where anything is possible.

Chapter 28

ETHAN'S CASE BACKLOG had now grown so large that he had to pile the stacks of manila folders on the ground. Sitting in his desk chair, he stared at the huge map of the United States that was mounted on one of his office walls. There were pushpins spread all over the western seaboard, throughout Arizona, and sprinkled in some of the western parts of Texas. The pushpins were the result of his most recent attempt to crack the identity theft ring that had been giving illegal immigrants the Social Security numbers of United States citizens. He picked up his phone and dialed Ryan's extension. "You got a minute to come see something?"

Ryan walked into Ethan's office and glanced at the map. "What's up?" asked Ryan casually, trying to ignore the tension between them since he witnessed the last illegal immigrant provide Ethan with an alternate form of payment for her immigration papers.

"What do you think?" asked Ethan.

Ryan squinted as he surveyed the map carefully. "Future vacation plans? What is it?"

Ethan stood up and walked over to the map. "This, Ryan, is the culmination of all our work."

Ryan was anxious to hear Ethan explain, since their investigation had gone nowhere. They had painstakingly gone through old case files to try and track down immigrants who had used Social Security numbers that did not belong to them. But the government had already deported all the immigrants they identified. The only people they had been able to get in touch with were the unfortunate American citizens who had been victimized. Ethan grew tired of calling these victims. All of them would use the opportunity to vent their frustration. Ethan knew they needed the catharsis. They could not find anyone who would help them. The local branches of their banks would say that it was not their problem because the fraudulent purchases were taking place in other states. The credit bureaus might put a security freeze on their credit reports, but this ended up causing more problems than it solved. The security freezes also prevented these citizens from securing loans or obtaining credit. The victims' local police departments had no interest or means to investigate a crime originating outside their limited jurisdictions. So Ethan would listen, and do his best to sympathize, and tell the victims that he was going to do everything in his power to help them. But the victims didn't know anything. They had no idea who had stolen their identities. All they knew was that goods and services were being purchased using their credit.

"Alright," Ryan said. "So what does the map have to do with our investigation?"

"I got to thinking," Ethan said, "what's the problem with how we've approached the issue up to this point?"

"Dead ends."

"Right. We find a Social Security number that sets off a red flag, and our investigation leads to a deported immigrant and a crazed citizen whose life has been ruined."

"Then what's with the map?"

Ethan smiled. "It occurred to me that some of the victims we talked to haven't had any problems with fraudulent accounts since the responsible immigrant was deported." Ethan pointed to the map. "But some have."

"And that tells you what?"

"It tells me that the criminal enterprise facilitating these identity theft scams are giving the same Social Security number to multiple immigrants."

"Are you sure?"

"Why else would the fraud continue? Why would a deported immigrant use someone else's Social Security number to buy a television on credit and have it shipped somewhere in California? It wouldn't make sense. I'm telling you, many of the immigrants using these Social Security numbers are still in the country. We just have to find them."

"And you've managed to find them?" Ryan skeptically inquired as he pointed to the pushpins on the map. "Is that what these pins are for?"

"I went back and reviewed my notes from the conversations we had with some of the victims. I focused on the victims still experiencing fraud after we deported the responsible immigrant. Then, I did some more research on those victims' Social Security numbers to find out where all the fraudulent items were being shipped to. These pins represent places, not people. Each pin is a location where some piece of merchandise was sent through the use of a victim's credit." Ethan sat back down at his desk and put up his feet. "So what do you think now?" he smirked.

"You think the responsible illegals are living at these addresses?"

"I don't know, but I'd like to find out. How about we rack up some frequent flier miles?"

"Run it by Jim?"

"Run it by Jim."

Jim Hazard had been Ethan's supervisor for the past four years. Although he initially green-lighted Ethan's identity theft investigation, he had become increasingly disgruntled with the lack of progress.

Ethan knocked on Jim's office door.

"Come in," said Jim, continuing to look down at his paperwork. Jim had a disproportionately large double chin that made him look more like a grandfather than a recent father. He sported a goatee in a feeble attempt to mask his neck pouch. "What's up guys?" asked Jim.

"I think I have a good lead in my ID theft investigation," Ethan said.

"It's about time. Go pursue it."

"We need to go out west."

Jim squinted at Ethan and stroked his goatee. "Sell me."

Ethan explained the significance of the pushpins and why he thought they were promising leads. Jim listened patiently, nodding his head occasionally. "So you have a bunch of pushpins on a map?" Jim summarized.

"Yeah."

"I'm certainly not sending you on a cross-country tour. Do you have any idea which pushpin you want to pursue?"

"A significant cluster of the addresses I found are located in San Diego. We can follow leads on all these addresses in one trip."

"San Diego," Jim said. "Interesting choice. Weather's nice out there this time of year."

"That's probably why all the illegals are there, sir," Ryan added.

Jim rolled his eyes. "I bet. Alright, here's what I'm going to do. I'm gonna send you two out there for ten days."

"Thanks, boss," Ryan interrupted.

"Not so fast. I'm sending you out there for ten days because you're gonna help our boys out there and pick up a few cases."

"Additional cases?" asked Ethan.

"Yes, additional cases. Both of you can spend a day in immigration court trying a case or two. It should take you no more than two days to prepare, which will leave you plenty of time to play detective, alright?"

"With all due respect, sir, is that really necessary?" asked Ethan, who shuddered at the idea of expanding his already significant docket of cases.

"I need to justify to our financial people why I'm sending two of my agents across the country to investigate a hunch on an identity theft racket that's well outside their regular job descriptions. So yeah, it's necessary. And since you two are here, do me a favor and run down to intake. A group of illegals arrived a little while ago. They've been booked already—just need you two to see if any of them have any legal claims that would stop us from kicking them out."

Ethan hid his frustration, thinking that any additional comments might cause Jim to dole out another assignment.

"Thanks for the invite to be on this taskforce," Ryan said sarcastically at Ethan as they headed down to intake.

Chapter 29

THE SNAKEHEAD DROVE in the right lane of the two-lane corridor of I-80 that stretched across Pennsylvania. Truckers driving big rigs sped by the van, gesturing their displeasure with the snakehead's adherence to the speed limit. A sign alerted drivers to a McDonald's half a mile off the next exit ramp. The van exited the highway, drove through several intersections, and parked in a space outside McDonald's.

Over the course of the past several days, the snakehead had occasionally pulled over at truck stops to sleep for two or three hours at a time. To keep pace with his schedule, he relied largely on heavy doses of caffeine to make sure he stayed awake, which accounted for the empty coffee cups and bottles of Mountain Dew that now cluttered the front dash of the van.

Turning around, the snakehead surveyed the passengers through a small opening in a divider that otherwise concealed the back of the van. "Who needs to use the bathroom?" he asked. Before anyone could answer, a policeman tapped his flashlight on the driver's side window. Startled, the snakehead lurched back around, smiled at the officer, and rolled down his window.

"Good evening to you, sir," said the officer. "Can I see your license and registration?"

The snakehead complied and handed the documentation to the policeman. "Did I do something wrong?"

"You turned right at an intersection when the light was red."

"I'm very sorry. I thought that was permissible."

"I'm afraid not, sir, not where you made the turn. You just stick tight here a moment. Okay?"

"Okay."

After the trooper walked back to his vehicle, the snakehead turned around. "You! Open that toolbox!" he barked at one of the passengers. "Hand me the hammer. No! Next to the drill. With the long wooden neck. The hammer. Quickly!"

With the tool in his hand, the snakehead banged the ceiling and broke the interior light bulbs that would have illuminated if he opened a door or tried to start the van. Stealthily, he proceeded to crawl over to the passenger side door and slither outside.

From their seated positions on the floor of the van, Lin and the other passengers could not see the snakehead fleeing the scene. But they quickly realized something was wrong when the officer returned five minutes later. "What in the hell?" said the officer. "You've got to be kidding me." A look of disbelief washed over the officer's face when he peered through the opening in the divider into the back of the van. "What do we have here?" The officer grabbed the keys from the ignition and walked to the back of the van. For a moment, all Lin could hear was the sound of keys jingling, then the back doors swung open. "Dispatch, we're gonna need the wagon. A tow truck too."

Lin and Shaoqing spent the night in a holding cell before local authorities turned them over to the Immigration and Naturalization Service. A bus waited outside the police station to transport them and the other captured passengers to an immigration detention facility in Elizabeth, New Jersey.

Sitting next to Shaoqing on the bus, Lin pulled out the crumpled piece of paper her mother told her not to lose before she left China. The humidity on the ship had taken its toll, making the numbers on the paper barely legible. Lin forced Shaoqing to repeat the numbers over and over until the bus grounded to a halt.

Officers placed Lin in a holding area with other female immigrants. Women and children with an array of different racial and ethnic backgrounds filled the benches—a Jamaican teenager twirling her dreadlocks, an Indian woman with a red dot in the middle of her forehead, a light-skinned grandmother from Albania. Lin tried not to stare, but during her childhood she had only seen the faces of other ethnic Han Chinese.

Ethan walked over to Lin and gestured for her to stand up and follow him. Three chairs surrounded a white circular table in the middle of the interview room. A Chinese interpreter was already sitting in one of the chairs. Ethan sat down and motioned for Lin to do the same.

"Hi Guyo," Ethan said to the interpreter. "Nice to see you again. Her best language?"

"Fuzhou," the interpreter told him, having had a chance to speak with Lin during the preliminary part of her intake interview.

"Okay," Ethan said, "let's proceed. I am going to ask you some questions to learn more about why you came to the United States. When I ask a question, Guyo will interpret it for you. Wait for him to finish interpreting my question before starting your answer."

Ethan asked Lin to explain why she departed China and why she fears authorities in China would harm her. Lin answered Ethan's questions as best she could. Ethan continued, "Do you know anyone in the United States?"

"I have an uncle."

"Where does he live?"

"New York."

"Where in New York?"

"I don't know."

"Do you have any way to get in touch with this uncle?" Ethan asked.

Lin pulled out the crumpled piece of paper. "I have a phone number."

Ethan reviewed his notes. "Alright. Based on your answers today, I have determined that you may have a credible fear of persecution if returned to China." Ethan knew he had not asked enough questions to fully understand Lin's story, but his mind was already focused on his trip to San Diego. So he decided to kick the can down the road a few years, when he would have to litigate the case before an immigration judge.

Lin was elated. "So I get to stay?"

"Remember what I said about interrupting. Just hold on one second." Ethan cleared his throat. "As I was saying, what I am going to do now is refer your case to the immigration court for a full hearing before an immigration judge. Okay?"

Lin nodded.

Ethan handed a document to Lin. "I want you to sign this document. It states the charges against you. By signing it, all you are doing is confirming that I have given you a copy."

After getting Lin to sign the document and providing her with a copy, Ethan continued. "Now, if your cousin—or uncle, whoever it was you mentioned before—or someone else can post a bond for you, I'm going to recommend that you be released from this facility." Ethan handed Lin a sheet of paper. "This is a list of organizations that provide free legal services. You can also hire an attorney with your own money to represent you. The government is not responsible for providing you with a lawyer. Okay?"

Pausing to make sure Ethan was done speaking, Lin nodded again.

"Right now we are going to give you a chance to make a phone call and then put you back into a holding cell until everything gets sorted out. Got it?"

"Where is Shaoqing?"

"Who?" asked the interpreter.

"Shaoqing," Lin repeated.

"What did she say?" Ethan asked the interpreter.

"I think she is asking about one of the other passengers. She said the name Shaoqing."

"What's the last name?"

Lin thought for a moment, shrugging her shoulders after realizing she didn't know.

"Shaoqing," Ethan said to himself. "Ah, I remember that name. He was in here before. Guyo, tell her that he is no longer at this detention facility."

"Where is he?" Lin asked.

"I don't know, ma'am," Ethan snapped as he stood up to leave the interview room. "Now, do you want to make a phone call or don't you?"

Chapter 30

LIN'S FRUSTRATION GREW with each unsuccessful attempt to get in touch with her uncle. Finally, she could hear ringing.

"Hello," a voice said.

"Long Shu?"

"Yes?"

Lin nearly broke down. "It's Lin, Chang's daughter. Lin!" she repeated.

"My beautiful niece, you have made it then! We have been worried." Long was actually Lin's great uncle, more than forty years her senior. As a young child, Lin remembered Long coming to visit from the nearby village of Xianyang to celebrate the Chinese New Year. Each year, she would wait anxiously by the window for him, eager to consume the ginger and honey candies he would bring her.

"Where are you?" asked Long.

"I'm in prison. I don't know where." The tears were now uncontrollable. "Please, can you help me? I don't know what's going on. I don't understand what everyone is saying to me. I don't know anyone here."

"Be calm, Lin. Be calm. Everything will be fine. I know what you are going through right now. Do you at least know the name of the prison?"

"No! I have no idea."

"Did you sign a piece of paper?"

"Yes."

"Do you have a copy of the paper?"

"I'm holding it right now."

"Now Lin, I know you don't understand what the paper says, but do you see a block of eight numbers anywhere?"

Lin scanned the document. "I do."

"That is a special number that the government has assigned to you. If you give me that number, then I can find out where they are holding you." The number Long was referring to is commonly known as an "A number" because the letter A precedes the eight digit sequence. The Immigration and Naturalization Service assigns one to every immigrant for record-keeping purposes.

"Be patient," Long said, copying down Lin's A number. "Nothing bad is going to happen to you. Just try to get some sleep and keep a positive attitude. You will be out of there before you know it."

"When?"

"Soon enough. I don't know exactly."

A surly immigration officer standing next to Lin tapped her on the shoulder. "You're out of time, ma'am," she said, motioning for Lin to hang up the phone.

Lin sighed. "I think I am not permitted to talk to you any longer."

"Remember, keep a positive attitude. I will see you soon."

Chapter 31

BY THE TIME Tesfaye found the auditorium in Seton Hall Law School, law students and members of the public had already filled the seats and lined the floor, awaiting the debate between Martin Holbrook and Professor Hugo Sandoval. Tesfaye found a sliver of free space on the back wall to stand.

On the stage, Martin folded his legs and took one last look at a crumpled page of notes he prepared the night before. Several months ago, Martin agreed to a series of three debates with Hugo on immigration policy. Hugo's reputation as a leading expert in the field of immigration had been growing since an article he wrote appeared in the *Harvard Law Review* two years prior. Several of Hugo's main points on the plight of the immigrant poor quickly emerged as staples for advocates pushing to ease immigration restrictions. Martin was not surprised when Hugo began with one of his most popular anecdotes.

"Imagine you are told that the government is trying to kick an immigrant out of the country." Hugo paused. "Would you care? Now imagine you know that individual. What if he is a co-worker? A classmate at school? A friend you have known all your life? What if this person is your spouse, or a parent, or a cousin? Put a face on this immigrant and you will see why those who try to demonize the plight of immigrants are overlooking the human aspect to the problem. When we uproot immigrants with longstanding ties to this country, we are not just deporting them. We are ripping apart entire communities."

Martin interjected. "Do we ask a criminal whether he has a family before deciding whether to convict him of a crime he committed? Of course we don't. And why not? Because we accept that a society of laws must punish those who do not follow the law."

"Right there is the problem with your argument, Mr. Holbrook. You are comparing immigrants to criminals."

"Not quite. I'm comparing *illegal* immigrants to criminals because they are both breaking the law. The key word is *illegal*, Professor Sandoval."

"But you still cannot compare the two. One commits a crime while the other comes here and for the most part contributes to the country, works, pays taxes, supports his family."

"Coming here illegally *is* a crime. Not agreeing with the law does not give you a right to violate it. Perhaps that sounds harsh," Martin admitted as he surveyed a handful of sneers in the crowd. "If you don't agree with a law, tell your congressman, vote for a politician who supports your position, start a grassroots campaign. The point is, there are plenty of legal ways to change a policy that citizens believe to be wrong."

"You are not accounting for the reality of the circumstances in this country," Hugo said. "There are more than ten million people living here illegally. I want everyone in the audience to think about that number. That is a lot of people! It's completely unrealistic to think that they're all going to just leave, which is why we need to focus on the best way to bring everyone out of the shadows."

"You mean give them all a legal right to be here, correct?" Martin asked impatiently. "Amnesty?"

"That is the *only* way to realistically address the problem. Otherwise, you are just pounding sand. There is simply no other way to find that many people, round them up, and then deport them. And Mr. Holbrook, you have forgotten another problem. There are many immigrants who have given birth to children in the United States and those children are U.S. citizens. How could you, in good conscience, justify ripping these families apart?

"It's arguments like that one that make a mockery of our immigration laws."

"Hardly. Why would you say that?"

"Well, immigrants illegally sneak into the country, right?" Martin asked rhetorically. "If they have a child while they are here illegally, that child is automatically a United States citizen. Right now there are millions of children in this country who are United States citizens because of this. So, the illegal immigrants who gave birth to children in this country get caught. One of them gets caught and the pro-immigrant groups say: *Wait! You can't deport her. She has a child. That child has a right to be here!* Having a child in the United States, you see, creates a safety zone that encourages people to disregard the law and decide they want all their children—and their grandchildren and so on—to be American citizens."

"Mr. Holbrook, you state my position as if it were a bad thing to want citizens of this country to grow up with their families."

"If citizens of foreign countries know that the government of the United States will allow them to stay if they give birth on U.S. soil, then what's to stop millions upon millions from coming here illegally? We are creating an incentive!"

"You act as if women are getting knocked up in Mexico, waiting until they are eight months pregnant, and then sneaking into the United States to give birth. That is not fair. It's just not accurate."

"You don't think taxpayers fork over millions of dollars so illegal immigrants can attend public school?" Martin asked.

"You don't think illegal immigrant parents are also paying taxes?" Hugo replied.

"You do realize that the average immigrant who even pays taxes in the first place does not make enough to even come close to covering the cost of their children's education?"

"Well do *you* realize that their pay is low because they do the jobs nobody else in this country wants to do?"

"Who pays the cost of their health care when illegal immigrants with no health insurance get sick and go to the emergency room?"

"Who cleans the toilets of the emergency room when nobody else is willing to do the job?"

Martin wiped the sweat from his brow. "Millions upon millions of people all over the world have filed applications in their home countries to come to the United States legally and they are waiting patiently for years, if not decades, while others are cutting the line."

"That is why we need to address the problem now, grant those who are here legal status, and then create a more systematic process."

"Amnesty!" Martin could hear his voice getting louder. "Amnesty never reduces illegal immigration. Illegal immigrants know that if they wait it out and hide in the shadows long enough, then they can take advantage of politicians who think they will be able to reform the system."

The debate continued for another twenty minutes before Martin and Hugo took questions from the audience. Afterwards, the students and other spectators slowly trickled out of the auditorium. The question and answer session went longer than Martin anticipated, and he worried he would be late for a meeting.

"Mr. Holbrook," an attendee queried.

Martin turned around. "Hi, yes, what can I do for you?"

"Mr. Holbrook, my name is Tesfaye Azene. I was wondering if I could have a minute of your time?"

"Sure, as long as it's only a minute because I have to catch a train."

"I was wondering if you would be able to help me. I was told that I have a good asylum case and I'm looking for an immigration expert to help me."

"Tesfaye was it? I think you have the wrong person. Didn't you hear my positions in the debate?"

"But that is exactly why you *are* the right person. An unchallenged consensus leads to complacency, but skepticism breeds creativity."

"I guess that's an interesting point," Martin conceded. "Why don't you try one of the organizations that provide free legal services? I think that would be your best bet."

"I did. I tried them all. I called numerous times. I went to their offices yet the answer was always the same. They told me they would like to help me, but they don't have the resources. They have full schedules. I even pleaded with a few regular immigration attorneys to take my case at a discount. Nobody was interested."

Martin was not surprised by Tesfaye's answer, knowing full well these legal services organizations are swamped. "I may know a decent amount of asylum law, but I haven't litigated a case in a long time. More importantly, Tesfaye, I'm actually from New York. I don't even live in New Jersey."

"Actually, I also live in New York."

"Well then what the heck are you doing here?"

"I came to see you, Mr. Holbrook. After I was turned down by a clinic at the New York University Law School, I took a copy of a flier in the hallway that listed upcoming immigration events, including this one. I hopped on a train to Newark for five dollars." Tesfaye retrieved a copy of the flier from his jacket pocket.

Tesfaye's story was starting to make a little more sense to Martin, since Hugo Sandoval was a professor at New York University Law School. Martin knew that NYU would have posted fliers all over campus. "I suppose I should be flattered, but I must say, I'm still a little perplexed."

"There was a time when I could shape the thinking of young men's minds and bend government leaders to see my point of view. I dare say that time has passed, but I still know the importance of sticking out in a crowd. In New York, they look at me as another sob story in a city filled with desperate immigrants. But here, it is just you and me, Mr. Holbrook. I came all this way, sir. Please."

Martin sighed. Accepting his inability to talk Tesfaye down, he unzipped the side compartment of his briefcase and removed a business card. "Call this number next week and my secretary will schedule an appointment. Tesfaye, I am agreeing to meet with you because you came all this way, but I am not making any promises."

Chapter 32

PRESSING HIS HEAD against the train window during the short ride back to New York, Tesfaye felt more at peace than he had for a long time. Even if there were no guarantees Martin would represent him, his ability to at least secure a future meeting with an attorney went a long way to help rebuild his badly bruised self-esteem. His pleas to Martin were reminiscent of the days when he was in a position of power—more so, perhaps, in his latter years in the Mengistu regime when his influence waned and his advice only led to half-measures, if it was not ignored all-together.

AYANA FIRST OFFERED the platter of beef cubes with spicy *awazie* peppers to Geteye before asking Yenee to pass the dish around the dining room table.

"Delicious as always, Ayana," Geteye said.

"Well thank you, Geteye. I'm not going to tell you which spices I put in the sauce. Otherwise we may never see you again for dinner."

"It has been entirely too long," Geteye agreed.

"And we know it's not because he has a wife at home cooking gourmet meals," Tesfaye joked.

"So when are you going to settle down, start a family of your own?" asked Ayana.

Tesfaye laughed. "The consummate bachelor? I doubt we'll ever see that day."

"Papa, what's a bachelor?" asked Yenee.

"A bachelor is a man too ugly to find a wife," Tesfaye told her, which made Afeworki start to laugh.

Yenee turned to Geteye. Deep in thought, she said, "I don't think you're ugly."

Geteye smiled. "I appreciate that Yenee."

"I'm just teasing, Yenee," Tesfaye said. "A bachelor is a man who is not yet married because he cannot find a woman as perfect as your mother."

"It's true," Geteye agreed. "How would I ever find someone as perfect as Ayana? Besides, being single gives me more time to travel. Have either of you ever been to Europe?" Geteye asked the children.

"No," both replied.

"We both know the political leanings of certain governments might make travel to some European countries a little dicey right now," Tesfaye said.

"That's true, but . . ."

"Here it comes," Ayana chimed in, Tesfaye nodding in agreement.

"Here what comes?" asked Geteye.

"*Italia*," Tesfaye said. Geteye had always had a mild obsession with Italy, which Tesfaye found peculiar since Geteye never developed a palette for Italian cuisine.

"I'm just saying—the canals of Venice, the Coliseum in Rome, *La Scala* opera house in Milan, the Amalfi Coast. Don't even get me started with all the artwork in Florence."

"You heard the man," Tesfaye said to the children. "He said not to get him started."

After dinner, the two men poured themselves a drink and adjourned to Tesfaye's study. Geteye patted Tesfaye on the leg. "It's good to see you old friend, it really has been a long time."

"Agreed, I have not seen much of you at the ministry lately."

Geteye took a sip of whisky and crossed his legs. "I've been busy on assignments."

"Assignments?" queried Tesfaye.

"Eritrea," Geteye responded. "I have been helping to oversee our strategy in the region." Hugging the western coast of the Red Sea, Eritrea was the northernmost province in Ethiopia. The rebels in Eritrea were particularly feverish because the province had a long history of independence before European colonization.

"Sometimes I wonder whether it's worth wasting so many resources on Eritrea," Tesfaye said.

"Without Eritrea, we would be landlocked. Eritrea is critical."

"Bah, let's just invade Djibouti," joked Tesfaye.

Geteye's face suddenly became more serious. "You haven't told anyone at the ministry that you think Eritrea is a waste of resources, have you?"

"If I did, it would only have been an offhand comment in jest. Why do you ask? I'm sensing another one of your famous words of cautionary wisdom."

"I'm just saying, Tesfaye, be careful. These rebellions in Eritrea have made Mengistu a little paranoid. There is no need to give him an excuse to question your loyalty."

"You worry to much, Geteye. Besides, I can't even remember the last time he convened a formal meeting of his military advisers."

"Does that prove your point or mine?"

Tesfaye swished the ice cubes in his glass. "So how are things in Eritrea? I've heard there have been some setbacks." The grumblings had been growing since President Reagan the previous year asked General Secretary Gorbachev to "tear down this wall" in a famous speech given at the Berlin Wall. The Soviets dismissed Reagan's comment as an inflammatory propagandist sound bite, but many at the ministry started to worry that Gorbachev might be more inclined than past Kremlin heavyweights to soften the Soviet's ultra-Communist ideals. There were also signs that the Soviets might consider turning off the spigot of steady military aid to Ethiopia, or at least slow it down.

"I assure you, things are going fine," Geteye remarked confidently. "When we redraw our military positions, it is purely tactical, aimed at stretching their forces."

"That is good to hear. We've been getting a lot of conflicting information at the ministry." Tesfaye sucked down a whisky-laden ice cube and spit it back into his glass. "Geteye, you would tell me if you knew things were not going well, wouldn't you?"

Geteye smiled. "Of course I would. You are still a top official at the Defense Ministry. I can't say there is much I am privy to that you do not hear about as well. You just project a positive attitude—and limit your grumblings to conversations with me and Ayana."

But things were not going well in the north. Tesfaye was being kept in the dark. The situation in Eritrea grew dire over the next two years. When the Ethiopian military redirected forces to Eritrea to combat the threat, the Tigrarian People's Liberation Front took advantage in the Tigray province and began their unstoppable advance toward Addis Ababa. Soon, they would be at the gateway of Tesfaye's home, the uniformed man's machete would slice Negasi's throat, and Tesfaye would be semiconscious in the back seat of a jeep.

Chapter 33

SOFIA JOINED ROSARIO in her backyard for a quiet afternoon basking in the dry sun with two cold glasses of lemonade. Having secured Dr. Garcia's blessing, Sofia would be starting her job at the Navajo crafts store tomorrow. She had been feeling much better in recent days and was not surprised that her most recent blood work showed a remarkable improvement in her T-cell count.

"So what exactly will you be doing at work?" asked Rosario.

"Stocking the shelves, maybe working the cash register, things like that. Down the road, they might let me work on some of the crafts, help create designs."

"That's fantastic, Sofia."

"For both of us. Hopefully I can move out soon, get my own place."

"With Fernando?"

"I guess."

"We should try calling the motel again, see if his mother left word."

"In a little while, I want to enjoy the day."

"Me too," Rosario said, lighting a cigarette.

"I traveled all this way to save my life and here you are intentionally doing things to end yours."

Rosario watched a mild breeze whisk smoke in different directions. "What can I say?"

"I'm not surprised. Everyone in this county takes so much for granted."

"But I smoked in Mexico. So did you!"

"I know, you're right," Sofia admitted. "Still, you must admit, there's a lot that people here take for granted."

"Such as?"

"Red lights for one. Cars actually stop at red lights."

Rosario chuckled. "It took me some time to get used to that."

"Could you imagine what would happen back home if someone waited at a red light, especially if there were no cars coming the other way?"

"Everyone would be honking and yelling, even the police!"

"The police," said Sofia, "that's another thing. Here, if you have an emergency, you call the police and they come to your house, quickly, and they don't expect money."

"You knew before you came here that the police weren't as corrupt as they are in Mexico."

"True," Sofia admitted, "but I didn't realize how different it makes everything feel. Don't you just feel more at peace with everything you do? Walking down the street to the park, driving to the market—I can't even explain it. It's like that feeling of uneasiness that's always in the back of your mind in Mexico, it's just gone."

"I do know what you mean."

"When I watch the news in this country, everyone complains about the smallest little things—the neighbor's tree is dropping fruit on my lawn, the police took eight minutes to respond instead of five minutes. We're lucky if they respond in an hour in Mexico."

"These things are small to you, but a few minutes can mean the difference between life and death."

"You don't think *I* know that?" asked Sofia, her thoughts drifting to her deceased husband.

"I'm sorry, I didn't mean to bring that up."

"No, don't be silly," Sofia quietly responded as she remembered the last time she frantically tried to summon the police in Mexico. "Anyways, you're right. I'm not trying to say it's not a big deal. I'm just saying that it's nice to debate how long it takes the police to show up as opposed to whether the police will show up at all."

Rosario raised her glass. "Here's to sweating the small stuff in the United States."

"*Salud,*" Sofia said, clanking her glass against Rosario's glass.

"*Salud.*"

Sofia didn't know it at the time, but the small stuff would soon be the least of her problems.

Chapter 34

PACING IN HER cell, Lin waited to hear from her great uncle. Manageable hours turned to boring days. Then weeks. Plenty of time to grow anxious. Too much time to contemplate whether the chipped cinderblocks confining her in the Elizabeth detention facility would be the only home she would ever know in the United States. And then there was Shaoqing. *Where is Shaoqing? What of Jiang and Ai?*

The solitude gave Lin time to think about all the other passengers on the ship. She mapped out elaborate narratives for each of them and all the wonderful things they were doing in the United States. She pictured Jiang and Bao racing to the top of the Statue of Liberty. Poor Ming Tso finding a tall, handsome American man and moving to a big mansion with lots of servants. *Ming wouldn't remember that I threw water on her. She wouldn't even remember the horrible trip from China at all.* Then there was Lin. Alone. Staring at all the patterns formed by the nooks in the cinderblocks.

At first, Lin didn't process the immigration officer opening the cell door and motioning for her to follow, or the sight of her great uncle in front of her. The bags under Long's eyes were darker than Lin remembered, but his gentle smile had not changed a bit.

Long reached out to touch Lin's shoulder with his trembling hand. "Look at you," he said, "all grown up, a beautiful young woman."

Lin broke down immediately. She embraced Long, digging her fingers into his back. A minute passed before Long loosened Lin's grip and escorted her away from the Elizabeth Detention Center to a bus stop nearby.

Long gave Lin the window seat on the bus so she could soak in her first glances of the United States as a free woman, uninhibited by the watchful eye of a snakehead. Once the bus entered the highway, Long reached into his coat pocket, pulled out a daisy, and handed it to Lin.

"What's this for?" she asked.

"Happy birthday, Lin," he said, kissing her on the forehead. "I know it was last week, but I guess this will have to do under the circumstances."

"I'd forgotten all about it," she said, stroking the daisy's soft petals. "Uncle, what took you so long to come get me?"

Long sighed. "It's complicated."

"Why?"

"I don't think your mother wants me to go into details."

"You've spoken to my mother? How is she? Does she know I made it?"

"She's doing just fine, Lin. And yes, she knows you are here. Your mother worked very hard to get you out of that prison."

"How did *she* get me out?"

"As I said before, it's complicated."

Lin was annoyed and equally curious. Her mother refused to tell her anything about her father. Now, this ongoing cone of silence was keeping her in the dark about *her* life—circumstances that might directly impact her future. *Enough*, she thought.

"No more secrets, Uncle. Please. I am not a little girl anymore."

"I know. Nobody who makes the journey you just made remains a child."

"Then tell me." Lin placed her palm on the top of Long's hand. "Please."

Long took a deep breath. "Oftentimes, snakeheads lure people to the United States by requesting a very small down payment and promising that the remainder of the money can be paid over time. Then, when the unsuspecting immigrant arrives in the United States, the snakeheads demand payment in full."

"*Ma* doesn't have any more money."

"That's true, but your mother is very resourceful. Have you ever heard of a loan shark?"

"No, but the name sounds scary."

"Loan sharks step in when people have debts they cannot afford to pay. The loan shark pays the snakehead."

"*Ma* borrowed money from a loan shark?"

"Yes." What Long did not tell Lin is that these money lenders had a notorious reputation for using any means necessary to make sure debts were paid on time and that many considered the tactics of the loan sharks even more ruthless than those of the snakeheads.

"And that is what took so much time?" Lin asked. "To get money from the loan shark?"

"That is certainly part of the reason." Long glanced out the window, losing his train of thought.

"Uncle?"

"Oh. What was I saying?"

"You were telling me why it took you so long to come get me."

"Right. Well, a lot of uncertainty surrounds these long trips to the United States. The snakeheads who help people—like you—make the journey expect to make a substantial amount of money each time. Any number of things can go wrong during these trips."

"Like getting arrested."

"Exactly. And when they do, the snakeheads raise the price of the trip."

"Raise the price?" Lin repeated indignantly. "It was their fault we were arrested." She shook her head in disbelief. "All they have done since the start of this trip is humiliate us, let us practically starve, sleep on cardboard . . ."

"I know Lin, I know. You don't have to convince me. It's not fair, but someone had to pay to get you out of the detention center and someone has to pay for an attorney to help you with your court case. Your mother was not able to get enough money from loan sharks to cover all the costs."

Lin's stomach sank as she contemplated a slew of horrible scenarios that could have led to her release. "So how did she raise the rest of the money?"

Long chuckled, which alleviated Lin's anxiety. "It took some negotiation. I was able to help out a little, too. And we were able to negotiate a small payment plan."

"I thought you said all the money had to be paid right away."

"That is typically the case, but your arrest changed that. The snakeheads knew after weeks of threats that your mother and I could not get any more money. They know that they will not be paid in full unless the only additional source of money was out of the detention facility and in the country."

"You mean me—I'm the additional source of money."

"That is why the snakeheads agreed to front the money for your bond. And that is why they hired an attorney for you."

Long paused. He debated whether he should be disclosing all of this information to Lin. Having no children of his own, Long had no means to gauge whether Lin could handle what he was saying to her, and the ramifications the arrangement would have on Lin. Looking at her sitting attentively next to him—*a young woman*—he could tell by the sharpness of her questions, and the way she digested so readily every word he said, that it was only right to explain to her the current situation.

"I will not lie to you," Long continued, "the amount of money you need to pay them back is considerable and it will take some time."

"What if I am not permitted to stay in the country and they deport me? How will they get paid?"

Despite Lin's maturity, there was a limit to the details Long was willing to disclose. The consequences of her being deported were not something he cared to discuss.

"Perhaps we shouldn't dwell on such things now," Long said, pointing out the window. "Look."

The Statue of Liberty jutting out of the Hudson River was eclipsed by the skyline of downtown Manhattan, buildings that appeared so tall and massive to Lin that she could not fathom how they didn't all sink into the ground. The breadth of these buildings from afar did not prepare her for the vertical inflation of the city once her bus exited the Holland Tunnel and headed toward Chinatown. A few minutes later, Lin was seemingly transported back home. Chinese characters were printed on awnings above small shops selling merchandise that poured out onto makeshift tables on the streets. Baskets of soft shell crabs sat outside small fish markets. The smells of a thousand Chinese restaurants mixed with the odors of trash heaps piled on sidewalks.

After following Long down the streets of Chinatown, Lin watched him fiddle with his keys in front of a six-story walk-up. After he opened the door, Lin followed him down a set of steps to a basement apartment. "Here we are," Long said, knocking on the door.

The hinges creaked as the door swung open. As Lin made eye contact with the man on the other side, she smiled in disbelief.

"What are you doing here?" asked Lin.

Shaoqing smiled. "You're surprised to see me?"

Chapter 35

ETHAN AND RYAN grabbed their bags and walked through the terminal of the San Diego International Airport to the car rental window.

"Steak and a beer?" Ryan asked as they tossed their bags in the trunk of a Chrysler Sebring.

"We've got a lot of ground to cover. I'd rather take advantage of the sun while we still have it." They got in the car and opened Ethan's map. "See these two addresses on Montrose," Ethan said, "they're practically next to each other."

"Good a starting place as any."

They drove out of the airport, cut over to route 94, and then headed east toward Montrose. The neighborhood was not what Ethan expected. There were upscale homes with well-maintained stucco exteriors and gardens that featured an array of exotic flowers planted in nurturing beds of mulch. They parked in front of the first house on their list. There were no cars in the driveway and a For Sale sign was staked into the front lawn. The grass wasn't as well maintained as the other houses.

"Looks like nobody's home," Ryan said.

"Only one way to find out."

They walked up the stone pathway and rang the bell. No answer. They waited another minute and rang the bell again.

"I don't see any lights on," Ryan said.

"No one's here," Ethan said. "Let's try the address two houses down."

Shortly after Ethan rang the doorbell of the second house, a heavy-set Hispanic woman opened the door. "Hello," she said with an accent.

"Good afternoon. I'm Agent Shaw and this is Agent Bard. Is this your house?"

"No."

"Do you live here?"

"No. I clean, feed the children."

"Is there anyone else here now?"

"Yes, the Misses."

"Can you get her for us?"

Moments later, Ethan and Ryan were greeted by a slender, young mother dressed in a business suit. "Can I help you?" she said.

"Hello, ma'am. My name is Agent Shaw and this is Agent Bard. Is this your house?"

"Yes."

"We're with a special immigration task force in the Department of Justice," Ethan embellished, as he and Ryan showed her their badges.

"Is Adrianna in some sort of trouble?" she asked softly, looking back in her house to make sure the maid had walked away.

"No, ma'am," Ethan said assuringly. "Have you noticed any of your mail missing? Maybe something you were expecting to get that never came?"

"Not that I recall."

"Have you ever had something appear in your mailbox that you didn't order, any electronics or something like that?"

"Funny you should ask. That actually did happen a few weeks ago."

"Was it a digital camera?" asked Ethan, checking his notes.

The woman crossed her arms and scrunched her brow. "How could you possibly know that?"

Ethan didn't feel like explaining how he spent many months compiling his collection of pushpins. "Do you still have it?" he asked, avoiding her question.

"No. I mailed it back to the return address and told them they had the wrong house."

"Did you ever get charged?" asked Ethan.

"No."

Ethan figured that she hadn't been charged. He suspected that the bills were all being amassed on credit from accounts taken out in the identity theft victims' names. The shipping address was just where the perpetrator would go to pick up the merchandise. "Were you home when it was delivered?"

"I did happen to be home that day. It's unusual that I am."

"And your maid is here during the day when the mail gets delivered?"

"Adrianna's here Monday to Friday, but I typically get the mail after I come home from work."

"Get the mail?"

"From the box," she said, pointing to a big mailbox perched atop a metal pole near the front of the lawn.

"Is Adrianna legal, ma'am?"

She remained silent for a moment, contemplating the implications of her answer. "Honestly, I'm not sure. She pays taxes though. I have a W-4, or a W-2—some form that I give to her."

"Could we see a copy?"

The woman came back a few minutes later and handed the form to Ethan. Ryan took out a notepad and copied down the maid's Social Security number. When he finished, Ethan handed the form back to the woman, along with one of his business cards. "If you think of anything else you would like to share with us, please feel free to call me anytime."

Ethan and Ryan walked back to their car. "So what are you thinking?" asked Ryan.

"That homeowner didn't have a clue. She's not involved."

"She looked nervous to me."

"Yeah, she was nervous because she doesn't want to get in trouble for hiring an illegal. She knew that woman wasn't legal."

"Do you think the maid's involved?"

"I don't know. We have to investigate the Social Security number she put on her W-2." Ethan looked around the neighborhood at the immaculately primmed lawns and the cars he could never afford to buy. "You see what's going on, don't you?" Ryan didn't say anything, waiting for Ethan to continue. "We have merchandise being delivered to a vacant house. Merchandise delivered to a house with its mailbox on the street."

"All places where it would be easier for someone to come and take it."

"I'm telling you Ryan, it's all local."

"What do you mean?"

"Whoever is ordering this stuff knows this area. They know when these houses are vacant, which ones have mailboxes on the street. They know where to send the merchandise. Think about how easy it is. They use someone else's Social Security number, create a fake identity and then send the goods to other people's house, where they go to pick it up. No way to trace it back to them."

"That means there's an illegal responsible for each pushpin cluster on your map."

"Exactly."

"There's no way we can bust them all."

Ethan squinted as he surveyed the neighborhood. "I know," he said. "That's why we have to get to the source."

Chapter 36

TESFAYE WALKED INTO the lobby of the Institute for Sensible Immigration Control on Lexington Avenue. He waited on an outdated sienna-colored ottoman next to the receptionist until Martin was ready to see him.

"Mr. Azene," said the receptionist. "He can see you now. Down the hallway, last door on the left."

Stacks of papers littered the desktop and floor in Martin's corner office. "My apologies for the mess," Martin said, clearing some papers from a chair in the middle of the room. "Please, sit."

Tesfaye gave Martin an overview of his time in Ethiopia when he served as an advisor to Mengistu. Martin listened as patiently as he could, fidgeting with his pen and sneaking glances at his watch. After absorbing Tesfaye's story for several minutes, Martin cut him off.

"You're giving me a bunch of details about your role in the government and the Red Terrorists . . ."

"Terror, the Red Terror campaign."

"Right, the Red Terror campaign. To speed things up, why don't I tell you a little about the asylum process and you can tell me why you think you would be eligible."

"That sounds fine."

"First thing's first, to be eligible for asylum, you have to face persecution. Nobody knows exactly what that term means, but it has to be serious harm. Very serious. I'm talking about a risk of death or fairly serious injury. Being beaten to a bloody pulp will do it, but a few slaps to the face or punches to the stomach will not."

"Like this?" Tesfaye said, holding up his severed index finger.

Martin bit his lip to keep himself from wincing at the sight of Tesfaye's finger. "Probably," he said. "But that's not enough. You also need to establish *why* you were persecuted. There are only five grounds that will get you asylum protection—you absolutely must face persecution on account of one of these five protected grounds. The person harming you must do it *because* of your race, or your ethnicity, or your political beliefs, or your religion, or your social group."

Tesfaye tried to digest Martin's words. "You mean someone has to come up to me and tell me that they are about to smash my head in because I am a Christian?"

"Well, that will do it, but they probably don't need to be so explicit."

"What if I'm going to be tortured by someone because he doesn't like me?"

"No asylum."

"But what if someone tries to rob me and ends up bashing in my skull?"

"Nope, you wouldn't be eligible. Suffering an injury because someone wants your money doesn't fall under one of the five grounds."

"I don't understand. Why does the United States care *why* someone chooses to beat me—as you said—to a bloody pulp? Isn't it enough that my life is in danger? Isn't that why this is such a great country, because you protect people in such situations?"

Martin thought about the best way to explain to Tesfaye why the United States had an asylum process that appeared to play favorites. "Picture a bunch of old men sitting around a table after World War II brainstorming a list of reasons why someone should be eligible for asylum. Their opinions were colored by the war."

"I see."

"Now, it is possible to avoid deportation even if you don't get asylum."

"How is that?"

"Under the Convention Against Torture. You have to show that it is more likely than not that you will be tortured if deported."

"I'm not sure I follow."

"It means you have to show that the chances of you getting tortured are greater than fifty percent."

"I'm *still* not sure I follow. You're saying that if there is a forty percent chance I will be tortured, I will still be sent back?"

"That's the law."

"That's outrageous! I don't understand these laws."

"A lot of shitty things happen to a lot of good people in this world. You can't expect the United States to take *everyone* in." Martin felt his anti-immigration sentiments hardening.

"I suppose not," Tesfaye said, conceding Martin's point.

"Back to your case," Martin said, trying to wrap up the conversation as expeditiously as possible. "I got the overview of your time serving in the government. No harm there, right?" Tesfaye reluctantly shook his head in agreement. "And you mentioned that you were treated badly after your butler was killed."

"He was my driver. Actually, he was my friend."

"And it sounds like you were mistreated for political reasons. So, you may have a case, I'm not positive. Now, don't get me wrong, it's not that I don't want you to get help. I just don't think I'm the man for the job."

Tesfaye lowered his head. "I am embarrassed, but there is one more thing I want to show you."

Martin watched in horror as Tesfaye lifted up his shirt.

"Sweet Jesus! How does something like that happen?"

TESFAYE'S JAW ACHED from the force of the rebel's AK-47 smashing against his face. His neck was gradually swelling. Shooting pains circulated through his body each time the jeep traversed over a rock or sank into a ditch. The vibrations coming from the jeep's worn skeleton drowned out a conversation between the rebels, who were gloating about how easy it had been to take control of the airport and finally topple Mengistu's regime.

"Hey," one of the rebels said to Tesfaye. "Hey!" he repeated, tapping Tesfaye on the arm. "Can you hear me in there? Shut up already." Tesfaye was unaware that he was repeating Negasi's name.

The vibrations dulled and eventually disappeared when the jeep came to an abrupt stop. Tesfaye was again airborne out of the backseat. He winced when two of the rebels each wrapped one of his arms around their shoulders. There were whispers and grumblings, then the sound of metal clanking. With a push from the rebels carrying him, Tesfaye's body plunked to the floor of the cell, his face grating along the grimy concrete beneath him. He prayed for sleep. He prayed he would awaken to discover this was all a bad dream. But surrealism plagued reality and Tesfaye knew his eyes were being truthful.

A slow, painful transition back to full consciousness swallowed the next two days. Like a fidgety schoolchild eyeing the classroom clock, each second bore its own identity. There was little time to recoup. The man in the army uniform with the eye patch who callously ended Negasi's life stood cross-armed in front of Tesfaye's cell. He motioned to a guard who walked over to the rows of evenly spaced metal bars confining Tesfaye, and unlocked the door.

"Follow me," said the man in the uniform. Accompanied by two guards, Tesfaye followed the man past several other cells to a room at the end of the hallway that contained a rickety table and two chairs. "Sit," he ordered. It did not escape Tesfaye's notice that the corner of the table appeared bloodstained.

The man in the uniform lit a cigarette. "I must admit, I found it rather amusing that you asked me for my name. That you, as a minion in Mengistu's poor excuse for a government, would want to know the identity of the enemy after you spent so many years killing us with no regard for who we are. I suppose it's always a little different when you're on the *receiving* end, no?"

"Sir, I . . ."

The man inched his chair closer to the table and pointed his cigarette at Tesfaye. "Before you say another word, I want you to understand something. You cannot ask me for mercy, you cannot beg me to appeal to my conscience. I don't care if you have a family who will miss you dearly and I spit on any God you may invoke for compassion. My soul is blacker than my skin *comrade*. Geteye made sure of that."

Tesfaye swallowed, forgetting what he was about to say. The uniformed man dragged out an uncomfortable silence before he continued. "I have waited a long time, Tesfaye, a long time to exact my revenge. You hold the missing piece. So I ask you again, where is Geteye Tge?"

"Sir, please, I don't know."

"Very well," the man said, rising to his feet. "I will only ask you one time." He stormed out of the room and gave an order to the guards.

The blow to Tesfaye's eye knocked him off his chair. A guard grabbed his arm and pinned it to the tabletop. Two more guards held Tesfaye's body. The fourth guard pulled out a machete and positioned it a yard above Tesfaye's hand. "Stick out one of your fingers," he ordered.

"What?"

"You can lose a finger or your whole hand, it makes no difference to me."

The pros and cons associated with the potential loss of each finger raced through his mind. Tesfaye quickly discarded the idea of voluntarily giving up his thumb. For a moment, his pinky seemed to be the most logical choice. However, as he stared up at the guard wielding the machete, Tesfaye thought twice about trusting this man to chop off his smallest finger without inadvertently slicing through his hand. *The ring finger*, Tesfaye reasoned. But he found himself unable to extend it out by itself. That left his middle finger and index finger.

One of the guards grabbed Tesfaye by the jaw. "Stick out a finger!" shouted the guard, squeezing the pressure points below Tesfaye's ears. Without further contemplation, Tesfaye stuck out his index finger, immediately regretting his choice.

"Please, please don't!" Tesfaye begged, his heart racing so fast that he thought he would pass out from the anticipatory anxiety. He wanted to substitute his middle finger for his index finger, but it was too late. Instinctually, he tried to pull his arm away as the guard lifted the machete high above his head—a maneuver that ended up saving part of his finger. A split second later, the blade came hurling down, almost directly at the first knuckle a centimeter below Tesfaye's nail, slicing through his finger like butter.

The next events seemed to happen in slow motion. Blood spewed out the top of his finger, running down his hand onto the tabletop. The machete-wielding guard smirked as he cleaned the edge of his knife with a piece of cloth. Tesfaye looked back down at the mangled stump of tissue and bone that resembled the side of a slab of meat one could pick up in a butchery, a circumference the same bright red as an artificial cherry, surrounding a miniscule white joint that no longer served any purpose. The other guards laughed as Tesfaye screamed.

Soon, he was back in his cell, his adrenaline overworked as his body went into shock. A package of gauze was thrown on his lap. "I suggest wrapping that finger if you want to stop the bleeding," said one of the guards.

The man in the uniform let Tesfaye lie dormant in his cell for two more days before bringing him back to the room at the end of the hall. Sitting across the table, he swiped a match and lit another cigarette. Tesfaye was surprised the man wore his gloves when performing tasks that required such dexterity. "Are you going to tell me what I want to know?" he asked.

"I want nothing more than to cooperate with you, sir, I . . ."

The uniformed man abruptly slammed his matches on the table, stood to his feet, and headed for the door. "If you haven't died from infection, we'll talk in a week."

Infection? "Wait. You didn't even give me a chance to respond." Tesfaye felt the urine running down his leg. "You didn't let me answer the question!" he shouted as loud as his nerves would let him.

But it was too late.

One of the guards placed a hood over Tesfaye's head after removing his shirt. The ropes securing his hands to the back of the chair chafed his wrists. The liquid drizzled on his chest was cold. He could barely breathe in the heavy hood, but the smell of gasoline filled the air. "Oh God," Tesfaye whimpered when he heard the distinct sound of a matchstick set ablaze. The smell of smoke filled his nostrils a moment before his brain registered that flames were now consuming his chest. But when the flames did register, Tesfaye knew what would be coming next. It was an all-consuming wave of pain like none he'd ever felt before. Accidently brushing up against the stove, multiplied a thousandfold. He kicked the table in front of him then jumped in the air and fell to the ground, unable to do anything else with his hands tied behind his back. The guards eventually used a blanket already bunched in the corner of the room to put out the flames.

Tesfaye was surprised someone came to his cell to tersely treat and bandage his wounds, even if the medical supplies used were rudimentary at best. The pain emanating from his chest and abdomen was overshadowed by the difficult time he had keeping his wounds clean. Tesfaye knew his only chance to avoid infection was to make sure his chest came nowhere near the dirty floor. So he lay in his cell, on his back, for days.

True to his word, the man in the uniform returned one week later. Tesfaye again found himself in the room at the end of the hallway, sitting on that fear-inducing chair. The man in the uniform stared at him.

"You are frightened, Tesfaye. You are a strong man, but I can see the fear in your eyes." He pushed out his chair and paced around the room. "Before I ask you again—ask you that question I know you are dreading—I am going to tell you a little story."

An intense burst of fear gripped Tesfaye momentarily when he heard the sound of the matchstick ignite as the uniformed man lit his usual cigarette. "My family lived near the town of Samre. You know where that is?"

"In the north, in Tigray."

"Correct. In the Tigray province where the crops failed in 1983. Where the crops again failed in 1984. I suppose my family was luckier than most. Hungry, but nobody starved. When the rains came the next summer, things actually seemed to be getting better. They should have gotten better, Tesfaye, but they did *not*. Instead, most of my family was ripped from their homeland by the Derg and forced to move to Illubabor. They shot my cousin when he refused to go. My father got sick in the middle of the long trip south and died. Do you know what the Derg did when he died?"

"No," Tesfaye said, trying to sound sympathetic.

"*Nothing,*" said the uniformed man, grading his teeth. "They left him on the side of the road to be picked at by hyenas like a discarded piece of meat. And when my family finally arrived at their little piece of paradise, they were ordered to farm corn on fields many kilometers away from the disease-infested shantytown where the Derg forced them to return each night. Do you know who ordered this, Tesfaye? Do you know who ordered that my Tigray brothers and sisters be forced to leave their homes?"

It occurred to Tesfaye that this man would not bother telling him this story if he knew where the original idea came from. "Mengistu, sir."

"It was Mengistu's idea, but do you know who was in charge of orchestrating the migration?"

Tesfaye stared perplexed at the uniformed man. "Geteye?"

"That's right. It was Geteye who decided to mercilessly rip these Tigray families apart. It was Geteye who made sure nobody could leave the shantytowns. It was Geteye who permitted my father to be left on the side of the road."

"No," Tesfaye pleaded. He had known Geteye his whole life. Geteye Tge was an honorable man who had watched over him and gotten him out of trouble since their years at Holetta Military Academy. How could Geteye have been the person responsible for implementing the migration of the Tigray without Tesfaye knowing? "That's impossible," Tesfaye exclaimed.

"Impossible? Was he not a senior military advisor? Did he not have Mengistu's ear? Who then, if you have all the answers, was in charge?"

Tesfaye had no idea and he then realized for the first time just how much he had been kept in the dark after the famine.

"I will assume by your silence that you don't know the answer. You see, we cannot get to Mengistu now because he knew his efforts to fight the resistance were futile. Did you know he fled the country?"

"Fled?"

"You had no idea, did you?" asked the uniformed man as he let out a boisterous laugh. "He is now comfortably kicking back his feet in his own private residence in Zimbabwe, the esteemed guest of President Robert Mugabe. But Geteye is not with him."

"Were you forced to go to Illubabor with your family?" Tesfaye asked, taking advantage of an apparent lull in the uniformed man's desire to dole out punishment every time Tesfaye opened his mouth.

"You are jumping ahead. Perhaps you think the death or near death of most of my family would be enough to motivate me to find the man responsible. But there is more. Much more."

Tesfaye fought the urge to scratch the bandages covering his burns as the uniformed man proceeded with his story.

"I was not near the Samre region with my family when they were forced to march south," the uniformed man said. "I was fighting with the Tigrarian People's Liberation Front. When I returned home, I found everyone gone, except for my son, who told me what happened, and how he managed to hide when the Derg rounded up the villagers."

Inhaling one last puff, the man in the uniform dropped his cigarette butt on the floor and put it out with his foot. "My son was enraged and he begged to come fight with me. But I didn't let him. I didn't want freeloaders to steal *my* land. I don't care what Mengistu thought when he nationalized all the land, that was always *my* land."

Tesfaye's concerns about the government's land policies came to life before his eyes.

"The work proved too daunting for my son. He couldn't manage the land and care for all the animals. Two years later, I finally agreed to let him come join the rebellion. We took the animals to the market in Hausien to sell them. We were negotiating a sale when we heard the first helicopters approaching. Then I saw the Soviet MiGs flying low. The bombing continued for hours. Helicopters gunned down anyone who attempted to run out of the town for safety. I assume you've heard of white phosphorous?"

Tesfaye nodded.

"Then you must know what happens when a bomb laced with white phosphorous explodes."

"Smoke. It creates smoke."

The man in the uniform leaned in close to Tesfaye. "Then you must know what happens when the phosphorous comes in contact with flesh."

Tesfaye knew very well. Instructors at the military academy taught him about the use of white phosphorous as a tool that provided cover by creating a smokescreen. The smoke itself was poisonous if inhaled, but the properties of white phosphorous also made it highly flammable when exposed to oxygen. Water was powerless to put out the flames.

Fiddling with the buttons on his right cuff, the uniformed man slowly rolled up his sleeve and removed his glove, revealing a thin, reddened layer of scarred skin. "You know where this story is going, don't you?"

It took all of Tesfaye's willpower to avoid recoiling at the site of the uniformed man's hand and forearm. "I don't."

"You know who decided to drop phosphorus-laced bombs on a peaceful marketplace for six hours?"

"Mengi—"

"Geteye!" the man shouted. "If it weren't for Geteye, I would not be sitting in this room with you right now. That means Geteye is responsible for burning *our* flesh." Tesfaye looked down at his chest. "Geteye is responsible for the death of my son and thousands of other innocent people who died that day in Hausien."

The uniformed man rolled down his sleeve and put his glove back on. "I am not going to try to convince you again how I know that Geteye planned the bombing of the Hausien marketplace. Either you were ignorant of what was going on under your nose or you are trying to play dumb with me. But you now know the seriousness of my convictions and that I will not stop until you give me the information I want, even if I have to rip off every single one of your fingernails or throw you into a pot of boiling oil."

"Kenya," Tesfaye said. "He's in Kenya."

"Before I took you into custody, you told me you were driving to Kenya for business. You actually were on your way to Kenya, weren't you?" he chuckled. "You were on your way to meet Geteye!" When Tesfaye didn't answer, the uniformed man began to scowl. "*Where* in Kenya?" he asked forcefully.

"I am going to tell you," Tesfaye said sternly, "but you must give me your word about something."

"I must give you my word? I don't think you are in any position to negotiate."

"What's your name, brother?"

The man looked strangely at Tesfaye, wondering if he remembered what happened the last time he asked the same question. Admiring Tesfaye's brazen courage, he abdicated. "Demissie. My name is Demissie."

"Demissie, your soul may have been blackened, but it is not black. I can see when you talk about your family and others who have died that you still feel sadness and compassion; it is not just anger. I swear I didn't know about the things you have just told me, but I admit Geteye has always been a close friend—so close that I have entrusted him with the lives of my wife and my children. Please, as you grieve for all those innocent people at Hausien, I beg you, my family is innocent too."

"I am only interested in Geteye. Nothing more."

"So I have your word?"

"I am only interested in Geteye," he repeated. "Innocent people around him are of no concern to me. The next words to come out of your mouth better be the information I want."

"Thika. The last thing I heard was that he was going to Thika. That is all I know."

Tesfaye hoped his answer was specific enough for Demissie, especially since he truly did not know any more details. Although the prospect of endless torture was enough to break even the strongest of wills, Tesfaye still felt like Judas.

"If you are lying to me, I will hack off your arms."

"I am telling you what I know, I swear."

SITTING IN HIS office at the Institute for Sensible Immigration Control and listening to Tesfaye's story, Martin was flabbergasted. "Why didn't you mention all this right away? I mean, *this* is your case. Your time serving in the government is important background information, but this . . ." Martin rubbed his hand over his forehead and pinched the bridge of his nose. His curiosity immediately turned to Tesfaye's family and Geteye. "Did this guy . . ."

"Demissie."

"Demissie, did he ever find Geteye?"

"No."

"When did he release you from prison?"

"He didn't."

"He didn't?"

"No."

"Then how did you get out of Ethiopia?"

Chapter 37

LIN WEPT AS she embraced Shaoqing in the doorway of her great uncle's apartment. After a minute, she felt him delicately try to loosen her arms, which were wrapped around his back.

"It's okay, Lin," Shaoqing said assuredly.

"I thought I would never see you again."

"*Never* see me again? We're not in China anymore. People don't just disappear."

Lin smiled. "The officer at the prison said you weren't there anymore. I didn't know what to think."

Basking in his ability to refrain from spoiling the surprise, Long stood contently next to Lin for a moment before placing his arm on her shoulder. "Why don't we sit down and have some tea?"

In the kitchen nook of Long's scanty, one-bedroom apartment, Lin watched a man she had never seen before clumsily pour cups of tea, spilling the hot liquid all over the counter as his shaking hands labored to control the heavy teapot. Long grabbed a cup from this man and handed it to Lin.

The four sat in a circle, legs crossed, in the middle of the floor. The tea trickling down Lin's throat brought back memories of the morning she fled China and the tea *ma* forced her to scarf down. She quickly re-emerged from her daydream and stared at Shaoqing in disbelief. "What are you doing here? I mean, how did you get to my uncle's apartment?"

Shaoqing looked surprised. "You don't remember?" He repeated the digits of Long's phone number that Lin made him say over and over again on the bus ride to the Elizabeth Detention Center. That day seemed surprisingly distant to Lin, even though it had only been a few weeks ago.

"But what happened to you?"

Shaoqing's face turned glum and he glanced over at Long.

"We discussed the snakeheads' methods on the bus ride over here," Long said to Shaoqing.

"Tell me, Shaoqing. What happened?"

Shaoqing took a deep breath. "One of the officers asked me questions for a while and then said that I would have to go before a judge who would decide if I could stay in the country. I was put into a jail cell for a short period of time. Then another officer came to my cell and told me that it was time to go, that my cousin had paid my bail and was waiting to take me."

"I didn't think you knew anyone here," Lin said.

"I don't. It was one of the snakeheads. He drove me into this city and brought me to some apartment. I later found out I was in a place called Brooklyn. There were a bunch of snakeheads there, three or four I think. They were very nice to me at first. They offered me food and water, and let me take a bath. Then they started demanding money. I didn't know what to say. Obviously I had no money. For a while, they yelled at me, calling me a deadbeat and telling me I should be ashamed for failing to live up to my obligations. I tried to reason with them. I told them about the arrangement I had worked out with the snakeheads in China and how I was told that I could repay my debt over time in the United States. Initially, I think they found my responses amusing, but they must have been getting frustrated with me because all of them started to take turns beating me."

Shaoqing paused and took a sip of tea. "After they beat me for a while, they dragged me down a staircase and locked me in a room with others from the ship."

"Was Jiang there?" Lin prodded. "Did you see Ai? The Tingjiang apes?"

"Ai was there."

"What about Jiang?"

"As I soon found out, the only people in the room were those who had not paid the snakeheads in full. Jiang's parents paid for his journey before he left China. The Tingjiang apes bought their freedom on the ship. We didn't know it at the time, but they agreed to be enforcers in exchange for the snakeheads forgiving some of their remaining debt."

"I thought Dong agreed to do it for fun."

"I guess he was a little smarter than we thought," Shaoqing joked.

"So how did you escape?"

Shaoqing started biting his lip and his gaze veered down to the hook on the tip of his nose. "I didn't. We were locked in that room at all times except when we had to use the bathroom. The snakeheads would come in and yell and beat us for not paying our debts. They asked everyone to call anyone they could think of in China—parents, other family, friends—who could fork over money. They beat people when they were on the phone so that the friends and family on the other end would know they meant business. It worked. Slowly, they began letting people go after they received the balance of the travel fees. Even Ai managed to get in touch with several relatives who agreed to loan her money. After a week or so, there were about ten of us left, everyone who hadn't yet managed to pay, and the snakeheads were getting more and more pissed off at us."

"What happened to Ai?" Lin interjected.

"I haven't seen her since the snakeheads let her go and I have no idea how to get in touch with her. It was all so chaotic. I'm grateful that Ai was able to get out when she did." His voice began to quiver. "If she was still there for what happened next, I would never be able to forgive myself."

Chapter 38

MARTIN RUBBED THE outer corners of his eyes in small, concentric circles, trying to soak in all the information Tesfaye was telling him. "What I'm hearing you say is that you escaped from prison?"

"Sort of, well, not exactly," Tesfaye said.

"And then managed to walk out of Ethiopia?"

"I was in the back of a truck."

"So you *sort of* broke out of prison and drove out of Ethiopia?"

Tesfaye's eyes wandered up to the ceiling. He leaned back and put his hands behind his head. "In a strange dose of irony, the last twenty years of my life had come full circle."

A STIFF COCKTAIL of boredom, grief, pain, and anxiety greeted Tesfaye each morning in the confines of his four by eight cell. Boredom from the endless days waiting in isolation for one of the two meals brought to him by the guards. Grief spawned by Negasi's pointless death and the Ethiopians who suffered because of his actions as a military advisor. Pain from his chest, finger . . . everywhere. And anxiety. *Did I put my family in danger?* The unquenchable apprehension of not knowing whether his family was safe—the worst feeling of all. It was true that his family and Geteye were originally going to Thika, but Tesfaye prayed they would be long gone by the time any rebels came looking for Geteye.

The guards occasionally dragged Tesfaye to the interrogation room to ask him questions about his time in the Mengistu regime. There were slaps across the face and occasional beatings, but nothing even remotely approaching the torment that Demissie put him through so many months ago. *The guards are probably just as bored as I am*, Tesfaye imagined. To his relief, he had not seen Demissie for some time, although part of him worried that Demissie's absence was a sign that he accomplished his mission and found Geteye.

The summer wet season lived up to its name, adding an unwelcomed layer of sludge to his cell floor. When summer passed and the insufferable heat finally broke, a younger, more energetic pack of guards took over. Tesfaye previously embraced the sight of a fading sun give way to darkness and sleep. Now, he dreaded the nighttime, for that was when the guards would begin drinking. With their unruly ways came more frequent beatings.

Tesfaye prayed for a painless night as he listened to the guards cracking jokes. Their raucous banter subsided after several hours. It was two-thirty in the morning and only one guard remained. Tesfaye finally started to drift to sleep, but a muted conversation grabbed his attention. Sitting up in the nearly pitch-black jail cell, he used the sound of the footsteps he heard to pinpoint the location of the people engaging in this atypically late conversation. The footsteps stopped right in front of his cell.

"Is this him?" said one of the voices.

"Yes, sir."

"Open it."

"The interrogation room, sir?"

"Yes."

With a flashlight in hand, the guard led Tesfaye to the interrogation room. Tesfaye could have made it on his own with his eyes closed; he knew the route well. Again planted in the chair, he watched the shadowy figure emerge in the doorway, the dim light of the interrogation room illuminating the man's military attire.

The man shut the door behind him, but continued to stand in the dark corner of the room. "This is quite a situation you've gotten yourself into," said the man.

"I suppose."

"You don't look very good."

"Is that supposed to be a joke?" Tesfaye quipped impatiently. "I have no more information to give, so if you're going to beat me, please spare me all these dramatics and just get on with it."

"Beat you?" the man said as he let out a baritone laugh, sounding offended by Tesfaye's insinuation. "You mistake my intentions. I want to help you, *Professor*."

"What did you say?" Tesfaye squinted at the shadowy corner of the room. "Who are you?"

The man took a few steps into the light and sat in the chair across from Tesfaye. His face had aged considerably since the last time Tesfaye saw him. If it weren't for his distinct auburn curls, Tesfaye probably would not have recognized Beniam. Yet here he was. One of the students he met with every Monday afternoon for a year and a half. The boy who Tesfaye and Ayana believed was another statistic in Mengistu's Red Terror campaign nearly fifteen years ago.

"I thought you were dead," Tesfaye said.

"I had to leave Addis Ababa."

Tesfaye shook his head. "I should have."

"Then why didn't you?" asked Beniam.

"I didn't have a choice."

"We all have choices, Professor, you taught me that."

"Your hair is still auburn."

"I stopped dying it for many years. Some think I'm going through a midlife crisis. But I'm not. This is me."

"As long as you feel comfortable in your own skin."

"Just as you told me, Professor, it's all about confidence."

It was strange to hear someone call him Professor. The title brought back memories of a much happier time. A long forgotten time. "Beniam, what are you doing here?"

"I already told you, Tesfaye, I am here to help you, to get you out of Ethiopia."

"You are going to take me out of this room and just send me on my way then?"

"It is much more practical for me to smuggle you out. Less of a headache for you too. Transportation has already been arranged. We should go."

"Transport me where? I have no money, no passport. I have nothing. I can barely stand on my own feet anymore."

Beniam smiled. "Don't worry about those things. I have taken care of everything. And when you get to Nairobi, you will talk to this man." Beniam handed Tesfaye a piece of paper. "He will make sure you are taken care of. Now please, we should go."

Hobbling behind, Tesfaye followed Beniam down the hallway, past his old cell. "What about the guard?" asked Tesfaye.

"I told you, you don't need to worry about anything."

The guard stood tall and saluted Beniam as he and Tesfaye walked out of the jailhouse.

The sensation of cruising in the passenger seat of Beniam's Jaguar was overwhelming, and slightly nauseating. The car ripped through the war torn streets of Addis Ababa as Tesfaye watched Beniam flawlessly synchronize the gearshift with the clutch.

"Why are you doing this?" asked Tesfaye after a few minutes of silence.

"When I was a young boy, Professor, I was average in everything I did until I came to the university."

"I think you're being a little modest. You had a way about you, Beniam. A charisma. I remember all the other students were drawn to you. You were engaged in the classroom like few I'd ever seen."

"I was not always like that, I assure you. It was you who inspired me."

"Inspired you?"

The Jaguar slowed to a stop in front of a light brown cargo transportation truck. Beniam shut the lights. "During the Red Terror, on a day of no particular importance, I arrived early to some English class— Advanced English Language if I'm remembering correctly. In the corner of the classroom I saw a girl crying. When I asked her what was wrong, she told me that her mother had found her brother's body in the street. A sad occurrence, yes, but nothing out of the ordinary for that period of time in Addis Ababa. I had never heard this girl talk before. I had barely even noticed her. But when I looked into her eyes, Professor, I saw the sorrows of an entire country, and I was overcome by sadness. My sadness turned to anger. And right then, it hit me, everything you had taught me about seizing the moment, pursuing your goals with a passion, formulating a clear strategy, outthinking your opponent. It was a moment of clarity like none I'd ever had. So I left school, me and Kaleb, Hakim, the entire group that used to meet with you every week and steal chunks of your honey bread."

"You left for where?"

"For Tigray. We went to Tigray to fight, to take back our country."

"You joined the Tigrarian People's Liberation Front?"

"No, Professor. We started it."

"You started the TPLF? I don't believe it."

"They don't call me Beniam anymore. Nobody has for a long time. I want you to know, Tesfaye, that I did not sanction what happened to you when you were first captured. It wasn't until recently that I discovered your whereabouts." Beniam stuck out his hand until Tesfaye reciprocated. "God-speed, Professor. I believe we are even now."

"SO LET ME get this straight," Martin said. "You inspired the man, who started the rebel movement, that overthrew the government, that you belonged to?"

"Do you have any idea how often I have thought about the chain of events that led a simple university professor to have to flee his country entirely? For years in Kenya, time was all I had. I don't have the stomach to rehash the irony again."

"I understand." Martin played with his pen as the two sat in silence. He was apprehensive to ask any more questions, feeling uncomfortable prying so deeply into another man's past unless he had the intention to help him. Right then, he made the decision.

"Tesfaye, I just want you to know that I have decided to take your case. I am going to represent you."

"You will?" Tesfaye asked happily. He nodded his head and smiled. "That is great news. Truly, Mr. Holbrook, you don't know how grateful I am."

"I hate to say you sold me, but your story is—well, it's quite compelling. You mentioned that—you'll have to excuse me, I'm not good with names—the guy who murdered Negasi?"

"Demissie."

"Right, Demissie. You said that he never found Geteye and your family."

It had been nearly seven years since the last time Tesfaye cried. Locking his jaw and breathing hard, he tried to stop it. But right there, in front of Martin, Tesfaye lost it. He knew he would have to tell Martin what happened in Kenya, and he wasn't sure he would be able to utter the words.

Chapter 39

THE CARPET HAD compressed down in the spots where Sofia paced back and forth for the past hour. She felt physically sickened by her conversation with her sister Miranda. The thought of Guillermo talking to her children was too disturbing.

If anyone could stand up to Guillermo the drug pusher, Sofia knew it was her sister. But the timeline of events was troubling. Guillermo had waited all this time for Sofia to be out of the picture before approaching the kids. *That had to be what happened*, she reasoned. It was too coincidental that Guillermo approached them for the first time a few weeks after she left Mexico. If Guillermo purposefully waited, then he must have something up his sleeve. *What the hell does he want?*

Sofia felt guilty. She yelled at her sister for a good ten minutes, beside herself that Miranda would wait so long before telling her that Guillermo had accosted Eva and tried to recruit Manuel. The anger was misplaced and Sofia knew it. Her sister was looking out for her, waiting until her health improved before sharing what had happened. "Besides," Miranda had reminded her, "there's nothing you can do anyway from the United States to help them."

It was all starting to make more sense to Sofia. Manuel had been distant on the phone with her, and Eva mentioned that Manuel had been acting out more recently. It must be hard enough for him on the farm without his parents, but his little chat with Guillermo apparently put him on edge.

Miranda was wrong about one thing. Even though Sofia now lived in the United States, she was not entirely powerless to help her children. Like a bear protecting her cubs, Sofia's mind focused with laser-like precision on what she would have to do. Now that her health had improved, she would dedicate all her energies to getting her children into the United States as fast as possible.

Chapter 40

THE ONLY TIME Lin had ever seen Shaoqing display any emotion was when he brandished a gun and scolded Dong on the ship. She had never seen him express anything remotely resembling this overt sadness that she was now witnessing. She reached out for Shaoqing's hand as he stared aimlessly at the dusty floorboards. "It's over, Shaoqing," she said comfortingly, wondering why he was so apprehensive to speak about the time when he was held in Brooklyn by the snakeheads. "You can tell me."

Shaoqing flexed his jawbone. "The snakeheads considered the remaining passengers to be the biggest deadbeats of all—I guess they were right. So they hardly fed us. And the beatings got worse. No more bare hands. They started using whips and iron poles." Shaoqing rolled up his sleeve to show Lin the deep purple bruises on his forearm. "Then . . ." Shaoqing closed his eyes. "Then they made *me* beat the others."

Lin was taken back. "What?" she asked in disbelief.

"They took one of the Changle City boys, stood him up against the wall, and removed his shirt. I was directed to stand and one of the snakeheads forced me to hold the whip. When he ordered me to use it, I refused and then they beat me. I kept refusing and the snakehead kept beating me until I couldn't take it anymore. So I did it. I whipped him as lightly as I could, but the snakehead wasn't satisfied. He said I had to keep whipping him until red gashes appeared on his back. When the snakehead left, everyone was cursing at me. I thought they were going to attack me. But over the next few days, they came to understand that I was doing everything I could to help them. That I would use the least amount of force necessary to satisfy the snakeheads."

Shaoqing looked straight into Lin's eyes, as if he was seeking approval. "You don't understand, Lin. If I refused, the snakeheads would have beaten everyone even harder. Or forced someone else to do it." Lin's look of understanding comforted Shaoqing. "I had to beat everyone, even the girls."

Lin couldn't blame Shaoqing for his actions, but a part of his story still bothered her. "Why you?" she asked. "Of all the people who were left, why did they make you beat the others?"

"Because I refused to make any phone calls."

Lin shrugged. "Why?"

"The remaining people were being held because their families were having a hard time getting money. But they were trying to get money. I refused to make any phone calls."

"Even if your family has no money, why not at least try to contact them?" Lin asked.

"Because my family doesn't know I'm in the United States." Shaoqing had always lived with his uncle, who begrudgingly took him in after his mother died during childbirth. His uncle regularly told him that his mother had brought shame on the family by conceiving out of wedlock. Shaoqing's father never had any interest in raising him. Shortly after his mother became pregnant, his father abandoned her and moved north to Hubei to feed an opiate addiction.

Lin was perplexed. "You didn't even tell your family you were leaving?"

Shaoqing pictured the smug look on his uncle's face after his uncle swiped the gun from his hand that night in the study of the mansion after calling him a coward. But the incident that *required* Shaoqing to flee China was not set in motion until the next morning.

ICING THE BRUISES caused by his uncle's beating the night before, Shaoqing sat quietly in the kitchen of his uncle's mansion, slurping down soybean milk soup. By the time he finished, he had come to a decision. His uncle's factories would have to be destroyed.

Shaoqing's uncle had built a conglomerate in the Guangdong Province of China. He produced numerous products sold throughout the world, from home insulation and knock-off furniture products, to canned goods and hood ornaments.

With an almost inhuman work ethic and a gift for pouncing on a good business opportunity, Shaoqing's uncle had become one of the most feared businessmen in China. It was a running joke that he had secured the loyalty of more government officials through bribes than the ruling party itself. Greasing government officials allowed Shaoqing's uncle to cut corners and vastly grow his profits. It was this unrelenting drive for profit that led Shaoqing to his decision.

Shaoqing's uncle had insisted that he spend at least one day a week in the factories, learning how the businesses work. For a brief moment, it had occurred to Shaoqing that his uncle might be training him as an "heir apparent"—it was a very brief moment. More likely, Shaoqing thought, his uncle wanted him to bask in the glory of a lifetime of accomplishments as a means of making Shaoqing more appreciative and respectful. The result, however, was certainly not greater respect for his uncle. Sulfur dioxide in the drywall, improperly wired lamps, and lead on toy products were among the first "cost-cutting" measures Shaoqing learned about. And many more followed.

The final straw for Shaoqing was a handwritten letter he found on his uncle's desk from the head of the company's research laboratory. The letter concerned a chemical called melamine, which was capable of artificially boosting the measured protein levels in any food or drink it was added to. Among the products the research department thought might benefit from melamine additives were canned soup, dog food, and even baby formula. The "hiccup," as the letter described it, was that melamine was poisonous. Among its potential negative effects was kidney failure, which seemed a rather large price to pay for a cup of soup, Shaoqing thought.

Shaoqing confronted his uncle about the letter. Snatching it from his hands, his uncle put on his reading glasses and stared expressionless at the piece of paper.

"Do you think I would just put this chemical into my products?" his uncle asked.

A wave of relief washed over Shaoqing, but only for a moment as his uncle continued.

"The cost savings could be astronomical, but we have to do more tests. Will it cause death or merely illness? Can it be traced back to our company? How long does the chemical composition of melamine last in the bloodstream? These are all important questions, and it will take time to get all the answers."

Shaoqing felt sick. His uncle was willing to cause the injury or death of countless numbers of people if he could be assured he would get away with it.

There was little time to sleep over the course of the next few weeks. A lot of planning had to be done. Meticulous planning. Shaoqing would need an exit strategy, a means of escaping China. Getting in touch with a snakehead was the easy part. Paying the snakehead was more complicated. Shaoqing carefully surveyed his uncle's mansion, noting items of value that he could sell to raise the necessary funds. While almost everything in his uncle's mansion was valuable, only certain items could be sold off without his uncle becoming wise to the plan—sterling silver serveware in the kitchen that his uncle rarely used, a diamond studded watch he had not seen his uncle wear in years, and a gold cuff link his uncle thought to be lost that was wedged into the corner of a sock drawer.

Sabotaging the factories would be easier than Shaoqing initially suspected. He spent weeks gathering information on security at the factories. Basically nonexistent. The access he could obtain as the nephew of the owner was all he needed. *Perhaps my uncle thinks his reputation for ruthlessness is enough to stave off thieves*, Shaoqing thought. Some basic research on combustible chemical agents proved sufficient to carry out the plot.

With less than three days before Shaoqing planned to set his plan in motion, another problem occurred to him. Factories can be rebuilt, production lines restarted. In retrospect, the problem was fairly obvious. If anything, Shaoqing thought, the financial hit his uncle would take would only make him more inclined to favor any measure that would cut costs and increase profits.

Recognizing that his plan would only serve as a means of delay, Shaoqing took out a pen and paper. He wrote a letter. Then, he wrote the same letter again. In all, Shaoqing drafted twenty-two copies of an anonymous letter documenting his uncle's shady business dealings and the potential repercussions of adding melamine to food products. The letter, Shaoqing thought, coupled with the destruction of one of the main factories, should be sufficient to garner media attention.

When the day arrived, Shaoqing mailed a copy of the letter to twenty-two different media outlets across the country. As he sped away from one of the factories, he glanced at his rearview mirror to witness a fireball blast out the windows of the blazing structure that had brought his uncle so much pride. He drove to a rendezvous point previously fixed by the snake-heads. Sitting in the back of a van next to a young woman who had just introduced herself as Ai, Shaoqing had never felt so at peace in his life.

SHAOQING HAD NO idea whether his uncle knew he fled China. But he certainly had no intention of calling him at the behest of the snake-heads. Whatever fate the snakeheads had in store for him would pale in comparison to the retribution his uncle would inflict on him if given the chance.

Lin stared intently at Shaoqing, waiting eagerly for him to explain why he hadn't told his family about his voyage to the United States. But Shaoqing was at a loss for words. "I don't have much family in China," he said.

"That doesn't answer the question, Shaoqing," Lin persisted.

Shaoqing knew she was right. "Let's just say certain family members would be much happier knowing that I'm no longer in the country."

Not feeling satisfied by his answer, but sensing Shaoqing's intentional elusiveness, Lin stopped prodding. Looking up, she quickly blushed, realizing that she had not introduced herself to a stranger who had been listening to her talk with Shaoqing for a good half an hour.

"Don't be upset," the man said. "Your voyage to this country gives you a pass on the usual good manners I know you typically display." The man extended his arm and patted Lin's knee. His fingers were disfigured. Lin followed the blistered skin of his arm back up to the stranger's eyes. Scars lined his face and the brim of a fisherman's hat covered his forehead. The stranger removed the hat. "You don't remember me, Lin?"

The voice was familiar. Sharpening her senses, Lin stared at the stranger. She couldn't pinpoint the face. Then, moving her eyes back down to the stranger's hand, Lin's heart sank. Instantly, she was transported back to China, her father's arms wrapped tight around her. Through a small opening between her father's chest and arm, she relived the piercing sound of the cadre smashing each of his fingers. "Guozhi?"

Chapter 41

MARTIN WAS NOT used to people crying in his office and he wasn't sure what he said to make Tesfaye break down. All he asked was whether Demissie ever found Geteye in Kenya. He gave Tesfaye as much time as he needed to regain his composure before continuing his story.

EVEN FOR SOMEONE accustomed to squalid living conditions, hiding in the back of a truck between stacks of cardboard boxes was a challenge for Tesfaye. The heat trapped in the thermal tarpaulin cover of the back of the truck only intensified as the driver approached the equator that sliced right through the middle of Kenya. Few roads in Kenya were paved, and the recent storms had further eroded the dirt roads, adding a few inches to the already considerably sized ditches that littered the route to Nairobi.

As the truck made its final ascent to the city of Nairobi, Tesfaye could smell an array of distinct odors. The stench of burning garbage was pleasantly overshadowed by the sweet aroma of eucalyptus leaves that locals threw on the fire to mask the blazing trash heaps. Food cooked outside on makeshift grills produced a hint of charcoal in the air.

Shortly after the smells began to subside, the truck stopped moving. Tesfaye immediately felt better as he got out and stretched his legs. Looking around at the well-kept lawns in one of Nairobi's wealthier districts, Tesfaye thought the neighborhood bore remarkable similarities to some of the districts populated by affluent Ethiopians near Addis Ababa.

"This is it," said the driver. "I was instructed to take you here." He pointed to a ranch-style home lined with brown panels and white trimmed windows.

Tesfaye pulled out the piece of paper Beniam handed to him in Ethiopia and looked at the name scribbled on it. "Is that where Chege Thuku lives?" asked Tesfaye.

"I was told to drop you off at this exact address. That's all I know. If you don't mind, I need to get to the bazaar with all this stuff." As the driver sped away, Tesfaye stood in the middle of the road without a possession in the world. Apprehensively, he walked towards the house the driver had pointed out, continuing up the walkway to the front door. He tepidly knocked.

Through a narrow glass panel lining the side of the door, Tesfaye could make out a man approaching the door. He had a receding hairline that magnified his dark complexion. His skin was only a shade lighter than his black facial hair.

The man surveyed Tesfaye through the glass paneling. "You must be Tesfaye."

"I am, sir."

The man unlocked the deadbolt. "I'm Chege—I imagine you knew that," he said as he shook Tesfaye's hand. "Please, come inside. I've been expecting you." Chege led Tesfaye to a home office in the back of the house. "Can I get you anything?"

"Thank you, but no," Tesfaye said, although he badly wanted a glass of water.

"Please, sit," he instructed Tesfaye, pointing to a couch hugging the wall. "How was your trip?"

"It was fine, but very long."

"I imagine any trip would feel particularly long in the back of a truck. The important thing is that you made it. The roads in Kenya can be a bit unpredictable, as can the police." Chege sat next to Tesfaye. "It appears we have a mutual friend who has taken a strong interest in your future. He believes that my contacts with certain United States immigration personnel in the consulate here may help you get out of this chaotic continent."

United States immigration personnel. "To the United States?" asked a smiling Tesfaye, his eyes widening.

"Indeed." He reached into a cabinet next to the couch, pulled out a stack of neatly rolled bills, and handed it to Tesfaye.

"What is this?"

"This, Tesfaye, is five hundred thousand shillings." The equivalent of about seven thousand American dollars, Tesfaye strained to remember the last time he saw so much money. "And it is for you."

"Why are you giving me this?" Tesfaye asked dubiously.

"Don't think of me as a generous person. You can thank our mutual friend for the donation. He understands that it can take years to get all the documents necessary to get you into the United States legally. You will need to use this money very wisely."

"Where can I buy a car?"

"A car," Chege repeated in disbelief. "Did you hear what I just said? You have to be conservative, Tesfaye. Use the buses, the *matatus*."

"You don't understand, I *need* a car. My family is somewhere in Kenya, and I am going to find them."

"This country is almost as big as Ethiopia. Do you have any idea *where* in Kenya?"

"Last I heard, they were in Thika, but I haven't spoken to them for some time."

"Thika?" asked Chege curiously, raising his eyebrows.

"Yes," Tesfaye said, observing Chege's expression. "Why are you making that face?"

"Do you know what is in Thika?"

"Besides people and houses?"

"It's a refugee center," Chege explained. "The United Nations set up a reception center there for refugees."

Tesfaye was slightly taken back. When he thought of refugee centers, he pictured people of meager means, not someone with Geteye's comfortable economic circumstances. Certainly that was not the type of place he pictured his family going to when they left Ethiopia. "A refugee center?"

"Yes."

"In the middle of the country? That doesn't sound very efficient."

Chege laughed. "As I said, it's the United Nations. If I may ask, how did your family manage to get to Thika of all places, if you didn't know about the refugee camp there?"

"A friend. Somebody I knew in Ethiopia who was supposed to keep them safe for a few weeks."

Chege smiled. "If your friend decided to take your family to Thika, I don't think he was planning on going back to Ethiopia any time soon."

Tesfaye stood to his feet. "All the more reason why I need to start looking now, Mr. Thuku." Tesfaye placed the money in his pocket. "Would it be too much trouble for you to drive me to a reliable car dealer?"

"I cannot dissuade you from buying a vehicle?"

"Not a chance."

"Then I suppose I should make sure you don't get swindled."

By nightfall, Tesfaye was the proud owner of a 1987 Suzuki Samurai. Dark blue with a plastic roof, the two-door SUV was not likely to win any awards for aesthetic prowess, but the engine was in good working order and the price was right.

Tesfaye reluctantly agreed to wait three days before leaving Nairobi so that Chege could obtain a doctored identification card for him. Without any identification, Chege assured him, he would end up in a prison cell in no time. It was hard enough to deal with police when you could prove you had a legal right to be in the country. The truth was, despite Tesfaye's eagerness to start looking for his family, his body badly needed the time to rest and rehydrate.

With his identification in hand, Tesfaye loaded the Suzuki with canned food, loaves of flatbread, gallon jugs of water, and several spare canisters of petrol. He placed a map of Kenya on the passenger seat of the Suzuki and drove out of Nairobi, heading northeast on a semi-paved road to Thika.

Within two hours, Tesfaye was at the outskirts of Thika. Barbed wire surrounded the gates of the United Nations refugee center. Policemen brandishing rifles guarded the entrance to the gate. Tesfaye approached and rolled down his window.

"What is your business here?" asked one of the guards.

Tesfaye looked at his own reflection in the policeman's aviator sunglasses. "I am looking for someone. Someone I believe is inside this camp."

"We are all looking for someone, brother, but I can't let anyone go through these gates because they tell me they are looking for someone."

"It's not just someone. I'm trying to find a close relative of mine."

"Let me see your identification."

Tesfaye nervously handed the policeman his newly acquired card. He could see one of the other policemen staring at him through the passenger window.

The policeman handed the card back to him. "The conditions inside are not good, brother. Everyone is in need of food. Perhaps you would like to make a donation."

"Yes, of course. How much?"

"Fifty shillings."

"That would be . . ."

"For each of us, brother," he said, motioning to the other guards. The policeman tucked the bills Tesfaye handed him into his front shirt pocket and pulled out a walkie-talkie. After a short exchange with a voice on the other end, the policeman waved at his colleagues to open the gates. "Go to the main building down the road," he said.

"Which building?"

"Don't worry, you will not confuse it with the other houses."

Tesfaye immediately rolled up the windows to cut the smell of trash lining the entire camp. The small, wooden houses were barely held together by compressed mud. Naked children played in the dirt while their parents congregated in small groups.

The policeman was right, Tesfaye thought. There was no mistaking the squalid living conditions of the refugees for the United Nations welcome center building. Compared to the other houses it looked like an oasis. It had cream painted wood turned slightly brown toward the bottom with an actual screen door to block out the mosquitoes. *How could Geteye bring my family here?*

Tesfaye parked the Samurai next to the building and walked inside. A ceiling fan helped cut the heat and diffuse the stench. Still, the light-skinned portly man sitting at the desk vigorously fanned his graying hair with a paper plate. "You eventually get used to the smell," he said with a slight British accent. "That is, until you leave the camp and come back. Byron Hatchfield," he said. "And you are?"

"Tesfaye Azene."

"That is your real name?"

"Yes."

"Would it match the name on the identification card you handed the guards."

Tesfaye hesitated. "Probably not."

"Why am I not surprised? I've found that many people in this country are not who they say they are. So what is your business here?"

"I am looking for my family. They came here in 1991, March or April I think, early in 1991."

"Early 1991 you say?" Byron walked over to Tesfaye and gazed out the front door. "This place was originally built as a welcome center for refugees, a place where we could process them and send them somewhere else. The total capacity was supposed to be no more than five hundred. We are now up to five thousand. But, if your family came here in 1991, we probably tried to relocate them somewhere else. Things were running a little smoother back then."

"Where?"

"That's the question, isn't it," Byron said, walking back to his desk and pulling out a stack of books. "We require every refugee to register when they get here. Since this center opened, we have recorded each person in one of these books. What names am I looking for?"

"Ayana Mengesha, Afeworki Tesfaye, and Yenee Tesfaye." Peculiar to most Westerners, Ethiopian children take their father's first name as their surname, while women do not change their names after marriage.

Byron ran his fingers down the names covering the book's yellow, college ruled pages. "Here we are," he said after a few minutes.

"Where are they now?" asked Tesfaye, trying to control his excitement.

"Looks like they were here for several months. They requested refugee status and permanent relocation in . . ."

"In?"

"In Italy."

Italy? Tesfaye thought about Geteye's repeated insistence that the Amalfi Coast was paradise on earth. "So they are in Italy?" he asked.

"Not quite. You can't just go to a country because you want to. They have to agree to take you in. Look around, could you imagine if all the refugees here could just go wherever they want? The truth is, most of them just want to be able to go home and live in peace."

Tesfaye was in no mood to discuss the plight of the refugee masses. "Then where are they? Where is my family?"

"Another refugee camp, up north I imagine."

"You imagine?" asked Tesfaye.

Byron scratched his head. "I . . . I'm not sure."

"Well what does it say in your book?"

"It says that they were relocated."

"So how do you even know they are *up north?*"

"The U.N. recently opened a refugee camp up north in Kakuma because of the influx of refugees pouring in from Sudan. The nationality listed next to your family's names is Ethiopian, which of course also borders Kenya's northern side. Our first mission is to repatriate citizens to their home countries when it is safe. So it would make sense to send them to a camp closer to their home country, right?"

"What about a man named Geteye Tge? Do you see his name in the book by my family's names?"

Byron stopped fanning his sweaty brow with the paper plate and remained silent.

"Well?" Tesfaye prodded.

"I dare say I just had the strangest case of déjà vu. Another gentleman who was here asked me that very same question."

"When?"

"A few months ago, maybe."

"What did you tell him?" The urgency in Tesfaye's voice was now unmistakable, and Byron was growing suspicious.

"Tesfaye—if that's even your real name—are these people actually your family?"

"Yes. Of course."

"You realize how unusual it is to have multiple individuals walk through my front door and ask about the same person so insistently."

"I met Ayana when I was a professor at Addis Ababa University. She chose the name Afeworki for our first child out of respect for her grandmother. Ayana and I agreed that I would name our child if it was a boy, but we decided that we only wanted two children. So when she gave birth to another girl, she let me choose the name Yenee. I assure you, this is my family. Now tell me what you told the person who came looking for Geteye?"

Deep in thought, Byron chewed on his inner lip. "I believe I told them that Geteye left the camp and that I didn't know where he was. It was a long time ago, I can't be sure what I said."

Them?

"Wait here," Tesfaye said sternly, dashing out the front door to his Suzuki. Retrieving his map, he placed it on Byron's desk. "Show me the fastest way to get to the Kakuma Refugee Camp."

With his course plotted, Tesfaye drove toward the gates of the Thika Reception Center. The policeman came to greet him. "You didn't find what you were looking for, brother?"

"No, not exactly."

"Best of luck then. But before you go, I will need twenty shillings to open the gate. It's a little rusty, we are raising money to buy some grease for the hinges."

"Twenty shillings?"

"For each of us, brother."

As Tesfaye sped away, it occurred to him that flashing money in Kenya was a sure way to incur one of the many "taxes" policemen so readily levied from their own personal tax code. Tesfaye hid some of the shillings in slits he made in the seats of the Suzuki. The rest he put in his socks and above the soles of his shoes, leaving only a small amount of pocket money in case of an emergency.

Heading north to Kakuma, the stretches of pavement ended, leaving nothing but strips of bumpy dry dirt. Tesfaye hoped the Suzuki's suspension could handle the punishment. Nomadic tribes herded goats along the side of the road. A speeding bus would occasionally pass him, driving so fast that dips in the ground would send robed passengers airborne. But for the most part, Tesfaye would drive for hours on end without seeing a single person or vehicle.

After a bad night's sleep slumped over in the driver's seat and another full day behind the wheel of the Suzuki, Tesfaye finished his thirteen-hour journey to Kakuma. Sporadic vegetation and prickly bushes helped cut the dreariness of the brown, barren landscape. A breeze whipped up dust clouds over the snake-infested desert. The town itself was comprised of no more than a few dozen huts. And there, overshadowing the town, was the out-stretched fence surrounding the refugee camp.

The Kakuma Refugee Camp was enormous, a small city onto itself, bottling the collective despair of tens of thousands of refugees. The atmosphere was noticeably tenser than Thika. Armed convoys patrolled the perimeter, an unequivocal deterrent to anyone thinking twice about fleeing.

Tesfaye drove to the entrance of the camp, several hundred shillings in hand. The U.N. security personnel didn't wait for him to reach them. Several guards walked briskly toward the Suzuki. With outstretched arms, they ordered Tesfaye to halt.

"What is your business here?" asked one of the guards.

"I am looking for my family. I believe they are in this camp."

The guard shot one of his colleagues a skeptical glance. "And you think you can just drive in and look around?"

"Of course not, friend. I was hoping you could tell me what I should do."

"Come back tomorrow, the sun is almost set."

Tesfaye reached into his pocket and pulled out a wad of shillings. "Are you sure there is no way I can pass now? I'm desperate."

The guard looked around and sneered at Tesfaye. "Who do you think I am?" he asked firmly. "Put that away. What good will that do me when my superiors ask me why an unidentified man has been found dead in the middle of camp next to an abandoned hatchback?" The guard pointed to a hut on the perimeter of town. "Go there in the morning."

Another night in the driver's seat of the Suzuki. Another night thinking about his family. Another night of worrying.

As soon as Tesfaye could feel the sun's rays hovering around his closed eyelids, he jumped up, drove closer to town, and went to the hut the guard had pointed to the night before. He knocked. No answer. He propped himself against the door and sat there for hours. Curious locals starting their day looked him over and whispered to each other. Around nine in the morning, the handle of the door turned and a man emerged to find Tesfaye at his feet.

"What in the bloody hell are you doing there? Was that you knocking on my door before?"

"I'm sorry, sir," Tesfaye said, rising to his feet and brushing the dust off his pants. "I was told to come find you in the morning."

"Told to come find me," he repeated. "Is this some sort of bloody joke?"

"No, sir. I told the guards at the gate that I was looking for my family. They said you could help me."

"I bet they did," he said, already walking briskly toward the refugee camp. "Do you know why they told you to come see me?"

"No, sir."

"Because they didn't want to bloody deal with you."

"Wait," Tesfaye said as he tried his best to keep pace. "Please, just wait one second." He pulled the shillings from his pocket. "I'm not trying to bribe you. I'm showing you this money so that you'll understand that I'm not looking for any handout."

"That's too bad, I could use the money."

"Take it! Here, it's yours."

"Put that away. Haven't you ever heard of sarcasm?" he asked, getting into a U.N. vehicle parked by the camp's entrance.

Tesfaye ran around to the other side of the vehicle and opened the passenger side door.

"Hold on there. Do you have any weapons on you?"

"No."

The U.N. official turned to one of the guards. "Make sure."

"He's clean," the guard said after frisking him.

"Alright, hop in."

The interior of the Kakuma Refugee Camp felt like a larger version of the Thika Reception Center. Five-foot tall straw huts blended into the ground. Other, more secured structures featured makeshift wooden front doors and tin roofs. Many refugees stacked bushels of straw in front of their homes to maintain some level of privacy from the steady stream of foot traffic kicking up dirt on the wide, rocky dirt paths.

"Here we are," said the U.N. official, parking the vehicle next to a U.N. station secured by more guards. Tesfaye followed the man through the front door. "Those are the files, they are chronological, based on when a refugee enters the camp. Good luck to you," he said, whistling to one of the guards.

"Yes, sir," the guard said.

"Watch him and make sure he doesn't do anything suspicious. If he does, shoot him."

"What?" asked Tesfaye.

"Sarcasm," said the U.N. official as he headed for the door.

Tesfaye sifted through the refugee files, pausing each time he came across a name beginning with 'A.' After thirty minutes of searching, his pulse increased. He found it. *Ayana Mengesha*. And next to her name, *Afeworki Tesfaye, Yenee Tesfaye*. All three checked into the refugee camp. Next to each of their names, the same entry—COD-MNG. *Some region in the camp*, Tesfaye suspected. The entry next to Ayana and Afeworki's names were written in the same handwriting, but the writing next to Yenee's name was different.

"Excuse me," Tesfaye said to the guard. "Can you tell me how to get here?" he asked, pointing to the cryptic entries.

The guard walked over and looked at the entry. "What are you asking me? Get where?"

"This entry. What does it mean?"

"Cause of death, meningitis. You knew these people?"

Tesfaye fell to the floor, tucking his head between his legs. He wept, tuning out the guard's feeble attempt to comfort him and explain that a strain of meningitis had run through the camp several months ago.

AFTER TESFAYE RECOUNTED how he came to learn the fate of his family in Kenya, Martin sat patiently while Tesfaye used the bathroom.

"Are you okay?" Martin asked when Tesfaye returned.

Tesfaye did not answer. He just kept taking deep breaths while he gazed down at the carpet.

"Why was the handwriting different by Yenee's name?" asked Martin.

"Because it was written by different medical personnel. The guard told me that the U.N. doctor at Kakuma was replaced a few weeks after Ayana and Afeworki died." Tesfaye looked up at Martin with his bloodshot eyes. "Do you know what that means?"

Martin shrugged his shoulders.

"It means," Tesfaye began to explain, getting choked up. He took another deep breath. "It means that Yenee died several weeks after her sister and mother. It means that she had to watch them die, and then suffer alone until her little body couldn't take it anymore."

"Alone? What about Geteye?"

Tesfaye's agitation spiked as he rigorously scratched his scalp. "His name was not listed."

"So he didn't catch meningitis, I guess?"

Tesfaye sighed. "He never set foot in the Kakuma Refugee Camp."

Chapter 42

BY VIRTUE OF his fisherman's hat, Guozhi's recognizably winsome eyes had initially eluded Lin. It was Guozhi's mouth, however, that confused her the most. His nearly toothless smile was one of his most distinct features, but he now bore a new set of dentures—an expensive addition Lin found as uncharacteristic of a rural Chinese farmer as the elegant interior of Guozhi's former home in Fujian.

Lin didn't know where to start. There were so many questions she wanted to ask. "What," she started. "I mean, how . . ."

"How did I get here?" Guozhi said.

Lin's thoughts immediately turned to her father. "Do you know where my father is? What happened to him?"

With the tip of his tongue, Guozhi fiddled with his new teeth for a moment. "I'm sorry. I honestly don't know where he is. I didn't even hear that cadre had also taken him away until after I arrived in New York."

Lin sighed. The often-recurring knot in her stomach returned, but it was overpowered by her curiosity. "So how did you get here?"

"I escaped with the help of Falun Gong practitioners."

"But how did you get out of prison?" Lin asked.

"As I said, with the help of Falun Gong practitioners." Guozhi struggled to take a sip of tea, gripping the cup between his palms to take the burden off his mangled fingers, which had recovered very little of their dexterity. "After I was arrested, cadre placed me in a holding cell and beat me all night. The next day, a doctor came and tended to my fingers. I thought it was quite peculiar that they would bother treating my wounds, but I was not about to point that out. That night, after—let's just call it an unpleasant afternoon—I was curled in a ball in my jail cell when I heard a tapping on the door. One of the guards motioned for me to come toward him. He whispered that he was a fellow Falun Gong practitioner and that he was going to help me escape."

"There are Falun Gong practitioners among the ranks of the cadre?" Shaoqing asked.

Guozhi nodded. "There are Falun Gong practitioners *everywhere*, all over China, tens of *millions* of them, including government leaders, military people, and yes, cadre too. One of these cadre snuck me out of my cell. He provided me with altered travel documents and helped me get a seat on a plane that landed in New York the next day."

"How did he already have these documents?" asked Shaoqing.

"Good question," Guozhi conceded, sitting quietly for a moment as he debated how much he wanted to reveal. Few people knew that Guozhi was one of the followers responsible for coordinating the Falun Gong movement in southeastern Fujian. Not even Lin's father had known, and Guozhi was grateful that Lin's father never asked about the furniture and ornaments in his home that might appear a little too lavish for a local farmer to own. Guozhi's status in the Falun Gong movement afforded him some additional income, which he used sparingly in order to avoid attention. Having grown up under the watchful eye of The Party, the ingrained paranoia shared by Guozhi and other high-ranking Falun Gong members cautioned them to formulate a contingency plan in case something went wrong. The doctored travel documents were part of this contingency plan, and the guard knew who to contact in order to retrieve these documents.

After mulling over Shaoqing's query about the origins of the travel documents, Guozhi convincingly said, "Honestly, I don't know the answer."

"You didn't mention how you ended up in this apartment," Long reminded Guozhi.

"I was just getting to that. On the way to the airport, the cadre asked me if there was anyone he should contact for me—to let them know I would be leaving the country. I thought of my nephew and what must have been going through his mind when he came back from the fields to find the house in shambles and me gone. I didn't know for sure whether the phone in my house was still working after it was ransacked by the cadre." Guozhi directed his attention to Lin. "So I gave him your father's phone number, hoping that your father could relay the information to my nephew. As it turns out, unfortunately, it was your mother who relayed the information."

"Mei also called me here in New York," Long added, "and gave me Guozhi's flight information."

Shaoqing was confused. "When you arrived at the airport, they let you enter the United States?" he skeptically inquired. The thought of traveling to the United States by boat unnecessarily was not sitting well with him.

Guozhi smiled. "The agent who looked at my travel documents and passport couldn't have been more disinterested. The whole process took a matter of seconds. Maybe he took pity on me because my fingers were in such bad shape that I could barely hold my passport. I had no idea what to do next, or where to go. I followed everyone else out of the customs area. It's a good thing Long was there to greet me. Otherwise, I'd probably still be walking aimlessly around the airport."

The question had been burning in Lin's mind since the cadre took her father. Seeing an opportunity to finally get some answers, she was unable to wait for the issue to come up naturally in the conversation. "What is Falun Gong?" she shouted. "Is my father a member of Falun Gong? Did he try to overthrow the government?"

Startled by the forcefulness of Lin's questions, Guozhi looked toward Long for guidance on where to begin. Long smiled tenderly at Lin as he leaned closer to her and put his hand on her forearm. "Do you actually think your father would try to overthrow the government?" Long asked.

"No," Lin replied. "I mean, I don't think so. But *Ma* wouldn't tell me anything, so I don't know what to think. I suppose I just assumed the worst." Guozhi and Long shared a glance of mutual understanding about Mei's notorious reticence.

"Your father most certainly had nothing to do with any plot to overthrow the government," Guozhi said assuringly.

"Then why did the cadre say that Falun Gong followers were trying to overthrow the government when we were in your house?" she asked Guozhi.

"Perhaps we should back up a little," Long suggested. "Have you ever heard of *qigong*, Lin?"

"Yes, of course. My father used to practice *qigong* in the house all the time."

"Did he ever tell you anything about *qigong*?"

"Just that it makes you healthier. I watched him do all the meditation exercises."

"That's right. The improved health comes from an energy source in the human body," Long explained. "That inner energy is called *qi*. It flows throughout the entire universe and in every living being. The meditation exercises you saw your father practicing were designed to help him control the *qi* within him and harness its powers."

Growing up with her father, Lin had come to develop an open mind about matters of spirituality and philosophy. But the idea that a person could gain control over an energy force sounded a little too far-fetched. Guozhi could see the apprehension on Lin's face. "You don't believe that *qi* is real?" he asked.

Lin shrugged her shoulders.

"But it does exist," Guozhi remarked confidently. "Scientific studies have proven that it exists as an actual, physical force." Guozhi was referring to a scientific experiment conducted by a Chinese researcher in 1978 that supposedly isolated the electromagnetic waves emitted from *qigong* practitioners during their exercises. *Qigong* exploded in popularity after word spread that a scientist had identified *qi*.

"That's not the only reason why *qigong* became so popular," Long added. "It became popular because the government permitted it to grow." Guozhi knew that Long was right. The discovery of *qi* was also critical to the *qigong* movement for more nationalistic reasons. The Communist Party was eager to shed the perception that China was a backwards nation relying on ancient superstitions. Combining ancient elements of spirituality and metaphysical understanding with scientific proof was the perfect formula to grow a movement in China at the time.

"What does any of this have to do with Falun Gong?" Lin asked impatiently.

Guozhi stiffened up. "Because the leader of the Falun Gong movement started as a *qigong* master."

Lin searched her memory, picturing herself back in Guozhi's house with her father. She visualized Guozhi standing defiantly in the middle of his house with Yending, the cadre leader, hovering over him. "Li!" Lin exclaimed, "he has brainwashed you." Shaoqing and Long sat perplexed, but Guozhi nodded his head. "That's what he said to you," Lin said to Guozhi.

"You're right," Guozhi agreed. "He said I had been brainwashed by Li Hongzhi. Li is the *qigong* master who started the Falun Gong movement. When the movement grew, the government felt threatened and tried to discredit Falun Gong. Newspapers and magazines all over the country published stories denouncing Li Hongzhi as a fraud and comparing Falun Gong to a superstitious cult."

"So what did you do?" Lin asked.

"We protested. Falun Gong practitioners staged hundreds of protests all over the country."

"So the government attacked you because you protested?" Lin asked.

Guozhi stroked his chin. "One particular protest. Thousands of Falun Gong practitioners gathered outside the Communist Party's headquarters in Beijing, the *Zhongnanhai*, to silently protest the aggressive tactics that police had been using against us at our gatherings. They didn't take too kindly to this. After the protest, The Party spent months planning a coordinated effort across all of China to arrest hundreds of thousands of Falun Gong practitioners. At the same time, they began a massive campaign to discredit the movement. Any local cadre who failed to arrest suspected Falun Gong practitioners would be kicked out of The Party."

"Or sent to a reeducation camp," Long added.

"Unfortunately for your father, this campaign against Falun Gong took place the day you came to visit me."

After the Communist Party's initial crackdown on the Falun Gong movement, many members of its leadership who managed to escape fled to the United States. A handful of practitioners living in New York City in 1995 quickly grew to seventy thousand. The Falun Gong organization in New York was highly organized and well-funded, fueled by an educated Chinese middle class that had migrated during the previous two decades to Chinatown, Sunset Park in Brooklyn, and Flushing, Queens. The New York contingency of the Falun Gong movement was able to help Guozhi and other fleeing practitioners get on their feet when they arrived in the United States. A practitioner specializing in dentistry even provided Guozhi with dentures free of charge.

Lin watched Guozhi continue to play with his new teeth. She struggled to process everything he was saying to her. The strong hand of the Communist Party was nothing new. It was all she ever knew growing up in China. But such a country-wide reaction to a simple protest seemed a bit much. "Why would the government go through all that trouble just because a few people protested?" she asked.

"Tiananmen Square," Shaoqing answered confidently. "That's why." Guozhi and Long could see what Shaoqing was getting at. The Party's use of military force to quash the Tiananmen Square demonstrators became a symbol used by activists all over the world to illuminate China's poor human rights record. Shaoqing continued, "The Communists wanted to cut off the movement swiftly and mercilessly to avoid another Tiananmen Square."

The government was even more fearful than Shaoqing realized. Before the protest at *Zhongnanhai*, party leaders knew little of the Falun Gong movement. Learning for the first time that these protesters belonged to a group that had tens of millions of followers did not sit well with a government willing to avoid the embarrassment of another Tiananmen Square at any cost.

"Control," Guozhi said softly.

"So my father wasn't involved in a plot to overthrow the government?"

"No," Guozhi replied, "he wasn't even a Falun Gong practitioner." Guozhi lowered his head. "It was my fault. If I hadn't let him borrow my copy of *Zhuan falun*, I doubt he would've had any trouble with the cadre." Teary eyed, he exhaled slowly. "I'm so sorry."

Lin felt numb. She had no more tears. "There's nothing to be sorry about," she said. "More than anything, my father wanted the education he never had growing up. Your generosity with all the books you gave him went a long way."

"I know this is a lot to take in," Long said comfortingly. "Perhaps you should get some rest. You have to prepare for immigration court."

Chapter 43

TESFAYE WAS VISIBLY upset as he told Martin that Geteye never even set foot in the Kakuma Refugee Camp.

Martin did not understand. If Geteye was with Tesfaye's family, then there should have been some record of him entering the camp. "Maybe the U.N. folks just forgot to put Geteye's name on the list when he entered Kakuma," Martin speculated.

"I suppose that could have been a possibility," Tesfaye said, "but that's not what happened here."

"How can you be so sure?"

Tesfaye took a deep breath. "I'm sure."

THE OVERWHELMING SADNESS Tesfaye felt when he learned that his family was gone soon turned to anger. Walking on the dirt path back toward the front gates of the refugee camp, Tesfaye's blood was boiling. Absolute rage created a vacuum that sucked all the humanity from Kakuma. The helpless exiles walking barefoot through the refugee camp morphed into unsympathetic freeloaders. Through the lens skewed by his recent trauma, all he could see were squalid beggars and con artists wearing the masks of genuine refugees, ungrateful parasites gorging at the trough of the U.N.'s generosity.

Storming out of the camp, Tesfaye got into the Suzuki, slammed the door shut, and punched the steering wheel. He screamed as loud as he could. *How could this have happened? How could Geteye let them come to this place alone? Why wasn't he with them?* Nothing was making sense.

Pressing down on the clutch, he gunned the Suzuki, speeding away from Kakuma. After eight hours behind the wheel, driving back toward Nairobi, Tesfaye heard the front right tire pop. When he purchased the Suzuki, Chege had insisted that it come equipped with a working full-size spare tire, believing that a flat tire on the back roads of Kenya was not a matter of *if*, but rather *when*.

Struggling to loosen the wheel lugs, Tesfaye continued to rehash the sequence of events causing his family to end up in the Kakuma Refugee

Camp. *Ayana and the kids left Thika with Geteye, but there is no record of Geteye ever entering Kakuma. Either Geteye never made it to Kakuma or his name was not recorded for some reason. What if Geteye's name was not recorded but he's at Kakuma right now? Should I go back and search for him?* But then, as he removed the blown-out tire, it hit him—Geteye taking his family to Thika of all places, a relocation request to Italy, someone else searching for Geteye—it all didn't add up; it couldn't add up.

Knowing what he needed to do, Tesfaye threw the jack and tire iron in the trunk and finished filling the Suzuki with the last jugs of petrol before heading back to Thika. When he couldn't keep his eyes open anymore, he pulled to the side of the road to rest. Unable to sleep more than a few hours, Tesfaye continued his drive, still relying on his headlights to illuminate the way. Shortly after dawn, the Samurai again pulled up to the front gates of the Thika Reception Center.

"You are back, brother," the policeman said, seeming almost happy to see a familiar face.

Tesfaye was in no mood for small talk. "Here," he said, handing the policeman five hundred shillings. "This is for driving in *and* out, okay?"

The policeman smiled. "We already fixed the squeaking gate, brother, but we appreciate your generosity to the cause." After a moment on the radio, the gates were opened, and Tesfaye was again heading for the main administrative building.

"Back so soon?" asked Byron as he greeted Tesfaye at the door.

Without hesitation, Tesfaye snatched the walkie-talkie from Byron's hand and threw it across the room, smashing it to bits. Grabbing Byron by the shirt, Tesfaye pushed him backward until Byron was pressed up against his desk. Wrapping his fingers around Byron's throat, Tesfaye slammed him onto the desk.

"What are you doing?" Byron shouted, his eyeballs bulging, his legs dangling in the air.

"You are a liar!"

"Whah," he said, gasping for air. "What are you talking about?"

"Don't hold out old man. My family is dead, there is no record of Geteye ever setting foot in Kakuma, and you led me to believe that he left here with my family. Do you expect me to believe that he *happened* to die on route to Kakuma, or that he *happened* to be the only name not recorded by the U.N.

at Kakuma? That someone else *happened* to be looking for him here and that you know *nothing* else? I've known Geteye a long time. There is no way he would execute a plan like this."

"He was trying . . . to get . . . everyone . . . to Italy," Byron managed to squeak out. "Even you."

Tesfaye loosened his grip. "What do you mean?"

"Check, check the book, the logbook. It's still on my desk from the last time you were here."

"Where?"

"I believe it's underneath my spine," Byron quipped.

Tesfaye let go of Byron's throat. Coughing uncontrollably, Byron slouched over until he caught his breath, then he reached for the logbook. Flipping through the pages, he again found the page listing Geteye, Ayana, Afeworki, and Yenee. "Here," Byron said, pointing to an entry in the book.

Tesfaye couldn't believe what he was seeing, but there it was, right above Ayana's name. *Tesfaye Azene.* "Why is my name in here?"

"I'll explain, okay? But I need to back up a little so you understand what I'm going to tell you. So please, just don't attack me again until I explain," Byron begged.

"I get it, start explaining!"

"Last year," Byron began, "a well-dressed man walked into my office. He said I should not be fooled by his attire, assuring me that he had fled his home country and that his life was in danger. Before I could say anything, he put a million shillings on the table. I asked him what it was for and he said it was to get him legal status as a refugee in Italy."

"This well-dressed man was Geteye?"

"It was. Geteye then said he would need me to relocate four other people as well, and he then put four hundred thousand more on the table. He said three of the other people were here, and the other—presumably you— would be arriving any day."

"And of course you took the money?"

"I tried explaining to him how challenging relocation could be, especially when you have a specific country in mind with no relatives already living there. But he said that Italy was not negotiable and that it had to happen soon. He put another hundred thousand shillings on the table, telling me the extra money was to make sure his paperwork was fast-tracked. So now I have one and a half million shillings on my desk. A lot of money. But then he put another five hundred thousand on the table."

"What for?"

"To keep your family safe. Geteye said he wouldn't be able to stay in Thika, that it wouldn't be safe for him here."

"Where did he go?"

"He wouldn't tell me. All I knew was that he would be somewhere in Nairobi and that he'd be coming back to the camp every so often to check in.

Smart, Tesfaye thought. *If Byron didn't know where to find Geteye, then he couldn't be forced to disclose his whereabouts, no matter how much pressure he was under.*

"We even created a code," Byron said. "I dare say I felt like some sort of undercover agent. When Geteye would approach the gate to check in, he would have the guards radio that Ato Russo was here to see me. If all was well, I would radio back to let him in. If I didn't think it was safe, I would tell the guard to let Ato Moretti in. You see, he wanted to go to Italy and these are Italian names."

"I get it. What of my family?"

"I provided them with accommodations here in Thika, in the village outside the gates of the refugee center. It wasn't a palace, but certainly not comparable to the conditions inside the camp. I made sure they had plenty of food and drink."

"You mean you fed them until it became easier to ship them to Kakuma."

"That is a vast oversimplification," Byron said as he reached for one of his desk drawers.

"Don't fucking move!" Tesfaye shouted, worried that Byron was trying to get a gun.

"Alright," Byron said, "you open it."

Tesfaye slowly opened the drawer. "The picture," Byron said, "take it out."

Tesfaye stared at the picture for a moment and then locked his squinting eyes on Byron. "What are you doing with a picture of my family?"

"I wasn't lying the last time you were here. Several men did come looking for Geteye. I told them I hadn't seen him. Then they put this picture of your family on my desk and asked me if I'd seen your wife and daughters. I said there were some other people with Geteye when he was here, but that all of them had gone to Nairobi after I said I couldn't provide any assistance. So I think the question you should be asking is what were *they* doing with a picture of your family?"

But Tesfaye already knew the answer. There were dozens of pictures of his family spread throughout his old home—the home that Demissie and his rebel posse no doubt ransacked after taking him into custody. Staring at the picture, a wave of guilt washed over Tesfaye as he thought about the role he inadvertently played in this nightmare by pleading with Demissie to spare his family.

"They searched the entire camp," Byron said. "They went into every hut, every makeshift church, looking for any sign of Geteye or your family. You want to know why I sent them to Kakuma? Well, it's very simple. I panicked. So when the U.N. started relocating refugees to the new camp in Kakuma two days later, I had them take your family as well." Byron paused, extending his arm to plead with Tesfaye. "It was only a matter of time before they came back and searched the town. I was trying to protect them."

"You mean you were trying to protect yourself."

"In my drawer, there's eighty-thousand shillings in an envelope given to me by the people looking for Geteye. One of them said I'd have a decision to make the next time I saw Geteye or your family. Either I could get in touch with him and keep the money, or . . ."

"Or?"

"Or he would gorge my eyes out after he kills my family in front of me so that the last thing I'd ever see would haunt me forever. So yes, maybe I was trying to protect myself and *my* family."

"So you shipped my wife and children to Kakuma?"

"Like I said, I panicked, I didn't know what else to do."

Trying to make sure Byron wasn't holding back any information, Tesfaye persisted. "But why Kakuma? Why not Nairobi or anywhere other than a refugee camp?"

"Because the men who told me they'd kill my family also said someone would be watching me at all times."

"What does that have to do with Kakuma?" Tesfaye asked impatiently, astounded that Byron actually thought the men would keep him under twenty-four-hour surveillance.

"On the day the U.N. relocated refugees to Kakuma," Byron explained, "there were thirty U.N. jeeps here, at least twenty buses, and several other security vehicles. It was an absolute zoo. If ever there was a time to get your family out of here undetected, it was then."

Byron paused to gather his thoughts, visibly drained from the nonstop questioning. "Geteye told me he would kill me if anything happened to your family, a machete-wielding maniac is threatening to remove various parts of my body, and everyone is throwing money at me. I saw an opportunity when the convoy was leaving for Kakuma and I took it. I mean, what the hell was I supposed to do!"

Byron wiped his brow. "Do you know what would happen to me if there was an incident in this camp? If my superiors ever found out I was taking bribes? I would go to jail, for a very long time!" Byron shook his head. "I never should have taken the money. I should have told Geteye that there was nothing I could do."

"But you know that would have been pointless. Geteye would not have believed you." Everything was starting to come into focus. "Geteye knew before stepping foot in this camp what you could and could not do. I assure you he knew who you were and how much money it would take to get you to do what he wanted. You can try to play innocent with me, but we both know this isn't the first time someone has gotten a favor from you in exchange for some money. And if this was the first time you took a bribe, then you must have recently come into some financial problems, financial problems that Geteye knew about."

Again wiping his brow, Byron sat speechless. The look of a deer in headlights said it all.

"Did you ever see Geteye again?" asked Tesfaye.

"No. But I spoke with him a few weeks later. He arrived at the gate and I told him I didn't think it was safe for him to come in." Byron pointed to the corner of the room. "I spoke to him on that radio you so thoughtfully destroyed."

"What about your silly code name for when it wasn't safe?"

"I used the code name, but he demanded to know what happened."

"And?"

"And what? I told him what happened as quickly as I could. He said to keep working on the materials for Italy and then he left."

"That's it, he just left?

"Yes, he drove away."

"You haven't seen him since?"

"No, and that's the God's-honest truth."

WITH A NOTEPAD on his lap, Martin tried to shield the notes he was scribbling about Tesfaye's unfolding story. "All this information about Geteye and your family, it all took place in the early 1990s, but you didn't come to the United States until recently. When was it exactly?"

"October. October 1999.

"Which means you spent a few years in Kenya."

"It felt like a lifetime."

"But that guy—the contact you had in Kenya . . ."

"Chege."

"Right, Chege. He eventually came through for you."

"He did."

"Was the money Chege gave you enough to get by during your time in Kenya?"

"*Getting by* is a relative concept in Africa. It would have been nice if I had all the money he had given me."

"You mean if you hadn't spent so much money on a car?"

"That. And other complications."

BEFORE TESFAYE HAD spoken with Byron in Thika, he was motivated by the hope that one day he would again embrace his beloved Ayana and the children. In prison, the thought of being with his family prevented him from imploding into a state of total hopelessness. They were the reason he was able to endure all the pain and brutality.

But now, as he drove back to Nairobi, Tesfaye searched unsuccessfully for an anchor. The only motivating force he could hypothesize was survival. Actions geared for no purpose other than trying to stay alive. Living for the sake of living. The tentacles binding him to friends and family had all snapped. He was alone.

Nairobi itself was home to tens of thousands of refugees. Camped out in the vast slums of the city, many refugees lived in conditions comparable to the Thika Reception Center. Each neighborhood in the slums had its own proper name, places like Mathare Valley, which conjured images of an area more hospitable than was actually the case.

Refugees flocked to sections of the city dominated by others who shared a common nationality. There were Ugandans in the Ngando neighborhood, Ethiopians in Mathare, and Rwandans in Riruta and Dandora. The men in these neighborhoods congregated in small groups, chain smoking and exchanging rumors about their home countries. The women cooked whatever food they could find on heated charcoals, as they tried to keep an eye on their children who were scavenging about, looking for anything to play with.

Tesfaye decided to avoid the Ethiopian neighborhoods. His plan was to keep as low a profile as possible and pray that nobody would recognize him. At the outskirts of the Dandora neighborhood, he struck a deal with a Rwandan landlady to rent a small apartment.

The next two years were filled with a steady flow of rumbles and rumors from fearful Rwandans who believed that something horrible was happening in their home country. Then, in April of 1994, Tutsi Rwandans began pouring into the camp, fleeing a systematic effort by the Hutus to wipe them all out.

At first, Tesfaye used what little resources he had to try and help the onslaught of Tutsis settling down in Dandora. But word of his generosity quickly spread and he found his apartment inundated by requests for assistance. The stories began to sound very similar and Tesfaye suspected that many who came to see him were regurgitating a script they heard had led to a handout. Recognizing his efforts were also thwarting his attempt to keep a low profile, he started to become more reclusive.

Tesfaye would check in with Chege every so often to see whether Chege secured the paperwork Tesfaye needed before he could migrate to the United States. "Be patient," Chege kept telling him, "it shouldn't be much longer now." Tesfaye would have liked to believe him, but Chege always said that it "shouldn't be much longer."

The city of Nairobi was notoriously unsafe. There was an ongoing debate about who were the most dangerous characters, common street thugs or the police. The public's mistrust of police led many refugees and other slum dwellers to take matters into their own hands. Mob justice. Tesfaye once witnessed a crowd bash a man's skull in with jagged rocks simply because a store owner yelled out that he was a thief.

Police were more of a nuisance. They had issued Tesfaye several driving tickets, fines collected on the spot, for such infractions as driving too slowly and failing to yield to an imaginary pedestrian.

Driving home from Chege's one night, Tesfaye kept an eye out for policemen. Up ahead, his headlights illuminated the body of a young injured man, crying out for help. He had barely shifted the Suzuki into park next to the man by the time two thugs barreled out from behind the nearby bushes and pointed a loaded shotgun at his face. Tesfaye knew better than to put up a fight. He walked the rest of the way home.

The loss of his Suzuki was bad enough, but Tesfaye had also stashed some of his money in the seat cushion. His funds were running low, so he did what many others tried to do—develop a trade to make some money based on any skill set they brought over from their home country.

The only thing that came to mind for Tesfaye was metalwork, a skill he picked up during his days at the Holetta Military Academy. He created intricate crosses that he would sell at the bazaars to embassy workers, tourists, and a steady influx of missionaries.

As the years went by, Tesfaye began visiting Chege less often, in part because he no longer had his prized Suzuki. He started to accept that he would live out his last days alone in the slums of Nairobi. But then, on one of his long treks to Chege's house during the Christmas holidays in 1998, all that changed.

"I have good news, Tesfaye," Chege said. "You will be in the United States within a year. Here," he said, handing Tesfaye a detailed roadmap of New York City. "You will need to memorize all these streets."

"SO YOU KNEW well before coming here that you'd be driving a taxi?" asked Martin.

"Yeah."

"I see."

"So what now?"

Martin put down his notepad. "Now, we fill out an asylum application. We'll have to appear before an immigration judge and present your case. You're probably looking at two to four years until the actual trial. In the meantime, you and I will keep in touch. I'll work on setting you up with some doctors so we can document all your physical injuries. Your job for now is to keep driving your cab, save some money, keep in touch, and above all else, stay out of trouble."

Chapter 44

IT WAS QUARTER to midnight. Ethan and Ryan rested on the hood of Ryan's Ford Explorer in the parking lot in back of the Friday's restaurant in Hackensack, New Jersey. "We have to start charging more for these papers," Ethan said. "Five thousand isn't going to cut it anymore. I'm thinking we should jack it up to seven thousand. Plenty of people are willing to pay that."

Ethan would have been fine with five thousand if he could split the whole amount with Ryan. But two thousand went to their partner. She worked on the immigration benefits side of INS. Since Ethan and Ryan worked on the enforcement side, they knew they needed someone with greater access to the benefits databases to legitimize the paperwork they were generating. Their partner knew the importance of her role and leveraged it to get the biggest share of the fee.

"Seven thousand," Ryan thought. "Might as well, it's not like there's a chance I'll get promoted any time soon." Ethan and Ryan's identity theft investigation had stalled. They had begun to piece together the components of the scams, but they had not made any progress tracking down the source of the forged documents. Their supervisor had grown impatient. He had sent them out west two times and they did not come back with anything tangible. He said that they needed to find another angle or drop the investigation, since he couldn't continue to justify the cost.

A woman pulled up in a Dodge Caravan. She got out of the car and looked around, noticeably nervous. She walked over to Ethan and Ryan and handed them an envelope. Ryan counted the money and placed it in his jacket pocket. "Here you go," Ethan said, handing the woman her brand new green card.

The woman kissed the back of Ethan's hand. "Bless you, sir. Bless you."

"Just remember," lectured Ethan, "if you commit one crime while you're here, I don't care how small it is, I'm going to make sure you're on the next plane back to El Salvador. Okay?"

"Of course, sir," she said assuringly. "You'll see. I will be good. I swear." She walked briskly back to her car, looking over both shoulders a few times, and then drove away with a big smile on her face.

"Perfect," Ethan said, "a single, anxious woman who knows she's doing something wrong and feels bad about it. She won't so much as run a stop sign."

"You believe that or is that what you need to tell yourself to justify what we're doing here?" Ryan asked.

Ethan thought about all the anger he had been harboring toward immigrants since the incident when he was younger, but also that the government paid him next to nothing to try and keep them out. He contemplated Ryan's question as he tried to reconcile his feelings. "To be honest, I don't know anymore."

Chapter 45

SOFIA TOOK IN a deep breath of the dry Arizona air and slowly exhaled through her nose. She knew it was silly, but this millennium smelled different. Sweeter. When she awoke on January 1, 2000, she began to cry. She felt like a newborn bird that had just managed to break out of its shell. The drugs were working better than she ever imagined.

But Sofia was always bothered by the fact that she left her children in Mexico. She wanted them to enjoy the United States with her, away from corrupt police and unhinged drug dealers. Even though her children understood that she would have died if she stayed in Escuinapa, she still felt as though she had abandoned them. Her feelings of dereliction intensified by springtime as her body continued to respond well to the medication. *Who am I to experience such joy when I left my children behind?* It was parental guilt exacerbated by Catholic guilt.

The wheels were already in motion. She had painstakingly saved every penny she could to pay for Eva and Manuel's trip up north. A coworker at the crafts store told her about a coyote who uses a much shorter route to smuggle people into the United States. Instead of trekking through the desert—which Sofia had no intention of letting her children do—this coyote starts out in *San Luis Rio Colorado*, a Mexican town near Arizona, and drives to the border near the tiny town of Gadsden, Arizona, inhabited by no more than one thousand people, mostly Hispanic.

Located near the Colorado River, Gadsden was tucked in the southwest corner of Arizona, close to California. Once her children made it to the United States side of the border, the only obstacle before reaching the heart of the town was an adjacent levee. All her children would have to do is swim across a canal and find her. No endless desert, no scorpions or snakes, and no bandits.

Sofia figured it would be too risky for the kids to walk straight into town, so they formulated a plan to rendezvous at the corner of one of the streets that crisscrossed the vast farmland surrounding Gadsden. She mailed Eva and Manuel a map of the Gadsden area so they could study the route they would have to take once in the United States. Everyone agreed on the corner of I and 19th Street, located no more than one mile inland from the border.

Sofia picked six in the morning as the time they would rendezvous. She reasoned that it was early enough to minimize the chances they would encounter any people, but not so early that her idling car would draw suspicion from anyone who happened to be on the road at that time. The exact date was yet to be determined. Sofia still had to raise more money. But with a new swing in her step, she had no doubt her rejuvenated body was up to the task.

Chapter 46

FOUR MONTHS. THAT'S how long it took. Exactly one hundred nineteen days after formulating the plan, Sofia had raised enough money to finance her children's journey to the United States. Even though Sofia had a driver's license, Rosario did not feel comfortable letting Sofia borrow her van; she did not want to be implicated if authorities caught Sofia near the border.

Hating to say no to her best friend, Rosario agreed to pay for the rental vehicle. Sofia decided to rent a maroon van that looked just like Rosario's. It was the only vehicle she felt comfortable driving and she reasoned that her attempt to smuggle illegal immigrants into the country was not the time to test out different models.

It was five in the morning. Driving across Arizona on Route 8, Sofia reviewed the plan, pondering all possible contingencies. *Please God, let me succeed.*

EVA AND MANUEL were crouched behind a fence. Much to their surprise, the coyote left them near the border after pointing to the canal in the distance and sarcastically wishing them good luck in their swim across.

Manuel looked around. "We're not the first people to cross here," he said, noticing the discarded clothing and used feminine products scattered around piles of empty plastic jugs and crushed soda cans. "I wonder how many made it?"

"All of them," Eva quipped.

"No way."

"What's the point of your question? We're here and we are going to make it."

"I know, I'm just saying, it's an interesting question."

"No wonder Mama wanted me to leave you in Mexico and come by myself."

"What?"

Eva smiled at Manuel, making sure his gullible disposition knew she was being sarcastic. "Are you ready?" asked Eva.

"As ready as I'll ever be."

The siblings sprinted in the direction where the coyote had pointed. They followed the sound of running water until they were standing at the edge of a canal. Water rushed through the middle of two steep concrete walls that formed a U shape.

"How do we get down there?" asked Manuel.

"Get on your butt and slide down."

"Here goes nothing," Manuel said, stripping down to his underwear. He stuffed his clothes and shoes into a garbage bag with his other possessions, using duct tape to seal off the opening of the bag. Eva stripped down to her bra and underwear, duct taping a garbage bag of her own. They carefully crawled down, sliding half the way. Manuel stuck his toe in the water. "The current is strong."

SOFIA MADE HER way into the Gadsden area. She was early. It was only a quarter to six and she didn't know what to do. After driving around town for a minute, she pulled into a dirt parking lot and shut off the engine.

EVA STUCK HER foot in the water. "You're right, the current is *so* strong," she said sarcastically to Manuel as she jumped into the water with her garbage bag.

"Very funny," replied Manuel, watching his sister forcefully paddle to the other side with her one free arm.

"*Andale*," Eva whispered, already on the other side. "It's almost six."

Manuel got in the water, his left arm gripping his garbage bag. Expecting the weight of the garbage bag to impede his progress, he was surprised that his left arm so effortlessly overcame the current.

"Manuel!" Eva whispered urgently, flailing her arms. "Look!"

Treading water, Manuel turned around to see his clothes floating downstream, freed by a gaping hole in his bag caused by him dragging it on the concrete during his slide to the bottom. He reached out and managed to grab his shoes, the only items still remaining in the bag. "Shit!"

SOFIA LOOKED AT her watch. It was five minutes to six. *Time to go.* She drove past the corner of I and 19th Street, hoping her children had arrived a few minutes early. Nobody was there. To avoid drawing attention to the rendezvous point, she decided to circle the block.

EVA AND MANUEL could see the town to their left. They scurried across the street and headed down a side road. Despite her fear of being seen, Eva could not stop laughing.

"You think this is funny?" whispered Manuel. Having lost his clothes, Manuel was forced to borrow an extra pair of shorts that Eva had packed. Seeing Manuel in nothing but women's shorts and a pair of wet shoes was enough to cut the tension of any situation.

"I'm sorry," she said, genuinely sympathetic to Manuel's situation. "You just look so ridiculous."

IT WAS EXACTLY six o'clock. Sofia pulled over at the corner of I and 19th Street. Her heart started to beat faster. The kids were nowhere to be seen.

"WHAT TIME IS it?" asked Manuel.

"Exactly six, on the nose." She looked up at the street sign. "This is it, I and 19th, where is Mama?"

FIVE MINUTES PASSED. Sofia was breaking out in a cold sweat. She did not want to stay in one place for too long. Torn about what to do, she decided to circle the block again.

MANUEL WAS TAPPING his foot and fidgeting with his hands. "Should we walk around?"

"Walk where? We don't even know where we are and you want to go walking around. Not to mention you're wearing nothing but my shorts." There was a faint humming in the distance. "What's that?"

"Look," Manuel said, pointing to the road illuminating in front of them. A van slowed down at the corner. "Is that her?"

"She said she was going to ask the rental place for a van. That looks like a van to me. C'mon."

Manuel knocked on the passenger window, startling Sofia. "You scared me," Sofia said, rolling down the window. "What are you doing standing over here? We agreed on I and 19th."

"This is 19th Street."

Sofia looked at the sign. "No, this is 19 and a *half* Street."

"What the heck is a half street?"

"This is why I told you two to study the map." Sofia looked down at Manuel's shorts. "It's a good thing I got you out of Mexico, not a moment too soon I see. Enough talk, get in, we have to get out of here."

Eva and Manuel climbed into the backseat of the van, and Sofia immediately drove away from the border.

"Look at you two, you made it! I can't tell you how relieved I am."

"I don't know what you were complaining about Mama," Eva said, "crossing the border wasn't so bad."

"Easy for you to say," Manuel said, "these shorts leave nothing to the imagination."

"Trust me, that's not the way I went," Sofia assured them.

The headlights flickering in Sofia's rearview mirror blinded her momentarily. She made a left-hand turn at the next intersection. So did the car behind her.

"What's wrong?" asked Eva.

"I think that car is following us."

"*Policía,*" Manuel said to Eva.

"What did you say?" asked Sofia.

"The SUV behind us has police lights on its roof."

"Shit." Sofia gradually pressed down on the accelerator. The SUV behind her also increased its speed. "Okay," Sofia said calmly, "let's not panic."

"I'm panicking," Manuel responded.

Eva glanced out the back of the van. "Me too. The SUV is definitely following us."

Sofia took her cell phone out of her pocket. "Take this," she said, keeping her eyes on the road as she extended her arm backward.

Eva grabbed the phone. "What are we supposed to do with this?"

"Rosario's number is in there, in the contacts section. Do you see where it says contacts on the screen, Eva?"

"Yes."

"Click—Eva, listen to me very carefully!"

"I'm listening!"

"To call her, click on the contacts button, use the arrows to scroll down to Rosario's name, and then press the green send button. Do you understand?"

"Yes, I understand."

"I want you to call her number when you get to a safe location."

"Safe location?" asked Eva.

"When I stop the van and give you the word, I want both of you to jump out and run as fast as you can into the fields. Don't stop running until you're so tired that you can't take another step and you've found a place to hide that's out of sight."

"Wait, Mama, what are you going to do?" asked Eva, startled by the seriousness of her mother's tone.

"Both of you, hang on." Sofia gunned the accelerator. The sirens on the SUV began to blaze, red lights flashing from its roof.

"What are you doing!" shouted Manuel. "You don't even know if you were going to get pulled over!"

At that moment, the only thought occupying Sofia's mind was the need for her to make sure that Eva and Manuel have an opportunity to stay in the United States. *I will not let anything happen to my children,* Sofia told herself. She flew through the streets, ignoring stop signs on the dark, deserted roads, making a sharp left turn onto a long straightaway. "I'm going to turn right up ahead and make a quick stop. When I do, I want both of you out of the van faster than anything you've ever done in your life, okay? Manuel, put your hands on the door handle and get ready to open it. Eva, put a hand on your seatbelt and the other hand on Manuel's. I want you to undo both of them the second we stop."

Sofia broke slightly and forced the old van to the right so sharply that two of the wheels momentarily left the ground. "Now!" she shouted.

Eva and Manuel raced out of the van, and Sofia quickly sped away. Seconds later, the SUV was back behind her in hot pursuit. She led them several blocks away from the spot where she dropped off the kids before reducing her speed. She knew she'd have to stop soon, but she needed a little more time to concoct a story. Before leaving Phoenix, her instincts told her to take her fake Social Security card out of her wallet, a decision that now provided the only silver lining in a very dark cloud. After two more minutes coasting down the road, Sofia pulled over, got out of the van, and raised her hands in the air.

"Don't move!" shouted a border patrol agent. He kept his gun pointed at her until his partner kicked the back of her knee, buckling her legs. A knee in her back forced her to the ground and the agent then cuffed her hands behind her back.

"Lady, you're in a lot of trouble."

Chapter 47

SOFIA SAT IN a windowless interrogation room in the Yuma border patrol station. Across the table from her, two border patrol agents filled out a form based on Sofia's answers to the questions they were asking her.

"Okay," said one of the agents. "So you have no legal status in this country and you have no family here. Is that correct?"

"Yes."

"Where do you currently live?"

"Phoenix."

"What are you doing in Gadsden?"

"I went for a drive to clear my head."

The two agents looked at each other. "Do you always need to drive so far from Phoenix to clear your head?"

"Was it that far? I must have lost track of time."

"Does being in a rental car help you clear your head?"

"What?"

"Enough with the games. You were in a rented van near the border and you were coming here to smuggle illegal aliens into the country."

"That is ridiculous."

"I want you to pretend you're me," said one of the agents. "It's five forty-five in the morning. I'm sitting in my office with my partner. A light goes off. That light tells me that someone just set off one of the motion detectors aimed at a strip of the border. Then, a few minutes later, when I go out to investigate, I find you, a resident of Phoenix, driving around the roads for no apparent reason in a rental car, and then leading me on a high-speed car chase."

Motion detectors! That had not even occurred to Sofia and her friend from work certainly never mentioned anything to her about motion detectors.

Sofia was caught. She knew there was no way for her to get out of this predicament, but she needed the agents to believe that she was not a smuggler. More importantly, she needed them to believe that she was alone. She was never much of an actress, but the emotion of the situation helped her conjure up some fake tears.

"I have AIDS, okay? Do you know what that's like? I spend all day trying to find odd jobs to support myself and pay for my medicine. I don't have any time to myself during working hours and I don't have my own car. I'm sorry if what I'm doing sounds a little suspicious to you, but I'm still coming to grips with my illness, and I don't know how far I wandered from Phoenix. And I admit, I panicked when I saw you, because, as you know, I don't have any immigration papers. But I can't go to jail. My medicines are at home and I cannot skip a single dose."

The skeptical agents impassively surveyed Sofia's tears before conferring with each other. Sofia could not tell if they were at all receptive to her pleas for mercy.

"Wait here," one of them said as they left the room.

Sofia would take whatever punishment they decided to dole out to her. She just hoped her children managed to avoid detection.

Chapter 48

*C*ONTENTMENT IS A *relative concept*, Lin thought. When suffering from severe dehydration on the ship from China, all she wanted was to make it to the United States alive. During her incarceration at the Elizabeth Detention Center, Lin prayed for an opportunity to walk the streets of New York as a free woman, even if her freedom would be short-lived; a brief moment to enjoy life on the busy streets as everyone else does, so that she could store the sensation in her memory banks and revisit the experience during one of life's many unexpected downturns. Now, Lin thought, all she wanted was a new boss. She needed to escape Dragon Lady.

Dragon Lady was the name Lin had given to the manager of the Prancing Dragon, a Chinese restaurant in the heart of Chinatown, where Lin had worked since Long got her out of the detention facility ten months ago. Barely five feet tall, Dragon Lady spent most of her time greeting patrons with a wide grin, then finding them a suitable table. Lin knew her unassuming appearance and mild manner with patrons was an act. Many of the other employees were also in debt to snakeheads and loan sharks. Dragon Lady relished the power she wielded over her employees, regularly threatening to "place a call" at the slightest perceived infraction of Prancing Dragon etiquette.

Lin worked twelve-hour shifts, six days a week. On a good day, she was responsible for pushing around the *dim sum* carts, serving mini-platefuls of shrimp dumplings, stuffed eggplant, and sticky buns. But the majority of her time was spent in the kitchen, washing pots, scrubbing pans, and cleaning the deep fryers.

Fiddling with the water temperature in one of the kitchen's industrial sinks, Lin heard the kitchen door swing open. She could feel the penetrating eyes of Dragon Lady sizing her up, looking for any excuse to lash out.

Math was never Lin's strong suit and she hoped her calculations were incorrect. At the rate she was repaying her debts, she would need to spend the next five years fearing the wrath of Dragon Lady.

"Stop wasting water!" scolded Dragon Lady. She would rather Lin burn her fingers if it could save a few pennies on the water bill.

Lin nodded submissively, trying to calm herself down. She knew there was no point in her getting anxious every time Dragon Lady yelled at her, since Dragon Lady yelled at her every day. But Lin couldn't help it. Whatever confidence she latched onto after making it to New York safely had been short-lived. Her internal demons had again taken hold, beating her into submission as if she were a stray dog taken in by an abusive owner. Part of her wished that she would lose her looming asylum hearing. That she could go back to China, her father would be there, and everything would return to normal. But it would never be the same. It couldn't. If the government deported Lin, the snakeheads and loan sharks would not get paid in full, and things would get even worse.

The door to the main dining room opened again and Lin's nerves finally settled down. Dragon Lady was gone.

It was almost quitting time. Lin hoped Shaoqing would not be too tired to meet. His job was even more demanding than hers.

"Three more pots," Lin said to herself, closing her eyes for a momentary escape. "Shaoqing better be free."

Chapter 49

IT WAS DECEMBER 8, 2000. Sofia's favorite day of the year, *el Día de la Inmaculada Concepción*—the Day of the Immaculate Conception. Work and school took a backseat today. In honor of the Virgin Mary's immaculate conception of Jesus, communities all over Mexico got together to partake in a feast in her honor. Sofia was not going to let her move to the United States get in the way of her favorite holiday, especially since she was too sick to celebrate last year. Living in a small apartment with three children now, Sofia was glad Rosario agreed to host the festival at her house.

There was much to celebrate. Eva and Manuel managed to stay hidden in Gadsden for five hours until they and Rosario found each other. Sofia's reckless behavior would typically be a reason to recommend detention pending a hearing before an immigration judge, but the border patrol agents did not want to take responsibility for depriving Sofia of her medication. The show she put on during the interrogation didn't hurt either.

Sofia's now-pending immigration proceedings were worth the opportunity to again be reunited with her children, but it was hard for her to compartmentalize her legal woes. She underestimated the feelings of uneasiness created by the uncertainty of her legal status. Now, she had to find an attorney willing to present an asylum case on her behalf.

There was a feast laid out on Rosario's kitchen table. Platters filled with tacos, *tostadas*, and *gorditas* surrounded a big bowl of Rosario's famous *posole*, a chili base, red soup with beef. A few other guests joined the two families in the feast, taking advantage of a temperate December afternoon under a cloudless sky. Rosario's husband grilled steaks in the backyard, scolding the children as they ran around with water guns, sending beams of water too close to the grill. Ranchera music blasted from the kitchen, filling the backyard with familiar horn ensembles.

Rosario and Sofia sat down on two of the lawn chairs scattered throughout the backyard, the paper plates on their laps overflowing with food.

"Thank you for hosting this," Sofia said.

"It's the least I could do, after being such a fusspot." Sofia and Rosario had gotten into an argument over Rosario's unanticipated role in the unfortunate events surrounding the morning of the kids' border crossing.

"Nonsense. Like I told you a million times, I shouldn't have put you in that position."

"And like I told *you* a million times, we're best friends, and if the situation were reversed, I know you would've done everything you could to help me." Rosario lit a cigarette. "How's Eva adjusting?"

"Good. Great. She got a job at a hair salon downtown. She used to cut all her dolls' hair when she was younger. I always thought she was just being destructive. Maybe she has a talent."

"Maybe."

"I can't tell you how nice it is to have a second income."

"I'm sure."

"She's much smarter than me," Sofia said as she watched Eva flirt with a handsome teenage boy trying to show off his dance moves. "The extra money is good, but I'd like to see Eva go back to school one day, get a real education. I could see her becoming a very successful lawyer. Lord knows she can argue."

"Or a doctor. The sky's the limit here."

Rosario's husband grabbed a bat and walked over to the piñata hanging from the lone tree in the backyard. "Everybody line up," he said, "it's time to test your strength!" Fernando hit the piñata twice, barely denting the side of the paper mache horse. Seeing Fernando struggle, Manuel stood behind him, helping him swing the bat with greater force. Candy began pouring out of a small hole in the horse's torso.

"Nice shot!" cheered Rosario's husband.

Sofia clapped. "Manuel's getting better," she said. "It was really tough when he first got here. It didn't even occur to me that school had already started. By the time I got him enrolled, all the kids had already formed their little groups. He really felt like the outsider."

"He looks happy to me," Rosario said.

"Fernando's had quite an influence on Manuel. Manuel looks out for him, like a father figure. They have a bond."

"They both know what it's like to lose someone close to them. Manolo couldn't have been much older than Fernando is now when you lost Israel."

"He still cries at night—Fernando that is. Not as much as he used to, but he does. Kids at that age can be very cruel. He tells me all the names they call him at school. For some reason they pick on him more than the other Mexican boys. It breaks my heart."

"That's what kids do." Rosario threw her cigarette butt on the grass and put it out with the sole of her sandal. "Let's be honest, that's what adults do too. You know how Mexicans feel about our neighbors to the south. We can be just as cruel."

"Not like this," Sofia said defensively.

"Really? How do Mexicans refer to people from Honduras?"

"Squash-growing mountain people who aren't smart enough to join NAFTA," Sofia said half-jokingly, causing Rosario to start laughing uncontrollably. "But we don't really mean it," Sofia continued.

"Neither do Americans when they make fun of Mexicans."

Sofia raised her eyebrows. "Really?" she asked sarcastically.

"Well," Rosario said, "I suppose some of them mean it."

"Some of us probably mean it too," Sofia conceded.

Rosario and Sofia sat in silence as they polished off the beef, tortillas, and guacamole mixed together on their paper plates.

"Should we try calling the motel again?" asked Rosario.

"It's been more than a year. She's not coming back."

"I know, but we haven't called in a few weeks."

"I wonder where she is right now?"

"I'm not sure I want to know." Rosario tilted her head back, letting the sun coat her already tanned face. "Did you find a lawyer yet?"

"No, but why let my immigration troubles spoil such a beautiful afternoon." Following Rosario's lead, Sofia laid back and let the sun's rays massage her closed eyelids. "Today belongs to the Blessed Mother."

Chapter 50

"I'M GOING DOWNTOWN, Millennium Hilton on Church Street." Tesfaye helped the elder gentleman place his suiter in the trunk.

"Where are you from, sir?" inquired the man in an exceptionally cordial manner.

"Kenya."

"Never been. I went on safari with the wife about ten years ago, before she passed away. I think it was in Tanzania. Great time. The whole family went, even the grandkids." After a few seconds of silence, he continued, "How do you like it here in the States?"

"What's not to like?" Tesfaye enjoyed the moments when the truth matched up to the answers passengers wanted to hear. He was indeed pleasantly surprised by his assimilation to life in New York. He even picked up some of his passengers' ruder habits, getting into the occasional shouting match with cars that veered too close to his pristinely maintained taxi.

The priest who helped Tesfaye start his search for an asylum attorney proved to be an invaluable source of motivation, coaxing him to join a group dedicated to helping people who were suffering from Post-Traumatic Stress Disorder. Tesfaye did not like to think of himself as being inflicted with a "disorder," but he could not deny that he was experiencing many of the symptoms associated with PTSD—a raised heart rate and sweaty palms when he thought about Demissie, recurrent nightmares about Ayana and the kids, and heightened feelings of guilt and shame that never seemed to dissipate. Even in these PTSD meetings, Tesfaye kept his hand close to his chest, hesitant to reveal too many details of his lurid past.

Martin had not called Tesfaye in the past few months with any updates about the upcoming asylum hearing. The communication vacuum was a welcome reprieve for Tesfaye, who was more than happy to put the whole thing out of his mind.

Traffic downtown was bumper to bumper. Tesfaye resisted the urge to let out a muffled curse or two, as he had taken to doing in front of his grittier passengers.

"What's going on?" asked the gentleman.

"It's New York, there's traffic. If you're in a hurry, it might be faster to walk. We're not too far from the hotel."

"I spent the first seventy years of my life in a hurry. I'm more than happy to slow down the pace."

"I don't mind if you don't." Tesfaye heard the sound of sirens blazing. "Must be some kind of accident." In his rearview mirror, he saw the older gentleman lowering his head, looking out the front windshield.

"You see that," said the older gentleman. "There's smoke coming from the World Trade Center—a lot of smoke."

When the second plane hit the other building, the gentleman opened the back door of the cab. "That was no accident."

"It didn't appear to be," agreed Tesfaye, joining the man outside. Other motorists got out of their vehicles and lined the street. His arms folded, Tesfaye looked around the eclectic mix of onlookers collectively gasping at the events they witnessed next. He shared in their sorrow. And for a moment, it didn't matter who amongst them was living in New York illegally.

Chapter 51

THE ONSET OF winter sent cold winds howling between skyscrapers, forcing Tesfaye to shut the windows of his cab and expend the additional gas needed to keep the interior warm enough for his passengers. The Christmas tree at Rockefeller Center did little to brighten the somber mood of the city. A sizable portion of southern Manhattan was still blocked off, piles of debris waiting to be removed. Unfortunately for Tesfaye, business was way down and he found it necessary to work longer hours.

Driving up Tenth Avenue, he saw an elderly woman on the side of the road trying to hail a cab with her trembling hand. Signaling, he darted over two lanes of traffic and pulled over by the sidewalk. As he stopped, Tesfaye could hear the screeching of brakes a second before the car behind him plowed into his cab.

For a moment, he was transported back to Addis Ababa, flickers of light flashing in his peripheral vision after Negasi slammed on the brakes to avoid barreling into the rebels' jeep.

"Son of a bitch," Tesfaye heard the man behind him shout as he opened the door of his car. Tesfaye joined him outside to survey the damage. When he got out of the car, the middle-aged Asian man was already wagging his finger in Tesfaye's direction.

"Why would you stop short like that?"

"Stop short?" asked Tesfaye. "I signaled and pulled over. That's what taxis do. You came out of nowhere."

"Nowhere? It's called *behind* you. That's where cars come from when you stop in the middle of the road. They come from *behind* you," the Asian man repeated, caustically emphasizing his words.

"Don't you worry," the elderly woman said to Tesfaye. "I saw the whole thing." She pointed at the Asian gentleman. "That man was driving like a lunatic."

"Listen, ma'am," said the Asian man. "Do I look retired? Do you think I can just leisurely cruise around the city and stare at fluffy clouds? No. I have work to do. And today I have to drag my ass to New Jersey. So please, I would appreciate it if you could mind your own business."

The elderly woman was taken back. "In all my years, I've never heard such disrespect."

"Well that's probably because you weren't listening."

Tesfaye attempted to reason with the man. "How about we just take a minute here to cool down."

The Asian man took a step toward Tesfaye and spoke quietly in his ear. "Listen buddy, I deal with jerkoffs like you everyday, so I know you're probably not in this country legally."

Not expecting such a comment, Tesfaye found himself lost for words.

"I'll gather from your silence that I'm on the right track. We both know that you veered over erratically and I might have been driving a little fast. So why don't you tell that lady to mind her own goddamn business, get in your car, and just drive away. If you do that, I won't call INS and get you deported back to Zanzibar or wherever."

Tesfaye stood defiantly with his arms crossed. "Listen asshole, I already have an immigration attorney."

The Asian man snickered. "You think that means they can't detain you? Especially after you caused an accident. You think they give a shit about you with 9/11 fresh in their mind?"

"*You* caused the accident."

"Fine. How about you explain that to INS. I'll call them right now. Look," he said, holding up his phone, "I have their number right here. Or how about I write down your license plate number so you can worry for the rest of your life whether you'll be waking up to the sound of an immigration agent knocking on your door."

Maintaining his composure, Tesfaye backed away toward the driver's door of his taxi.

"Where are you going?" asked the elderly lady.

"I'm sorry, ma'am," Tesfaye said. "I won't be able to take you, I'm off duty."

"Shouldn't we call the police?"

"No need," Tesfaye assured her. "You'll get another cab in no time."

Chapter 52

A FTER A VERBAL lashing from Dragon Lady for failing to provide enough advanced notice, Lin took the afternoon off from washing dishes to meet with her attorney. The Broadway law office was right on the outskirts of Chinatown. Lin pleaded with her uncle to join her and he reluctantly agreed.

Taking the elevator to the fourteenth floor, Lin and Long walked into the law office of David Kon, who greeted them at the door. David led them back to his office, wincing in pain as he sat down in a ripped leather chair behind a particleboard desk designed to look like real wood.

"Are you okay?" Long asked David.

"You'll have to excuse me," David said, "my neck is a little sore. I was in an accident yesterday. Some crazy taxi driver cut me off."

"Nothing serious I hope."

"I'll live," David joked, turning his attention to Lin. "You are a very lucky young woman. Your mother has done a lot of work for you back home." He took out a stack of documents. "She went through all this trouble for you—your household registration, identity card, pictures of your house and family, all these medical records, affidavits from friends and family and doctors. She even found a notary to swear that all these documents are genuine."

"She did all that?" asked Lin, not even sure what a notary was.

"As I said, you are a very lucky little lady. I've had clients who can't even find their identity card. Could you imagine trying to prove you were persecuted when you can't even prove who you are? Especially now after 9/11, it's very important to have identity documents. One of the 9/11 hijackers used the asylum process to get into the country legally."

"Really?" asked Long.

"Well, you have nothing to worry about Lin, unless you're a terrorist," David said sarcastically as he let out an unusually high pitch, extended laugh.

"What?" Lin asked, fearing David might have a screw loose.

"Just kidding," David said, reining himself in. Looking serious now, he handed Lin a form. "I want you to look this over. This is an asylum application. Your mother has filled in most of the information for you. All the biographical information, everywhere you've ever lived, all the bad things that happened in your life, why you fear going back to China. In the end, you are responsible for making sure that everything in the application is accurate. So take it home with you, read it over, and add anything that she forgot. If you could mail it to me when you're done, I'll have someone translate it and then give you a copy to sign. How does that sound?"

Lin flipped through the pages of the asylum application, becoming increasingly confused as she read the answers her mother filled in, especially when she got to the part of the application that asked her to explain why she feared returning to China. "But Mr. Kon, I . . . ."

"I know," David interrupted, turning his attention to Long. "It's often very traumatizing for people to have to read over all the terrible events of the past." He returned his attention to Lin. "You need to be strong. If you're reading something that makes you uncomfortable, just put it down and take some deep breaths. We'll get through this. The most important thing is that you tell your story at trial *exactly* as you have it in your asylum statement. The last thing you want is an ill-tempered immigration judge questioning whether or not you're telling the truth. Do you understand?"

Lin nodded.

"Fantastic. I do apologize, I spent the morning lying in bed trying to rest my back, so I haven't had time to make copies of all these documents, but when I do, I'll send you a copy of all of them. I'm sure you'd like to look these over as well. You might take solace knowing how many friends and family have written to support you."

Friends and family? Lin thought as she grew more confused. "I guess," she responded, not knowing what else to say.

David stood up and shook Lin's hand, then he bowed toward Long. "I appreciate both of you taking the time to come here today. I have your phone number. Don't worry, Lin, in no time you'll be able to tell your full story to the immigration judge, the judge will grant you asylum, and we'll all walk out of the courtroom happy."

"You're quite the optimist," Long said.

"I've never heard of someone winning a case through unbridled pessimism, have you?"

"I suppose not," Long said, as he headed for the door with Lin.

"Don't forget to mail back that asylum application."

Chapter 53

E THAN KNOCKED ON his boss's door. "You wanted to see me?"
"Take a seat," Jim said. Ethan never liked the sound of that. "Have you been working at all on the identity theft cases?"

Ethan tried to read Jim's face to sense which answer he wanted to hear. The truth was that Ethan could not bring himself to stop gathering information on the identity thefts even though he had not been authorized to actually pursue any of the leads for some time. He assumed that Jim was going to give him a hard time for continuing to add pushpins to the map still mounted in his office. But this time, Jim's face did not appear as menacing.

"It's pretty much dead."

"Well, it's time to do some mouth-to-mouth."

"What gives?"

"9/11. That's what gives. The powers that be have decided that they want to make sure the people living in this great nation are who they say they are. Quite a novelty. That means tracking down identity thieves is now a matter of national security. Any other hotspots in mind, according to your map?"

"I have a few in mind."

"Pick the most promising one that's close to an immigration court."

"Close to an immigration court?"

"You know the deal. I send you out there to play detective and you take on a few cases while you're there."

"But I thought you don't need to justify my trips. Right? National security and all."

"Close the door."

Ethan didn't like the sound of that either. He got up and closed the door.

Jim leaned forward and clasped his hands together. "I don't think you're some hothead that goes around causing problems. But I know why you chose to join INS—or Homeland Security Department, or whatever the heck they are calling us now—instead of another law enforcement agency."

"With all due respect sir, *that* happened a long time ago and it has nothing to do with how I do my job."

"That's bullshit and you know it. Don't get me wrong. I'm not saying it as a negative necessarily. You bring a lot of passion to the job and that's a good thing. But, I want you to have some regular appearances in immigration court while you're out there just to keep you grounded."

"Sir . . ."

"It's not negotiable. Have your itinerary ready for me to sign off on by the end of the week."

Chapter 54

AFTER JIM APPROVED their itinerary, Ethan and Ryan were on a plane to Phoenix, Arizona. They retrieved their bags and set out to investigate another cluster of Ethan's pushpins. The first two houses fit the most common profile. They were located in neighborhoods that had mailboxes on the street and owners who claimed to be in the dark about any transgressions. The third house they visited was in a quiet, ethnically diverse middle class neighborhood. Ethan and Ryan pulled up to the front of the house.

"No mailbox by the street," Ryan said.

"No For Sale sign either."

They walked up to the front door and rang the bell.

Rosario struggled to her feet when she heard the doorbell, gaining momentum as she headed for the front door, her hips swinging back and forth. She looked out the peephole at two men standing on her front porch. "Can I help you?" she shouted without opening the door.

"Good afternoon, ma'am," Ethan shouted back. "My name is Ethan Shaw, I'm an agent with the United States government. I was wondering if I may have a moment of your time?"

Rosario was skeptical. These men were not wearing uniforms, nor did their appearance give any other indication that they were federal agents. "Do you have any identification?"

Ethan took out his badge and placed it a few inches from the peephole. Rosario squinted to read the writing on the shiny silver badge. She grew lightheaded when she made out the word 'immigration' on the badge. She slumped over, feeling as though she was about to throw up.

"Ma'am, you still there?"

Rosario took a few deep breaths and regained her composure. She unlatched the deadbolt and greeted the agents with a smile as she opened the door.

"I didn't mean to startle you," Ethan said reassuringly. "I just have a few questions I want to ask you regarding an investigation I'm involved in."

"Okay."

"Does anyone else live here with you?"

"Yes, my family."

"So you're married?"

"Yes."

"Is your husband home?"

"No."

"What does he do?"

"He's a truck driver."

"Is he a United States citizen?" asked Ryan.

"Yes."

"What about you?" Ethan followed up.

"No, I don't drive trucks."

"I mean are you a United States citizen?"

"Yes, I'm a citizen," Rosario proudly responded, trying to force a smile.

"Are you a United States national?" Ethan asked.

"What?"

"Were you born in this country, ma'am?"

"No."

"Where were you born?"

"Mexico."

"Did you grow up in Mexico?"

"Yes."

"You still have a lot of friends from Mexico, that you keep in touch with?"

"Sure, I have some."

"They ever come to visit you in the States?"

Rosario felt her face flush red. "What do you mean?" she asked, stalling for time, not wanting to give an answer that could get her in trouble.

"It's a simple question, ma'am. Any of your friends or family from Mexico ever come visit you in Arizona?"

"No. They can't get papers. So I go to visit them."

"Have you noticed any items being delivered to your house that you didn't order?"

"Delivered, sir?"

"You know, from the post office. Like a television set or a camera, anything like that?"

"No. Nothing like that."

"You own a computer, ma'am?"

"No, I don't know how to work them."

"You ever buy a computer, maybe as a gift for a friend?"

"Sir, I don't have the money for that."

Ethan skimmed his notes. "According to our records, three laptops were delivered to this address on September 26, 1999."

Rosario felt her chest caving in as she thought about the laptops Sofia had sold to pay her back when Sofia first came to the United States. Rosario never fully believed Sofia's story that she won the laptops in a raffle, but she had looked the other way at the time, burying her head in the sand and hoping that she would never find herself in the predicament she was now in. "I don't know anything about that. Are you sure you have the right address?"

"We definitely have the right address," Ryan insisted. "Do you have a maid?"

"No."

"Have you ever employed anyone illegally living in this country or let anyone illegal live in your house?"

"Heavens no," Rosario said indignantly, praying that the agents did not have any evidence that Sofia had lived with her.

"Are you sure? We're not here to get you in trouble if you did. Frankly, we could care less."

"I'm sure."

"Do you have any idea why someone would have signed for three laptops at this address?"

"I don't know, honestly."

"Were you working in September of 1999?"

"Yes."

"Where?"

"At a beauty parlor in town."

"You still work there?"

"Yes."

"Then what are you doing home right now?"

"I have a day off," Rosario said, momentarily relieved that she was able to provide a truthful answer.

"If we talked to your employer, they could verify that you worked there in September 1999?"

"Yes."

"And whether you were working during the day on September 26, 1999?"

"I suppose so."

"Would you mind writing down the address of your employer?" asked Ryan as he handed Rosario a pen and turned to a blank page in his notepad.

After Rosario had written down the address, Ethan handed her his business card. "If you think of anything else, anything at all you might have forgotten to tell us, would you please give me a call?"

"Of course."

"If someone is using your house for illegal activity, I'm sure you would want to put a stop to it as well, right?"

"I certainly would."

"Thank you for your time, ma'am," Ethan said.

As she shut the front door, Rosario crouched down, her hands trembling, and immediately started to cry. She wanted to call Sofia right away and start yelling at her. More importantly, she wanted to find out exactly what Sofia had done, so that she could better answer any follow-up questions the agents might have. But she decided against it. Despite her anger, Rosario did not want to upset Sofia right now. Sofia's trial was rapidly approaching and Rosario knew that Sofia was particularly anxious about it. After all, Rosario thought, if Sofia lost her trial, then she would be deported and the agents could never find her. For a moment, Rosario wished that Sofia would lose her trial so that this whole mess would go away. She slapped herself across the face in a symbolic effort to cast out her guilty thoughts and repeated the sign of the cross several times with a clenched fist.

"So what do you think?" asked Ethan as he and Ryan walked back to their car.

"Doesn't fit the typical mold of houses we've seen."

"I'd like to verify her story with her employer."

"You want to do that today?"

"Yeah, let's make a quick trip down there. Then I gotta get back to the hotel and prepare for these stupid hearings."

Chapter 55

THE FIRST HALF of 2002 had been a mixed bag for Sofia. She was overjoyed to be reunited with her children and to see them take to their new school. But her health was deteriorating. Dr. Garcia could not definitively pinpoint the cause. "Sometimes," he had told her, "the virus just manages to build up an immunity to the drugs." He altered the composition of her drug cocktail, but admitted that his options were limited. The tragedy of 9/11 had unwittingly created its own side effects for the Helping Hands Medical Clinic. Financial contributions and surplus drug donations to immigrant groups had plummeted, limiting Dr. Garcia's prescription choices.

Dr. Garcia had another theory to account for part of Sofia's faltering health: stress. Unwavering stress. Stress from the upcoming trial, wreaking havoc on her immune system. Sofia knew the trial was pushing her blood pressure higher and she was not surprised when she woke up nauseous on the morning of her trial. The day had finally come.

The courtroom at the Phoenix immigration court was nothing like Sofia had pictured. The law programs she watched on television gave the impression of huge courtrooms lined with mahogany and two-story tall ceilings. But this room was small and there was no mahogany. The white walls of the courtroom surrounded a slightly elevated judge's chair positioned four feet away from two tables. A few benches for the public lined the back of the room. Rosario took a seat on the front bench. Although Eva and Manuel wanted to come to court to support their mother, Sofia knew it would be a bad idea. The immigration authorities did not know about her children. She wanted to keep it that way.

"Good luck," Rosario said as they embraced, Sofia then taking a seat at the table she hoped was for her.

Ethan walked into the courtroom, his papers packed in a worn leather briefcase slung over his shoulder. He was looking down at some of his notes as he walked past Rosario.

When Rosario saw Ethan's profile, she nearly fell off the bench. She remembered him from their conversation a few days ago, the conversation that had hindered her ability to sleep through the night ever since. Instinctively, she put her head down and pretended to fiddle with her shoelaces as she contemplated what to do next. Seeing no other option, she sneaked out of the courtroom, praying that Ethan did not witness her precipitous departure.

"No need to stand up," said the judge as she entered the courtroom from a door behind the judge's bench. "Okay," the judge continued, "this is the deportation hearing of Sofia Vargas. We have Peter Amarios here as the interpreter," she said, pointing to a smiling Hispanic man who sat down next to Sofia, "and Ethan Shaw for the government. Now Ms. Vargas, I see you don't have an attorney."

"That is correct, *Señora* Judge," Sofia responded after the interpreter translated the judge's comments into Spanish.

"Would you like some more time to try and find one?"

"No."

"Are you sure?"

Sofia did want a lawyer. She made several calls to immigration attorneys only to find that each charged a minimum of five thousand dollars. Although she had become rather savvy in finding creative ways to obtain money in a bind, the cost just seemed too daunting. Weighing even more heavily on her decision, Sofia did not think she could physically handle any more delays. The anticipation of this day was eating her alive. The thought of living with the anxiety of not knowing whether she would get asylum was too much for her frail body to endure.

"I'm sure," said Sofia. "I just want to tell my story."

Ethan looked at Sofia with disdain. He thought about how the formalities of a court hearing were a waste of his time. All he had in front of him was a report from the border patrol agents who had arrested Sofia, which included a little background information and a few jumbled notes that basically consisted of Sofia saying she had HIV and begging to stay in the country. He did not have anything else to go on other than the fact that she was from Mexico. No Social Security number had been provided, no tax returns, and no statement about why she thought she was entitled to stay in the country under the law. If she had hired an attorney, Ethan figured, then maybe he would have an embellished statement to pounce on. He could see just by looking at Sofia that she was frail, but he was still irritated that he had to waste his morning sitting through the hearing when she did not even have an attorney, and he was annoyed that the government had to front the bill for a courtroom, and a judge, and a government attorney, and an interpreter, just because some lady from Mexico did not feel like following the rules like millions of other perspective immigrants, who were waiting patiently all over the world to come to the United States. Instead, because she didn't have an attorney, Ethan knew that the immigration judge would take control of most of the questioning and coddle this woman, while he sat muzzled at his table.

The immigration judge asked Sofia to explain all the reasons why she thought she would be persecuted if she was deported to Mexico. Sofia described what Guillermo did to her, how everyone treated her like dirt after word of her sickness spread, how she could not get any medication in Escuinapa, and that her journey to the United States was the only reason why she was still alive.

"Ms. Vargas," the judge said, "don't get me wrong. I'm not under any delusion that the medical system in Mexico is comparable to ours here in the United States. But the way you're describing it makes it seem incredibly primitive. Is it possible that perhaps you are exaggerating the situation slightly?"

"No," Sofia said assuredly. "I am *not* exaggerating."

SOFIA HAD NOT opened her eyes since Guillermo ripped off her underwear. By the time the third man was done with her, tears were streaming down her temples, soaking a small area of the couch cushion that her head was pressed against. Blocking out the men's cheering, she didn't hear Israel sobbing as he lay on the floor, forced to watch what was happening by whichever gun-wielding drug-pusher was not raping his wife at the time.

Finally, when it was all over, Sofia lunged up to retrieve her clothes. Her heart sank further when she saw blood streaked across Israel's face. He had repeatedly wiped away the tears with the bloodstained hand that he had used to cup the bullet still lodged in his shoulder. And now there he lay, the father of her children, the only man she had ever loved, relegated to the floor, forced to watch three men rape her, and laugh while they did it.

Sofia thought about all the bickering between her and Israel over the years, all the little disagreements that inevitably come up in any relationship between two people who decide to share a life together. They suddenly seemed like such an unnecessary waste of the limited time she now realized life gave her to spend with Israel, this wonderful, caring man who now looked as helpless as an infant.

Guillermo wagged his finger at Sofia, who was struggling to put on her underwear with her shaking hands. "Let this be a lesson to anyone who thinks twice about fucking with my money," he said as he raised his gun and pointed it at Israel.

"Please," Israel pleaded, defensively extending out his hand as if it would be able to protect him against a bullet.

Guillermo just smiled. "You shouldn't have fucked with *El Memo*."

The loud bang echoed through the house as the bullet pierced Israel's chest. When he slumped over, blood trickled out of his mouth.

"No!" screamed Sofia.

"Make sure you let everyone know what happens to thieves," Guillermo said, kicking over a vase when he left the house with the other two.

"No!" screamed Sofia a second time, forgetting momentarily that the kids were in the next room. She rushed over to her husband's body. *"Mi amor!"* Sofia gasped for air, trying to figure out what to do. "No! No!" she kept repeating. "This can't be happening!"

She put her shirt on and rushed to the children's bedroom. "It's still not safe," she yelled into the room through the closed door, her voice trembling, "stay under your beds."

"Mama," she heard Eva whimper.

"Nobody's going to hurt you, just stay under your bed."

Her body aching, heart racing, Sofia stood paralyzed in the hallway. *What do I do now?* She stumbled to the phone and called for an ambulance. For a few moments she stood motionless, succumbing to the powerful malaise fogging her perception. The room was spinning. She tried to gather her composure. Despite feeling humiliated, she could not handle the situation by herself. She picked up the phone and called her sister Miranda before rushing back over to Israel.

"Israel," she whispered. *"Mi amor."* She kissed him on the forehead, blood rubbing off onto her lips. His eyes were shut and he wasn't moving. Sofia checked for a pulse. She couldn't tell. Her clouded mind was slowly reconnecting to her body, but the connection was still frail. Nothing felt real.

Five minutes later, Miranda ran into the house through the open front door. "Oh my God!" she gasped. *"Ay,* Israel," she said, too shocked by the situation to cry. "What happened?"

There was no answer. "Sofia! What happened?"

"Guillermo," Sofia moaned in the midst of her sobbing.

"We have to get him to a doctor."

"I called an ambulance."

"We can't wait for an ambulance! Who knows how long it will take them to get here if they even bother showing up. We have to bring him to the doctor." Miranda looked around. "Where are the kids?"

"In their bedroom."

"Okay. Okay," she said, trying to assess the situation. Overwhelmed, Miranda collapsed onto the sofa and lowered her head between her legs to alleviate the sudden lightheadedness that was overpowering her will to act quickly. "Oh my God!" she repeated.

"Miranda, what are we going to do?" shouted a panicked Sofia, unsympathetic to her sister's sudden state of shock.

"I'll call Edgar to come watch the kids. You and I are going to get Israel in the car and take him to a doctor. I'll call and tell the clinic we're on our way. You just go grab a pair of pants."

The two struggled to load Israel into the car. They sped to the *Centro Medico Cruzroja*—Red Cross Medical Center—the only health clinic in town. Sofia ran into the clinic. "Help! I need help!"

Two men wearing white robes walked briskly to the front of the clinic. "The supervising doctor is on his way, let's get him inside." The two men helped carry Israel to a table in the back of the clinic.

"Is he alive?" asked Sofia.

One of the men held his hand to Israel's mouth. "I think I can feel a little breath."

The other doctor brought over a container of rubbing alcohol and started to pour it on Israel's forehead.

"What are you doing?" screamed Miranda.

"You aren't allowed to be back here. Both of you need to go to the waiting room."

The front door of the clinic opened and slammed shut. The supervising doctor ran into the back room. "Out of the way," he said, "give me some space." He sniffed the air around Israel. "This man is drunk, he must have stumbled and fallen down."

Sofia grabbed her hair and stomped on the floor. "What are you talking about?"

"I need you to wait outside." He turned to one of the younger doctors. "Can you please escort them out of here."

"He's been shot!" screamed Sofia as one of the men pulled her away. "He was shot in the chest! He's not drunk, he's been shot!"

THE IMMIGRATION JUDGE paused for a moment, pondering her next question. "What about other places in Mexico? Bigger cities. Surely you must be able to get treatment there?"

"A couple of years after I was raped, when I first noticed something was not right and the Red Cross in town could not figure out what was wrong with me, I went to a hospital in Mazatlán. That is when I first found out I had this disease. They put me on a . . ." Sofia pointed to the veins in her arm.

"An IV?" asked the judge.

"Yes, yes, an IV. And I started to feel much worse because the doctors and nurses were messing with me. After they found out about my condition, they put different drugs in me—bad drugs, not drugs to help. I saw them all laughing when they didn't think I was awake."

"Why would they do that?"

"Because they looked at me like a piece of garbage. When a man has HIV in Mexico, everyone thinks he got it because he is gay."

Ethan stood to his feet, feeling the need to say something to pass the time. "Your Honor, not to state the obvious, but she is not a man."

"I was just going to follow up on that point, Mr. Shaw." She directed her attention to Sofia. "Ms. Vargas, I don't see how that is relevant to your situation."

"If you are a woman with HIV, all that means is that you've been with a gay man—it's just as bad."

"Here's the problem as I see it, Ms. Vargas. The law is very clear. We don't just let people stay in the United States because they've been wronged in the past. The harm has to be on account of one of five grounds—political opinion, religion, ethnicity, race, or social group. These men did not rape you or kill your husband for any of these reasons. It sounds like they did it because they thought he stole their money. That's just a run-of-the-mill criminal act. So while I sympathize with your situation, I cannot grant you asylum simply because you were raped by criminals. Do you understand?"

Sofia was feeling despondent. She turned around to look at Rosario's comforting face for support, but the benches were empty. Suddenly, she felt as alone as she had in the desert, when she was lying on her back letting the sun bake her dehydrated skin.

"Ms. Vargas? Do you understand?"

"I'll die if you make me go back. What about my condition, the HIV?"

Ethan sneered at Sofia as he thought about all the people around the world dying of AIDS. *Are we supposed to take them all in?* He wanted to scream at her.

"I'm not saying that you won't be discriminated against," the immigration judge politely acknowledged. "I believe what you're telling me and I've heard many cases from people who report similar discriminatory conduct for a variety of reasons. But we can't let you stay simply because you may be harassed or because the medical clinic in your town isn't that good. After all, the clinic doesn't let people die *because* they have HIV. It sounds like they just don't have the money to treat your condition. That just doesn't have anything to do with asylum."

"But what about the doctors in the city who were making fun of me?"

"Did those doctors have some of the more current HIV medications?"

"I couldn't afford them."

"See right there, that's the point. It's a money issue. They didn't deny you the drug because you're Catholic or because you're Mexican. Do you see what I'm saying?"

Sofia started to cry. "Isn't there any way you could show me mercy? Any way at all, after everything I've been through?"

The immigration judge thought about Sofia's question. "We do have something called humanitarian asylum." Ethan perked up as the immigration judge continued. "It can be used when there is no risk of persecution in the future, but an exception is made because the past harm was so awful. But that is really extreme. It's granted in very, very few cases."

"Yes! What you just said—humane asylum. *Señora* Judge, I am at your mercy."

The immigration judge turned to Ethan. "Mr. Shaw, care to respond?"

Chapter 56

E VA COULD NOT understand Sofia's behavior. It didn't make any sense. In the three weeks since the immigration judge denied her mother's asylum claim, she had witnessed Sofia's mood get *better*. Much better. Sofia was initially heartbroken when the judge graciously told her that her circumstances were not extreme enough to warrant a grant of humanitarian asylum. Seeing her mother so depressed initially, Eva decided to hold off on discussing an appeal. She and Rosario read the slip of paper the clerk at the court handed Sofia after the trial. It said that she had thirty days to file an appeal.

Time was winding down. Eva decided she could not hold off any longer. Her mother's curious jubilation should have made it easier for her to approach Sofia, but it didn't. Eva was skeptical. Her gut told her that Sofia was a house of cards waiting to tumble at the slightest tug.

"Mama," said Eva, who was helping Sofia wash the dishes. "I need to talk to you."

"Sure, dear."

"Can we sit down?"

Sofia removed the rubber gloves she was using to scrub the pots and took a seat at the kitchen table next to Eva. "What's on your mind?" she asked, rubbing Eva's knee and smiling from ear to ear.

"Mama, I want to talk to you about your asylum case." She unfolded the piece of paper that the clerk at the immigration court had given to Sofia. "According to this paper, they can deport you unless you appeal the decision in the next nine days."

"I know," Sofia said cheerfully. "I'm not going to appeal."

"You're not? Why?"

"Because this is how God wills it to be."

"That doesn't make any sense. Why wouldn't you want to stay here with me and Manuel, and Rosario, and Fernando?"

"Of course I want to be here with you. Nothing would make me happier than to watch you and Manolo grow older, get married, for me to be a grandmother."

"Then why not appeal? Maybe you could win. I was talking to a friend at the salon, she told me that one of her friends was ordered to leave the country, but then she appealed and now she has a green card."

"Eva, we both know I'm not going to grow old and I'm not going to be able to see you get married."

"Not with that attitude. They're coming out with new treatments all the time. Who knows, maybe soon they'll come out with a cure."

Sofia sat back in her chair, the wobbly legs creaking beneath her. "It feels like it did before. Remember in Mexico when my health started to fail all of the sudden." She took a long, slow breath, allowing her chest to fill up completely, and then she exhaled just as slowly. "It's attacking me right now, I can feel it. There are so many germs in the air all around me that are destroying my weakened immune system." Sofia smiled. "My body put up a pretty good fight though, didn't it?"

Eva started to choke up. "I don't care what you say, you are a fighter. You made it across the desert, you can handle a little appeal."

"Maybe, but this is how it's meant to be."

"Why do you keep saying that?" asked Eva, growing frustrated.

With her fingertips, Sofia played with the cross around her neck. "Think of all the horrible things that have happened to us these last seven years. Yet here we are, all of us, in the United States. Do you remember when your father got you a Cabbage Patch Kid for Christmas?"

"Sort of."

"You were so happy that night. You had this look in your eye, you couldn't believe the doll was actually yours."

"It was just a silly toy."

"No Eva, it was more than that. That night, you were playing with the same doll as all the little girls in the United States. Just think, if I didn't get sick, we wouldn't be here right now. You and Manuel wouldn't have the opportunity to make a life for yourself in the United States. You'd still be in Escuinapa growing tomatoes."

"Are you crazy? You're trying to tell me it was a good thing that *Papa* was killed and that you got HIV? No fucking way!"

"Eva, watch your mouth."

"I'm sorry, but you're not making sense and it's really starting to scare me."

"I'm making perfect sense. When I was in the desert, I thought I was going to die. I hadn't seen the coyote in hours because I was too weak to keep up. If I was able to keep up with the group, I would be dead right now, killed by bandits, and my body would be lying in the middle of the desert getting eaten by little critters."

"Don't say such a thing."

"But it's true. My illness saved my life in the desert. And you know what else? If it wasn't for Fernando slowing down his mother, I probably wouldn't have made it out of the desert. If she kept up with the others, the bandits would have killed her too. But she was there to guide me, to encourage me to continue when I thought I lost the will to live. And look at me now. Because of my illness I am here, taking care of the boy who saved my life, with both of my real children by my side. And Fernando, who had to run around Tucson, trying to find his lost mother, he is now thriving with the help of Manuel, because he also had to endure the trauma of being around when a parent disappeared. These are not coincidences, Eva, it's part of God's plan. These are the sacrifices God wanted me and your father to make in order to give you and Manolo a better life."

Eva refused to accept Sofia's reasoning. "No! God does not want you to leave yet!"

"He does." Sofia grabbed her daughter's hand. "Eva, I don't want to die here in front of you. I should die in Escuinapa and be buried next to your father."

"Your purpose in life is not over," Eva said forcefully. "I am not going to let you just give up and go home. If you get sicker then I am the one who should take care of you. I'm sorry, I can't accept what you're saying. I'm calling Rosario. Maybe she can get you to see reason."

Chapter 57

ETHAN'S PERSISTENCE FINALLY paid off. He and Ryan fortuitously received the lead they were looking for. For many months, their door-to-door searches around the country had led to dead ends. They had almost given up during a trip to Los Angeles when they caught a lucky break. They tracked down an illegal immigrant who had used someone else's Social Security number to open a fraudulent account and buy a landslide of Christmas presents he had no intention of paying for. Ethan enjoyed watching the man begin to cry after he got caught, watching him beg for mercy. He tried to explain that none of his children back home in Mexico ever had any toys to play with and that he was just trying to bring them a little joy. He even tried to convince Ethan that one of his children was sick and might not make it through winter. Ethan did not believe a word of it. The illegal immigrant's pleas only angered him more.

When Ryan threatened the man with years of jail time, he quickly told them everything. He explained that there were organizations on the Mexican border that handed out Social Security cards to immigrants to entice them to use their coyotes to cross the border. But the real kicker for Ethan and Ryan was that this man had not gotten his Social Security card until he came to the United States. There was some mix up and he lost his card in the desert. The coyote told him that he could get another card if he paid double. When the man agreed, he was directed to an address in San Diego to get the Social Security card. He didn't see the person who gave him the card. Rather, he knocked on the door and the card was shoved through a mail slot. Much to Ethan's frustration, the man could not remember the address, but he did remember what the house looked like. Ryan was tasked with driving this man up and down the streets of San Diego because Ethan had to fly back east for a scheduled appearance in immigration court.

Even though Ethan had to try two cases the next day, he had barely looked at the case files. One of the files belonged to Lin. Ethan did not recognize the name. He'd seen a hundred cases of Chinese immigrants named Lin, or Jin, or Yang, or Yen, and he couldn't keep them all straight. He quickly glanced at the picture and had the same reaction. He read the transcript of the interview he performed during intake, slightly aghast at the brevity of his questioning. Then Ethan remembered that he was focused on his first trip to San Diego. He had known at the time that he was kicking the can down the road when he gave the interview short shrift. Now he was down the road, and his thoughts were still focused on the identity theft case and getting back to San Diego.

He turned to the other case file. A middle-aged Ethiopian man named Tesfaye. Ethan had not tried many cases that involved Ethiopian nationals, but he had quite a few from various countries in Africa. He considered them all to be remarkably similar. Some rebel government that did not obey the rule of law did something bad or authorized the police to do something bad. Usually the African immigrants' stories were so riddled with holes that Ethan would enjoy watching them unwittingly contradict themselves when they answered questions during direct examination. Then, Ethan would bring them all to the surface during cross-examination and watch the immigrants' faces change as they realized the proverbial stake was slowly being driven through their hearts.

Ethan read Tesfaye's compelling story for the first time and was intrigued. Tesfaye's story was different than the other cases from Africa that he was used to. Ethan could see that he would have his work cut out for him. The attorney who filled out Tesfaye's asylum application did so immaculately and with compelling detail. After scribbling down some notes, Ethan began to do some research on the State Department databases. After an hour, he started to smile. "Got him."

Chapter 58

TESFAYE WAITED IN the reception area of the immigration court in downtown Manhattan, the largest federal building in the United States. The immigration court was one of dozens spread throughout the country, where nearly two hundred judges would hear hundreds of thousands of cases each year. As he sat next to Martin, Tesfaye attempted to find a comfortable position in the attached seats that looked like they were swiped from an airport terminal. A sheet of printer paper for each of the courtrooms was scotch-taped to the walls around him, listing each case that would be heard that day, alongside a list of the languages that each of the immigrants would use to testify.

It had been more than three years since Tesfaye initially filled out an asylum application with Martin's help. Three years driving a cab, watching the city change around him, and listening in muted angst as the intensifying drumbeat to war in Iraq forced his own past experiences in Africa back into his thoughts.

"It smells like puke in here," Tesfaye commented, fidgeting with his thumbs.

"Someone must have been nervous," Martin said.

"I thought we were scheduled for 1:00."

"The judge had another trial this morning. I think these things have a tendency to go long."

The doors of one of the courtrooms opened and Ethan emerged, nearly running toward the bathroom. Shortly after that, Lin exited the courtroom, flanked by Long and Guozhi. Lin was crying, but Tesfaye could not tell if she was sad or if he was witnessing tears of joy. Shutting the courtroom doors behind him, out walked a man carrying a briefcase. When Tesfaye locked eyes with the man, his heart skipped a beat and he let out a grunt.

"You okay, Tesfaye?" asked Martin. "You look like you just saw a ghost."

More like an asshole, Tesfaye thought, picturing this man yelling at the elderly lady after rear-ending his cab.

With a big smirk on his face, David Kon winked at Tesfaye. "I knew you were illegal," he said, patting Tesfaye on the shoulder as he walked past him. "Don't lose your temper in there. Judge Lancaster will deny your claim in the blink of an eye. And don't lie. He's very good at spotting a liar."

"You know him?" asked Martin.

Before Tesfaye had a chance to answer, the immigration judge's law clerk walked out of the courtroom. "Mr. Holbrook?" asked the clerk.

"Yes," Martin responded.

"Is your client here?"

"Yes, this is him."

"Judge Lancaster is running a little late. He just stepped out for lunch so we're not going to begin for about thirty minutes, but feel free to get set up in the courtroom if you'd like."

Martin and Tesfaye walked into the courtroom.

"It's smaller than I thought it would be," Tesfaye said, observing the dirty, off-white walls of the twenty by twenty foot courtroom. "These benches look less comfortable than church."

Martin put his arm on Tesfaye's shoulder. "Are you nervous?"

"A little."

"Try to relax, all you're doing is telling a story."

"I was fine until the courthouse. All this sitting around, doing nothing, it's a little nerve-racking." Seeing David Kon didn't help Tesfaye's nerves either. Now all he could think about was the judge not liking him and deciding to deny his asylum claim.

"At least the delay will give us a little time to go over some last minute things. Now Tesfaye, as I mentioned before, an attorney who works for the government is going to ask you some questions after you and I are done talking. He is going to try and trip you up, get you to contradict yourself, test your credibility. Just tell the truth and everything will work out. Make sure you answer all the questions the attorney asks unless I make an objection. It's important that the judge believes you are being candid, so try not to act defensive. And remember, immigration proceedings are less formal than regular court cases, so don't be surprised if the immigration judge interrupts me or the other lawyer to ask you a question."

The doors to the courtroom opened and Ethan quietly strolled down the aisle. He reached into his leather briefcase that was already at the table from his morning trial and spread out a slew of papers. He then stepped over to Martin, introduced himself, and engaged in a short exchange of mindless pleasantries before returning to his table to review his notes.

The exchange between the lawyers was uncomfortable for Tesfaye. The surrealism of watching a casual conversation about the mundane details of weather and traffic, by men whose actions would literally determine the future course of his life. *Just another day at the office*, Tesfaye reflected.

Everyone stood when Judge Lancaster entered the room. The necessary procedural aspects of the trial stretched out for a good half hour before Tesfaye took the witness stand. The questions Martin posed were exactly like they rehearsed. Tesfaye's nerves settled around the time he began discussing his imprisonment. When Tesfaye lifted his shirt to reveal the scars that covered his chest and abdomen, the result was even more dramatic than Martin had anticipated.

There was a ten-minute break before cross-examination. Tesfaye stretched his legs and grabbed some water before retaking his place on the witness stand.

"Now, sir," Ethan began, "you were a member of the Derg, correct?"

"Yes, I worked for the government."

"And the government in power was the Derg?"

"That is true."

"And the Derg was responsible for the deaths of hundreds of thousands of people?"

"Objection," said Martin as he rose to his feet. "That is entirely too vague."

"I think I agree with Mr. Holbrook," Judge Lancaster said. "Please rephrase the question, counsel. What do you mean by *responsible?*"

"Very well, Your Honor," Ethan said, directing his attention back to Tesfaye. "Sir, was the Derg responsible for killing thousands of people during a campaign known as the Red Terror?"

"Yes," Tesfaye readily conceded.

"Was the Derg responsible for letting hundreds of thousands of people starve from 1983 to 1985 when there was a famine in the country?"

"People starved because there was no water."

"Did the Derg provide aid to the people who were starving?"

"They tried, they certainly tried."

"But isn't it true that the Derg failed to provide any assistance until the international media started exposing the famine?"

Tesfaye felt himself start to get defensive. Although he had not been prepared for this particular line of questioning, he usually felt comfortable thinking on his feet. He racked his brain for the perfect explanation that would illuminate this government attorney about a predicament nobody could fully appreciate without having lived in Ethiopia under the Mengistu regime. But the right words simply eluded him. All he could think about were the intentionally malicious quips of attorney David Kon before he entered the courtroom, making the judge out to be a judicial ogre waiting for the chance to pounce on any mistake and deny his asylum claim. Now, instead of concentrating on the answer to Ethan's question, Tesfaye was getting lost in the masquerade of the trial process. He was more worried about how the judge would perceive his answer than simply telling his story. It was the fatal transition that so often led witnesses down the road to a self-fulfilling prophecy.

"Perhaps the reaction of the government could have been quicker," Tesfaye said. "I would have liked it to have been quicker."

"Your Honor," Ethan exclaimed, grabbing a large folder of documents from the corner of the table. "I have in my hand documents that describe all the details of the government's brutal bombing campaign throughout 1988. It discusses dozens of incidents where the government attacked its own people. Its own people—not soldiers or fighters—regular Ethiopian citizens."

Martin stood to his feet. "Your Honor, I object. This is outrageous. The government has not provided me with a copy of any of these documents. I have never seen them before. It is well established that all evidence must be disclosed ahead of the actual trial."

Judge Lancaster looked over at Ethan. "Counsel, Mr. Holbrook is right, you can't just waltz in here the day of trial with some smoking gun or whatever it is you have in your hand. This isn't an episode of Perry Mason, it's a federal immigration court. We have clear rules about submitting evidence ahead of time."

"I apologize, Your Honor. I only recently discovered all this information." Ethan left out that he only recently discovered the information because he hadn't looked at the case file until a day before the trial.

"If you want," Judge Lancaster continued, "you can ask him if he knows anything about these events, but I cannot accept these documents. You might as well throw them in the recycle bin on your way out."

Ethan didn't care. He knew he was required to disclose the documents to Martin ahead of time and he knew that the judge would not likely let them in. But it didn't matter. The damage was already done. He had already alerted the immigration judge to the fact that there were a slew of atrocities committed by the Mengistu government, and he did it in a way that caught Martin off guard and didn't give him time to prepare. Ethan figured out after five minutes of researching Martin's background that he had not litigated in immigration court for years. That he'd probably come into court all sentimental, believing his client had a great case, and not thinking hard enough about the strategy involved in the trial itself.

"Sir," Ethan continued, directing his attention back to Tesfaye, "did you know that in 1988, the Mengistu government bombed aid workers in Dejena who were bringing food to starving people?"

"I did hear about that."

"And did you know that the Mengistu government bombed Samre twice in 1988, nearly destroying the town and killing dozens of people?"

Tesfaye remained silent. There was a lump in his throat. After a moment, he nodded.

"You have to give a verbal answer," Judge Lancaster instructed Tesfaye. "Are you aware of the incident the attorney for the government just described?"

"Yes," Tesfaye faintly responded.

Ethan persisted. "And were you aware that the government dropped phosphorous bombs on a market square in Hausien, killing or mutilating thousands of people?"

Tesfaye pictured Demissie searching for his son in the rubble of Hausien when the bombing finally subsided that day. "I only learned about that when I was in prison, years after it happened."

"But it happened when you were working for the Mengistu government?"

"That's true, but . . ."

"And you mentioned that you worked in the Defense Department?"

"Yes, I worked in the Ministry of Defense . . ."

"In fact," Ethan interjected, "you testified that you were a *senior* advisor in the Ministry of Defense, isn't that correct?"

"But not by choice, I . . ."

"You were being forced to help lead the military against your will?"

"Not against my will, but you have to understand that Mengistu was ruthless. I was living in fear. Everyone was. What else was I suppose to do?"

"Why didn't you leave the country?"

"And go where?" asked Tesfaye with open hostility. "Ethiopia is my country, the only home I had ever known."

"The only home you ever knew. But you *did* leave. And here you are," Ethan sarcastically responded.

"Objection," Martin said. "That was not a question."

"I apologize, Your Honor."

"You're apologizing too much, Mr. Shaw," Judge Lancaster scolded. "You need to be more careful with your questioning."

"I have no more questions, Your Honor," Ethan said. "I would just point out that based on the applicant's answers to my questions, it is clear that he is not eligible for asylum. The law explicitly states that you cannot obtain asylum protection in the United States when you yourself have engaged in persecution. It is clear that this man *did* engage in persecution. He helped run a government that murdered thousands upon thousands of people because of their ethnicity and their political affiliations."

"Response, Mr. Holbrook?"

Martin was already on his feet, waiting for the go-ahead from the immigration judge. "It is true that there is a persecutor bar to obtaining asylum, but that is not applicable here. Tesfaye cannot be held responsible for the viciousness of Mengistu Mariam. You heard from his testimony that he was largely kept in the dark about what was going on."

"He says he was kept in the dark," Judge Lancaster said, "but he did admit that he was a very senior advisor in the Ministry of Defense. It is hard to believe that someone in such a prominent position would be wholly ignorant of everything going on around him."

"It's not that he was *wholly* ignorant, Your Honor," Martin tried to explain, "but he did not actively participate in all those atrocities that counsel for the government rattled off before. He just didn't. And many of his responsibilities during his time in the Mengistu regime were carried out in fear—fear for the safety of his family if he disobeyed this crazy, paranoid dictator."

"Judge Lancaster," Ethan chimed in, "we didn't give members of the Third Reich a free pass during the Nuremberg Trials simply because they claimed they were taking orders when they sent the Jews to the gas chamber."

Martin let out a nervous laugh. "Nuremberg! You're actually comparing Tesfaye to SS guards. That's ludicrous! That's completely different. You've heard Tesfaye's story and you've seen the brutality he has suffered. The same people who did this to him still hold positions of power in Ethiopia. If this man doesn't qualify for asylum, I don't know who does."

Judge Lancaster stroked his chin for a moment and turned to Tesfaye. "I want to thank you for your testimony today. You may step down and go sit with your attorney. Gentlemen, we will stand in recess for fifteen minutes, at which point I will come back and announce my decision."

Martin patted Tesfaye on the knee. "You did well up there."

Tesfaye's hand shook as he poured himself a glass of water from the goblet on the table. Staring intently at the judge's podium, he took a sip.

"Tesfaye? Are you okay?" asked Martin. There was no answer. Martin tried again to grab his attention, but again no response.

A minute later, Tesfaye turned to Martin. "I didn't know the judge would be making a decision today. He will decide my fate in less than fifteen minutes."

The next few minutes were among the most nerve-racking of Martin's life. In his head, he replayed Ethan's arguments before the immigration judge, brainstorming different responses he could have given to better neutralize them. It was the inevitable reexamination that all attorneys experience after appearing in court. And the inevitable frustration that follows. The frustration of failing to perform on the stage of the courtroom floor, failing to articulate in real-time the perfect lines of legal gospel as if the merits of a case were solely based on an answer that comes to an attorney with only a second or two of contemplation. Having not litigated any cases in recent years and forgetting what it was like, Martin did not anticipate this internal rehashing of the trial, nor the most unwelcomed internal angst that it caused. He watched Tesfaye biting his nails and cuticles, the burden of his role as Tesfaye's attorney suddenly becoming all too real as he looked at this asylum applicant with the empathy of a parent wanting to protect his child.

Judge Lancaster returned and took his seat. "Alright, I will now read my findings into the record."

Chapter 59

THE IMMIGRATION JUDGE dispassionately recounted the facts of the case from notes he scribbled to himself during the hearing. Turning to his legal findings, he proclaimed that Tesfaye without question suffered persecution.

Tesfaye's momentary euphoria dissipated when the immigration judge continued to state his conclusions for the record. Judge Lancaster noted how deeply unfortunate it was that a man who had undergone such atrocities in his life would be ineligible to obtain asylum protection because of the persecutor bar.

The oral decision continued, but Tesfaye unwittingly blocked out the words. Time stood still. All outside stimuli were muted, as if a noise machine were pumping static between his temples. A dreamlike state of detachment produced the feeling of separation between his mind and body, and for a moment he was an observer watching a demoralized African immigrant clench his sweaty palms.

Standing outside the courthouse with Martin, Tesfaye felt profoundly sad, utterly beaten down. The expectation of success had made defeat all the more bitter.

"I know you're upset," Martin said comfortingly, "but don't think of this as the end. Judges make mistakes all the time. This was just one of those times. We're going to appeal this thing to the Board of Immigration Appeals. If we have to go to the federal appellate courts, we'll do that too."

Tesfaye sighed. "Maybe that attorney for the government is right. Maybe I don't deserve asylum."

"Don't buy into that crap."

"I could have done something, right? I could have taken my family and left Ethiopia."

"Someone else would have taken your spot, someone who wouldn't have tried to help people like you did."

"Maybe, who knows."

Martin hailed a cab, got in, and looked up at Tesfaye. "You want a ride uptown?"

"No. I think I'll walk for a bit."

"We all have skeletons in our closet, Tesfaye, things we would like to take back. But that doesn't mean this judge got the law right. We're going to appeal this decision and we're going to win, so you hang in there. Have a beer, be sad for the afternoon, and get some sleep. When you wake up, you'll realize that this is nothing more than a slight delay in your journey to becoming a legal resident of the United States."

Tesfaye wandered aimlessly through the streets of downtown Manhattan, taking Martin up on his suggestion that he have a beer. He sat on a strip of plush green lawn in Battery Park. The brown bag hiding his Blue Moon crunched as he raised it to his lips and took a sip. He watched the ferries zigzag through the Hudson River. The setting sun eventually cloaked the Statue of Liberty. Exhausted, Tesfaye followed suit, collapsing onto the grass.

Martin was wrong. When Tesfaye awoke the next morning on the lawn, he did not feel any better. The loss did not feel like a mere hiccup on some purposeful journey to a better end.

Tesfaye stopped showing up for his shifts at work, instead finding comfort in the smokiness of the Crazy Horse, a dimly lit neighborhood bar. After three days, he told his employer he would be undergoing a medical procedure, unable to resume his duties for an indeterminate amount of time. Tesfaye was wholly apathetic to his employer's skepticism about the legitimacy of his story and completely indifferent to the steady depletion of the little money he had managed to save.

Many times in the past, Tesfaye had forced himself to fight through the adversities and rise to the occasion. But this time, he found himself unable to summon any internal vigor. He was a sleep-deprived college student rereading the same paragraph of a textbook, unable to comprehend the words and advance to the next page. All he could do when he awoke in the early afternoon was stroll down the street to the Crazy Horse and indulge in eighty proof shots of self-pity.

Three weeks passed. Tesfaye fell deeper. Nursing a drink, his head bobbed back and forth as he focused on the television set in the corner of the bar. He joined the other bar patrons watching President Bush give Saddam

Hussein forty-eight hours to leave Iraq or face the consequences. "The day of your liberation is near," Bush declared. The bar patrons applauded.

"And when the dictator has departed," Bush continued, "they can set an example to all the Middle East of a vital and peaceful and self-governing nation."

Tesfaye watched the excitement around him. "We are going to fuckin destroy that motherfucker," said the bar patron sitting next to him. "Bush is not fuckin around."

"It's goddamn brilliant," said the patron's friend. "We'll turn Iraq into a democracy and all the other Arab dictators are gonna fall like dominos. Gore never would have had the balls."

"Fuck no."

Tesfaye let out a hiss and the patron shot him a flippant glance before continuing his conversation. "There's no fuckin way Bush is going to make the same mistake his father made. He will drop a shit storm on these guys."

"Where's your cousin at?" the patron's friend asked him.

"Been training in Kuwait for months. First Brigade Combat Team."

Listening to their conversation, Tesfaye pictured how sure Mengistu was that his political philosophy would unify all the different ethnicities in Ethiopia, even though many of them inhabited lands that were not even part of Ethiopia a century ago. He smiled as he tried to think of an Ethiopian ethnic group that had *not* had its own liberation front. "Your cousin is fucked," he mumbled to himself.

"What did you just say?" the patron asked Tesfaye.

Tesfaye looked over at the startled patron. "Hmm? Nothing."

"I distinctly heard you say something about my cousin."

Tesfaye raised his glass. "I wish him the best of luck," he said, smiling as he lowered his glass.

"Asshole, I don't know what your problem is, but if you don't mind your own business and stop insulting my family, we're gonna have a serious problem."

The numbing indifference created by a day at the Crazy Horse was not mixing well with the nagging cynicism that had been clawing at Tesfaye since he lost the trial. As he looked at this patron in utter disgust, he saw the unwitting target of all his pent up frustration and anger.

"Do you have any idea how many different ethnic and religious groups live in Iraq?" asked Tesfaye sarcastically as he tried to keep his balance on the barstool. Not waiting for a response, or caring if one was given, Tesfaye answered his own question. "No, you have no idea. You think we're going to drop some bombs, clear out Saddam, and everyone will just play nice together? Are you an idiot?"

The patron's friend got off his stool and stood cross-armed next to Tesfaye. "They will all start fighting for power or independence," Tesfaye continued, taking a sip of his drink. "And that, my friend, is why your cousin is *fucked.*"

Tesfaye was not sure whether he landed any shots before the patron and his friend started pummeling him. Because the three of them were so close together, none of the blows carried any significant force. The most painful aspect of the fight occurred outside, when the bouncer pushed him to the ground and ordered him to scram.

Stumbling to his apartment building, Tesfaye fiddled with the lock of the front door for a while before falling into the lobby. It took him an equally long amount of time to find the key to his mailbox. On the steps leading up to his apartment, he discarded a few mailers and coupon books, along with several other envelopes that looked like junk mail through the slightly blurred vision of his bloodshot eyes. Opening the unlocked door to his meager dwelling, he headed straight for bed. He had almost reached his destination by the time he saw the manila envelope with no return address.

There were two standard-sized envelopes inside the larger manila one. As he opened one of the envelopes, Tesfaye's eyes bulged. In his inebriated state, it took him several minutes to read the fine print. It was a plane ticket. In the other envelope there was a letter, written in longhand. Tesfaye sifted through the sheets of paper without reading them until he got to the end. And there it was. The signature of Geteye Tge.

Chapter 60

L IN SAT UP in her basement studio in Chinatown staring at the night-light flickering in the corner of the room. It was early, but she could not fall back to sleep. Her emotions had been in overdrive since the trial. On the morning of her asylum hearing, Lin joined the very exclusive club of immigrants who managed to puke in the hallway of the courthouse, a club the janitor was none too pleased to see Lin join.

Lin waited until the sun rose before banging on the front door of her uncle Long's apartment.

"I'm sorry," Lin said as Long opened the door. "I can't sleep again."

"Come in, I'll make some tea."

Lin waited quietly for the tea to boil. "Here," Long said, handing a cup to Lin. "When's the last time you slept through the night?"

"I can't remember. I know it was before the trial."

"You're still confused."

"Yes."

"The laws in this country are very complicated."

"It's not that, I—I just don't understand everything that happened, what exactly I said to get this outcome."

Steam evaporated off the mug as Long blew on his tea. "Well," he said, taking a sip, "there's a lot about the system here that I myself don't understand." Long waited for Lin to finish before bringing the empty cups over to the sink. "I'm sorry I'm not better company right now. I have a twelve-hour shift in a few hours. I should probably get in a few more winks."

"You should," Lin agreed, heading for the door. "Thank you for the tea."

Chapter 61

THE DRAW OF sleep overpowered Tesfaye's curiosity. He had passed out on his bed, fully clothed, holding Geteye's letter in his hand. When he awoke the next morning, he found the letter crumpled on the floor. Straightening out the pages, Tesfaye's heart raced as he digested Geteye's words.

Dear Tesfaye,

It has taken me a considerable amount of time to find you. I came close once in Kenya before you seemed to vanish off the face of the earth. Given the times we were living in, I must admit that I thought the worst and gave up my search for several years. I am grateful I decided to resume seventeen months ago, although I will leave for another time the events leading me to restart my efforts. If I had not managed to secretly get in touch with your former student Beniam, I dare say I might never have found you, given your new assumed identity in America. Even when I finally discovered that you were living in New York, I spent a number of days trying to figure out what to say in this letter.

More than anything, I want you to know how sorry I am. You cannot imagine how hard it has been to carry around the burden of my actions. I don't know what you have heard about me, about what I did back in Ethiopia. I have no doubt that some of what you heard is true, although gossip has a way of lending itself to exaggeration. While I am ashamed by many of my actions, you must believe me Tesfaye when I say that I did everything I could in Ethiopia to protect you. If there were rumors about your loyalty, I made sure they were quashed. When other advisors would question whether your advice was wholly candid, I would scold their remarks as petty jealousy. And when Mengistu contemplated your execution, I did everything I could to dissuade him.

I should have come up with a better plan before I asked you to entrust me with the lives of your family, a plan that would have better ensured everyone's safety. I suppose it is easier to see the deficiencies of a plan in retrospect, but not a day goes by that I do not think of them. I am haunted by images of Ayana singing the children to sleep in Thika. I relive the last time Afeworki hugged me goodbye. Sometimes I wake up in a sweat, thinking her arms are still around me and that this time I can save her.

My biggest regret is that I didn't try harder to get you to leave Ethiopia with Ayana and the kids, and that I waited so long before begging you to leave. All the signs had made it clear for some time that Mengistu's army didn't stand a chance. I wish more than anything that I had told you everything when I called you that morning. But I was ashamed, or perhaps I was scared. Maybe it was guilt that I had not been completely honest with you for so many years. The truth is, I know it was all these things.

I'm sure you have many questions, more questions than I could possibly answer in a letter. I know I have given you many reasons not to trust a single word I say and that the last thing you would expect from me would be to ask you for something else. But I must beg you to trust me this one last time. If any part of you remembers the two wild cadets who would have done anything for each other at Holetta Military Academy, then you will get on Alitalia Flight 603 from JFK to Rome, departing Wednesday, March 26. If my calculations are correct, you should have at least one week to get your things in order. In the other envelope, you will find the plane ticket. I assure you this ticket cost me a sizable amount of money, and I do not have unlimited funds. Perhaps that will help convince you to trust me.

> Ever your humbled friend,
> Geteye

Tesfaye took a moment to soak in Geteye's request. *Trust him? Is he serious?* During the first shower he had taken in some time, Tesfaye thought about Geteye's plea. Feeling hung over, but better than usual, Tesfaye headed for the door.

"Shit," he said, realizing he could not go back to the Crazy Horse.

He sat down in the middle of the dusty floor and rested his elbows on his knees. Biting his nails, he reread the letter. Studying each word intently, it soon became clear what he needed to do.

MARTIN SAT AT his desk, editing a brief he planned to file with the immigration appeals tribunal. The phone buzzed and Martin picked it up. "Yes? He's here? Really. Okay, send him back."

Tesfaye stood in the doorway of Martin's office, his hands in his pockets. "Tesfaye," Martin said. "It's nice to see you. You're looking well. Sit, please," he said, adhering to his routine of clearing papers off one of the chairs when a visitor arrived.

Tesfaye sat, and Martin continued. "I wasn't expecting you, but great timing. I was just finishing up the appeal brief for your case. It's due in a few days and I have to tell you, it's pretty good."

As Tesfaye remained silent, Martin started to feel slightly uncomfortable. "Don't you work during the day, Tesfaye?"

"Today is my day off."

"Everything okay?"

"What happens if I leave the country?" asked Tesfaye.

Martin squinted his eyes. "You mean *now*, what happens if you leave right now?"

"Yes."

"Well, the immigration judge entered an order of deportation against you. If you leave, then you have carried out the order. You've deported yourself."

"So we would not be able to appeal?"

"No, Tesfaye, we wouldn't. I imagine you wouldn't be asking me unless you were thinking about leaving the country. If you could hold off on that a little while, I think it would be best."

Tesfaye smiled. "I know it would, but I can't hold off."

Martin scratched the back of his head and let out a sigh. "We've spent a lot of time getting this brief together and—I'm not just saying this to be nice—I really think we have a shot at winning. Are you sure you can't hold off?"

Tesfaye nodded. "I'm sure."

"What the heck is so important that you would leave the country during your appeal?"

Given all the time Martin had dedicated to helping Tesfaye try to obtain asylum, Tesfaye knew Martin deserved to hear why he was leaving the country. But for some reason, he could not bring himself to do it. At least not now. It all sounded too silly, wholly ridiculous. "Mr. Holbrook, I wish I could answer your question better, but the truth is that I myself don't know the answer." He paused. "I am not a spiritual man, but I am taking a leap of faith." And with that, Tesfaye extended his arm.

"At least promise you'll keep in touch," Martin said as he hesitatingly shook Tesfaye's hand.

"You have my word. I will never forget the kindness you've shown me these last years. I am eternally grateful." Tesfaye patted Martin on the shoulder before heading for the door.

In a state of shock, Martin sat quietly in his office. He thought about his debate with Hugo Sandoval, replaying Hugo's point about how feelings can change when you actually know the immigrant the government is trying to deport. Martin wasn't a drinker, but he needed a drink. He flicked off the lights on his way out of the office and sighed as he dropped the appeal brief into the trash.

Chapter 62

THE HOUSE WAS confirmed. The judge had signed off on the no-knock warrant. The agents were in place, crouched around the inconspicuous raised ranch on the outskirts of San Diego.

One of the agents on Ethan's team broke down the door. They flooded in, guns drawn. There was a faint smell of marijuana in the air. A glass bong sat in the center of the coffee table in the living room. Unemptied ashtrays were scattered throughout the stained rug. A fifty-five inch television displayed the graphics of a video game that had been paused. Ethan thought it looked more like a college frat house than a criminal hideout, until he entered the dining room. It was filled with laptops and scanners and printers and laminating machines and special colored printer paper. And more unemptied ashtrays.

The agents methodically searched each bedroom, clearing them one at a time. Ethan heard the sound of a shower running. The agents gathered outside the bathroom door. The sound of running water stopped. There was a mild squeak as the shower curtain's metal rings ran across the shower rod. Ethan counted to three in a whispered voice. He swung the door open. A young kid stood in front of the mirror shaving, wearing nothing but boxers. Ryan and another agent swarmed in and pinned him to the ground. He screamed as his hands were handcuffed behind his back.

"Is there anyone else in the house?" asked one of the agents.

"No," whimpered the kid.

"Where are they hiding!"

"There's nobody here," the kid pleaded. "I swear, there's nobody else here!"

ETHAN STOOD OUTSIDE the interrogation room, shaking his head at the blond haired kid they had just arrested. The kid sat in the cold metal chair wearing nothing but his boxers and a tee-shirt the agents had gotten for him, a blanket draped over his shoulders. He was shivering profusely. Ethan could not tell if he was cold or petrified, but he imagined it was a bit of both.

Ethan let the kid sit and shiver while the agents compiled some background information. Ryan walked over to Ethan. "What'd you find?" asked Ethan.

Ryan handed Ethan a folder. "His name is Brody James. United States citizen. Attended UCLA for three years before dropping out a few years ago. No priors and no record of prior employment."

"No record of employment ever?"

"Nothing on the books."

"Whose name is the house in?"

"His."

"Let's have a little chat with Mr. James." Ethan and Ryan walked into the interrogation room. Ryan sat down in one of the metal chairs across from Brody, while Ethan stood to the side with his arms folded.

"You know why you're here?" asked Ryan.

Brody didn't answer.

"Some interesting equipment you have in your house," Ethan said. "Really high-tech stuff."

Brody looked up at Ethan, still shivering. "Not really."

"You pay for it?" asked Ethan.

"Yeah."

"How?"

"My parents help me out sometimes."

Ethan leaned over the table. "Your parents bought you a house too?"

"I've never hurt anyone in my life. I don't know what you think I've done."

"We know what you've done," Ryan said. "We just want to know who was helping you."

"Helping me?"

"Do you know the penalties for identity theft?" asked Ethan. "You're gonna spend ten years in a federal prison with a bunch of tough guys who can't wait to get their hands on you."

"Especially with that long blond hair," Ryan added. "How do you get it to be so shiny?"

Brody hunched over. "I think I'm gonna be sick." He took a few deep breaths. "I want a lawyer."

Ethan walked around the table and patted Brody on the back. "That's fine," he said, kneeling down. "That's your right. I'm almost glad that you said that. Because otherwise I would have given you one shot at a sweet deal to keep you out of jail. Now I'm gonna enjoy watching you squirm in the courtroom when the judge sentences you."

Ethan could see the fear in Brody's face. Brody was batting his eyelids as fast as he could to stop himself from crying. Ryan followed Ethan to the door of the interrogation room. "Have a nice life," Ethan said.

"Wait," Brody blurted out.

"Sorry kid," Ryan said, "you said you wanted a lawyer, so we can't talk to you anymore."

"Just give me a second."

"You want to talk to us?"

Brody was taking very slow, deep breaths as if he were willing himself not to throw up.

"Do you want to waive your request for an attorney?"

Brody nodded his head. "Can we just talk here—without the whole tough guy interrogation thing?"

Ethan and Ryan closed the door again and sat down across from Brody. "Sure," Ryan said. "What do you want to talk about?"

"I don't know what you think I did, but if you can guarantee I don't go to jail, then I'll tell you whatever you want to know."

Ethan could barely control his excitement as they spent the next few minutes hammering out an agreement and getting the go-ahead from the other federal agents who were listening to the interview outside the interrogation room. "Remember," Ethan said, "you lie about any detail or omit any important facts from your statement and this deal dies. Understand?"

"Yeah."

"The floor is yours."

"My junior year in college I went down to Mexico with a few friends to chill out for a few days and just get fucked up. One night we went to a donkey show and we were . . ."

"Donkey show?"

"Yeah. It's these shows where a girl lets a donkey have sex with her on stage while everyone watches."

"You paid to see this?"

"You just go to say you've done it. You know what I mean?" Neither agent responded. "Anyway, it smelled gross in there, the donkey shitting on the stage and all, so I went outside for a smoke. I got to talking with some dude out there. We started to talk about how it's bullshit that the drinking age in the United States is twenty-one and I was telling him how easy it was to make fake IDs for college kids who wanted to get into bars. I told him how much money I made doing it—charging like a hundred a pop for these piece of shit IDs. Then he asked if I could make fake Social Security cards. I said I didn't know because, you know, I'd never even seen one. He said he knew someone who would pay me a lot of money to make them, so I gave the dude my phone number in the States. I didn't really expect to hear from him, but I did a few days later. He offered to pay me like two hundred bucks for each one I did. So I asked my parents for my Social Security card so I could see what it looked like and I just started buying equipment and making a few on the side."

"How did you know how to make them?" asked Ethan.

"It's easy. I took some graphics classes in college because I wanted to be a video game designer, but honestly, anyone could do it. It's not hard. Soon I started making the IDs full-time."

"What do you mean by full-time?" asked Ryan.

"Not really full-time. More like an hour a day or so. I spend a lot of my time at the beach, surfing mostly. Like I said, it's really not hard to do. I mean, Social Security cards aren't even laminated!"

Ethan sat expressionless as Brody relaxed and began to divulge more and more irrelevant details about his daily routine. Ethan could feel his blood pressure rising with each irrelevant word uttered by Brody.

"Let's cut to the chase," Ethan said. "How does the identity theft organization work?"

"I don't know anything about identity theft and I don't know what you mean by organization."

"How did the Social Security cards get into the hands of the illegal immigrants?"

"I just made them and sent them to an address in Mexico. A few times I've given it to someone in the United States. That's it."

Ethan pointed at Brody. "You remember what we agreed to, don't you?" asked Ethan in a raised voice. "You bullshit me and our agreement is over."

"I'm not bullshitting you, that's all I know."

While Ryan got Brody to write down the address of his contact in Mexico, Ethan ground his teeth and squinted at Brody. Ethan thought about all the time he had spent over the last four years on these identity theft cases. All the times he had pictured himself busting up a huge criminal enterprise operating in the United States. Now, he was staring at a twenty-something surfer pothead, making more than he did, who only worked an hour a day. All of a sudden Ethan snapped. He bolted around the table and grabbed Brody by the shirt collar. The collar ripped as Ethan slammed Brody against the wall. Ethan grabbed Brody's shirt and started to shove him against the wall repeatedly until Ryan and two other agents ran over and restrained him.

Chapter 63

PROFESSOR HUGO SANDOVAL let out a deep breath as he hung up the phone. This was not how he pictured spending the majority of his free time. He had planned to write a book, teasing out further some of the pro-immigrant arguments from his *Harvard Law Review* article that he had used against Martin during their debates.

From his third-story apartment in the Chelsea neighborhood of Manhattan, he watched a pedestrian passing by below. He let the outside world occupy his attention, if only for a moment, knowing full well the circumstances he would have to confront when he forced his thoughts back to his wife sitting on the couch. It was a federal investigator on the phone, relaying news about his wife's case.

It started out as nothing more than an annoyance three and a half years ago, a call from a creditor asking when the company he represented could expect payment. Mrs. Sandoval had no idea what this man was talking about. *She* had not made the purchase and surely Hugo would have told her if he bought these items. It took several phone calls to resolve the issue, but two months later she was absolved of any liability, all evidence of the delinquent account erased from her credit reports at all three of the credit bureaus. Thinking the isolated incident was over, the Sandovals did not pursue the matter further.

Six months later, creditors again began hounding Hugo's wife. Numerous calls, at all hours of the day and night, claiming she owed money for all sorts of merchandise she never purchased. Some of the calls got ugly. They would call her a deadbeat, claim they were going to garnish her wages, and threaten to get her son's student loans cancelled. One creditor even called her a whore, advising her to become a prostitute to cover her spending habits.

It seemed that whenever she and Hugo managed to resolve one of these situations, another one would spring up in its place. The stress generated by this never-ending string of phone calls and letters had slowly taken its toll on Mrs. Sandoval. It wasn't just the time she had to spend on the phone, attempting in vain to explain to impassive creditors that she was innocent.

Nor was it the effort spent drafting letters to memorialize her position to create a physical record of her attempts to explain herself, a necessity she learned all too well after being caught flat-footed by the first creditor to take her to court. More than anything, Mrs. Sandoval felt violated. She had lost control. Her identity was being pimped out.

It was a strange feeling, Mrs. Sandoval thought, to lose control of your identity. Surely she was the same person. She held the same beliefs as she always had, the same values, the same affiliations. She spent money on the same types of items and worked for the same causes in her spare time. Even though in her mind Mrs. Sandoval hadn't changed, the experience taught her an important lesson. Identity is not internal. In a world where information is a commodity and a dossier of personal facts hold more weight than a person's word, others' beliefs about her turned into the *de facto* reality. She is who they say she is—who the piece of paper says she is—until she proved otherwise.

Getting authorities to take her claim seriously was a challenge. Every police department or agency she called said that a different one had jurisdiction. She was not surprised. The charges to credit cards and the bank accounts opened with her personal information, had appeared all over the country. Why would a police department investigating a fraudulent bank account in Boise care if someone opened a credit card in her name in Los Angeles?

And then there were the insurance companies. She tried to explain that it could not have been her who got the mastectomy because she never even had breast cancer. But someone with her Social Security number apparently did undergo such a surgery and she was told that she was on the hook for the bill.

The federal agent's words on the phone brought Hugo some much-needed relief. There was a break in the case. The federal agent assured Hugo that authorities had arrested the man responsible for furnishing the Social Security cards to the Mexican middlemen, and that they might even have a lead on the people in Mexico responsible for distributing the cards. The agent told Hugo that he was confident that the number of new accounts popping up all over the country would diminish. Unfortunately, the agent conceded that it would be much harder to track down the dozens of people already in the United States who were using his wife's personal information. "It's important to stay vigilant," the federal agent told him. *Stay vigilant*, thought Hugo.

All they tell me is to stay vigilant, as if spending your whole life on edge about your financial well-being is easy.

Despite the good news, Hugo felt betrayed. The same people he spent his entire career defending were responsible for the last four years of hell. *Did they know the information belonged to someone else? Would they have cared?* The questions were unsettling.

Mrs. Sandoval was sitting on the couch, looking at Hugo for an update on his conversation with the agent.

"They might have found the culprit," he said, "the thief who sold your information to all the others."

She began to cry, as she had done so often these last few years. Hugo sat next to her, kissing her on the forehead. "We still have to be vigilant, but hopefully now the end is in sight."

Mrs. Sandoval shook her head. "I just wish we didn't wait so long before we contacted the police. Maybe this whole nightmare could have been over by now if we acted when we saw that first charge."

"Those three stupid laptops."

The laptops Sofia had mysteriously acquired in Arizona. The laptops she sold to Rosario's friends at the beauty parlor to repay Rosario the nine hundred dollars. The nine hundred dollars Sofia gave to the coyote's smuggling cohorts when she tried to rescue Maria.

Chapter 64

ETHAN TOLD HUGO he would stay in touch and then he hung up the phone. He tried to sound as assuring as he could, but the address in Mexico that surfer Brody gave Ryan turned out to be the equivalent of a post office box in the United States. Even worse, Ethan's image of an international criminal enterprise had been replaced by the narrow eyes of a stoned twenty-something. Ethan figured that someone would probably just take Brody's place, given how easy it was to forge Social Security cards. He hoped he had not raised Hugo's expectations too high. But he knew his reassuring words were not just to comfort Hugo. They were also for him. He needed to fight the nagging feeling that had begun to fester recently. His career chasing illegal immigrants was beginning to feel as fruitful as weaving a rope out of sand.

Chapter 65

SHAOQING TOOK A sip of coffee and placed the mug back on the saucer. The table wobbled on the uneven sidewalk outside the bubble tea café and coffee bar. "I shouldn't have helped Jiang when we were on the boat, after he was stabbed."

"Where did that come from?" asked Lin.

"I've been thinking about it recently. Way too risky."

"Everyone thought you were very brave."

"I know," he said, watching tourists scurry around Chinatown with knockoff purses and sunglasses purchased from the Canal Street vendors. "But it was stupid."

"Maybe a little."

"I didn't really even know the guy."

"That's true."

"And I risked my *life* to help him."

"The funny thing is," Lin noted, "we haven't talked to him since." Jiang wasn't the only one whom Lin and Shaoqing had not seen. Neither had spoken with Ai, and Lin made no effort to find her, even though she heard Ai was working somewhere in Chinatown.

Lin and Shaoqing had each crossed paths with other passengers, including several of the Tingjiang boys. No words were uttered. None needed to be. Everyone was ashamed by what they had done or witnessed. There was an unspoken understanding that the events of the voyage were better left at sea, where they belonged.

Shaoqing continued, "When I helped Jiang, I think I was trying to prove something to myself."

"What would that be?"

"That I was a stronger person than my uncle." Shaoqing took another sip of coffee. "It sounds stupid when I listen to myself say it—that I wanted to prove I was stronger than my uncle—as if it really makes a difference. As if I need his approval."

"It's natural to want the approval of a parent, or an uncle."

"I remember running up the ladder to go find the medicine for Jiang after we distracted the Tingjiang apes. As soon as I got off the ladder, my body froze for a second. I was petrified. Part of me knew there was no way I could pull it off without getting caught, but I didn't listen to the voice in my head telling me I was crazy."

"My father used to tell me that it's important to trust your instincts."

"Have you heard anything about your father?"

Lin shook her head. "No."

"How is your mother doing?"

"Same as always. If she's sad that I'm not there, she sure has a funny way of showing it."

"You mentioned she has always been that way. I'm sure she misses you."

"The only time I ever hear her get emotional is when I don't send her the money on time, when the loan shark is hounding her."

Shaoqing put his hand on top of Lin's. "More importantly, how are *you* doing?"

Lin lit a cigarette, a habit both she and Shaoqing had recently acquired working long hours in the States. "I'm fine."

"Really?" inquired a skeptical Shaoqing.

Shaoqing had noticed how odd Lin had been acting since the trial, and she had shut out several of his prior attempts to find out what, exactly, she found so bothersome.

Lin knew she had nothing to feel bad about. She had done everything she was told to do, and in return, the immigration judge had granted her asylum. Still, she didn't understand why she was not permitted to tell her story.

She wanted to explain that she still has nightmares, horrific images of cadre smashing Guozhi's fingers, images of blood pouring out of his mouth. She wanted to tell the immigration judge that she cried almost every night in China after her father disappeared and that her mother refused to remove the broken bookshelves in the house that she would stare at each night as she tried to fall asleep. She wanted to explain that without her father, her mother struggled to put food on the table. Then there was everything that happened on the boat, and the crazy smugglers and loan sharks threatening to kill both her and her mother if they missed a payment.

Lin didn't tell that story. Everyone agreed that the trauma she suffered would not have been sufficient for her to get asylum. *She* wasn't a Falun

Gong practitioner. *She* hadn't been detained or beaten. Her circumstances just weren't covered by any of the five grounds. Instead, Lin was given the prototypical story to prepare, the golden goose of asylum claims provided as a gift to Chinese immigrants. Under the law, the only harm a woman could experience that would *automatically* qualify her for asylum protection was a forced abortion or sterilization procedure. And with China's restrictions on the amount of children couples could have, it was decided that Lin would play the coerced victim.

Three days before Lin departed China for the United States, her mother concocted the outline of the story with one of the snakeheads. Lin relayed this rehearsed outline to Ethan after she was arrested and brought to the Elizabeth Detention Center. From their document production factory in Fujian, the snakeheads provided Lin's mother with all the physical records that would be needed for Lin's asylum hearing—fake medical documents, forged attestations from the local family planning board, letters from nonexistent friends confirming the dates when she was forced to abort the pregnancy. Lin's mother, in turn, sent all these documents to David Kon, the lawyer in New York.

"It's very simple," her uncle Long had told her when he was helping Lin prepare her case in the months leading up to her trial. "Learn every detail of the story in these documents and there will be no way the judge will be able to deny your claim. Just don't contradict yourself. That's it."

Lin should have been less nervous about her trial after learning that Shaoqing had flawlessly executed his concocted story during his asylum hearing, playing himself up as a persecuted member of the Chinese Democracy Party. But his performance only made her more anxious. She had always felt that her aptitude could not match up to his unique ingenuity.

As she grabbed a napkin that had fallen onto the sidewalk, Lin playfully grinned at Shaoqing. "I appreciate your concern, but I'm fine." She threw the napkin onto the table. "I still don't understand exactly what happened, but I have no reason to be unhappy. So," Lin continued, changing the subject, "what should we do today?"

"I just had two cups of coffee and I'm still tired enough to go to sleep."

"No way, Shaoqing. It's so rare we both have the same day off. Let's take a walk up to Central Park."

Shaoqing grumbled.

"C'mon, don't be such a lazy bum," Lin said, grabbing Shaoqing's shirt. "Up you go."

They walked up Broadway, past the law office of David Kon, and cut over to Fifth Avenue. They darted past a young saleswoman in a storefront window dressing an ultra-slender mannequin in the season's newest fashion.

"Shaoqing," Lin said, "I still think what you did on the boat was very brave."

"Thanks, Lin."

Shaoqing and Lin held hands, as they had begun to do recently. Lin couldn't decide whether she was attracted to him or merely comforted by his presence. Either way, she welcomed his warm hand cupping hers.

Walking toward Central Park, Lin thought about the long work week ahead of her under the watchful eye of Dragon Lady, and the many months left until she repaid her debt. Tomorrow, she would be an indentured servant trying to break even in Chinatown. But right now, jockeying for space on the crowded streets by Rockefeller Center, she was just another aggressive New Yorker enjoying a beautiful spring afternoon.

TOMATO FIGHTS IN the rain. Mama scolding us for giggling in church. My first kiss. Papa snoring on the couch after Easter dinner. Kissing Manuel on the forehead when he was a baby. Burning my hand on the stove. Eating black licorice. Chasing after Eva when she was a toddler. Meeting Israel at the discothèque. Smoking my first cigarette with Rosario. Grandma's coarse hands rubbing over mine when she taught me how to sew.

Sofia lay in bed. Miranda sat next to her, doing what she could to make her sister comfortable. Bare feet, then two pairs of socks, then back to bare feet again. Drape another blanket over her, then turn on the fan. It didn't matter. Any momentary relief would be fleeting. Sofia tossed and turned, unable to find a suitable position. She dragged her heels back and forth on the sheet, exposing the mattress. Miranda did her best to fix the bed without disturbing Sofia, but there was only so much Miranda could do. She had seldom heard Sofia curse this much, or so coarsely, the irrelevance of everyday social etiquette never so pronounced.

Miranda cried as she stroked Sofia's clammy hands, but sadness did not have a monopoly on her tears. She was amazed and bewildered by what was coming out of Sofia's mouth. Images Sofia would likely not have been able to recall until recently. But now, as her body was giving out, the synaptic connections in her brain were firing and misfiring for the last time, unleashing myriad of memories locked deep in her psyche, waiting to be recalled by a triggering stimuli—or, in this case, an approaching eternal sleep.

There was no coherent timeline linking the recalled memories. Events from Sofia's years in the United States were interspersed with childhood follies. Sofia took on the characteristics of her former self. She *was* that little girl learning how to sew, asking her grandmother when Mama would be home. When she asked when Rosario was coming over to play, Sofia displayed the impatience of her childhood years.

Listening to Sofia's rants, Miranda felt humbled. How much of Miranda's own life would lie in the annals of her mind forever, never to surface again?

"I will not take life for granted," she said assuringly, promising herself she would focus more on the often overlooked little joys sprinkled throughout the day. Part of Miranda knew she would be powerless to stop an inevitable reversion to the everyday problems and worries that so frequently saturated her limited attention. But in her heightened emotional state, she needed to at least make herself that promise.

Despite Sofia's tossing and turning, Miranda felt relieved that Sofia had reached peace with her decision before the coherency of her thoughts began to fade. Rosario and Eva could not convince her to stay in the United States and keep up the fight. Sofia's mission was complete. She had done what few in Escuinapa had—singlehandedly given her children the chance to make it in the United States. There was lingering guilt associated with her use of the Social Security card to secure funds in emergencies. But she had no choice. And before she left the United States, she had to provide her children with a small nest egg so that they could get on their feet without her.

Sofia knew there were no guarantees. Her children could be deported if immigration authorities caught them. They would likely face discrimination. Limited job opportunities at first. But she told herself that the Blessed Virgin was looking out for them and that everything would work out in the end, just as it was meant to be.

Dios lo manda.

TESFAYE FIDGETED WITH anticipation during the entire flight to Rome. There were so many things he wanted to say to Geteye; it was not easy to decide which was the most pressing. Part of him did not want to say anything at all, imagining a situation where he would walk up to Geteye, punch him in the face, and then stand over him, arms folded, waiting for him to grovel for forgiveness.

Emerging from the secured zone in the airport terminal, Tesfaye scanned the crowd. Friends and family awaiting the arrival of loved ones peered around drivers holding up signs with names scribbled on them. There were only a few black faces and none of them bore any resemblance to Geteye.

Tesfaye waited. Ten minutes went by. Twenty minutes. *Could this be some cruel hoax?* he wondered, immediately dismissing the idea. *Geteye would have no motive for trickery.*

Thirty minutes, standing in the same spot. Tesfaye's mind began to wander. *What if Geteye didn't even write the letter? Maybe this is a trap*, he thought, picturing Demissie waiting for him outside the airport, or someone else who held him responsible for the execution of Mengistu's agenda. "An unlikely scenario," Tesfaye told himself, but he grew anxious. After one more scan of the crowd, he headed for the luggage carousel.

Tesfaye's faded blue duffel bag spun slowly around the nearly empty carousel. He grabbed the duffel and placed it on the ground. Squinting, he again surveyed the faces around him, focusing on the black men. *Where the hell is he?*

A young, dark woman caught Tesfaye's eye. She was walking toward him, smiling. Her high, defined cheekbones reminded him of the first time he saw Ayana in the library at Addis Ababa University. *Could it be?* he asked himself. She began walking faster, almost running. Before Tesfaye knew it, her arms were draped around him.

"Papa," she sobbed.

"Yenee? Is that you? How can this be?" The questions flowed faster than Yenee could answer them. "Where is Geteye?"

"He doesn't have the courage to look you in the eye."

"Ayana, Afeworki, are they with you?" he asked as he looked around, hoping they were waiting somewhere to surprise him.

"No, Papa," Yenee said, her voice teetering. "They didn't make it out of Kenya," she said solemnly.

His arms wrapped around her, Tesfaye buried his head in Yenee's neck, crying uncontrollably, just as Yenee had done to him the last time they saw each other twelve years ago, on that hot morning in Addis Ababa.

Yenee is alive. Tesfaye was piecing everything together. He thought about Geteye's letter to him. The handwriting. *How did I not see it?* It was the same handwriting that was next to Yenee's name in the logbook at the Kakuma Refugee Camp. The guard at Kakuma had misinformed Tesfaye. A change in medical personnel was not the reason why the handwriting next to Yenee's name was different from the handwriting next to Ayana and Afeworki's entries. It was *Geteye* who made the notation that Yenee had died.

Tesfaye wiped his eyes. "Geteye got you out of Kakuma?"

"Yes."

"He faked your death?"

"He was trying to protect me. Geteye was convinced he was being followed."

He was right, you were being followed.

"Where is he now?"

"I don't know. Before he called me a few days ago, I hadn't heard from him in over eight months. He won't even tell me the alias he is using."

"Alias?"

"He did some very bad things. Many people are looking for him."

The weight of his asylum trial was again falling on Tesfaye's shoulders. A lump formed in his throat as he recalled Ethan comparing him to an SS guard. "Yenee, I know many Ethiopians needlessly died when I was at the ministry, I just want you to know . . ."

Yenee interrupted, "I know, Papa, you don't have to explain." Wiping the tears from her cheeks, she grabbed his hand. "Come, there is someone I want you to meet."

Yenee brought Tesfaye toward a young man who appeared to be of Indian descent, carrying a toddler in his arms. The man handed the child to Yenee.

"Papa, this is my husband, Kaiv."

Kaiv extended his hand. "It's an honor to meet you, sir," he said, sporting a British accent.

"You're married." Tesfaye realized just how much time had passed since he last saw Yenee.

"Meet Adina Tesfaye, your granddaughter."

"*My* granddaughter."

"Do you want to hold her?" asked Yenee, placing Adina in Tesfaye's arms before he could answer.

"How old is she?"

"Seventeen months."

The reason Geteye resumed his search for me. "She has your mother's dimples."

Stuffed up from crying, Yenee blew her nose. "I know," she laughed.

Taking Adina back from Tesfaye's shaking hands, Yenee led the way to their car, Tesfaye and Kaiv walking behind her.

"Mr. Azene," Kaiv said, trying to secure the straps of Tesfaye's duffel over his shoulder. "A very close friend of mine, his father is a prominent immigration attorney. He has already started to look into your situation, to help get you settled here."

"You were sure I was coming today?"

"Well, yes, I suppose," Kaiv said, confused by Tesfaye's question. "Geteye said you would definitely be on this flight."

Tesfaye smiled. "I bet he did."

"It looks like my friend's father has some promising angles . . ."

"Kaiv," Tesfaye interjected, putting his hand on Kaiv's shoulder, "we can talk about all that tomorrow." He looked up at the sky and smiled. "Just in case I wake up tomorrow and discover this is all a dream, I want one day to soak it all in. They'll be plenty of time to worry about the years of legal issues I'll have to deal with."

"Years?"

"Unless they deport me sooner," Tesfaye responded, trying to pretend that he was joking.

Tesfaye didn't want to think about immigration issues for the rest of the day. For twelve years, he had been an immigrant in foreign lands, without any family, waiting for a chance to finally settle down again. His walk out of the Leonardo da Vinci Airport behind his daughter bore all the hallmark traits of the strange and unthinkable events that filled the latter years of his life in Africa. But for the first time in a long time, it was a surrealism he gladly welcomed.

Author's Note

Many of the historical events depicted in *Five Grounds* actually happened. In Ethiopia, Mengistu Haile Mariam did come into power as a result of a successful coup against the Emperor at the time. Mengistu launched a "Red Terror" campaign to strengthen his position and he governed the country through the tenets of socialism. The former Soviet Union was a strong supporter of Mengistu and there was a drought in Ethiopia in 1983 that led to widespread famine and suffering. Mengistu hosted a celebration during this time to commemorate his decade in power; many foreign dignitaries from Communist countries attended. Mengistu also made efforts to internally relocate many Ethiopians. The rebel liberation fronts discussed in the novel did operate in Ethiopia and a TPLF-led coalition eventually overthrew Mengistu in 1992. The Kenyan refugee camps that Tesfaye visited are also real (or at least used to exist).

In 1999, the Chinese government cracked down on the Falun Gong spiritual movement. Numerous incidents of abuse against Falun Gong practitioners were reported. The movement was started by Li Hongzhi, who was forced into exile. Large boats have historically been one of the modes of transportation used to smuggle people into the United States from abroad. Alternatively, these boats have taken passengers to Central America, where they then attempt to enter the United States through the southern border. The smugglers in China are often referred to as "snakeheads" and there have also been reports that the syndicates these snakeheads belong to have forced immigrants into positions of indentured servitude (although this predicament is certainly not limited to immigrants from China). Chinese immigrants have also reported that physical violence or the threat of violence are methods employed by the snakeheads in the United States to coerce money from relatives back home.

Mexican nationals regularly attempt to cross the U.S. southern border in even the most inhospitable areas. The extreme conditions have caused numerous people to perish on their journeys, from dehydration or otherwise. In parts of Mexico, there is widespread discrimination against individuals with HIV; beliefs about homosexuality are reportedly one of the causes. HIV medications are not always available, particularly outside major cities. (Many countries face similar resource problems.)

Immigrants placed in deportation proceedings appear before an immigration judge. They are not entitled to an attorney at the government's expense. U.S. immigration law only provides asylum protection for harm perpetrated on account of the five grounds discussed in this novel. The persecutor bar that the immigration judge applied to Tesfaye's asylum claim is real. Also, immigrants cannot obtain protection under the Convention Against Torture unless they can demonstrate that they are more than fifty percent likely to be tortured. The law also provides asylum protection for those who can prove they will be forced to undergo an abortion or sterilization procedure in their home country. In all asylum cases, immigration judges have to decide whether they believe the immigrants' stories are true or not. Numerous court cases concern the credibility of asylum applicants from China. Finally, although Sofia's case is fictional, identity theft is a recurrent problem in the United States. There have been instances where the individuals responsible for the identity thefts are immigrants who themselves lack proper documentation.

I would like to acknowledge several works that provided invaluable aid: *Revolutionary Ethiopia*, by Edmond J. Keller, published by Indiana University Press; *A History of Ethiopia*, by Harold G. Marcus, published by University of California Press; *Falun Gong and the Future of China*, by David Ownby, published by Oxford University Press; and *Smuggled Chinese: Clandestine Immigration to the United States*, by Ko-Lin Chin, published by Temple University Press.

About The Author

Scott Rempell is a native of New Jersey. He practiced immigration law in Washington, D.C. at the United States Department of Justice before moving to Houston to teach at the South Texas College of Law.

CPSIA information can be obtained at www.ICGtesting.com
Printed in the USA
LVOW04s0243260615

443909LV00012B/60/P